Secret Lives

SUSAN WELLS

outskirts
press

Outskirts Press, Inc.
http://www.outskirtspress.com

Paperback ISBN: 978-1-9772-2709-6

Outskirts Press and the "OP" logo are trademarks belonging to Outskirts Press, Inc.

PRINTED IN THE UNITED STATES OF AMERICA

I dedicate this book to an outstanding man, who has enriched my life and is my inspiration to be the best I can be, my husband, Ron.

CONTENTS

SECRET LIVES

He stared at his blood-spattered shirt. His eyes wandered downward towards his large hands dripping the red liquid on the carpet. That's when he saw her damaged body which lay at his feet, a knife protruding from her stomach. He couldn't move for fear of spreading sticky patches farther.

"What have ya done?" a voice behind him yelled.

He turned to see his father. Now he must do away with him also.

—➤《》◀—

Chapter 1

THE BUSYBODY

Wednesday 6:50 a.m.

Bernice Butzen pushed her rocker faster and faster and pet Felix. The feline purred contentedly as he lay across her potbelly. Her mind was focused not on her cat, but on her neighbor. Carolyn didn't come home last night. *Something's wrong next door. I just know it. I sense it.*

Yesterday morning Bernice heard her younger neighbor's alarm go off at five thirty through their paper-thin walls.

Then twenty-five minutes later she wondered, *why isn't Carolyn starting her shower as usual?* The seventy-year-old Bernice went about her usual morning routine and stepped outside to give fresh water to the neighborhood stray cats. That's when she saw Carolyn come bounding down the back stairs of their apartment building. Bernice thought, *why the rush?* Of course, she would ask, "Good morning Caroline. Where are you going so early?"

With a startled look, Carolyn spun around in their shared parking lot.

Bernice didn't realize her house coat, an unfortunate collage of bright colors and floral prints, was quite a shock. The older woman held a bottle of water in one hand with an orange cat in the other arm.

"Oh, I've got to run to the store," Carolyn said in a rush. She turned towards her car as she added, "I'll be right back." But she never returned.

Bernice thought she might have gone to work, then on to some activity after work, but she hadn't returned all night. Bernice was so worried, her heartbeat quickened. She couldn't sleep. Carolyn lived alone since her husband left. Bernice, a self-appointed neighborhood watch team of one, got out of bed at four a.m. She moved to her rocker in the small living room to listen for her neighbor's return. Her panic rose as the minutes ticked by. *Young people are always out 'til the wee hours, but she should have been home by now. She needs her sleep.*

"Should I call the police, Felix?" she asked the cat. "This just isn't right." One minute after seven, Bernice dialed the West Chicago Police Department as Charlie, her long-haired cat curled on a sofa cushion flicking his tail back and forth.

"9-1-1, what is your emergency?" the calm voice inquired.

Bernice yelled, "Carolyn didn't come home. I want to report a missing person."

"Is this a missing child?"

"Oh, no. It's my neighbor."

"Is this an elderly neighbor?"

"No. She's in her twenties." With her voice getting more excited she said, "On TV shows, sometimes they say they wait a day or two. Should I wait to call you?"

"That's just TV. There is no waiting period. However, we don't take missing reports over the phone. It would help if you came into the district police station to make a report in person. We'd like you to sign it."

Bernice's glasses were slipping down her nose, but she couldn't deal with that now. This was urgent. "Okay. I can do that."

After the clerk got Bernice's address and phone number, she disconnected the call.

Bernice turned to the nearest tabby sitting on the flowered carpet licking one foot with long elaborate strokes. "Hear that

Penelope? They want me to come in person."

Bernice Butzen fed her large cat family, that had become the children she always wanted. She and Victor had endured years of what doctor's had referred to as "uncomfortable tests" and fertility shots. Even Victor had put up with embarrassing tests, arriving home red faced. That was all behind her, but never forgotten.

She dressed in tight grass-green capri pants, pulled on her t-shirt with five cat faces stretched tight over her ample stomach, then drove across town. About an hour after her phone call, she waddled into the West Chicago Police Station. She carried an over-sized, plastic leopard print bag. She'd never been in a police station before, so her eyes darted around the room then stopped at a glass case of police paraphernalia in the lobby.

A young clerk at the front desk asked, "May I help you?"

Bernice Butzen declared, "Yes. A definite yes, you can help me. I want to report a missing person. They told me to come in, so here I am."

"Let's get you inside to see..." the clerk hesitated, looking inside the room where roll call had just finished. "Detective Garcia can take your report. Let me call him." She picked up the phone on her desk and dialed his extension.

"Carlos Garcia," the new detective answered on the first ring.

"I have someone up front who wants to file a missing person report. She called earlier."

————)(()((————

The words, 'she called earlier,' told him the entire call had been recorded.

"I'll be right there," the Latino detective said. His hand brushed the left side of his dark mustache. He pulled out Form M-829 used for documenting a missing person. Many of the veteran cops didn't use the form. They simply took notes. Garcia, new to missing persons, didn't want to miss any important questions. It didn't take him long to reach the front desk.

Smiling he stretched out his hand to the woman who barely reached his shoulder to introduce himself. "I'm Detective Garcia, Ma'am. Why don't you step in here, so we can get started?" He indicated a small room off the lobby.

Bernice didn't move. She stared up at him. "Are you a real cop?"

Detective Garcia didn't understand the question, "Ma'am?"

"Well, I heard on the news there are fake cops who try to scam innocent people. They even dress like real policemen. Some come right to your door to try to come inside." She nodded to agree with herself. "You're not a scam artist, are you?"

"No ma'am. You came into the police station." He pulled his jacket aside to reveal the West Chicago badge on his belt.

"Oh, you're right. You're probably okay then." Bernice swung her hips as she walked past the clerk's desk. The clerk turned her head with a quick look, noting the back of Bernice's t-shirt with five cat butts each with their tails raised, as Bernice passed by. That's when she saw Bernice raise her left hand to run her fingers through her dyed orange/red hair which Bernice called a delicious shade of strawberry blonde. The clerk noticed Bernice palm one foam curler she missed that morning in her haste to get to the police department. Bernice pulled it from her hair dropping it into the large bag she carried.

Detective Garcia showed Ms. Butzen into a small interview room. "Please sit here." The detective pointed to a chair near the corner table. He went around to sit in the other chair.

The visitor's straight-backed chair groaned under Bernice's weight as she settled herself in.

"Your name, ma'am?"

She hugged her large bag on her lap, pushed her glasses to the bridge of her nose as if to ready herself to be of utmost importance and looked directly at him. "Bernice Butzen. I've been living next door to this nice young couple ever since they moved in, about six years now."

"Who's missing?"

"My neighbor, Carolyn. Carolyn Fazzino."

The detective leaned forward. "What makes you think she's missing?"

"She's my neighbor. I'm worried. I know what she does. I know she does her laundry on Saturday mornings. She buys her groceries on Wednesdays after work. Carolyn said she would be right back Tuesday morning. It was quarter to six. I know because that's when I feed the neighborhood cats." Concern showed on her face.

"Was that the last time you saw her?"

"Yes, yesterday morning. She didn't come home last night. She didn't even ask me to pick up her mail, so she's not on vacation. I just know something happened to her." Bernice rattled on, "She always leaves the light on her back landing if she's going to return after dark, but no light last night. She told me; she'd come right back from the store. Those were her exact words, or something like that." Bernice was getting excited.

"Where do you live?" he asked in a calming voice to sooth her.

"I live over the medical building on Hampton Avenue." She smiled proudly. "I'm in apartment 202 and she's in 204."

"Do you have a photo of Carolyn?"

"No, but maybe you could break in to look around her apartment," Bernice offered. "She's probably got a picture of herself there."

Detective Garcia ran his fingers through his thick, black hair. "Can you describe her?"

"Well, she's cute. Shoulder length brown hair, pretty brown eyes."

"Color of her skin?" he prompted.

"Oh, she tans better than me. I stick my nose outdoors and burn. It's this Irish skin I have. It gives me a sunburn every time."

"No, I meant her race."

Bernice giggled. "Oh, she's white."

Garcia looked up from the form on his desk. "How tall is your neighbor?"

"About my height. I think I was taller a couple years ago, but I'm shrinking down."

The detective fingered his mustache as he sighed. "Her weight?"

"Oh, less than me, that tiny little thing, maybe a hundred pounds. I don't really know. I don't really watch my weight or anyone else's, if ya know what I mean. Don't even own one of those scales. Mine broke and who's got time for that nonsense?"

Garcia had a mental picture of her scale whimpering as she stepped on it. Instead the detective went on with his next question. "Earlier you said 'couple.' Is she married or living with anyone?"

Bernice leaned forward, cupped her hand around her mouth. "Her husband left her. He's a real dream boat, that guy is. But they fought all the time." She dropped her voice to a whisper and leaned in closer to Detective Garcia. "She doesn't want to have kids and he does. Wow, could they get into it."

"Really?" Officer Garcia prodded.

"Yeah. First, they had sex all the time. I could hear them right through the walls. Newlyweds. Reminded me of Victor and me when we were first married."

"Let's get back to your neighbors."

"Oh, of course. You've got to find her. Will you dust for fingerprints like C.S.I.?"

He ignored her question and asked his own. "What is her husband's name?"

"Vince Fazzino. I don't know his middle name. I called him Mr. Fazzino when I first met him. Sometimes she called him Vinny, but he asked me to call him Vince."

"Any chance she and her husband made up?"

"Well, she still wears her wedding ring. Hasn't taken it off even though he left four months ago. I would have taken it off; maybe even dated some new men. Ya know, many men." Bernice gave a knowing wink. "I wouldn't save myself."

Detective Garcia's eyebrows shot up as he mentally tried to block that image. "Does anyone live with her now?"

"No, that's why I watch out for her." Bernice nodded feeling very proud of herself.

"Could she have gone to stay with family?"

Bernice's face lit up. "Her mother lives here in town. Over on the north side, I think. But Carolyn told me she would be right back." Her face darkened. "She didn't return. I just feel something's wrong. Sometimes I get this sixth sense."

Detective Garcia doubted her psychic abilities. He quickly asked, "Have you called her husband or mother since Tuesday?"

"Oh, I don't have their numbers. I thought of calling you first. Was that okay?"

He sighed a little louder. "That's fine. We'll send out a squad car. Any broken windows in her apartment?" He resigned himself to listen to her unnecessary details.

Bernice unconsciously pushed her slipping glasses up on the bridge of her nose. "No, nothing like that. She just ran down the back stairs and didn't return."

"What was she wearing the last time you saw her?"

"Mmm," Bernice hummed. "Tight blue jeans like girls wear now, so she wasn't going to work. She didn't even have a shower yet. I can hear the water when they shower. Anyway, it was too early for her to leave for work. It was about quarter to six yesterday morning. She always leaves at seven twenty to drive to Lombard. She works at a college library. Good thing I asked her that a while back, because now you need to know."

Garcia interrupted, "Besides jeans, what else was Carolyn wearing when you saw her last?"

"Oh, tennis shoes. She couldn't dress like that for work. She dresses up kind of nice, like slacks and blazers for the college library, ya know. Usually those open toe things, like sandals. She told me she was going to the store. She was kind of in a hurry. Didn't say much to me. Normally she's really friendly to..."

Garcia had left the door to the room slightly ajar, like he had been trained when questioning a woman alone. Phones rang throughout the noisy police station distracting Bernice. Several officers were speaking into their cell phones. Detective Garcia pressed onward. "Did Carolyn seem confused?"

Bernice shook her head. "No, not her; and Carolyn told me she'd be right back. I believed her. She's kind of an artsy-fartsy person if you ask me." Bernice leaned forward to whisper, "She told me once, she wears moisturizer *and* sunscreen at the same time."

Garcia flipped to the second fresh page of the missing person form. His body growing more tense as he clicked the top of his city-issued pen. "Did she seem upset?"

"No." Bernice was shaking her head. "Just in a hurry. She didn't say much. Sometimes, she'll chit chat with me for a while."

The detective leaned backward and thought of a possibility. "Was she carrying anything with her, like maybe a suitcase or anything that didn't fit going to the store?"

"Oh no. She only took her little purse. Don't know how she gets everything in there. Not like me." Bernice patted the enormous leopard bag she held on her lap. "Now me, I have anything you ever want right with me. You just ask me. I bet I've got it, from Band-Aids to a paper stapler. Ya never know when you're going to need something."

"Tell me, does she have many friends over?" He drummed his fingers on the table.

"Yeah, sometimes she has a girlfriend over. No guys. I keep an eye on her."

"Have you seen anyone visit her recently?"

"Not in a couple of weeks," Bernice answered. Two policemen walked past the open door. One gave Garcia a head nod.

"Let me ask you this, does Carolyn wear glasses?"

"Oh no. Sometimes sunglasses. I've seen her wear those especially when she's driving, but it wasn't all that sunny when she left so early yesterday."

Bernice turned her head to look at a uniformed female cop with a tight expression on her face escorting a woman wearing a low V-necked red blouse and short tight black skirt. The handcuffed woman turned to the officer. "I make more than you do, sister."

To get her focus back to the matter at hand, Garcia asked, "Mrs. Butzen, did Carolyn leave with anyone?"

Bernice turned back to him. "No, she's been on her own ever since that husband of hers took off. I saw him carry suitcases out to his car the Saturday he left. She went out all by herself yesterday."

"When he was there, do you think there was any domestic violence?"

"What do you mean?" She looked totally confused.

Trying to rephrase it, he asked, "Do you think he might have hit her?"

Shaking her head, she answered, "I never heard any hitting. Never saw any bruises on her. I've heard them yelling at each other. Several times I heard her crying. I even heard doors slamming. They got so loud; they scared the bejesus right out of me. Once I got so upset, I phoned the police. Was it you, who came?" she asked him. "One policeman looked a little like you."

"No, Mrs. Butzen, however I can look up the record." He punched a few keys on his laptop computer.

His typing didn't slow her down. "Now Victor and I, we never ever yelled at each other. Oh." She paused. "I take that back. The time I scraped up the side of our car on the fence as I pulled into the parking lot, well he did yell at me that time."

Garcia changed the subject, "Does she own a car? Did she leave in that?"

"Oh sure. She took her car. I heard it start right up. We park in the back of our building."

The officer tapped his pen on the document in front of him, anxious to get her back on track. "What kind of car does your neighbor drive?"

"Oh Lordy, ya got lots of questions, I don't know." She looked thoughtful. "I'm not so good with cars. It's tan. It could be saddle brown you know. One of those fancy color names they give to cars to sell more of them. Now me, I'd just call it tan."

Garcia told her, "I can look up the make and model from their registration."

"Would the license plate number help you out?"

He looked up from his notes and quickly turned to face her. "It sure would, ma'am!"

"I see it parked behind our building every night. I keep an eye on our parking lot." Bernice started rummaging through her oversized purse, pulling a package of tissues and her keys out, placing them on the small table between them.

The bag is so big, she could have a cat in there, he thought as he looked at the cats on her shirt.

"Don't want anybody parking there who doesn't live in our building." Next, she pulled out an open package of Chips Ahoy chocolate chip cookies offering him one.

Just don't dump that thing out on the table. "No thanks."

"I've got it here in my purse. We have to keep those spots just for our own tenants." Both of her chubby arms were inside the bag now. "Oh my gosh, here's my cell phone." She placed it on the table. "I only have that thing for emergencies. I guess this is an emergency, but it's really for road emergencies. The numbers are too tiny. If ya know what I mean." She dug some more. Then finding her spiral notebook and flipping a few pages, she said, "Here's the Anderson's." She moved her chubby finger down the list. "Here are the Fazzino's two cars. Carolyn's license number is WC 8455."

Of course, she's got every tenant's number. "That's very helpful Mrs. Butzen."

"I've drawn a line through her husband's, but I can still read it. I don't cross them out completely when they move. Like in his case, ya never know if he'll come back. Vince's number was WC 7768."

Mrs. Butzen was a very reliable witness, sincerely trying to help. He wrote both numbers down.

A cop in horn rimmed glasses walked out of the break room with a Styrofoam cup in his hand shouting, "Who made this mud today?"

Bernice, distracted, turned to see who asked the question.

No one answered him.

Garcia in a slightly louder tone asked, "Did you see which direction she was headed that morning?"

"Oh no, Sir. Felix was meowing. He wanted his morning milk, so

I had to go inside."

"Anything else you can tell me? Like does she have any hobbies?"

"She reads a lot. I see her bringing in library books. Oh, she runs. Normally about six o'clock at night. You know, after work, but it should be her dinner time right then. I never miss a meal."

His brown eyes opened wide as he looked at her bloated face.

The front desk phone rang. Bernice turned to look as the clerk answered it on the third ring. Bernice started to lean in that direction to listen to the conversation.

To get her back on track Garcia said, "You were telling me about her hobbies."

Bernice reluctantly returned to their conversation. "Oh yes. Carolyn's a fair-weather exerciser. She only runs if it's not raining or snowing or cold. I can tell when she's going to run because she puts her hair up in a ponytail. If I see her brown ponytail swinging back and forth down the front steps, I know she's not taking her car." She gave the detective a knowing look.

She really knows a lot about her neighbors.

Bernice continued, "But she exercises more than me. Now I..."

He cut her off with his next question. "Is the entire building all apartments?"

"Oh no. The doctor on the first level told me he owns the building and rents out the apartments on the second floor."

"And what is his name?"

"Dr. Kennedy."

It took the detective a couple hours to learn as much as possible from Bernice who kept wandering off the topic. But in the end, she did sign the *report which was several pages long.* One thing for sure, she was *not* a reluctant witness. He tapped the M-829 form twice and rose from his chair to give Mrs. Butzen the clue it was time to leave. As the detective handed her his business card he smiled. "Thank you so much Mrs. Butzen for coming in today. Hopefully, we'll find your neighbor quickly. If she shows up at home, call me right away."

Bernice rose from the uncomfortable office chair. "Of course.

I do belong to the West Chicago Bible Church. Our prayer group meets on Thursday mornings. I'm going to pray for Carolyn. If she doesn't return tomorrow, I can just pray from home."

"That would be very nice of you," he responded.

Bernice smiled and put the card into her enormous bag. "I'll call you right away officer if I think of anything else. Just like the old Mission Impossible TV show. I accept." She saluted him.

As he directed her out of the interrogation room, he suspected this nosy neighbor would watch Carolyn's apartment day and night until she returned.

Bernice stepped out into the lobby but stopped. A teenage boy with a Mohawk, wearing combat boots, was being escorted by a stern looking policewoman, saying, "Settle down, or you're going to juvie."

A young black man in handcuffs was wearing a knit cap on this beautiful July day. He was arguing with two female officers saying, "Come on, coppers. I didn't do nothing."

Bernice leaned back towards Detective Garcia and asked, "Where are his parents?" Then her eyes shot open. "Oh my, he could be in a gang."

Garcia had to move her along. "Your top priority is to get home. Keep an eye on Carolyn's place. Duty calls, Mrs. Butzen."

She nodded and slowly walked towards the front door.

He sighed. *Mrs. Butzen might be overreacting. What a nut case. Or could this be domestic violence?* He tapped keys on his computer to look for any reports on the Fazzinos. *Had the husband beat her? Maybe he did, but the marks just didn't show. Did he do something horrible?*

Chapter 2

WELL BEING CHECK

POLICE STATION WEDNESDAY 10:00 A.M.

As Bernice waddled out of the station, Detective Garcia squinted at the form. *Should I take this nut job seriously? The last thing I need is another neighbor problem, like those two neighbors yesterday over on Gates Street arguing about dog poop and trampled tomato plants.* He wanted to tell those children in adult bodies he wasn't a babysitter. Instead he recommended they see a neighborhood mediation clinic.

He leaned back in his chair and fingered his mustache, a nervous habit. *Maybe the busybody wants to get the so-called missing person in trouble over something.* He frowned. Then again maybe Mrs. Butzen was on the level. She seemed sincere. Goofy as Hell, maybe, but sincere. *This could be important, maybe the big break I need to jump-start my career and impress the big bosses.* He glanced towards his supervisor's office. Through the glass door Garcia could see Sergeant Dodson. He still wore his hair 'high and tight' from Iraq, where he received a Silver Star for bravery in action. Garcia dialed Dodson's extension.

The special-operations supervisor's immediate response was, "Dodson."

"It's Garcia. I've got a reported missing woman. I'm going to run over to Hampton Avenue to do a Well-Being Check unless you've got something else for me to do."

Dodson was serious. "No, you're up at bat. I'll send Wilson over to Brown Street on an accident, however if you find a body or any signs of foul play, you call for backup."

Garcia knew they didn't want the scene messed up. "Sure thing," he answered. He grabbed the keys to a Ford Explorer from a departing midnight shift policeman. He was eager to get out to his car. Better than sitting around the office drinking too much coffee. More than anything he wanted to be a detective. Garcia went out the parking lot marked OFFICIAL VEHICLES ONLY to the car. The Hampton Avenue apartments were only five blocks from the station.

A second generation Mexican, the U.S. was Garcia's home. Carlos Garcia had never been to Mexico. Maybe someday he would visit his ancestor's homeland, however it wasn't a necessity. The detective passed a dollar store, the bank that held his parents second mortgage, in addition to the Mexican café where he ate lunch a couple days every week.

He pulled up in front of the two-story red brick building. A large sign read "Hampton Psychiatry." Garcia checked his notes - apartment 204.

All looked peaceful and quiet. A few cars parked out front had a look as if they were right at home. A man was putting golf clubs into the trunk of a Buick. Garcia quickly climbed the stairs to the second floor. As he passed apartment 202, he stepped over a large welcome mat decorated with paw prints. *This must be Mrs. Butzen's.* At apartment 204 he rang the doorbell. No answer. The landlord would probably have the key. The detective went back down and opened the office door. The sign on the glass read "Dr. Kennedy, Psychiatrist." He stepped into the doctor's waiting room.

A tired looking receptionist in scrubs narrowed her eyes as he walked in. "May I help you?"

As the detective flashed his badge, Garcia answered, "Yes, I'm doing a well-being check on Carolyn Fazzino in apartment 204.

Have you seen her lately?"

"No. She only comes in to pay her rent. Is there something wrong?"

Knowing he didn't need a search warrant for a well-being check, Garcia asked, "Would you or the good doctor open apartment 204, so I can check on her?"

"Oh, let me ask him." She pressed an intercom button and said into her phone, "There's a police officer here, who wants to see inside the Fazzino apartment." There was a slight hesitation as she listened. "He said he's doing a well-being check." Another hesitation. "Okay." She opened a drawer, pulled out a set of keys. Then she rose from her swivel chair. As she stepped around the counter, she turned towards a young man sitting in the small waiting room and told him, "I'll be right back."

She led the way up the stairs. This time as Garcia passed apartment 202, the front door was wide open. He glanced through the screen door and saw a large orange cat looking out the door. The cat meowed at them. He heard Mrs. Butzen say, "Sheba, get your darling little claws off the screen, dear."

There sitting just inside her front door with a long-haired cat on her lap, was Bernice. She had been scratching Charlie's head as it leaned into her chubby hand. Its bushy tail flowed over the edge of her lap falling straight down. She picked the hairy cat up, gently placing him on the floor. Raising herself, she smiled. "Yoo-hoo, Officer Garcia, you're here already."

"Yes, Mrs. Butzen."

Bernice looked concerned. "This *is* important, isn't it?"

Garcia shrugged. "It could be." He said as he turned from her front door.

The detective and receptionist walked on to the next apartment door. There he pressed Carolyn Fazzino's doorbell a second time. While he waited, he pulled on his latex gloves, just in case the police had to look for fingerprints later.

Bernice quickly opened her screen door to follow. The receptionist raised the set of keys, pulling number 204 forward and unlocked the solid wooden door. Then she stepped out of the officer's way.

"Mrs. Fazzino?" he called out. "This is Detective Garcia, West Chicago police department. Are you home?"

As the detective stepped over the threshold, busybody Bernice stepped forward, trying to peer inside. He could feel the older woman's heavy, excited breathing. "I think I've got this. You stay right here on the landing just in case she comes home. Okay?"

"Okey dokey. I can do that, but if you need back up, ya just call out for me." Then she quickly added, "Maybe we should leave this front door open, so we can hear you."

"I'll be fine." Garcia closed the door behind him. He could see Bernice's curious face trying to peek through a small window in the front door. He couldn't do anything about her, so he went about his business, looking around inside, in addition to taking an inventory. The room consisted of two leather loveseats, two cloth chairs, and a flat screen TV. A three-foot-high bookshelf was used as a room divider to separate a table and chairs in the corner. He walked through a galley kitchenette which was more like a wide hall. A few dishes dried in the rack to the left of the sink. The coffeemaker sat on the counter with its filter basket swung open. Garcia peered in to see a clean dry paper filter with no coffee grounds.

A black and white cat slowly came out of the bedroom. He wrapped his furry body around Garcia's leg, meowing. Garcia imagined the cat had done the same with its owner the day before. When he didn't bend down to pet it, the cat walked to its bowl. Garcia noticed the empty saucer sitting on the floor next to the cat's dish. *Looks like the cat hasn't been fed.* The cat mewed, then casually it strolled into the large bedroom, which was to the right of the kitchen. He rolled onto his side on a small throw rug and into a sunbeam like nothing was amiss. The detective walked into the room. A cheerful flowered bedspread was hanging off the end of the double bed. It didn't look like a struggle to him; simply, whoever slept here last, hadn't made the bed. He opened the sliding doors of Carolyn's closet. A flowered suitcase sat on the floor.

He turned to look closely at the bedroom. A closed laptop was on the desk with a lady's watch just to the left of it. *She might have left the apartment in a hurry to leave her watch behind or maybe she doesn't always wear it.* A tiny corner of paper was sticking out from under the laptop. With his gloved hand, he raised the computer to see a list of IDs and passwords. *This could be helpful.* He pulled out his iPhone and snapped a photo of the list.

Garcia opened the nightstand drawer to find antacids, a pair of fuzzy bed socks and a book, *Gone Girl*. His sister had talked about this movie. Anna said it was about a very dysfunctional couple where the wife goes missing. *Is this a coincidence or is something strange really going on?* Garcia picked the book up. He noticed a bookmark between pages 32 and 33. *Possible, however she's just started it.*

Then Garcia noticed a wedding photo under the book and wondered, *She's placed her wedding photo in a drawer where it doesn't show.* He took a photo of it. Just as he was about to close the drawer, he saw a small pill bottle in one corner. Raising it to eye level he read 'Carolyn M. Fazzino,' *the missing woman.* Under her name were the letters 'Zoloft Tab 50 mg. Take 1 tablet daily.' The prescribing doctor was L. Kennedy, Ph.D. *That's the doctor downstairs.* The detective could see through the brown bottle that it was practically full. He took a photo of the prescription label.

As he turned away from the bed stand drawer, Garcia spotted a mayonnaise jar half filled with change sitting on the dresser. Clearly this wasn't a robbery. Money and the expensive watch sitting out. TV still in the living room. He saw a suitcase in the closet. Signs that she hadn't planned on leaving.

He got down on the floor to look under the bed, but only found women's shoes. After getting back up, he tried the back door that went out to the balcony. It was locked. A small bathroom completed the apartment. Garcia noticed a robe hanging on the back of the bathroom door. He peeled the top of one of his gloves down a couple inches. With the top of his wrist, he touched the washcloth that laid on the sink. It was dry. Mrs. Fazzino hadn't used it today.

Still there was nothing in the apartment that suggested foul play.

Garcia opened the front door and stepped out on the landing. There was Bernice, looking hopeful and the receptionist looking bored. Impatiently, the cop said, "You're still here?"

"Unfortunately," said the receptionist who left out an exaggerated sigh. "I have to get back downstairs."

Then Garcia realized the neighbor *really cared*. He was getting a warm feeling from this kind-hearted woman. He knew Bernice was curious, so he told her, "Nothing out of the ordinary in there. Oh, there's a cat."

"That's Tuxedo. See, she didn't leave on a vacation, or she would have asked me to feed him," Bernice explained knowingly.

"You must stay out of her apartment just in case we have to investigate it more, however I could bring the cat to your place. Could you take care of him?"

"Sure, I'm really good with cats. When you say 'investigate,' do ya mean, look for fingerprints? I watch CSI, so I know how they do it." Her eyes seemed to light up with excitement.

Garcia wasn't going to explain how they really *do* it, so he stepped back inside Carolyn's apartment to scoop up her cat. He deposited it into the waiting arms of Mrs. Butzen.

The receptionist was impatiently tapping her foot during the switching of the cat. Then she locked up and headed back down the stairs.

The officer held up his phone showing the wedding photo to Mrs. Butzen and asked, "Is this Carolyn and her husband?"

"Yes sir. That's them. Don't they look sweet together? I just love weddings." She gave a slight smile. Then it disappeared as she added, "I haven't been to one yet this summer. Young people just live together nowadays; don't even plan a nice memorable wedding day with a photographer and all their family and friends."

He had to get her back on track, so Garcia asked, "Is there anyone else in the building that might know where Carolyn is? Can you tell me a little about your other neighbors?"

She took a step closer to him. "Sure, I can help you. What else have I got to do now? I'm on this side of Carolyn," Bernice said as she gestured with her left elbow because her arm was full of cat. "Mrs. Triston and her teenage son, who plays his music way too loud, live over on that side." She pointed with her pudgy right hand. "Well, after his mother gets home from work, he turns that loud stuff down, but boy from the moment he gets home from school and until she gets here, I can feel the vibrations right through the walls. Now I'm no prude or anything about bad language, but *he* has a foul mouth. He and his buddies like to stand around in the parking lot, back there." She pointed towards the back of the building. "And they swear. I mean they scream a particular four-letter word that I will NOT repeat, even for you."

Garcia stared at her in disbelief, as she went on, "But he's a kid, with no dad now, so I just put up with it. You got to give the kid a break. He only has his father on the weekends." She cupped her hand around her mouth and whispered, "They're divorced." Her hand came down from her face. "Maybe I should complain, but I want my neighbors to like me." She paused only the briefest of seconds. Then asked him, "Can I offer you an herbal tea? It'll only take me a minute and I can tell ya about all of these folks." She waved her beefy arm towards the entire building.

"I don't have the time."

"I could bring it out here, but then it's nicer to sit and relax with tea, ya know, calms the nerves and all."

"No thanks, ma'am." Garcia pulled out his notebook to scribble down a few notes and names of the other tenants.

Once Bernice saw him taking notes, her face seemed to beam with importance as the neighborhood watch. So, she went on describing the rest of the apartment occupants.

Garcia had been taught in basic training to let witnesses talk. They just might say something useful. The witness that wouldn't talk was certainly more difficult. Listening to Mrs. Butzen, Garcia thought maybe she was the exception to the rule.

"I've heard Dr. Kennedy." Bernice leaned against the outside wall and continued, "Drunk at night, throwing his bottles into the garbage bin downstairs. I've looked in the morning. He likes Vodka." She cupped her hand around her mouth. Leaned closer like she had a big secret to tell the detective. "I called Alcoholics Anonymous for him. I told 'em I was Mrs. Kennedy and asked if they could send my husband some pamphlets about AA meetings, but I don't know if he ever went." She lowered her arm because her big confession was out. "I've told my friends, if I ever need a psychiatrist, don't you take me downstairs to that old drunk. You carry me over to my doctor, Dr. Pearson, over on Gale Street. I don't care if it's farther. I just don't trust any boozer with my mind or my body," she said patting her ample hips. She continued, "Dr. Kennedy built this here building. Whole bottom floor is his practice with some medical doctors. He had these apartments put on the second floor. He told me himself, 'it was an investment.' Me and Victor, my late husband, when we moved in, we didn't know he was a drinker. He was just real nice, but then we heard him in the parking lot late at night, singing like a drunkard. Well, now where am I going to go?" She shrugged her shoulders.

But the question didn't slow her down. "I can tell ya about more people who live here. One wonderful lady, but I'm not telling you who because she's a baker, decorates beautiful fancy cakes for birthdays, weddings, and anything. I don't know if she has a license to sell from her house, so I'm not going to tell you who it is. I don't want her getting mad at me. If I tell on her, she might not ever make me those fancy cupcakes. She's a good friend of mine."

Garcia's eyes narrowed. He could tell she would certainly miss those pastries. "Who else have you got?" he prodded even though she didn't need encouragement to talk.

Bernice turned her head to her right. "There's Mrs. Alison, the church secretary in apartment 206. I don't remember which church."

"Oh, that's okay. Just knowing she's with a church will probably suffice." Garcia said as he shifted his weight to his left leg before the other fell asleep.

"The retired couple in 208. He's had forty years of service with

AT&T. They're not home now. Since he retired, they travel a lot. Number 210 has the newlyweds. Her hair is bleached to kind of a canary yellow frizz. They had a baby first. They do things so different now, don't they?"

He nodded his head, which was all the encouragement she needed. "George Manning, he's deaf, poor man. He asked me out for dinner once, but I told him, the love of my life was my husband, God rest his soul. I'm sure Victor is waiting for me up there. I don't want any three-way triangle going on in Heaven." Bernice glanced at the wedding ring on her left hand. "He's been gone nine years now. I had to yell that at Mr. Manning 'cause he's so hard of hearing."

Garcia tapped his pen on his notebook.

She simply went on. "He doesn't wear socks, even in the winter. Once I asked him 'why not.' Something about losing socks in our laundry in the basement. The old coot is just lazy if you ask me. I really don't want to go out with him."

Garcia perked up. "You have a laundry in the basement? Could you show me?"

"Of course, you can always count on me, Sir." She saluted him. She put the squirming cat in her apartment and got her key for the basement.

Garcia followed her down the back steps. He had her wait outside as he thoroughly searched the basement area where he found a row of three washers and three dryers. Each tenant also had a six-foot by four-foot screen-linked storage area. Each numbered and each padlocked, however he could easily see through the wire to view various sized plastic storage bins and cardboard boxes. He took a close look at number 204's storage locker, and saw a couple small plastic crates, a bicycle, and a large stew pot. However, nothing looked out of the ordinary. As he came back up the stairs, he told her, "Thank you, but I didn't find Carolyn."

"Over time, neighbors have come and gone, but only Victor and I remained. Well that is until poor Victor had that nasty heart attack. Bless his heart. We were married forty-three years, but then his heart gave out. We never had children. Guess the good Lord didn't see it that way. Anyways I had my job at Balls Seed Company. Nice people to work with. Victor, he worked at the Jel Sert Company right here in town. Where would I move? I said that to people then and I still ask, where would I ..."

Garcia cut her off with, "Have you ever seen anyone watching the building, looking at Carolyn's apartment? Or anyone hanging out in the parking lot?" There was no garage. Every tenant just parked behind the building.

Bernice shook her head. "No one. I go out of my way when I see a neighbor in the hall or downstairs. I come out to keep 'em company. Now I can't carry their groceries up for them, but I can walk along." Bernice leaned a little closer to the detective as if to tell him a secret. "Could terrorists have taken her? I hear about them on TV all the time."

Garcia struggled to maintain his cool as he told her, "I really doubt it, ma'am."

They both climbed the stairs to the second floor. He excused himself by telling her he had to start questioning the other tenants, saying, "Thank you Mrs. Butzen. You've been very helpful."

She nodded in agreement and waved.

Garcia spent the next two hours ringing doorbells. He tried every door in the building. No one had seen Carolyn yesterday. He was thankful no one was willing to talk as much as Bernice. Two other neighbors did verify that the doctor/landlord drank too much.

Chapter 3

NO BABY-SITTING JOB

Detective Waller seated at her desk studied a bank robbery report trying to figure out how she could get herself attached to the team of detectives on the case. It was mid-morning and already the air conditioner couldn't keep up in the station house. She was glad she had pulled her dark hair back into a ponytail that morning. Feeling perspiration in her arm pits, she pushed her navy sleeves up, revealing multiple tattoos on her arms. She wore no makeup. Alicia Waller's' coworkers knew Al as someone who believed in herself. Detective Waller had been with the police department long enough for a few of her police patches to fray.

She leaned back in her swivel office chair as she remembered the cutie, she met this past weekend at her favorite gay bar in Chicago. She smiled slightly as she recalled the mid-twenty-year-old dressed in lime green tights that walked up to her, bragging how she was a love goddess.

Waller did one better, telling Lime Green Pants, "I used to do cartwheels in grammar school recess to show off my panties. I believe in being an individual."

Now, at work, she opened her middle desk drawer and selected a miniature Hershey bar. It felt a little soft in this heat. She pushed one chubby finger under the wrapper as she glanced up in time to see her supervisor looking straight at her.

Sergeant Dodson's close-cropped hair buzzed to military

specifications was just beginning to grey. He had the new guy that looked like a fireplug with the drooping mustache in his office. However, Dodson, seated at his desk, wearing a white shirt and a dark maroon tie, looked past the standing Garcia out through the glass window of his office door and stared directly at her. Without warning, Dodson waved his meaty right-hand motioning for her to come into his office.

Shit, this will have to wait. She dropped the chocolate back into her drawer. As Waller, packed firmly into her dark suit, badge clipped to her too-tight belt, stepped into the office, their Sergeant said, "I want you two to work on a missing person case together."

Oh Christ, thought Waller, however before she could say anything, Garcia was explaining, "I didn't find anyone in apartment 204 on Hampton Avenue. None of her neighbors have seen her for at least two days."

Shit was Waller's second thought, but she turned to face her boss, her shoulders tensed. "Why do I have to train the new guy?"

Garcia jerked his head back in alarm at her words, but he said, "Just keep me on the case, Sarge."

Oh, for God's sake. Waller threw her arms in the air for special effects. "It's not even a case yet. Someone probably went on vacation without telling anyone. That's what normally happens." But she was thinking, *now, I've got to hold the hand of a new detective.*

Dodson rose from his desk chair. Just a hint of a gut showed. Actually, everything about him seemed large. He radiated physical power as he said, "Garcia's an experienced cop who knows his way around."

She faced Dodson with her hands on her hips. "What has he got? Two years on the force?"

"I'm right here." Garcia tried to defend himself as he brushed his hand over the left side of his mustache. "I can hear you bad mouth me."

"He's been reassigned from patrol after spending six years on the street in a squad. He's had over eighty hours a year of investigation in addition to the interviewing classes." Dodson defended his investigator.

Waller looked squarely at Garcia. "So, a position opened up and ta da, here you are in my lap." Then she turned to face her supervisor thinking, *I don't want to play nursemaid on his first assignment as a detective.* However instead of saying it, she just glared at Dodson.

He looked back at her. "You can show him the ropes." The sergeant raised his voice with more force. "I'm teaming him up with a veteran because you've got the experience. You're good Waller."

She hadn't asked for the compliment, however it felt good. "I'd rather get bank robbers or drug dealers," *because I don't want to be his teacher.*

"Waller." Dodson's voice lowered slightly, "You've been around the block."

Backing down slightly because she knew she wasn't going to win, her voice softened, "I could handle this myself with one arm tied behind my back."

"Garcia stays on the case because I want you two to work as a team."

Waller reluctantly nodded in agreement to their sergeant.

Dodson explained, "It's possible the woman just left town; however, I want you two to question people who know her. Check it out. I don't care if you don't get along, but you *will* work together."

"Sure," Waller mumbled, then turned to Garcia. "Alright let's go find a missing person."

Garcia turned to leave, then eagerly said, "I found a large suitcase sitting in her closet. Doesn't look like a vacation."

"Oh, you've already got a theory. She might have taken an overnight bag," the veteran detective said, sighing.

"There was a cat in her apartment," Garcia answered. "Animal lovers would get someone to feed their pet before they go away, however the dingbat neighbor said Mrs. Fazzino didn't ask her to take care of it this time."

"Maybe she just filled the food bowl up high knowing she would be home in a day or two," speculated Waller.

"The cat's dish was empty."

As Waller took a step backwards, she took in the sergeant's messy desk: some manila folders of current cases, a computer screen, a cheap pen set, in addition to his hat. Then she noticed the five-by-seven photo of Dodson's beautiful blond wife taken on a Paris runway. Her long legs looked perfect for an airbrushed glossy magazine. Of course, she looked at the gorgeous woman. *I probably just came across as a real SOB, better make peace with the boss man.* "How's your wife doing now?" *Everyone in the precinct knows what happened to her, but this new guy.* She turned towards Garcia to explain, "She was mugged."

Dodson let out a long sigh. Turning towards Garcia he explained, "Diane used to travel to Milan, the fashion capital of the world, however after she was viciously attacked last November, she won't leave the house. Her shrink calls it agoraphobia. She's so afraid, she won't go out in public."

"Wow, that's got to be tough for you both," Garcia sympathized.

"It's my fault." Sergeant Dodson said as he lowered himself into his desk chair. "I should have been there for her. Now she'll bear the damage forever."

"You couldn't have done anything." Waller tried to ease his guilt. "Any leads on who did it?"

"The detectives on the case have looked at everybody that could possibly have a grudge against her, even the competition. Nothing. The attack just doesn't make any sense; however, they're still working on the case and hopefully, she'll heal soon." Dodson leaned back in his swivel chair. "Go," he pointed out his door. "Work together."

The two detectives did as ordered. Waller lead the way out of their supervisor's office. As they walked towards their desks, Waller began popping the knuckles of her fingers one by one. She faintly smiled as she noticed out of the corner of her eye that each pop made him jump a little. Then with a brisk tone she told her new partner, "Right now, our missing woman is a mystery. It's our job to learn everything we can about her in addition to everyone in her life, so we can sort out the pieces to see if she took off voluntarily or someone forced her into leaving. However, we've got to find her dead or alive. You've only been on the detective squad a week. You're a pup, so you better listen to me."

Garcia corrected her, "Two weeks Ma'am."

She abruptly turned to face him. "Don't ma'am me, don't ever ma'am me. You got it?" But she was thinking, *He's completed his probation. Working himself up through the ranks, but why must he do his first case with me?* Waller tried the best glare she could give him. "I'm darn good at my job, so pay attention. If the Sarge had any doubts about me, he wouldn't have put me on this case. He knows I'm the best." Then she added, "You move into that empty desk by me, so we can get to work."

As both detectives sat at their side-by-side desks, Waller asked, "Find anything during the well-being check?"

"Her mail was still in the box when I looked. Her passport, bank books, in addition to the suitcase were all left in the apartment."

The veteran tightened her face. "Then we've got some work to do."

Chapter 4

FAMILY COMES FORWARD

A FEW MONTHS AGO

"He yells at *you*. What about?" Ruth said into her cell phone. It had been a calm evening up until her daughter called. Ruth liked her son-in-law. She had never heard him raise his voice.

"I don't want to talk about it, Mom. I just can't." Carolyn managed through her tears. "I just wanted you to know that we had a big fight today and he packed some stuff and left <u>me</u>."

"Oh, baby, I'm so sorry." Taking her daughter's side, she added, "You can come home, here with me. You don't have to be alone."

"No, I have to be here if he comes back."

"Of course, well, I can come over there."

"No. You'll get a better night's sleep in your own bed. There's nothing you can do here. It's late. I've got to get up in the morning. I just wanted you to know."

"He'll be back, dear."

"I'm not so sure. You didn't see how mad he was." Carolyn hesitated. "But I hope you're right, maybe after he cools down. I just don't know." Then she yawned. "I'm so tired. This whole day has drained me. I need sleep, but I'll probably just lie awake tonight."

"You try to rest. And I'll call you tomorrow night."

That's how their phone calls became an every night thing four months ago. But now it's been two days and Ruth hadn't heard from her daughter. Something was terribly wrong.

It took Ruth fifteen minutes to reach the Hampton Avenue apartments in the middle of town. She quickly took the stairs to the second floor. She was leaning on her daughter's doorbell when Bernice Butzen opened her screen door. "You're Carolyn's mother, aren't you?" Bernice asked.

Ruth spun around. "Yes, have you seen her today?"

"No. In fact, it's been a day and a half since I last saw her. It was early in the morning, out on the back landing." Bernice pointed her chubby hand towards the back of the apartment building. "We talked right outside our doors. She said she would be right back. But she hasn't returned."

Ruth's stomach lurched. "You mean she left? You haven't seen her?"

Mrs. Butzen stepped forward to place a comforting hand on Ruth's arm. "That's what I'm saying. But don't you worry, Dear. The police will find her. I've been watching close. The nice policeman told me to keep an eye on the place."

"What police?" Ruth's voice was filled with tension. Her eyes widened.

"The officer I told the whole story to this morning. He came here, looking for her. They really trust me with this assignment. I've hardly slept. I'm tuned to every little noise. I've set my clock to wake me every couple of hours. I get up to come out here on the landing." She pointed a finger towards the floor. "I can see if she turns lights on in her place. Well, that is, I see her *whole* apartment, except her bedroom. For that, I have to go out on the back landing." She grinned at the distraught mother.

Ruth was digging through the bottom of her purse for her daughter's spare key. As soon as she found it, she rammed it into the lock. Then she flung the door wide open as it banged on the wall doorstop.

Bernice replied, "She's not inside. The policeman looked already."

Ignoring that last statement, Ruth yelled loud enough to wake the dead, "Carolyn dear, you here?"

Both women peered in. Then Ruth ran through the living room with Bernice trying to keep up.

Ruth yelled her daughter's name again in the kitchen. Frantic with worry, she turned into the bedroom to look around. But finding no one home, she found herself asking, "Where would you go?"

Nosy Bernice was scanning each of the rooms as she tried to help the distraught mother. "The police and me, we just don't know. He even asked all the neighbors."

Ruth turned to find her daughter's neighbor at her shoulder. "Our West Chicago Police?"

"Yes, that's the ones. I went right there, to the police first thing this morning. I just knew this wasn't right." Bernice pushed her slipping glasses to their rightful place on her nose.

Ruth turned quickly and headed back to the front door, saying, "I'm going right over there. Surely they found her by now."

Bernice offered, "Ya want me to come with you?"

Mrs. Hendricks stopped at the door to wait for the slow-moving neighbor, sensing Bernice wanted to be more involved. "I, I just don't know." Thinking she could get down the stairs faster without the older woman, she added, "I'll let you know what they say."

"Oh, that would be great. They haven't called me back or anything yet." Bernice assured her, "And I'm taking good care of her cat. Don't you worry about Tuxedo."

As soon as they were both out of the apartment, Ruth locked up. She passed Bernice on the landing, then quickly took the stairs down to her car. It didn't take her long to reach the police station on Freemont. She hurried inside up to the desk clerk, shouting, "I can't find my daughter."

"What is your daughter's name?" asked Bonnie Parnell, the

police station records clerk.

"Carolyn Fazzino. She's not in her apartment. Don't just sit there. Look for her!" Her voice was rising.

"Your name?" the clerk asked as she tapped the keys of her computer.

"Ruth Hendricks."

"Sergeant Dodson has assigned Detective Waller and Garcia to work on this case."

"She's not a case! She's my daughter!" Ruth's voice was getting higher.

Calmly the clerk said into her phone, "Carolyn Fazzino's mother is here."

⬥

"Good," was Detective Waller's brief answer. She hung up. Turned towards her partner, and said, "Maybe it's time we get some real answers."

Garcia had carefully filled Waller in on the missing person report this past hour.

Detective Waller stood, revealing navy blue trousers pulled tight by the pants zipper over her protruding mid-section. Her collapsible metal baton, marked with scratches from years of street work, attached to her belt. They both walked to the front, where they found the distraught mother. Detective Garcia reached out to shake hands. Ruth's eyes darted between the two of them. She didn't raise her hand.

The mother's too upset to even notice my friendly gesture, thought Garcia.

Instead Ruth screamed, "I can't find Carolyn anywhere!"

In a soothing voice Waller asked, "Can you come inside so we can get started right away at finding her?"

Ruth with her shoulders slumped simply nodded in agreement.

"Please come this way so we can help her." Once inside a smaller interview room where it was quieter, the detectives introduced themselves and Waller said, "Please have a seat. Would you like a cup of coffee or water?"

"Nothing. Just find her." Ruth caught a fast breath. They could hear the painful rasp where her throat was closing.

Waller turned towards Garcia and ordered, "Get her a bottle of water anyway." Much quieter she said, "I'll take this, woman to woman."

Garcia glared at his partner with a look of 'why me,' however she was the leading officer. Just maybe Waller had a point. He got two bottles of water and knocked lightly on the interrogation door. As he stepped back into the room, he found his partner sitting across the table from Mrs. Hendricks. He handed water to each of them smiling. The interview was being taped. Later they could view the tape to watch the Mother's body language when asked certain questions.

Waller asked, "How old is Carolyn?"

Ruth's voice was starting to wobble. "Twenty-nine."

Garcia noticed Mrs. Hendricks expensive white veneer teeth, that hadn't grown in her mouth. "When did you last see or hear from her?" asked Detective Garcia as he sat next to his partner.

Ruth sniffled, but explained, "Monday afternoon. Carolyn didn't go to work that day. She was getting a crown in the morning. She phoned me that afternoon saying she was home from the dentist. Her mouth was still numb, but she was going to take a couple Tylenol and lay down."

Waller used a gentle, but firm voice prodding, "Do you remember anything else?"

Mrs. Hendricks shook her head nervously, her voice filled with anguish. "No, not really. I said something about calling me if she needed anything. She said she wanted to sleep. She hadn't slept much the night before because her tooth hurt. So, I told her I wouldn't bother her that evening when I usually call her. But we talk every day. Why hasn't she called me back?"

Garcia smiled and asked, "What kind of phone does she have?"

"She uses her cell," the mother's agitation showed in her shaking hands.

"Any other phones?" the detective questioned leaning forward.

"No." She was wringing her hands on the table.

"What kind of phone and what's her number?" Waller pulled out a small pad of paper and pen to write it down.

"An iPhone." She gave them the number without looking it up. Tears were running down her cheeks.

With concern in his voice Garcia questioned, "How would you describe your relationship with your daughter?"

"We're close. We talk every night. I really enjoy hearing her voice, even though sometimes it's only a few minutes, but Carolyn didn't answer last night. I don't understand what's going on." The worry cracked in her voice. "I call her, hoping she'll tell me Vince came back. But it's been two nights of no return calls. Something is very wrong. I even tried Carolyn's work number, but another woman answered instead, even asked to help me. When I told her, I was Carolyn's mother, she said they haven't seen her since last Friday because of her dentist appointment. Then I went to Carolyn's apartment and now here."

"Does she live with anyone?" asked Waller.

Garcia knew the answer to that question already. He knew Waller just wanted Mrs. Hendricks version of her daughter's marriage.

Ruth looked down towards the tabletop. Her voice quivered, "Well, she's separated from her husband. I always liked Vince. He's handsome, charismatic, Italian. I could easily see why Vince made Carolyn so happy. But after they were married a few years, I sensed something was wrong."

"Wrong?" prompted Waller.

"He was nice, full of flattery when they started dating. I liked him right away, but it seemed like he was trying too hard at first," Ruth answered. "I could see how happy Carolyn was." She paused and lowered her voice. "Then suddenly he left. I should have been there for her when he moved out. I feel so guilty." Ruth wiped her eyes with the back of her hand.

Waller was staring at the mother with a concerned expression on her face as she asked, "Was there any abuse between them?"

Her shoulders tensed. "Oh, I don't think so." Ruth paused. "Carolyn did say, he yelled a lot."

A gut feeling tells me she could have hidden her husband's physical abuse, thought Garcia but he asked, "Why did he leave?"

Mrs. Hendrick's body tensed up. "I," she sniffed. "I don't really know. I guess it was all the fighting."

Waller had to push. "But what did they fight about?"

Ruth's forehead wrinkled with concern. "I don't know."

This is heartbreaking for her, thought Garcia. "Any guess as to what they were fighting about?"

Silent tears dribbled down her cheeks as she shook her head. She pulled another tissue from her purse and blew her nose.

Waller's voice softened as she asked, "Mrs. Hendricks, do you think it was about money or could one of them have had an affair?"

Her voice went shrill as she answered, "Really I don't know. I tried to ask her, but she wouldn't talk about it." Ruth nervously fiddled with the water bottle in front of her.

Waller leaned closer to ask, "Could she have gone back to her husband?"

"Vince?" Ruth leaned back in her chair. "Oh, I hope so." Her eyes softened. "Maybe that's it. They finally spoke and made up. That has to be what happened."

Garcia knew they needed to talk to the husband. "When was the last time you spoke to him?"

She threw her hands in the air as she said, "I couldn't call him. How could he leave my daughter? As a mother, I had to take her side, no matter what it was about. I haven't spoken to him since." She pulled a tissue from her purse and blew into it.

"We'll do it, Mrs. Hendricks. We need more than a character reference." Detective Waller's tone was firm. "We need proof." The officer gave a slight smile. "We don't even know if there's actually been a crime. She's just missing. Maybe she went on a trip."

Ruth's eyes were pleading for help as she frowned. "But it's been two days. Surely Carolyn would have told me if they decided to go away together. She's my baby, my only child. This *is* serious."

"Do you have her husband's address?" asked Garcia.

She scratched the base of her chin with a manicured nail and thoughtfully said, "No, no I don't know where he's staying, but he works for ECHO Global Logistics."

"Do you have his number?"

"Oh, yes. I have that." Ruth reached for her purse. Taking her pink cell phone, she pressed the icon for contacts and found her son-in-law's number. "Here it is."

Garcia jotted the number down. "Has your daughter been seeing anyone since her husband moved out? Possibly a new boyfriend?"

The tone of her voice shaky as Ruth told them, "She's never mentioned it to me, but Melissa might know."

Calmly Waller prompted her, "Who is Melissa?"

"Oh, her best friend, Melissa Tomlin. I even called her to see if she's heard from Carolyn, but she hasn't." She paused slightly, but then went on, "Melissa is a bit of a wild woman, full of life, exciting to be near. They're like sisters. When she didn't know where Carolyn was, I just knew something was wrong."

"We'll need to talk with Melissa. What's her number?"

Ruth gave it to the detective, then glanced at her watch. "She'll be at work now. She's the manager at Victoria's Secret in Stratford mall."

Waller placed a hand on the table close to Ruth. "Does Carolyn have any other close friends?"

Tears streamed down the mother's face as she managed to say, "She has friends where she works."

"Where does Carolyn work?" asked Garcia.

Ruth's voice was trembling, but she said, "At Morton Medical library."

"The one in Lombard?" Waller questioned.

"Yes."

As soothing as Waller could manage her voice she asked, "Could she be working overtime? Maybe worked so late last night she just didn't have a chance to call you?"

"She always has time for me." Her voice was sounding hysterical again. "Carolyn told me, she explained to Mr. Herman, she wasn't sure she would be at work on Tuesday."

"Who is Mr. Herman?" Garcia automatically pulled at the left side of his mustache.

"Oh, her boss." Ruth was wringing her hands. "Carolyn didn't know how she would feel the day after a crown. She's never had one before." Suddenly she wailed, "I should have driven her to the appointment. What kind of mother am I?" Then she caught her breath and slowed down, but her eyes were still filled with fear. "She got home after the dentist appointment. I talked with her."

Seems like she disappeared immediately after the neighbor saw her leave. "Has she ever gone away before?" Detective Garcia questioned.

"She and Vince took vacations when they were together. Before she was married, she and Melissa would go on short trips, but nothing in the last few months since she's separated, but never, ever without telling me." Ruth's hands trembled uncontrollably.

Waller glanced down at the missing person report her partner had filled out earlier asking, "Any identifying scars or birthmarks?"

Ruth snapped, "She's perfect."

Waller's head pulled back as she responded, "Of course."

However, we must ask, thought Garcia.

Alicia Waller reached into her pants pocket and came up with a few miniature Hershey bars offering one to the irritated mother.

Ruth strongly shook her head 'no,' so the detective unwrapped the melted chocolate for herself. After swallowing a bite, she continued the questioning with, "Mrs. Hendricks, does your daughter ever take the train anywhere?"

"Only when she's going into the city. Like who wants to drive in there?" The pitch of her voice rising.

Waller placed her hands on her hips and asked, "Does she owe money?"

"Not that I know of." Ruth was shaking her head. "She could

have asked me for money if she needed it."

Garcia could hear the terror in her voice; however, he went on, "Does she have a weapon in her home?"

Ruth's eyes opened even wider. Her hands were trembling, but she managed a weak, "I don't think so."

She was startled by that question, but we must know.

"Is she suicidal?"

"No. No. She's nothing like that." The mother's voice was near hysterics. "She would never do that."

Garcia sensed the mother was coming unglued.

Waller changed the subject, "Where is Carolyn's father?"

"Just find my daughter. Don't worry about him, he's dead! Heart attack five years ago," she snapped. The fear was obvious in her eyes. Her body was shaking.

Wow, a verbal attack. She's starting to hyperventilate. She's losing it. Is the father a trigger? Does her daughter have an old issue with him?

Detective Waller asked for phone numbers of Carolyn's friends in addition to co-workers. Then went on to ask about her place of work, and how long she had been there. After getting as much information about Carolyn Fazzino as she possibly could from the mother, Waller thanked Mrs. Hendricks, promising to let her know when they found anything more. Waller rose from her chair and handed over a business card as she said, "Here's my phone number if you think of anything else."

Then reassuringly Garcia added, "Please keep in mind even people who are regular in their habits can get stuck in traffic, caught in a long line at the supermarket, or they can run into an old friend on the way home from work. Most people go missing because they want to be missing. They want to get away from something or someone."

"Not Carolyn!" Ruth wailed as she reached for her purse to pull out a tissue. "That's not my baby. She wouldn't leave without telling me." Her voice was shaking right along with her hands. "She's my only child." Crying, she swallowed and found her voice again,

"You *have* to find her!"

"Missing persons and their vehicles are entered into the federal NCIC computer system. If any officer runs their name or license plate, it's flagged as being associated with a missing person." Waller was trying to reassure her.

Ruth screamed, "You have to go look for her!"

Waller took a step towards the mother. "We have enough for today. Would you like a ride home, or can we call someone for you?"

Ruth blew her nose again. "No, I can drive."

In a patient tone Garcia said, "Be cautious when speaking with the media. We don't want them compromising sensitive information or evidence that may be needed later."

Ruth nodded her head and stood.

Reluctantly she left the police station and shakily drove home. People in town everywhere around her were doing ordinary things, driving cars, pushing buggies, and walking dogs, as if life was exactly the same, when it wasn't. It was all wrong. Her daughter was missing. Ruth poured herself a glass of white wine wanting to calm her shaking nerves and sat down in an easy chair. Using her cell phone, she started making calls to her friends she had just given to the police. She wanted to give them a heads up before the police would call each one. She had to do something. She just couldn't sit idle. Between calls, Ruth cried so hard she could barely breathe, her sobs bursting from her throat as if they came from the bottom of her soul. She kept thinking; *I can't fall apart. I must find her*. This was so unlike Carolyn. Something was very wrong.

Chapter 5

INTERROGATION

They took separate lunches. Right after lunch, Detective Garcia tried to hide his doughnut as he walked into the station house because the cliche' embarrassed him. Little did he know that no one truly cared. He stepped past a twenty-something guy, thick-necked thug. Carlos Garcia thought, *he could be in the mafia, if we have any of them here in West Chicago.* As he walked by, he turned to see the back of the thug's t-shirt which read, "Mafia." Laughing to himself he thought, *maybe we should brand all gang members.*

Waller was busy herself watching a brunette giving a report of disturbing the peace. Just as Waller got back to her desk, Sergeant Dodson strode past the confusion straight towards them. Once he was close enough to the pair, he said, "You two, in my office."

The three walked into his domain. Waller and Garcia stood facing their supervisor. As Dodson sat in his desk chair he spoke up, "Who have you talked with so far on the case?"

"I've spent a lot of time with the nosy neighbor. Even questioned many of Carolyn's other neighbors," answered Garcia.

Waller said, "We've interviewed her mother." With the detective's mouth full of chocolate, she turned towards Dodson saying, "I believe her. She's truly worried. The father was some financial bigwig at AT&T. He died before he retired, so she got a year's salary for death benefits and health insurance."

"It's possible a kidnapper thinks she has money," speculated Dodson.

"However, her mother is going through the insurance money quickly: new teeth, furniture, and likes traveling first class," Garcia answered, as the strong scent of chocolate filled the air between them.

Waller handed a file folder to barrel-chested David Dodson. The sergeant, with his flat-top haircut, was easily three inches taller than Garcia and thirty pounds heavier, but not overweight like Waller. The sergeant's desk chair squeaked as he straightened up reaching forward with his broad hands to take the manila folder. He raised his eyebrows, furrowing his whole forehead. All three knew a missing adult was not an amber alert like a child would be. "Twenty-nine-year-old, Caucasian, separated from her husband," explained Waller.

Dodson swung around slowly and heavily in his swivel chair. He put his size thirteen feet flat on the brown office carpet.

Waller turned her face to him with a sort of lunge. She was the type to speak up to contribute ideas, so she asked, "Would you watch for a ransom note?"

The powerful, but graceful, Sergeant Dodson was reading the report, so he didn't answer immediately.

Garcia waited a few minutes, then said, "Her husband is a semi-truck driver. They've been separated approximately four months. We're looking at him next."

Dodson with the report still in his hand said, "Good." He looked up at Garcia. "Bring him in for questioning. Maybe that will shake him enough so we can get his story. Also check to see if she boarded a small plane from the DuPage Airport. Let me know what happens." With that brief comment, he dismissed them.

The two partners drove to ECHO Global Logistics headquarters. They got lucky. Vince Fazzino had just returned from his first haul of the day. They met up with him in the dispatcher's office.

"Vincent Fazzino?" Waller with her dark hair in a sleek ponytail, pulled back her jacket to reveal her badge.

"What?" Irritation was obvious in his voice. Vince had Italian features with cocky self-assurance.

"I'm Detective Waller of the West Chicago Police Department and this is my partner, Detective Garcia."

Vince turned on the charm with the female detective. Winking at her he said, "Hi Babe."

Garcia reached out his hand to the clean-shaven man saying, "This is about your wife, Mr. Fazzino." They all shook hands. "Have you seen her lately?"

"No. We're not living together." Vince smirked before he asked, "What's happened?"

"We'd like to talk with you. Could you come with us into the station?"

"Talk about what? I haven't seen her." There was a superior tone to his voice.

Waller tensed her shoulders and said, "That's why we need to talk."

Vince's voice mounted in annoyance as he added, "Well, I got to tell my boss."

"We've already spoken with him Mr. Fazzino and he says you can go with us."

He answered with slow emphasis, "I guess it's okay then."

───────≈《◎》≈───────

Fifty-five minutes later, broad shoulders pulled back, Vince Fazzino, looking like he owned the place, even though he was sandwiched between Waller and Garcia, stepped inside the police station. The thirty-four-year-old was dressed casually in a light blue button-down shirt, no tie, and tan chinos. His unruly black hair toppled onto his forehead. With head held high, the athletically built man was ushered into the interrogation room with its stark white walls. A small table sat in the corner with three straight-backed chairs, a room designed to sweat out the truth. What Mr. Fazzino didn't see was a video camera mounted inside a vent located high in the corner.

Waller expressionless, snapped, "Sit down Mr. Fazzino." She gestured towards the chair facing her partner.

Vince sat down, then tilted his chair back, clasping his hands behind his head, elaborately casual. Did he realize there were eyes staring at him through a monitor on the outside of the room? He didn't look threatened, instead he held his chin high.

"Would you like some water or coffee?"

"Sure, make it bottled water." Vince crossed his arms.

Garcia went to fetch water without being told.

Wanting the interrogation recorded, Detective Waller casually asked, "Okay with you Vince, if we tape this talk? I'm pretty slow taking notes."

"Sure, I don't care."

Waller pushed a sheet of paper towards Vince saying, "This form is your consent to tape this." Then she shifted in her seat because her trousers were tight at the waist.

As Vince quickly signed, Garcia sat a bottle of water in front of Vince and commented, "July has been nice weather so far." He tried to develop a rapport. If the person starts talking to the police about harmless things, it will become harder to stop talking or start lying later when the discussion turned to the crime.

However, Waller just jumped right in. "Carolyn hasn't been seen for a couple days."

"What happened to her?" His voice hard.

"That's what we're trying to find out. Is it like your wife to go missing for a day or two?"

Vince crossed his arms in defiance again. "No, she's never been gone, 'er, missing."

"Okay, Vince, we need Carolyn's date of birth."

"August 5th, 1985," Vince quickly answered, then looked rather proud of himself for knowing his wife's birthday.

Still using casual conversation to create a non-threatening atmosphere, Garcia asked, "Your birth date?"

"April 3rd, 1980." Vince told Garcia.

"How tall is your wife?"

Vince turned to smile at Waller. "Five foot three."

Detective Garcia scribbled on his pad of paper. "Thanks. How long have you known Carolyn?"

"We met in college. We lived together for about a year before our wedding." Softness had seeped into Vince's voice. It sounded like a lover's voice of low light and drifting music for only one listener.

Garcia leaned back in his chair, tapping his pen off his teeth. "We have some domestic disturbance reports here on file, so I just want to go over some details."

Vince grimaced. "Oh Hell, that nosy neighbor called the police every time we got loud. We had a couple fights. Those apartment walls are paper-thin, but the crazy woman next door was a royal pain in the ass. She called the police on us. Her apartment smells like a litter box. I don't even know how many cats she has in there."

"When did you last see your wife?" asked Detective Waller.

"I haven't seen Carolyn in four months. I don't know where she is."

Garcia kept his eyes on Fazzino. "What did you fight about?"

"Oh everything, but mainly, I want kids and she doesn't."

Waller stared impassively at Vince. "What upset you the most during those fights?"

Vince's alert brown eyes moved to the right. "I'm Italian, come from a big family. I wanted children. I've always pictured myself playing catch in the backyard like my dad did with me when I was a kid. It was hours of throwing the ball back and forth. I thought I could talk her into it in time." Sarcastically, he added, "But Queen Carolyn didn't want any of that. She can't handle a hangnail. It's always, all about *her*."

Waller made a mental note of Vince's eye movement. She had been taught that when the suspect is remembering something, his eyes will often move a certain way which is a manifestation of his brain activating the memory center.

Domestic abusers are often charming to others, thought Garcia as he leaned forward and asked, "During the arguments, did you ever hit her?"

Vince's eyes flared wide open as his voice got louder. "Damn it, of course not." He balled his fists tight. His eyes flared momentary with anger. "We just have to find Carolyn."

The detective suspected if Vince truly was violent, he'd take a swing at him then.

"I couldn't convince her. You know, it was just useless to argue anymore. No one was budging. I wanted children. It meant..." His voice trailed off.

Waller prodded. "It meant what, Vince?"

Vince raised his voice, "You can't treat me like this. I willingly came in here." Then he looked at Garcia and asked, "You ever been married?" His voice was hard.

"We're not talking about me, Vince. We need to know what <u>you</u> think of marriage."

Vince looked down at the plain tabletop and stared at his hands. His voice softened as he said, "Marriage is only perfect to those that have never been married." Then he focused on the detective and answered, "I walked out of the apartment. Hell, I thought she'd call me right away, tell me to come back. I was hoping she'd give in." His voice trailed off, "But she never phoned."

"Have you started divorce proceedings?"

Vince's voice sounded depressed, "No, I just didn't get around to it. I was heartbroken for her months ago, but now I really don't know what happened to her."

Waller asked, "What happened after you left?"

"Nothing. She's bull-headed." Slowly he added, "We both are."

Garcia ran his hand over his chin. He needed a shave. He would always need a shave. "After you left her, you ever talk to Carolyn at all during those four months?"

"No." Vince balled up his fist.

"We'll check your phone records, so you want to rethink that answer?" prodded Waller. She leaned a little closer.

Vince shook his head and looked straight at her. "I want clear-cut answers. She can't just vaporize. I don't know anything." He tried to square his shoulders. "I've got regrets. I wish it had worked out, but now we just have to find her," Fazzino said matter-of-factly.

"She belong to any churches, or maybe join a cult or other religious organization?"

"No. No. This is so off base. I mean, we got married in her parent's church, but we just didn't get around to going on Sunday mornings yet. That doesn't make us bad people."

Practically interrupting him, Garcia said, "No, no we're not saying you're bad. We're just looking for all the facts. Mrs. Fazzino have any tattoos?"

Vince looked surprised. "Carolyn? Tattoos? She's so afraid of needles she would never get a tattoo. You don't know her like I do."

"We'll need to contact her dentist to get dental records."

With a shocked look on his face, Vince screamed, "Oh my God! You think something awful has happened to her!"

Waller patted his shoulder. "We just don't know yet, Vince." She paused a second, then watching his eyes closely, she added, "We'd like your permission to go back to the apartment to collect her toothbrush and hairbrush for samples of DNA. We'll lift her prints from the apartment, too."

Vince's shoulders tensed as he tried to suck in air.

Waller continued, "I'm not suggesting foul play here, however once we have all the facts about the potential disappearance, we'll be better equipped to respond appropriately."

Garcia assured him, "We'll keep her records on file here."

Vince let out a long sigh.

"Tell us what you did yesterday Mr. Fazzino?" Waller asked looking directly at him.

"You think I saw her?" he shook his head 'No.' "I just want to find her."

"Okay Vince, let's have it from the start." Waller said firmly.

Vince sighed, like he was resigned to go through this. "I left my room at the Blossom Hotel and reached the yard at eight o'clock like I do every mor..."

"Which hotel?" interrupted Waller.

"The one on Lake Street, but it still takes me a good hour to make Chicago that time of the morning."

Garcia moved closer. "After you got to work, what happened?"

"They sent me up to Milwaukee to get a load." Fazzino started to say something, then checked himself, but he fidgeted in his seat. Instead he said, "I took it to South Bend."

Waller pushed a few dark strands of hair behind her left ear. "What did you do there?"

"Unloaded, then I went east to Elkhart."

"What happened then?" Waller was really watching his face.

"It took them a while to load me up, but I brought that haul back into Illinois, to Darien."

"Then what happened?"

"I was done for the day. So, went back to the hotel."

"What about your evening?" asked Detective Waller.

"Oh right. After work, I called a buddy, then met him for a burger and beer in Elgin."

"Vince, we're going to need his name and number."

"Jerry Ridder." And gave the number to them.

"How long were you with him?"

"I guess we drank a few beers. Probably talked till after nine o'clock. Then I went back to the hotel, watched the news and went to bed."

"We'll check with your friend. What about Carolyn's family? Would she go visit someone?"

"Her mother is the only family she's got. Ruth Hendricks. Her dad died a few years ago."

"You get along with your mother-in-law?" Detective Waller asked.

Smiling, Vince answered, "Sure. Ruth always liked me. She seemed thrilled that Carolyn and I got married."

"Does she work?" asked Garcia.

"Well, she used to clerk at a law office until Carolyn's dad had a heart attack. Then she took care of him. But he had a second attack eleven months later and then, he didn't make it. But Ruth and I get along great."

"Does your wife often go on trips, go overnight anywhere, with a girl friend? Another man?"

"I don't know if there's another guy since I left. Melissa would know. Melissa Tomlin is her closest friend. Maybe she and Melissa went somewhere."

"Tell us about Melissa," encouraged Waller.

"She's a store manager at Victoria's Secret inside Stratford Mall. They've been friends since they were kids. They're best friends." Suddenly he had a thought, "Maybe they're in this together. Melissa runs around loose, new guy every week. She'd probably encourage Carolyn to date since I left. In fact, I can easily see Melissa taking her along to those bars she goes to all the time."

"Do you know which bars they might have gone to?"

"There's a sport's bar on Wise. I don't remember the name."

Waller said, "We'll look into that idea. Does Carolyn have any enemies?"

He jerked backwards in his chair with shock. "What? No one."

Garcia added, "Like anyone who's mad at her?"

"No." With annoyance he said, "Hell, I don't know. What do ya mean?"

"For anything at all, like maybe she took someone's parking space?"

"Damn it," he yelled. "You're wasting your time here. I don't know where she is. You need to be out looking for my wife."

"Sometimes asking the right questions, gets us to the right answers."

"I'll take a lie detector test." Then Vince's teeth clenched. He was rapidly blinking his eyes. His lips clamped shut; his body was taut as a cornered animal.

The detectives both stared at him.

Vince clenched his fists into balls at his sides. Looking intense, he turned his brown eyes on Detective Garcia and answered, "I can't think of anyone who would want to harm her."

Both cops stared at him as he shut down.

Waller stood and said, "Mr. Fazzino, we're going to give you a moment to compose yourself so you can tell us the truth."

They left Fazzino sitting in the interview room. Once the door closed, Waller flicked on a machine that made white noise in the interview room. Then she explained to Garcia, "So the suspect can't hear us here in the hallway."

Chapter 6

SUSPECT THE SPOUSE

Detective Waller and Garcia stood facing each other outside the interrogation room. Garcia shot her a surprised look as he heard the word 'suspect.' "Is that what you really think, Waller?" Detective Garcia had the feeling that for all the dramatics, the man was sincere. Thinking, *he's concerned about his wife.*

"Those tears were so fake." Detective Waller began pacing in tight circles in the corridor. Every muscle in her body seemed to be twitching from sitting still at that table so long. "Who's he trying to fool? He's hiding something. I can feel it." Waller reached inside her trouser pocket to pull out a small candy bar. In frustration, she exclaimed, "It's impossible to know what happened behind closed doors, like what really went on in the Fazzino home." As she eyed the chocolate in her hand, Waller replied, "Domestic violence is the worst call ever. I had one a few weeks ago where the couple suddenly started arguing with me. Even the grandmother took their side. She was arguing with me too. I considered taking all three of them in, the nut cases."

Garcia saw the Fazzino situation a little differently than his untrusting partner. He wrinkled his nose and faced his partner. "Even though they split up, he's not heartless. He seems to have feelings for her. And even his mother-in-law loves him."

Waller unwrapped her chocolate while she caught her breath. "Vince Fazzino gives the impression of being a thoughtful and reasonable man. I've found time and again that's exactly how abusers appear to the outside world." She popped the chocolate into her mouth. "That's camouflage." She chomped hard on the candy. "The Fazzinos didn't have happily-ever-after like Vince expected. He sounds desperate to have kids. Their marriage went south. Maybe he's so frustrated with his wife, he does away with her and his problem." She placed her hands on her hips. "He may be abusive. His motive could be revenge. You ruined my life, or a more complicated scenario, the Mrs. isn't doing what Vince wanted. He's desperate for kids. In his mind, Carolyn's broken the marriage contract. She's not doing her job. His life isn't perfect anymore. He wants a lovely family, or while smacking her around, he killed her, maybe accidently, however it's a done deal. Abusive spouses can progress to killing. How about the Pederson guy in Bolingbrook? He had a missing wife and said she left their children." With no talent for finesse, she rolled her eyes.

Garcia doubted his own partner. "Hmm, how do you get from leaving her, to killing her?"

"I believe the man was desperate. He was clever, didn't do anything to her in their own home. He waited and grabbed her when she was out. He's good or we've got to find out if he lost his marbles." She waved her hand towards her own head.

"Possible," but doubt sounded in his voice.

The more experienced officer took this as another opportunity to educate her newbie partner. "We had this old cop who used to talk about his brothers with whomever we brought into question. I'd hear him say to a burglar, 'Well, you know, I can understand your problem 'cause I have a brother who's a burglar. Then he'd be talking to a rapist about his brother the rapist. This guy could bond with them, but he had more brothers. One night he's talking about his brother the car thief to this guy we caught with a slim-jim, and the guy confesses to a murder."

Garcia's eyes shot open. "You want me to tell him I have a brother who got rid of his wife?"

"No, I'm just telling you what this guy did to get them to open up. Ninety percent of this job is jawbone. You've got to know how to talk to people, from the high-end lawyer to the gangbanger on the street. Did you see how he looked upward when he was telling us what he did yesterday? He's hiding something." The corner of her mouth gave a slight smirk.

Garcia ran his free hand through his dark hair. "Are you sure?"

"Fazzino is accessing different parts of his brain. He looked to his right when he was remembering the truth, like when he was talking about his dad. During simple recall questions, his eyes rolled. Experience has taught me that listening is important." The know-it-all Waller added, "He's arrogant, even abusive and he's hiding something."

Garcia rolled his eyes. "He's an arrogant Italian, but I'm sorry Waller, I just don't buy it. There's absolutely no physical evidence against him. He's a person of interest, not a suspect yet. However, you've seen more of this then I have."

"When he's making up an alibi, he's thinking, so his eyes move up." The tiny chocolate morsel was gone, so she rummaged through her pockets for more, but added, "There's some deception going on here."

"Well, getting someone to confess to a crime, when we don't even know if it's a crime, isn't going to be easy," he answered her back as he tugged on his mustache in a nervous gesture.

"He knows more than he's telling, and he's in the system," said Waller nodding her head up and down.

Garcia ran his hand across his mustache. "Only the domestic fighting reports. Other than that, he's clean."

In a very cocky tone Waller said, "In my book, they all did it. Each one is guilty until I prove them innocent."

Garcia mumbled, "I'm not that tough on people." He raised his voice slightly as he said, "I get the feeling, they were a happy couple, however they haven't been that way for a while."

"He could be acting like he cares, to throw us off."

"Maybe. . . it's a desperate attempt to win back his wife, to prove to Carolyn he loves her. It's just an impression I got. He's upset, but not that angry. There's normal anger."

Waller crossed her arms. Contemplating out loud she said, "Then there's anger that can hurt. I'm not a psychologist, however in my opinion those two needed a therapist."

Garcia quickly had an image of his know-it-all lesbian partner meeting with a therapist but brushed the image from his mind. "Fazzino doesn't come across as a destructive bully. He left four months ago. Why would he come back now to do something to her? We don't have any evidence it's him." He thought, *Al you've been around for a while, longer than me, however you're not always right,* but said, "We can't arrest him for anything yet."

Waller threw up her chubby arms and announced, "I don't like him, too good looking. Besides, that thick chain of gold around his neck is distracting."

You don't like any men, Garcia thought, but answered, "People that have been arrested for a violent crime, even if released, are stigmatized for the rest of their lives, whether they did it or not. We can't charge him. We can't even hold him for long. In my opinion he's genuinely concerned about her."

Waller patted him on the cheek. "I know. It shows all over you. Maybe that's why Dodson made us work together."

Garcia pointed a finger at his own chest. "Good Cop." Then he turned the same finger towards Waller. "Bad Cop."

"Whatever works." Waller shrugged. "You need sharp eyes when questioning these characters."

"And an open mind," finished Garcia. "So, what's our next move?"

"We go back in and ask him again."

"Okay, Kemosabe." Garcia gave a nod of his head.

They both turned and walked back into the interrogation room. They knew they had to get tougher.

Vince sat right where they left him, but he had rolled his sleeves up. He was so tense that when the door swung in, he jumped. As soon as the door closed, Waller barked, "Where is your wife, Fazzino?"

Vince's left leg began to tremble, his eyebrows arched, and his teeth clenched. "I told you, I don't know, damn it. I want to find her."

Detective Waller's hands tightened into fists. "I don't know what you're up to. You say, you never saw your wife, nor heard from her in four months?"

"Never. We're separated." A firm answer, but he fidgeted in the straight-backed chair.

She raised her voice even louder. "Husbands are always under the microscope when women go missing, if they are living together or not. Your wife is missing. You're starting to look like a suspect, so tell us what's going on."

"No, you're not getting it. It wasn't that way. I mean, I...I don't know." Vince noticeably gulped.

"How was it?" The AC cut off. Without it's hum, the room fell silent. The thin sounds of their breathing filled the silence.

Detective Garcia cleared his throat and said, "We could work with your bank to see if she used her credit cards. Does she use the State Bank on Washington?"

"Yes, anyway we did use that bank when I lived with her." Trying to be helpful, Vince gave the policemen a list of her credit cards she used when they lived together.

With patience Garcia explained, "By the end of the day, we'll obtain a search warrant to look at her personal records."

But Waller impatient snapped, "She's your wife, so why haven't you seen her in months?"

Vince looked away from her prying eyes, saw his bottle of water and took a sip. "It sounds odd, I know..." His voice trailed off then. He couldn't hold her gaze. He looked at the table. "I was angry." He gasped for air again and again.

"How angry, Vince?"

His head lowered. "I, I needed some breathing room. A little time to think it over, that's all." His upper lip was sweating.

"You're gone a lot on your trips for work? Rough life, huh?" Waller accused. She pulled her chair nearer, leaned in till their heads almost touched.

"Not really." Vince rubbed his chin. "Usually, I'm home every night."

Waller made a mean face as she studied Fazzino. "Your wife ever take off before?"

He shook his head 'no.' "Not while I was there."

Already knowing the answer, however the detective asked anyway, "Where does she work?"

"In Lombard, at the library on the college campus." His hands were shaking so, he shoved them into his pockets.

"She ever take time off from work before?" Garcia sat directly on the table, close enough that his thigh pressed against Fazzino's arm.

Vince pulled his arm off the table. "Only vacations. She's dependable. It isn't like her to disappear." Sweat glistened on his arms.

"Could she have left for a better job or a different place to live?"

His left hand was trembling. "No. She liked her job. She's been there for seven years, but it doesn't pay well enough for her to move into a larger place."

Waller kept firing the questions at him, "Where does Carolyn shop?"

"For clothes, she goes over to the Stratford Mall in Bloomingdale. She likes Melissa's opinion on clothing."

Since Vince already told them about Melissa, Waller asked, "Where else does she shop?"

Sweat dripped off Fazzino's face. "Well, for groceries she goes to Aldi's on 59 or Diamonds on Roosevelt Road."

Waller leaned forward and stared hard into his eyes and said, "You saw her somewhere, didn't you? You met her. The two of you talked, and it grew into an argument. Maybe you accidently hit her. We know you didn't mean to do it."

Vince's face suddenly turned stone white. "No. I'd never do that." Then he wiped perspiration off his forehead with the back of his hand, despite the fact, the air conditioning was back on and working fine.

Persistently she pried, "You just weren't thinking clearly."

Vince's head shook slightly. "Nothing like that."

"Anything can happen in a split second."

"Hell, no!" he screamed.

Waller cocked her head to one side and squinted at Fazzino. "In fact, it could have been her fault. She asked for it. Didn't she?"

His adam's apple shook slightly as he gulped. "No, that's not what happened. She's a prima dona, not a bad person. Why don't you believe me?" His eyes were pleading with them.

Waller slammed her palm hard on the table for emphasis and insisted, "She lied to you, gave you the impression she'd have your babies. I want to know where Mrs. Fazzino is."

"She didn't tell me the whole truth at first, but I tell you, I don't know where she is." His face looked troubled.

"Jesus man, you walked out on her. Can you contact her?" Garcia stood and leaned over Vince as he thought, *don't lawyer up on us.*

Vince yelled, "It wasn't meant like that. I'm telling ya the truth, damn it!" He tightly balled his fists like he might punch someone. "I just couldn't stay that day. I couldn't call. Maybe I wanted her to give in first, but she didn't call."

Garcia tried to calm his voice as he said, "Vince, if you love her, now's your time to show it. Now's your time to get it right."

Vince wouldn't look at the detective's face.

"I happen to believe that basically, deep down, you're a decent guy." Garcia explained. "I may end up regretting this, however I think you're a good guy who somehow ended up in a shit situation."

That got a tiny twitch from Fazzino's eyebrows.

Garcia continued, "I don't like being wrong about people. These interview rooms have seen men and women spill out things that should never happen in this world. You do give a damn about Carolyn."

"I, I want her found."

Waller chose to be blunt. "Come on Fazzino, you've been lying ever since you entered this room." She paused for effect, then went on, "Do you think Carolyn might have been depressed because you left her? Maybe even try suicide in a remote location to spare her family the mess at home?"

Vince's eyes darted back and forth, visually shaken, then he hung his head.

Waller raised her voice, "Your wife's disappearance is some serious shit. We have to sort this out."

Vince began to tremble; his nervous fingers actually making a tapping sound off the tabletop. "I've told you, I don't live with her, so I don't know where she goes."

The police needed to probe at Vince's feelings for his estranged wife, but they were random questions, shots in the dark. Garcia knew they had no trump card, no evidence, no tool to pry into this man's soul. They were hoping he would fear their authority enough to give up his darkest secrets. "You living with her or not doesn't make any difference because, legally, she's still your wife."

Vince's eyes widened in fear.

Waller pulled her chair forward and stared at him. "I've been doing this job a long-time man and a whole busload of people who lied to me in this very room are on Death Row now." Even though, she knew the death penalty was abolished in Illinois in 2011.

"I'm really worried about her." The words came out sounding stilted because his jaw was jetting.

Fazzino might be cooperating the best he could, so Garcia touched his shoulder to offer feigned comfort. "I know you loved her."

"Hell, I still do. I really care what happens to her." It was out of his mouth faster than he had a chance to deny it.

Garcia wanted to come across as a friend, so he moved a chair around the table closer to Vince. Calmly, he asked, "Then help us, Vince. Where were you yesterday morning?"

Vince gave his work schedule to Garcia once again.

Waller suddenly realized there was over an hour and a half lunch break during his workday, enough time for him to have traveled the thirteen miles from Elgin to West Chicago, grab Carolyn, and do who knows what and get back to Elgin. "That's a long lunch, Vince."

"I, I was really hungry," he stammered. He chewed his knuckle and stared at Waller.

Waller kept at him, "Where did you eat lunch, Mr. Fazzino?"

Vince couldn't look at her anymore and turned his head downward. "It doesn't have anything to do with Carolyn!" he said, his voice wobbling.

"Let us be the judge of that." She glared, moving closer to the guy's face. She knew getting in his personal space, would increase his discomfort. She was going for his jugular. "Your story sucks. You had time to drive to West Chicago, didn't you?"

"No, no that didn't happen!" he yelled. He was shaking his head 'no.'

It was time for the good cop to step in. Garcia, trying to show he's a friend softly said, "Vince, there's clearly something you're not telling us. We need to talk about it."

Sweat broke out on Vince's forehead, his face ashy. With his shoulders hunched, he bent his head down. His posture collapsing. Vince wouldn't look at either cop. He said in a tentative voice, "Okay, okay. I'm seeing someone. Jenny Maxwell. We went to a hotel in Elgin at noon yesterday, so I have someone else. I had nothing to do with Carolyn's disappearance."

"How long have you been seeing her?" Garcia asked in a soft, soothing voice to appear non-threatening, but thinking, *he was holding something back.*

"Just a couple months. She's nice," Vince answered.

Waller said, "You must put everything on the table, so we know what we're dealing with. Is *she* the reason you left your wife?"

"Oh, no." His shoulders slumped farther. "I didn't even know Jenny until I was on my own. I know she'll vouch for me. She's a real sweetheart." He pulled out his cell to give the policemen Jenny's work number. While he had the phone out, Garcia asked for the names of Vince's family members and close friends. He cooperated fully. They spoke of Carolyn's usual activities, her schedule on weekdays and weekends. He told Garcia about the places Carolyn usually frequented and her hobbies.

Then Waller straightened up and asked the *big* question, "Did you do something to your wife, so you would be free to be with your girlfriend?"

"No. Don't ya get it yet? I didn't do anything to Carolyn!"

Waller wanted to upset him more. "What did Carolyn think of you having a lady friend?"

"I didn't tell her, because we haven't spoken in months." Vince shook his dark head of hair, then exasperated with their questions he yelled, "I've got nothing to hide."

Waller moved closer, into his space again and sneered, "However you did try to hide the girlfriend from us."

"That's nonsense. Are you accusing me of something? If ya are, I don't like it a damn bit. I've told you all I know, which is nothing."

After hours of questioning, Vince looked defeated and tired. "I don't know anything. I'll take a lie detector test or a polygraph or whatever you call it. I don't know where she is." He rose to his feet.

Waller's eyes widened.

Vince said, "This is stupid. You can't keep me here." He started to move away from the table. "I watch crime shows on TV." He stopped walking, as if rooted to the spot near the door. "I came in to help find Carolyn..."

Waller interrupted. "Wait a minute Vince. We need to look at all possibilities to rule you out."

Vince opened the door. Suddenly he stopped and turned to look at them. "Me, I didn't do anything to her. You should get out there to look for her."

Detective Garcia realizing they couldn't keep him at the station, stood saying, "I want to thank you for voluntarily coming in today. We may have more questions, so don't go far."

"But my job requires me to drive into Chicago every day."

"Work trips are okay." Garcia reached towards Vince as they shook hands. "I must warn you; the press could be out there. They'll want to ask you questions."

"I don't know what to say to them."

Trying to help the man, Garcia said, "They have her on the air now. You can ask local newspapers, radio, and television for help in finding your wife. You can distribute posters, however, do not put your telephone number or address on the posters to avoid hoaxes. Tell them to contact us."

Vince swallowed with a dry throat. His jaw clamped tight, then he walked out. Hearing the babble of voices throughout the police station and worried someone would try to stop him, Vince walked rapidly down the mud-colored corridor of the station to the front door. He would drive around town for a while, looking for her himself since these cops weren't doing it.

Garcia jotted something on a pad. "Should we get a search warrant to look at his Blossom Hotel room?"

Waller's face was pale and hard in the yellow glare of the suspended electric bulb. "We don't have probable cause; however, I'd like to see if she's there. We'll just drive through the parking lot. Maybe we'll get lucky."

By now it was late in the day when Vince Fazzino stormed out of the police station. Detective Waller turned to her partner saying, "He looks *really* guilty. However, we've got to keep looking." Then she explained, "The best time to do a canvass of the area where Mrs. Fazzino was last seen would be the same time of day."

Garcia didn't even look at his notes before answering, "The neighbor said she saw her on the landing of their apartment building at five forty-five Tuesday morning."

Then the lead investigator said, "Let's meet here at five o'clock tomorrow morning. We'll go directly over there. I want to look at the parking lot some more."

Chapter 7

LAST SEEN

Twenty-four hours after Detective Carlos Garcia had done a well-being check at this apartment, he found himself back here again; this time with an experienced partner, Detective Alicia Waller. By five twenty they parked their unmarked Ford Explorer in front of Carolyn Fazzino's apartment building. The street was cast in pale blue-gray light of early morning, a hint of sunrise. They circled around to the back of the building. Waller looked for cameras, however there were none. The parking lot was surrounded with a high gray board fence with a garbage bin at each end. Very enclosed. No way anyone from the street could see into the parking area. At five forty-five they heard the sound of a door opening and turned to see Mrs. Butzen step out on her back landing. She was wearing a bright fuchsia flowered house dress with fuzzy blue slippers. Her red hair was pulled into pink foam curlers and she was carrying an animal's dish. Under her breath Waller mumbled to her partner, "Now that woman could scare the dead."

"Here kitty, kitty, kitty," Bernice sang out as she lumbered down the back stairs. Once she reached the gravel parking lot, she placed the food dish just to the side of the steps. When she raised herself back up, she saw the detectives. Only slightly startled, she quickly smiled. "Well, well, if it isn't that nice Detective Garcia and you've brought a friend." She reached her hand out to shake.

"I'm Detective Waller, ma'am. We're working on the

disappearance of your neighbor."

"I've been watching her apartment just like you asked me." Bernice winked at Garcia. "There's been no action. Oh, except for the mailman at ten thirty yesterday morning. He really didn't come up to her door. He leaves our mail down on the lower level in our mailboxes down there." She pointed in that direction. "Her cat, Tuxedo. Well, he hid in my bathroom last night. Maybe he's not used to so many other cats around him. He's a little bit of a loner, if ya know what I mean." She nodded her head towards Waller. "Have you found Carolyn, yet?"

"No ma'am. Where does Carolyn normally park her car?"

"Oh, just anywhere back here. There are just enough spaces for us all to park, but if we have company, then the guests must park out front, on the street. They don't get to park back here." She swung her flowing fuchsia draped arm towards the front of the building. "I don't get too many guests."

"Did Mrs. Fazzino have visitors?"

Bernice planted her feet firmly on the gravel and stated, "Well, she did yesterday, her mom came, and we searched her apartment. She's not in there, just like you said, Detective Garcia. She's not at home. I know because there weren't any lights turned on last night. No one, I mean no one I know sits around in the dark without their lights on or their TV on or something going."

Waller shifted her weight to her other leg, then asked her, "When you come out in the mornings to feed the cats, do you ever run into anyone else out here?"

"Let's see." Mrs. Butzen seemed to be thinking hard about this question. "I've seen Samantha Petersen leave really early for work because she's a baker. They start really early." Suddenly she placed her pudgy hand over her mouth and said to Garcia, "I wasn't going to tell you her name, because she bakes special treats for me sometimes."

"That's okay, Mrs. Butzen. We're only here to look for Carolyn," Garcia reassured her.

"Oh, good. Well, the only other one that leaves that early for work is Mrs. Triston. If you ask me, she leaves that son of hers alone way too much. He could get in trouble, if ya know what I mean."

Concerned that this could be a young child left without care, Waller asked, "How old is the son?"

"Hmm, now I don't know for sure, but I do know he goes to West Chicago High School. I just don't know which grade for sure."

"That's okay Mrs. Butzen. Anyone else ever been back here in the morning?"

She shook her head of curlers. "Nope, can't think of another soul. You want me to keep an eye on this parking lot too, for you? I don't mind. I can do it."

"That probably won't be necessary," said Waller.

"It's no trouble at all. In fact, I could even come back to the station to look through some mug shots for you."

"Not at this time, Mrs. Butzen. We don't have any possible suspects for you to identify right now." Garcia patted her hand.

She looked disappointed but said, "Okay then."

"We're going to look around here for a while. We don't want to hold you up if you're busy with your cats." Garcia told her.

"It's no trouble. I could even help you. I'm not really so busy right now."

"We'll investigate back here, if you could watch the front for us." Waller suggested.

"Oh," disappointment sounded in her voice, but she said, "Goodbye." She started up the stairs, then stopped after a few steps to look back at them.

They could tell she was reluctant to go back to her apartment, but eventually she did. Once inside, Garcia saw Mrs. Butzen pull her curtains apart to watch them. Waller pulled out her cell phone and started taking photos of the license plate numbers of all the cars in the parking lot.

Suddenly another back door opened. A black Scottie dog immerged, followed by an elderly man. He attached a black leash to the dog's collar. They slowly made their way down the back stairs.

Garcia walked to the bottom of the stairs to meet him.

Just as soon as the dog reached the gravel, she squatted to relieve herself.

"Good morning sir. You usually walk your dog at this time of day?"

"Wha'd ya say, young man?"

Garcia pulled his jacket back to reveal his badge clipped to his belt and repeated himself, raising his voice this time.

"Oh, sure. This is how Maddie and I start our day. First, I get to the head and then I bring her down, so she can too." He chuckled at his own humor, then added, "I'm an old navy guy myself, Korea."

Still shouting the detective asked, "You ever see your neighbor Carolyn Fazzino down here?"

"Yah, sometimes," the old Navy man responded.

Waller stepped closer to talk to the new witness. "You see her two days ago? Tuesday morning?"

"Not yesterday, but the day before; she was just pulling out of the lot." The old guy pointed towards the driveway that lead out to Hampton Ave. "She works, so she was probably going to work."

"You see her most mornings?" asked Garcia.

"No, now that you ask young man, she usually doesn't leave that early. Maybe she wanted to get into work early. Make some overtime money or something."

Waller asked, "Did you talk to her on Tuesday?"

"Oh no. She was already in her car, pulling out when I saw her. She didn't stop, didn't even wave. Maybe she didn't see me. Ya know, young people, always rushing around, in a big hurry all the time." The little Scottie was pulling at the leash. "Oh, I gotta walk Maddie. This is our routine."

With a smile and a nod of his head Garcia said, "Thanks for your help, Sir."

With the dog pulling, slowly the old guy moved towards the driveway himself, then out the parking lot entrance.

Garcia turned towards his partner. "That confirms what Mrs. Butzen said."

Waller got the receptionist to open up the Fazzino's apartment again. Nothing had been disturbed. This time she picked up a hair-brush in the bathroom and a toothbrush hanging on the brush holder. She placed them each in separate new paper bags, so the lab could collect DNA samples. Then she picked up a lap-top she saw sitting at a small desk in Carolyn's bedroom. She could get IT to look through any calendar Carolyn might have kept.

Meanwhile Garcia knocked on a few doors to speak with neighbors. But no one had seen Carolyn or her husband. After an hour of walking around the area and finding nothing out of the ordinary, Detective Waller spoke up, "First, we'll drop this computer off at the station, so our computer forensic specialist can start looking for any calendar she might have kept. We must question people who know Mr. Fazzino and his family. Let's get in the saddle, cowboy, to check out his alibi. Then we'll check with her dentist, the landlord, and her employer. We've got to do more digging into this couple."

The detectives left the apartment building, stopped at the police station to turn over Carolyn's laptop to Jake Nelson. The geeky twenty-five-year-old rubbed his hands together in excitement, eager to snoop into someone's life.

Chapter 8

IPHONE

Detective Garcia and Waller sat facing each other. Their desks side by side. Garcia said with compassionate dark eyes, "I've looked at her bank accounts: one savings in addition to one checking. No big withdrawals. No criminal records on either of the Fazzinos."

Waller opened the folder and saw the photo Garcia had printed of Carolyn and Vince Fazzino on their wedding day. The bride was sweet-faced with shoulder length chestnut brown hair, brown eyes, and girlish round cheeks. The groom was handsome in his tux, black hair, and brown eyes. The kind of guy, women would be falling all over. His arm wrapped tight around his bride's waist. Their smiles were pure happiness as they looked at each other. "If this photo could talk, would it say, 'this is a happy loving couple?' The likelihood of you breaking up is nil, so what went wrong with you two?" she asked no one in particular.

Garcia brushed his left hand over his mustache. "She's been missing over forty-eight hours. There's no credit card usage and we've got no clues."

"Did you check the train depot?"

"Yeah, I took her photo over there. There's no record of her purchasing a ticket. We're looking at surveillance cameras now to see if she boarded a train or bus. Our IT guy is checking her internet history to see if she was chatting with somebody about leaving town, or if she was doing any unusual searches, like a cheap hotel in Vegas. I found her doctor's name on a package of birth control pills. Oh, there was the Zoloft from the psychiatrist, however the bottle looked pretty full."

Waller squared her shoulders as she sat at her desk. "Did you check with her doctor?"

"Yes, actually got a subpoena to see her medical files. Birth control and a Zoloft prescription are the only medications. Small scar on her right knee from a bicycle accident when she was a kid in addition to a birthmark on her left hip. No mental illness or confusion. No memory loss ever reported that would cause her to forget where she lived," Garcia responded.

The experienced detective suggested, "Apple phones have a *Find My iPhone* app."

Garcia offered hopefully, "I'll search her number."

Waller's forehead wrinkled as she instructed, "This is such a wild shot in the dark. Keep in mind it's not even possible to locate the device if the *Find iPhone* function wasn't activated."

While she warned him, he was already tapping the green circular icon on his home screen.

Fairly sure this was going to be a futile waste of time; Detective Waller opened her left top drawer, where she kept her stash of chocolate. She pulled out a Kit Kat bar and ripped off one end of the wrapper. She broke off a piece. Placed it in her mouth while her partner typed in the phone number the mother had given them.

Garcia pulled out his cell for the list of IDs and passwords he photographed the day before.

Waller glanced over at him. "Where did you get the passwords?"

"Found a list in her apartment."

She wasn't about to give the new sleuth too big a compliment so simply murmured, "Mmm."

They got lucky. Carolyn had written her iCloud login credentials on her list of passwords. He tapped the blue *Go* option located in the pop-up window. Once logged in, he selected *AT&T iPhone 6* from a list of devices. Within seconds, Carolyn Fazzino's name in addition to her home address on Hampton Avenue in West Chicago popped up.

Waller with her mouth full of chocolate managed to mumble, "Her phone battery is probably dead by now."

Garcia, not to be discouraged, activated the *Find iPhone* feature. He leaned back in his chair to wait. The curser started circling; suddenly the computer brought up the cell tower right in town on South Hale Street. Garcia's eyes opened wide as he stared at his screen and out loud questioned, "Her phone's last known location is right in town?"

Waller surprised to hear him say that, quickly turned to look. They both stared at the Route 59 and Franklin intersection. "Diamond's is on that corner. Good work, partner." Her face broke into a grin.

"Yeah, but could she be at a grocery store for two days?" doubted Garcia.

"It sure looks like she is. Let's go." With no time to waste, Waller crammed the rest of the chocolate bar into her mouth.

He carried the laptop with them as they hurried out to their Ford Explorer. Waller went straight to the passenger's door saying, "You chauffeur me. I've earned it."

Carlos Garcia didn't want her pushing him around, so his comeback was, "Then you can ride shotgun." He got in the driver's side. "How many years you got in?"

As Garcia merged their vehicle into the traffic, Waller explained to him, "Fifteen. In the police academy, they tell you, 'The only way you become a good cop is through experience, and you," she pointed a stubby finger at him as he drove. "Never really obtain your street degree credibility without years of work."

With the siren blaring, it didn't take them long to reach the large busy store. It was 12:05 p.m. as they parked right in front of the main entrance. Both police officials walked through the front automatic doors. Once inside, they went directly to the service desk where they asked for the manager.

A tall, thin man stepped forward. "I'm the manager, Steve Sturgis."

Waller flashed her badge, introduced herself in addition to her partner, without mentioning anything about a search warrant they hadn't bothered to obtain. She said, "We're looking for a missing person and tracked her phone to this store. We'd like to search the premises."

Steve nodded his agreement as he said, "Sure. Don't want any trouble with the police."

Garcia opened the laptop device and logged in again. "Hasn't moved," he reassured his partner. Both cops separated going up and down the aisles. When nothing out of the ordinary was discovered, they asked the manager who had been following along with Waller about viewing back rooms. A thorough search reveled nothing.

The manager offered, "We have the Chef's Kitchen area."

"Show us," instructed Waller. The manager led the way as the two detectives followed. The officials went behind the deli counter. Three Diamond employees dressed in white looked up to see their store manager with the two detectives.

"Anyone been back here other than you three?" asked their supervisor.

"No, just us since five o'clock this morning," one hair-netted employee replied.

After searching the kitchen with no luck, Waller spotted a side door and commanded, "Maybe outside."

Steve opened the employee door. The three stepped into the bright sunlight in the side alley.

Several large stacks of wooden pallets leaned next to the brick building. With no one in sight, all three looked at a large garbage bin close to the wall. Detective Garcia held the laptop device while saying to his partner, "I'm going to try to activate the sound button."

He tapped the gray *Play Sound* button featuring the speaker to force the missing phone to play. He turned towards the fascinated store manager to explain, "This only plays for two minutes."

Suddenly a high-pitched ping sounded inside the dumpster. Waller reacted first. Looking at Garcia, she said, "I'll give you a boost."

"Dumpster diving?" was all Garcia could mutter, however he knew he was younger and in better shape than Waller, so he sensed the inevitable.

Dread sounded in Waller's voice as she said, "Our vic could be in there."

Garcia brushed the left side of his mustache as he said, "There's a folding step ladder in the back of the Explorer."

The store manager stayed in the alley as the two detectives hurried back to their car.

Garcia took the compact ladder out of the trunk while Waller took a cigar out of the glove compartment. Garcia saw her place the cigar in her front shirt pocket. He gave her a quizzical look.

Her face hardened and darkened as she narrowed her eyes. She slowly explained, "In case there's a stink-o dead body in there. It's July, ya know."

Garcia's eyes widened; his bushy eyebrows furrowed almost together as he thought of finding a body.

She continued, "That stink will last in your nostrils for days." She pushed her right hand into the glove compartment again and took out another cigar, handing it to him. "For you. Don't say I never gave you anything."

He took it hesitantly with dread, but just in case; he placed it in his shirt pocket.

Detective Waller advised, "If you don't smoke, Vicks VapoRub right under your nose works too."

At the dumpster Garcia placed the stepladder beside the steep metal side. All police officers in addition to investigators wear a pouch attached to their gun belts that contain at least one pair of latex gloves. He put on his rubber gloves and climbed to the top rung. He looked in at mounds of broken cardboard boxes mixed with papers. His voice sounded relieved as he said, "So far no body," however he knew he had to look under all of it. *Just hope there's no rats.*

He swung over the metal side. As he sank down into the debris, he reached out to hold onto the metal side to get his balance. Even though it was daylight outside, it was shadowy and gloomy in the garbage bin. The pungent smell of rotting onions in addition to potatoes was strong. He wanted to cover his nose, but instead, he tried to hold his breath while he used his hands to pull a flashlight from his pocket. Shinning the beam around in the piles of decaying trash, he heard his partner yell, "Find her?"

"No." He started kicking some squashed milk cartons. A mouse darted under some dented cans. Garcia started digging at the waste where the pinging sound was coming from. The continuous irritating noise echoed inside the metal container. Suddenly he yelled, "There's a purse in here."

He could hear pinging coming from inside the purse. Some sticky liquid was smeared on one side of the bag, but he wrenched it free of other garbage. Then fumbling with the zipper, he got it opened. There it was, a sleek, shiny silver phone.

Waller yelled back, "Did you find a body?" as she watched the store manager's look of horror.

"No." After a few attempts Garcia was over the side and standing in the alley. Not soon enough for him. He took a breath of clean air. "We're getting closer to finding her." He handed the dirty purse over to his partner.

Waller put on plastic gloves to avoid messing up any possible fingerprints. "This means more paperwork."

As she took the soiled bag, she warned her partner, "Don't stand too close to me."

The store manager took one look at Garcia's pants and white shirt dirty with what looked like eggs and some other unknown goo. He muttered something about getting back to work and he vanished inside.

As Waller watched the manager turn away, she caught movement out of the corner of her eye. She jerked around to see action behind the wood pallets. "Who's there?" she shouted. The movement stopped, so the detective ordered, "Come out here, where I can see you."

"I-I'm not doing notin'," a shaky voice answered.

"Let me see you, then," Waller commanded as she put her hand on her gun.

Slowly a dirty, bearded man crawled out from behind the broken crates. "I-I didn't do notin."

Detective Waller looked him over, small in stature, could be fifty or older, wearing some sort of suit, although it was so dirty it was hard to tell what was shirt and what was jacket. He was clutching the front to keep it closed.

Garcia immediately thought of Pig Pen in the Snoopy cartoons. As the cops walked closer to him, Detective Garcia asked the vagrant, "How long have you been there?"

A strong foul-odor of dirty laundry, sour sweat and possible vomit surrounded the homeless man. His left eye twitched uncontrollably. "Huh? Oh, I dunno," he stammered.

"You see anyone throw this bag in the dumpster?" asked Detective Waller.

"Naw, nobody, no one here. Jus me."

"Have you been sleeping here in the alley?" asked Garcia.

"Uh-uh. I been awake awhile."

"What's your name?"

He hesitated, then said, "They call me Pete, Pete Phelps.

Waller slowly said, "I remember him, a petty criminal. He's known for minor burglary. She turned on Pete. "You're hiding something. We can take you in, Phelps, if you don't tell us what you know."

A frightened look crossed the old man's dirty face as he looked at the purse Waller was holding. "Uh-uh, no don' do that. I found it. It wasn't anybody's. It was just there, all day."

"What was *there*?" asked Garcia.

"A bag, just sitting there all day."

"Where?" questioned Waller.

"Over there, in a car." He pointed a long dirty fingernail towards the parking lot.

Detective Garcia pulled Pete's arms behind his back to put carbon steel handcuffs on his wrists. He was glad he was still wearing the latex gloves as he patted down the vagrant.

While Garcia was busy with him, Waller called the precinct to let their sergeant know they found the missing woman's purse and cell phone. Then she looked through the purse to find Carolyn's driver's license, two credit cards in addition to a checkbook.

Waller yelled, "Pete, you show me right now where you found this bag!" She shoved him forward.

"Yeah yeah, ya always the boss. Ya police always bossing' me around. Yeah, I do what cha want." He took a few shaky steps forward. Waller went to one side of the old man as Garcia walked on his other side to keep the petty criminal between them. Pete dragged his feet, slowly trudged through the alley and into the nearby parking lot, but finally he walked up to a tan Honda Civic.

Garcia read the license number, "WC 8455." Turning to Waller, his brown eyes opened wide, he exclaimed, "It *is* Carolyn Fazzino's car!"

Waller was excitedly talking into her phone again. "We got the missing woman's car, right here at Diamonds."

Garcia looked down and pulled a piece of tomato off his pants leg. He looked up at his partner and said, "We're getting closer to her."

Waller saw him trying to clean himself off and remarked, "You smell almost as bad as Pete here. I'm tempted to smoke the cigar in my shirt pocket." Instead, she turned away quickly, started to circle the four-door vehicle but stopped near the passenger side. The side front window was broken. Shattered glass lay across the front seat. Waller yelled at Phelps, "Did you do this?"

"I, I hungry. I see that bag just sitting there, 'bout all day, on the seat. So, I find me a big rock."

"What day?" asked Garcia.

"Don't know." He was glancing around the parking lot then back towards the alley. Maybe looking for a hiding place.

"You think really hard. Did you break that window today or yesterday?" Waller was stern.

"I, I guess it was morning. Ya' know, just getting light."

"You take anything out of her bag?" questioned Garcia.

"No, no I don' steal."

"Yes, you do, you old bum! You do too steal. This is a robbery!" Waller yelled at him.

"I need to. I told ya, I real hungry, so just took the cash." He turned to leave.

Waller took a hold of his arm to keep him put. "Where's the woman?"

Pete Phelps's left eye was getting more nervous. "What woman?"

Garcia tried to help him remember. "The lady that owns this purse."

"I, I don't know no lady. No one here by that car. I watch all day, all night. No one, so, finders' keepers. I find it."

"You spend all the money?" Waller questioned.

"Yeah, get me a bottle of Jack, the good stuff an' I shop at the Dollar for some food."

"The Dollar?" questioned Garcia.

"He means the Dollar General store, don't you?" helped Waller.

Garcia asked him, "The one across the street in the strip mall?"

Pete bent to scratch his thigh, "Uh-huh, that the one."

Out loud, Waller speculated, "Could she have planted her car here to throw us off where she really went?" Waller moved farther around the car. "There's a muddy smudge on the outside of the driver's door. Looks unusual because the rest of the car isn't that dirty."

"It could be a boot print. Kind of looks like someone kicked the door closed," Garcia speculated.

"We need to find out what kind of boot, maybe even get a shoe size from it," explained the experienced cop.

"Mrs. Butzen, the neighbor, said the missing victim was wearing tennis shoes when she left."

Within minutes another Ford Explorer pulled into the parking lot and stopped near the tan Civic.

Sergeant Dodson lifted his muscular body out of his car. He was a prince who asked only competence in addition to loyalty from his team. Pulling on gloves, he walked the few steps to Carolyn Fazzino's Honda.

Garcia continued circling the car when he yelled, "What's this stuff here on the blacktop by the driver's door?"

Waller quickly came to his side of the car and looked down at the pavement. "It could be blood." She squatted down near the stain to look closer. "That's a lot of blood. Maybe she's hurt." She pulled out her cell phone and snapped a couple photos.

"Should we call in Homicide?" asked Garcia.

Dodson, who provided his shift with support in a quiet manner said, "No one, I mean absolutely no one, knows this is a murder, so this is a missing person until I declare it isn't." The sergeant spoke into his phone, "Get some more uniforms out here." Careful not to step on any evidence, he took a step toward his men. "Get that trunk opened." Then he really saw Garcia's dress shirt and pants. "My God, what happened to you?"

Garcia explained to his boss, "We found the missing purse and cell phone in the dumpster on the side of the building." He gestured towards the tramp. "Phelps admitted he broke into the car and stole it."

Garcia reached in through the broken window to unlock the car.

Waller, the closest to the driver's door, opened it with her gloved hand and released the trunk button. The trunk popped open.

Waller had managed to creep Garcia out a bit when she talked about a dead body, so hesitantly, he stepped forward. He raised the lid. They all stared in to see a gym bag, however no body. Concerned there could be a head or body part, he slowly unzipped the canvas bag to find exercise clothes. Relieved Garcia turned to Dodson and suggested, "Maybe she tripped, hit her head and wandered off."

Waller looked at him like he just grew a horn out of the top of his head, then she said, "Maybe, however I don't think any woman would leave her purse, credit cards, check book, in addition to her phone in her car. Wouldn't she need it inside the store to pay?"

Garcia speculated out loud. "It's possible she just took one check or one credit card inside. You know, stop herself from overspending."

"There's a cup," Waller pointed. They both looked at a cardboard cup sitting in the cup holder between the two front seats. Waller reached in with a gloved hand and carefully raised it exposing a Kup logo on its side.

"That coffee shop is approximately two blocks from here."

Another police car pulled up near them. David Dodson turned to the two newly arrived policemen. "Canvass the store for witnesses," he said as he pointed to the Diamonds Food Market. "See if our missing woman was inside shopping and what time? See if there's a camera over this parking lot. Rope this car off." They all knew he meant the yellow police tape. He continued, "I'll call for evidence techs to go over this car and purse for prints." He turned facing Waller and Garcia, "You two get back to the station, so *you*," he pointed at Garcia, "can change." Dodson raised his voice, "The clock is ticking people. We've got to find her."

"Copy that boss." Waller gave him a head nod.

Dodson ordered his staff to check every surrounding building. "Start within sight of this parking lot, then fan out." He pointed across the street. More officers were sent to check anywhere that was secluded like the back yards and forest preserve on Route 59. "I want house to house searches. Maybe she got into someone's car and they took her to the nearest medical facility. It's not a robbery because her purse was here. Take Phelps in, maybe he assaulted her and stole the purse. He's our firmest lead." The sergeant was barking orders to get this case solved before the media made any negative comments about the police department.

Waller turned to her partner. "Let's go back to our house."

Garcia instinctively knew, she meant their police station. He gave her a head nod.

As he nudged the handcuffed vagrant towards their Ford, Pete argued, "That's not fair at all."

Back in their cruiser, Waller sarcastically teased her stinky partner, "Do you mind sitting in the back with him?" Then she added, "We've got plastic cover-ups at the station, but I didn't mention it earlier because we didn't have time." She giggled.

Garcia glared at her. *Now you tell me. What kind of a partner are you?* "Ha Ha. Very funny. Just for that, I'm riding up front with you." However, he could tell the two of them were building team rapport.

"At least I can close the window on him," she said as she closed the Plexiglas opening between the front and back seats. The metal frame allowed a gap on each side of the partition, so the homeless man's sweat, and urine could still be noticed. Then she reached in her pocket for a Snickers, which turned out to be quite soft. "We *need* a chocolate smell in here." Getting serious she said, "We must find out if our missing woman owes money. Some people will take off to hide from someone they owe. We'll follow her credit card usage."

While Waller and Garcia returned to the station with Pete, they knew a thorough search would be made of the Honda Civic including removal of the seats. Photos would be taken of the entire car inside and out, including the mud smeared on the driver's door and the surrounding area of the parking lot. The police listed all evidence and who they turned it over to. They had to prove or disprove the petty criminal's story.

Detectives Waller and Garcia stepped out of their police car. Waller warned, "I'm going to puke if you don't change your clothes, so I'll take him to lock-up." She took hold of Phelps' arm pulling the slow-moving man from the back seat.

It took Waller longer to admit Phelps to a cell downstairs, than it took Garcia to shower in the station locker room and put on fresh clothes he had in his car.

Dodson met them at their desks. "The subpoena you put in for Carolyn Fazzino's cell phone records shows no usage since Monday evening. The only fingerprints on the purse we can match are Pete

Phelps."

Waller nodded towards Dodson. "He's a petty criminal who saw the purse on the front seat of her car. He admitted he broke the window and took the purse. He took only the cash for food and alcohol. Left the phone and cards inside, then tossed the bag in a garbage dumpster. He also said he saw no one else around the car. Funny, there was over a half cup of coffee in the car's cup holder. We asked Phelps why he didn't drink it if he was looking for money for food, but he said he doesn't like coffee."

"Good thing you found her phone. Now you two need to interview everyone in her contact list to try to locate her."

Chapter 9

CAROLYN

THURSDAY AFTERNOON

Where am I? I stir, feeling uncomfortable as the spinning engulfs me. It's a struggle to move my arm. Am I laying on something hard? What is this? My hand moves across what feels like a rough dirt-packed surface. The smelly dank ground feels cool. Something is completely wrong. I need to focus. I blink my eyes more. The dampness overwhelming. Trying to raise my head, throbbing pain shoots down the back of my neck. Gradually I become aware of the rest of my body. Slowly reaching a hand to my head, I feel an egg-sized lump and my hand feels sticky. "Ouch," I want to yell, but my mouth won't open. Where am I? What stupid thing have I done?

Staying calm is not one of my strong suits. I breathe heavily through my nose as panic takes over. Smells of earth and grass fill the air. My heart pounds as a shudder of overwhelming terror goes through my body from head to toe. My head throbs, my mind fills with questions. I roll onto my side, curl up my arms and legs tightly, folding them close to me in a fetal position. I hear a distant moan of trees. Am I outside? Is there dirt around me? I lose consciousness.

Chapter 10

QUESTIONS

The West Chicago police listed Carolyn Fazzino as officially missing. This meant her specs had gone out to all northern Illinois police agencies and the Illinois State Police. The all-call included her name, address, age, photo, verbal description, last seen and clothing worn.

Next the detectives drove to Diamond's Grocery Store to canvass the area where they found Mrs. Fazzino's cell phone, purse, and car. They talked with each person going in or out of the store. They each had a legitimate reason for being there. No one said they recognized the picture of the missing woman. A couple clerks did remember her, but said they hadn't seen her this week.

Next, they went to the Elgin company where Vince said his girlfriend, Jenny Maxwell, worked. They parked out front of Plastic Equipment Inc. and walked inside. Six office workers sat at their desks on this busy Friday morning. Startled, the workers raised their heads to look at the two police officials who showed their badges.

"May I help you?" asked a smiling receptionist.

A couple people who had been on their phones were politely, saying, "I'll call you back in a few minutes."

"We're looking for Jenny Maxwell," Detective Garcia explained.

The red-headed receptionist gulped; her eyes opened wide. "Why?" She hesitated, then explained, "That's me."

Her co-worker at the next desk cocked his head of well-groomed dark brown hair and openly stared at the cops. Jenny, as well as the police, saw him lean her way to hear what was going on.

"I'm Detective Garcia and this," he tilted his head. "Is my partner, Detective Waller." Then noticing the faces looking their way, asked, "Could we speak with you in private?"

Both police detectives smiled to put Jenny at ease, but it didn't help.

"I guess," was her hesitant answer. "There's a small conference room that's available right now. Let me get someone to watch the front desk for me." She looked at her nosy co-worker. "Ray, do you mind?"

Once the three were inside the small meeting room, Garcia closed the door for privacy.

"Let's sit," said Waller, as she pulled her chair up close to Jenny's and softly asked, "Do you know a Mr. Vince Fazzino?"

"No," Jenny answered, way too fast, but her eyes told another story. Her body stiffened. Guilt hung in the air, like smoke in a closed room.

Waller placed her right hand on Jenny's left arm and calmly said, "We heard that he delivers here quite often."

Jenny's fair skin paled as she stared at the cops. "Oh yeah, I just forgot. He works for ECHO Global; I believe."

"Mr. Fazzino says he's been meeting you," Waller informed her.

Jenny's eyes jerked open at the detective's statement. Then she squirmed in her seat. "Oh no. Why would I go out with anyone? I'm, I'm married." Nervously she played with her wedding ring.

The detectives watched as she became uneasy and shifted her weight in the chair. They glanced at each other. Waller cleared her throat as if to speak, but then said nothing.

Garcia still standing gently asked, "Did you have lunch with him?"

Jenny's upper lip glistened with perspiration. "No, I don't go out with anybody. I never saw him Tuesday."

Waller kept her face completely blank but calmly stated, "We never said anything about Tuesday. In fact, we never said anything about *this week.*"

All three heard Garcia's pencil scratch over his pad of paper in the quiet that followed.

Jenny gulped. "Sorry, did I say, *Tuesday?*"

That's when Waller placed her palms on the table and said, "We'd like a little more information."

Garcia sat on the other side of Jenny and looked her right in the eye. Softly he said, "I know you don't want to get involved."

The gentle appeal didn't work. That's all they could get out of her. Even though they kept asking questions for at least another thirty minutes, she said, she didn't know anything about Vince.

Finally, Waller let out a long sigh and stood ending this interview.

Garcia sensed her frustration. Once back in their unmarked car, he spoke up. "There goes Vince's alibi."

Waller nodded. "Or did the two of them do something to the little wify, so they can be together, and they just didn't plan their cover stories very well?"

Garcia's left hand unconsciously played with his mustache. "They're not going to be happily ever after if we can prove it was them."

She looked straight at him as she agreed. "Nobody's closet is skeleton free. Digging out their dirty little secrets is what we do. We'll check Vince's phone records. Maybe he made some calls to Jenny and then we can prove he was in contact with her; however, she certainly won't support him." Her face formed a knowing smirk as she offered, "You want a Hershey bar? I got two."

Garcia looked at her mid-section and said, "No thanks."

She said, "I knew you'd say no. You always turn down my candy. Just like *I know* people after years of police service. I'm telling you, Jenny Maxwell just lied big time."

"So does the husband have an alibi or not?" Garcia asked the more experienced cop.

"Phew, who knows?" She shrugged her shoulders.

Next, they went to Jerry Ridder's home. The man that opened the door to their knock had a panicked look across his face as the two police officers displayed their badges.

Garcia wanted to put him at ease, so quickly asked, "Mr. Ridder, do you know a Mr. Vince Fazzino?"

Jerry's face relaxed slightly as he invited them in. "Oh sure. I've known him since college. We were Frat brothers. Hey, ya want a beer?"

Waller said, "No thanks, Mr. Ridder. We're on duty."

Waller and Garcia stood next to each other just a short distance inside Jerry's front door.

Jerry wore a blue and white checked shirt that casually hung outside his jeans. "Oh yeah. Well, I work from home, write game software. I'm at work right now." He chuckled. He reached for a pack of cigarettes from an end table and took one out, asking, "You mind?"

"It's your home."

He lit up and told them, "In fifty, maybe seventy years game software might be one of the great art forms."

They chose to stand in his living room of miss-matched furniture even though Jerry waved at the couch.

Waller told him, "We're investigating the disappearance of Carolyn Fazzino."

Suddenly Jerry's calm face changed to a look of shock. "What happened to Carolyn?"

Garcia noticed the beer bottles on a counter's half wall separating the living room from the kitchen, and asked, "You didn't know Carolyn Fazzino is missing?"

"Missing?" Jerry shook his head slightly. "Maybe she's on vacation or something."

Garcia looked at a tread mill and a comfy tan easy chair both facing a large screen TV, as Waller asked, "Did you see Vince Fazzino Tuesday night?"

"Yeah, we went to the Stone Eagle in Hoffman Estates for a few beers." He flicked ashes into a pizza box laying open on the coffee table containing only a few chunks of cold cheese stuck on the bottom.

"Lots of people there who might have seen you two?" Detective Waller asked as she removed a small notebook from her back trouser pocket.

"Sure. It's a meet-up place. The place was crowded." He waved his right hand in the air as he said, "Those twenty-and-thirty-year-olds were checking and swiping on their phones to see if someone tried to call them in all that noise."

"Did you actually talk to anyone that might remember you both?"

"Maybe, I talked with four women at a table right in front of us for a little bit. They're in college. Vince wasn't interested in meeting them, though."

"Why not?" Detective Garcia asked, his voice even.

"He told me he was seeing a woman from Elgin, a red head. Even said he wanted me to meet her sometime."

"Did he tell you her name?" Garcia probed.

"Jenny something. I don't remember her last name. Sorry. I was drinking and trying to get phone numbers from the girls at the next table."

"Jerry, did Vince tell you the last time he saw Jenny?"

"No." He chuckled. "But he sees her for funch."

Garcia felt confused.

But Waller winked knowingly towards Jerry as he said, "Yeah, lunch time fuck buddies."

Garcia turned his head and stared at the lesbian cop thinking, *the less I know about Al's personal life, the better it is.*

Jerry saw the look between the cops, so explained, "That's not what Vince called it, but that's what I think."

"Was he seeing this woman while he was married?"

"Look, before Vince got married, he got more ass than a toilet seat at a girl's school." Jerry grinned. "Then he met Carolyn. He really fell for her and didn't talk about anyone else. After they got married, it went sour." His smile vanished. "It happens. He moved out. It didn't take him long to find someone else." Jerry gave a little shoulder shrug.

"Vince's got a knack with the ladies?" Garcia raised his eyebrows.

"Oh, I'll admit it." Jerry responded, "I envy how smooth he is. He knows it, the cocky S.O.B. If only I'd been born Italian."

"One more question, Jerry, did Vince use a credit card when you guys were leaving Tuesday night?" asked Waller.

"Yeah, we split the bill," was Jerry's answer.

Waller gave him a head nod saying, "Thanks for your help, Mr. Ridder."

Once in their car and away from the man they were interviewing, Detective Garcia asked, "Why the question about the credit card? Who cares how they paid?"

The more experienced cop explained to her novice partner, "So we can check out his credit card usage to verify where he was the night his wife disappeared. We can check security cameras at the Stone Eagle to see if there is footage of her husband there too."

Garcia said, "Okay Jerry backs up Vince's story, so maybe the husband didn't do anything to his wife, but then who did?"

"What?" Waller raised her voice. "He's got a girlfriend." She pointed a finger at Garcia. "Motive for this woman, Jenny, to get rid of the wife for good. She didn't even want to admit she knew him."

"Or if the wife confided in her friends about her husband's cheating, then maybe she wanted to scare him, then get out of town to think things over," Garcia speculated.

Waller looked doubtful at the very idea. "It's possible Vince did away with his wife during the day, then went out partying with Jerry that night. But maybe Carolyn left on her own, or someone did something. We're going to find out who and how. Jenny Maxwell lied to us, so maybe she's guilty of more. Carolyn was last seen leaving her apartment, so let's talk with her landlord, Dr. Kennedy," Waller said.

As usual she's telling me what to do, however she's right, thought Garcia.

"Then we'll talk to her neighbors next," said Detective Waller as Garcia pulled away from the curb.

As she said 'neighbors,' Garcia got a quick image of Mrs. Butzen again. He frowned as he envisioned her. Must *we listen to Chatty Cathy again? But it's got to be done.* He sighed.

Waller called into headquarters to let their sergeant know they were planning to visit the missing woman's landlord.

Sergeant Dodson agreed that questioning him was a good idea, but informed them, "Records show Kennedy had a DUI eight months ago. He attended a couple court-ordered AA meetings, however that's all."

Waller turned to her partner and said, "He hasn't done the recommended year of AA meetings. Could a drunk landlord have grabbed our victim?"

Garcia parked the Explorer in front of the Hampton Avenue medical building. The detectives went to the front door and stepped into Dr. Kennedy's waiting room. There they showed the same tired-looking receptionist their badges and asked if they could see the doctor. "Tell him, it's about one of his tenants," Garcia added, but thought, *so he won't get scared and take off.*

The receptionist made a quick phone call explaining that two policemen wanted to see him. As she set the receiver back into its cradle, she slowly rose from her chair. She yawned, saying, "Please follow me," then shuffled down a hallway past patient rooms.

She took them to a walnut door marked 'Dr. Kennedy, Private' at the end of the hall. She knocked briefly, then held the door open for them. They went in and shut the door on the hall corridor and the low energy receptionist. The corner room was large with windows on two sides. The office was paneled in a dark wood. A mahogany desk was at the far end, so they had to walk across an expanse of blue carpet to get to it.

The tall man leaned slowly across his desk, then stood. The room was dim; however, they could still see his face. His sagging skin made him look a decade older than he probably was. He stood with his legs spread. He looked trim and corporate in an expensive dark brown business suit, a white shirt, a garish diamond ring on his third finger, and a diamond studded pin in his lapel. Stiff points of a paisley handkerchief decorated his outside breast pocket. His nose beamed Johnnie Walker Red through his fake tan. As they got closer, they could see even his eyes were flecked with red veins. He greeted them, "Please sit." Spreading his hands, he motioned at the two chairs in front of the desk.

As they shook hands, Detective Waller made the introductions. Then they sat facing him.

"How can I help the fine police department today?" His very faint smile hardly moving his mouth.

Detective Garcia responded, "There's been a little trouble, Doctor. One of your tenants is missing, a Carolyn Fazzino."

The gentleman before them had a stony look to his brown eyes as he questioned, "Missing?"

"She hasn't been seen since Tuesday morning," explained Waller.

The landlord seemed to be thinking.

Waller continued with, "Sir, have there been any disturbances from apartment 204?" Meanwhile, her eyes were going over his ruddy face, line by line.

He looked at them with an absent expression as he repeated, "204?"

"Mr. and Mrs. Fazzino," Waller prompted.

The property owner worked his lips slowly, rubbed one over the other, then slid his tongue out to moisten them and worked his jaws. A spark of light snapped into his eyes, held a moment, and faded out again. "I've been here a long time. I've seen tenants come and go, but now I remember her, actually she and her husband. They always pay on time."

"That's good, however did you ever have any problems with either of them?" asked Waller.

His head was cocked as he remembered. "Oh yeah. Well, their neighbor, Mrs. Butzen, used to call me all the time, but what am I supposed to do about 'two screaming banshees,' like she used to call them?" He shrugged his shoulders and raised both hands in helplessness.

Garcia kept his eyes on the landlord, the hint of a frown between his eyes. "Did you personally ever hear them fighting?"

"No. I'm two floors below. I stay down here." His thick-coated tongue moistened his lips again. Both detectives stared at him as his hands shook ever so slightly. "But I sent my maintenance man up there one night because the heat wasn't working, sometime last winter, I think. I take care of my tenants."

Garcia noticed one of his office windows looked out to the

back-parking lot. *He could easily have seen Mrs. Fazzino walk to her car the morning she went missing.* "Were you here in your office early Tuesday morning, Doctor?"

"I don't remember."

"You could check your schedule since you don't know," Waller's sarcasm was thick.

"I normally start seeing patients about ten o'clock. You can check with my receptionist for that particular day."

Garcia remembered the pill bottle he had seen in the drawer of Carolyn's bedside stand. "Doctor, did you prescribe Zoloft for Carolyn Fazzino?"

Suddenly the doctor's eyes flashed open. "Carolyn Fazzino," he mumbled. "Now I remember." While sitting in his chair he tapped a few strokes on his keyboard. He read quickly and told the police, "She came to see me once, on a professional basis."

"When Doctor?"

"Approximately three, maybe three and a half months ago, however doctor/patient confidentiality prevents me from telling you anything more about my client." He smiled a big toothy grin.

Garcia jumped in, "We could get a court order doctor."

Waller wanting to add more clout to her partner's statement so threatened, "We could make a lot of trouble for a psychiatrist who drinks but doesn't attend AA meetings."

The psychiatrist's grin faded. "Well, when you put it like that." Dr. Kennedy hesitated like he was thinking how to say his next words. "I can tell you; Mrs. Fazzino was nervous when she talked to me. She kept wringing her hands and twisting her wedding ring. She frequently diverted to lighter topics. I prescribed a medication to calm her. We really didn't get far. I only saw her once because she cancelled the next appointment."

As Detective Waller leaned forward in her chair, she asked, "Can you tell us the nature of her problem?"

"I must respect my patient's confidentiality."

"Of course, Doctor. We understand, however we need more." Garcia hoped he sounded calmer than he felt.

Waller added to her partner's threat, "You could help us out here, or we could make sure your license isn't renewed, Doctor." She said the last word with a sneer.

An intercom buzzed on the doctor's desk. A woman's voice sounded, "I'm sorry to interrupt Doctor, but your next patient is here."

"Okay, Connie," he answered towards the phone. He faced Garcia as he said, "Really, I don't know anything that could help find her." Then he reached into his desk drawer. "Here's my business card. Please ask Mrs. Fazzino to call me when she gets home."

Garcia accepted the card as they rose from their seats. They thanked him for his time and left, closing the door to his office. They asked the receptionist what time the doctor came into the office on Tuesday, but she couldn't remember or chose not to. They checked above with Carolyn's neighbors, but no one could shed any more light on the missing woman.

Bernice Butzen was enthusiastic and smiling when they rang her doorbell, but she hadn't seen Carolyn come home yet; promising, "I'll continue to keep a close watch on both the Fazzino's front and back door for you. I'm doing round the clock surveillance. Even watching our parking lot like you asked me."

Before they left the premises, they walked around the entire medical building to the back-parking lot once more eyeing the outside stairs to the apartments above. Garcia looked up to see a Weber grill on the Fazzino's back landing. He imagined the couple barbecuing hamburgers and serving cold beer with friends before Mr. Fazzino moved out. As soon as they arrived at their car he thought, *maybe I'm just getting hungry.*

As their unmarked car drifted quietly along the shaded street of homes, Garcia said, "The landlord dresses nice to keep people from looking at his red, puffy nose, however his liver has been pickled in port wine."

"The good doctor seems a tad vain to me." Waller answered, "People have secret lives. They either confess to their priest or to a shrink. They aren't all Catholic, so he'll be in business a long time." Despair sounded in her voice. "Meanwhile he's got the sins of the world on his shoulders. It can't be easy. He has to keep it all inside. Having a drink once in a while might keep him sane."

"Yah, maybe," was all Garcia commented.

"However, he's going to taste water sometime, just for the Hell of it." Waller unwrapped a Milky Way and asked, "What was that drug name you found in her home?"

He steered the Ford around a corner, as he answered her, "Zoloft."

"Good thing he's not a surgeon with those tremors." She pulled out her iPhone. "Google says it's most commonly used for depression."

Exasperated, Garcia turned to face her and asked, "Was she so depressed she could take her life?"

"Possibly," answered his partner. "However, we also found out Carolyn's a reliable tenant who pays her rent on time even after her husband left her. She's usually predictable, so why would she suddenly take off now, four months after her husband left?" Slowly she added, "This doesn't feel right."

As he stopped the Explorer for a red traffic light, Garcia turned to his partner. "You think the drunk landlord could have grabbed her when she went out that morning or when she came back home? From his office, he can see right into the tenant's parking lot." He hesitated, then thinking out loud added, "But then her car should have been at the apartment building."

Waller looked at him. "The drunk could've been watching his cute tenant. He probably knew that her husband moved out, then the doc tried something stupid."

Garcia finished her thought, "it could have backfired."

"Everyone has secrets in their lives. It's our business to find the truth."

Chapter 11

CAROLYN'S PANIC

Unknown location Friday morning

My pounding head wakes me. My eyes seem fuzzy in this gloom. Where am I? I sit up too quickly, my head spins. Heart banging in my chest; irrational fear grips at my insides. Slowly I sit up. My face feels uncomfortably tight. Instinctively I raise my hands to feel what's wrong. There's tape over my mouth; using a trembling fingernail, I loosen one corner. How did this happen? The duct tape pulls, hurting my skin. *Ouch!* Little by little I pick the tape off. It seems to take a long time. Have I been in an accident? But tape over my mouth, how did that happen? No, no accident.

Next, I run my hands over my scalp. There's a lump on the right side of my head, too painful to touch. My hair is matted with old-dried blood. I must have hit my head. Dark hues are pulsing in and out of my vision. There's pain in my right knee. Instinctively I feel where it hurts. My jeans are torn. My leg sticky with blood. The lacerated flesh hurts like Hell, but not like the throbbing pain in my head.

Looking at my blood smeared hands, they start trembling more violently. I wipe them on my t-shirt trying to clean them the best I can. I realize I'm holding my breath; I exhale. My lungs gulp hysterically for air. Then all I can hear is my own breathing.

Groaning, I turn to my right. There's dirt. *Why dirt?* I look around. There is dirt everywhere, dirt barriers all around me. I'm sitting on a hard-packed dirt floor. I reach my right arm out to make sure I'm seeing correctly. The dirt smells dank and musty. Am I in a ditch? Or maybe I've fallen into some kind of hole. I can't be here. What's happening to me? I need to figure this out. What did I do? I take a few shallow breaths wishing I was back in my apartment, safe.

Don't panic. There should be people stopping at the grocery store. Someone should come by to find me in a hole in a parking lot. I lift my head to scream, but a wheeze comes out instead. I feel as if I need to cough up a puff of dust. Finally, words, "Help! Help me!" I shriek. I continue to shout and scream. Begging for mercy goes unheeded. After a while I begin to wonder if I'm making any sound at all since there is no response. I just scream and scream for someone, anyone until my throat feels raw. Then the terror takes my voice, so my once hearty yells and piercing screams become a strange strangulated rasp as the cries for help are lodged in my dry throat. Okay, okay, stop it.

I look around me. Occasionally there's a small thin root sticking out of the dirt. Then I realize this is a hole in the ground. Must be ten, maybe twelve feet across and just as deep. There are woody smelling leaves. Looking upward, it's lighter, with sky high above me. It's a big hole, open at the top. Birds chirping, tree branches and leaves above.

A breeze ruffles the treetops high up there. Filtered sun shines through the branches. I can see sky above. This isn't the grocery store parking lot with branches way up there. There's a dank woody earth smell. In utter panic and disorientation, claustrophobia takes over. I'm a prisoner, but where? Is the ground swallowing me? *Get out!*

The smell of green leaves and woody earth is everywhere. The light blue sky is far away. Gold shafts of light slant through tree branches above. Waking and shaking from the early morning chill, my teeth chatter. I've never been so cold in my life. Wish I'd worn socks. They would keep me warmer, but I was in such a hurry, I didn't even bother. When was that? How long have I been here? I clench my fingers into fists and bring them up to my mouth. I blow warm air into my cupped hands and rub them together. I force my cold hands into my jean's pockets for warmth. I jump up and down to warm my feet. Then run in little circles trying to work up a sweat and body heat.

I look at the dirt surrounding me and sit on the ground. What will happen to me down here? I start to hyperventilate. My lip begins to quiver. Adrenaline floods my veins. Heart thumps, hands sweat, my nose runs, and tears blur my vision. Instinctively I fold into myself, arms hugging my legs to my chest sobbing until my throat feels raw. It's not a pretty cry. I'm secreting from my eyes, nose, and mouth all at once. I cried on and on, more than I can ever remember. Well, maybe as much as when Vince left, and my world fell apart. Now I'm worried that I'll never stop crying. But the sobs finally turn into hiccups; my eyes feel like they are burning. I grit my teeth to keep from crying. I draw my arm across my eyes, wiping away tears. It feels like hours pass while I struggle with my fear.

Chapter 12

WORK ETHIC

FRIDAY 10:55 A.M.

Detectives Waller and Garcia were driving along Washington Street when they spotted a couple of children selling lemonade on the corner of Oak.

"Hey, look at those kids. You don't see that very often." Garcia tipped his head towards the children. "I want to stop." He slowed the car at the curb. Garcia got out. The air smelled of newly mowed grass.

Waller started to get out of the unmarked car but stopped. "Lemonade doesn't go with my chocolate." She turned back towards the Ford Explorer.

"What?" Garcia was shocked. "You're not going to help out a couple of kids?"

"You go ahead." She reopened her car door. Then as an afterthought she barked, "See if they have a permit." She got in but left her door open.

"They're just kids," he mumbled under his breath as he walked over to the card table. The kids grinned excitedly as Garcia approached. A little boy who was missing his two front teeth asked, "You wanna buy some lemonade? It's only fifty cents."

"Hey, I know you," the girl said, pointing a finger at Garcia. "You came to our school. You're Officer Friendly."

"Yes, I am." He smiled as he reached their small folding table. "I was explaining Stranger Danger and talking about safety at all the grade schools last spring. Do you go to Turner school? It's not very far from here."

"Yeah. I'm Sally, and this is my little brother, Nick." She smiled up at the police detective.

"We got work to do." Waller's voice cut through their conversation.

Garcia turned towards her voice and gave her a thumbs up response to let her know he heard her. He paid them each fifty cents explaining it was a tip for the Dixie cup of lemonade and drank it down. *I better not keep Bossy waiting.* "Thanks." He used his left hand to brush droplets of lemonade off his mustache.

Quickly Garcia was back in the cruiser. As soon as he closed the car door he beamed. "She recognized me. I was a little bored passing out coloring books at the elementary schools, however when kids like that remember you, it's worth it." He avoided the topic of the permit. "All good cops should be community oriented."

"Well, I'm not. You got to be tough on this job. I put my time and energy into getting answers, not hugs and sweet lemonade." Waller nodded. "Let's grab lunch, then check out where Mrs. Fazzino works."

Garcia knew the best Mexican places. "Changarro Cocina on Route 59 is on our way. Then we can take Roosevelt Road into Lombard."

Waller pulled out her cell phone and called into the station. "We've talked with a couple people who know Mr. Fazzino, then we questioned the landlord. Next we're going to grab a little lunch and then we're headed to Lombard to look where Mrs. Fazzino works." She clicked the phone off and turned to her partner. "Come on, I'll let you buy."

"No problem, just don't order anything that costs more than three bucks." Garcia smiled.

They parked out front of Changarro Cocina restaurant and

went inside. As the restaurant door closed behind them, Waller stepped forward, with Garcia following. She quickly walked to an outside wall and pointed an index finger at a table. Garcia thought, *now she's telling me where to sit in my restaurant, but don't make waves,* as he sat.

After lunch, they buckled themselves back into the unmarked vehicle. Garcia placed his hands at the ten and two o'clock positions on the steering wheel like he had been taught in basic training. He wheeled their car onto Route 38 as Waller asked, "Did I tell you I got a compliment last week?"

"No kidding," Garcia answered her.

"Yep, I was taking a drug suspect out of the Nora Lynn Apartments in handcuffs when someone in the crowd outside yelled, 'Good job. Get those crack heads out of our neighborhood.'"

"Wow. Nice to be appreciated."

"Yeah, however there are those domestics between neighbors that drive me nuts." Waller opened a Reese's candy wrapper and continued, "Like this one guy had some beer cans thrown into his yard a couple months ago, so he puts up this fence to 'protect' himself, he says, however he calls the police because he wants the neighbor to pay for it. Goofball. We're not going to help him with that."

Garcia continued driving, but asked his partner, "Don't you wish they would channel their energy into something like piano lessons?"

She chuckled. "Last summer I got a call about a couple having sex in a car when the airbag malfunctioned and deployed."

"What did you do?"

"I tried not to laugh as I gave them a citation for indecent exposure."

Garcia chuckled and then asked, "Carolyn drives this road from West Chicago to Lombard every day, twice, at rush hour? Yikes. Can you imagine this in the snow and slop?"

Waller disagreed, "The traffic never stops on this road, so there's no chance of snow sticking to the pavement." Suddenly she pointed to her left. "There's a drug deal going down."

"I didn't see it." Garcia answered turning his head in the direction she was looking.

"That was a guy slinging dope right there in the Seven Gables parking lot. It's out of our jurisdiction. I'm calling it in."

"I missed it." Garcia said, disappointed.

"That's because you're a newbie. I've got years of street time in and that my beginner, was a drug deal. You must learn to pay attention out here." After she called it in to their precinct who would pass it on to the Glen Ellen police, she bragged, "I've got street smarts. Veterans take in the whole playing field. You must always be alert. You could get killed or hurt or get somebody else hurt and it better not be me. However, you'll get there. You can learn from me. You'll get the ability to read what's happening on the street."

Garcia's happiest moment was the day he received his acceptance letter into the recruit academy class. Carlos Garcia wanted to learn from Alicia Waller, but right now he felt she was an arrogant SOB, always thinking she knew it all. He clenched his teeth.

"You must have alert interaction with your environment. A detective better watch every move the citizen makes to be able to react to any potential threat before it surfaces," she explained.

She did say I'd get there, so she knows I have the smarts to make a good cop. Suddenly he was glad he was partnered up with someone with so much experience. He craved the ability to really see the street. Meanwhile he sat there next to the veteran and tried to absorb as much as he could.

"If they pick him up, he'll have a stunted pharmaceutical career," she chuckled. Then added, "Another thing, you see a guy carrying a gym bag, but there's no gym around, you stop him. Mostly they're legit, but a burglar, he'll probably drop it and run." As she said it, Waller got fed up with the traffic suggesting, "Let's put the siren on to get through all these lights."

Cars pulled over once they saw the Ford Explorer's lights pulsing, however the loud siren prohibited their small talk. Soon Garcia was pulling into the college campus. The parking lot was quite full.

"Over there in handicapped. There's an empty." Waller was pointing.

Aggravated she would even tell him where to park, Garcia said, "Two-hundred-dollar fine for that."

"I think we'll get a pass," she argued.

Garcia came back with, "I was joking," as he parked the Explorer beside the curb in front of the largest building. It looked a little industrial with its rigidly upright windows and the American flag flying above the door. The detectives walked inside. Stepping into the round lobby, they saw a thirtyish woman at a desk marked INFORMATION. Their heels clicked sharply as they strode across the shiny marble floor. Garcia spoke first, "We're looking for Mr. Hubert Herman."

"The library is on the second floor at the top of the stairs." With a dry tight withered smile, she pointed to the steps at the right.

They proceeded up the staircase to the next level to find paneled walls, but no windows. A large glass door was on the left. Waller pulled the door open showing rows of books inside. A girl sat at the large circulation desk.

This time Waller asked for Mr. Herman and added, "It's about one of his employees."

The brunette smiled. "Right through here." She gestured for them to come behind the desk.

Garcia walked around the desk thinking *why would the director of the library be hiding back here, behind the circulation desk where patrons can't reach him?*

The library worker showed them into an inner office where a couple of clerks were processing new books. The chatter seemed to stop, and heads turned when the suited cops walked in. The circulation clerk lightly tapped at the next doorway, as she said to the detectives, "He's right in here." She stepped aside to let them enter.

Mr. Herman was picking his teeth as the cops walked in. He stopped but the toothpick dangled from his lips. They looked at the man's round plump face, with sweat beaded on his forehead. His pink scalp glistened through thin brown hair. He was thick necked and triple chinned. He stared at the detectives. His shirt had the snug fit of a horse-collar and was about the same shade of dirty brown. His chalky white skin was accented by steel-rimmed glasses that looked like they could have belonged to his grandfather.

There were no chairs in the office except the one Herman was using. Flashing their badges, they quickly introduced themselves and stood in front of his desk. Garcia said, "We're here to ask you about one of your employees, Carolyn Fazzino."

The head librarian leaned a little over his desk, but not far, because his stomach was in the way. With his chins quivering, he asked, "What kind of shenanigans did she get herself into?"

"We don't know, Mr. Herman. We're trying to find her."

He folded his short fingers on his desk, and said, "I don't see how I can help you." As he spoke, the toothpick slipped from his lips, dropping on the desk. "She didn't show up for work; no call, no text, no nothing. I didn't worry because she had a major dentist thing Monday morning. Last week she said she might take Tuesday off, too." His chubby fingers began to shake. "And now she could be using personal days that are coming to her."

Waller interrupted him, "When did you last hear from her?" as she and Garcia exchanged a look.

Mr. Herman swallowed nervously, made a disgusted sound in his throat, then said, "She was here working all day Friday, so I guess it was five o'clock when she left."

Garcia sensed the rising irritation in his voice.

Waller looked serious at the librarian to the point of stern. "Did you see her walk out at the end of her day?"

Herman was staring at the top of his desk. "Of course not. I'm back here in my office. I don't watch any of 'em."

"She's been MIA since Tuesday," Waller snapped at him. She kept her eyes on him to gauge his reaction as she asked, "Any problems with her? Like was she absent a lot?"

Hubert Herman waved a soft glistening hand. "Quite the contrary. She's reliable." He looked up at the ceiling for a brief second, then down at his desk again, like he was trying to avoid the two pairs of police eyes on him. "She's a conscientious worker." Herman put his arms down on his desk and drummed the fingers of both hands to hide the slight nervous shake. "I've never had a problem with her. But now she's brought the police in here."

The worried expression on his face made him look like a stone lion outside a public library. No one said anything for a full minute, then the tension got to him, so he added, "It's only Friday. If she doesn't show up, she's got a little vacation coming, a week." Lowering his eyelids until half of his irises were covered, he went on talking in a light stutter, "Mm,m-meanwhile her work piles up. If it piles up t-too much, I-I'll ask someone else to do it." Herman glanced at his watch too quickly to see the time, trying to show he had work to do. "I hope you will excuse me, I'm rather busy," he said. When they didn't move, he glanced at the door. Then he placed his pudgy fingertips to his left breast. "I feel faint. I have a heart condition."

Waller ignored what she deemed his fake illness. "Is she close to any of her coworkers?"

His eyes were sunk deep in the glistening sweaty flesh of his face. "She seems to get along with everyone." Then impatiently, he added, "I've had enough of your questions, so if you're finished, I think it's time for you both to leave."

Detective Waller sighed. This jerk wanted to get rid of them, so just to irritate him, she asked, "Were you here at the office on time Tuesday morning, sir?"

His face was turning pinkish. He pulled a handkerchief from his pocket and mopped his forehead, then his neck. In a bored, barely audible voice he said, "Sure. I'm always on time."

Garcia wanted to stay, but Herman really didn't seem to know or care about his employee. Garcia glanced at his co-worker, who rolled her eyes. They could have asked more questions, however there was no point to it.

Detective Waller said, "We're finished now. Thanks for your time." She started to turn towards the door, then turned back to the man sitting at the desk. "Do you mind if we talk to her coworkers?"

"Nope, go ahead." The heavyset man looked relieved the police were leaving his office.

Just to upset him, Waller added, "We'll probably be back with more questions."

At the outer office, they stepped around a cart of books as Detective Waller turned to a few employees and asked, "Have any of you heard from Carolyn Fazzino?"

"Not this week," a tall, dishwater blond answered.

Waller lowered her voice, "Does she get along with her employer in there?" pointing her thumb towards his office.

A tall woman with a head of blond curls motioned towards the outside door. Garcia and Waller both realized she wanted to talk, but not within earshot of her supervisor, so Waller nodded her head in agreement. Loudly the detective said, "Well, thanks anyway. Now, you all have a good day."

Waller and Garcia walked past shelves of books, then stepped outside the library. The blond and a second woman probably in her mid-fifties, accompanied them out into the hallway. As soon as the door closed, the blond said, "I'm Catherine Wells."

The older one replied, "I'm Irene Pelletier. Look, Carolyn's a sweet girl."

Catherine nodded in agreement. "She's really nice. It's just that I don't blame her for taking a few days off. I mean, I'm actually thinking of looking elsewhere for work." Then she turned to Irene, "Don't you tell Mashed Potato Head in there. Promise me?"

"Of course, I won't tell him anything," Irene agreed. Her hair hung in strips on both sides of her head, so her ears poked through. She turned towards the detectives. "That's what we call him behind his back. He's not popular with any of his staff. He's hiding in that office of his."

"He wrote me up," Catherine said, her face slightly flushed. "I'm the head of circulation and he wrote *me* up. He told me, I snapped at a student. I've never raised my voice to anyone."

The tall mid-thirties woman was nodding in agreement. "Right after he started, he accused the head librarian of technical services of being a peeping Tom. She's very popular with all of us. She can fix any computer glitch."

Catherine nodded in agreement. "She's married with a family for God's sake. Why would she spy on him in his office? He's just a weirdo."

"He's a stickler for getting back from lunch on time, too, not like our last boss. She was nice." Irene's voice rose with enthusiasm.

The detective knew these two women were unloading their feelings about their supervisor, but the detectives needed to know how it affected the missing woman. Garcia asked, "Did Carolyn feel the same way about him?"

"Yeah, this guy chews us out for nothing. He didn't even try to get on our good side when he started." The older woman threw her arms up in the air. "Carolyn didn't like it either when people got reprimanded for doing nothing wrong. She didn't like it when he stopped us from celebrating our birthdays. No more parties or cake in the afternoons."

Irene, a little calmer than Catherine, said, "He's not on speaking terms with half his staff. He refuses to fit in. Before he started here, we use to go out after work, but not anymore. He made it clear, he doesn't drink, and he doesn't think others should either."

Garcia saw Waller arch her eyebrows, to show don't interrupt, just let them talk. There might be a clue in their ranting. Garcia nodded to let her know he understood, as Waller raised her voice, "So he doesn't get along with any of you?"

"Right," answered Irene. "I figured Carolyn might be out looking for a better place to work, maybe out for interviews or something."

Garcia wondering how close these two ladies were to Mrs. Fazzino, but not wanting to disclose she and her husband were separated asked, "Did Carolyn ever talk about her husband or her marriage with either of you?"

They glanced at each other. Then Catherine, shaking her head, said, "No, not to me. She hasn't said anything about him lately." Then she looked over her shoulder. "We should get back before

Mashed Potatoes notices that both of us are gone."

All four stepped back inside the library. The detectives asked around; however, the other library workers were of no help in finding Carolyn. The two police officers didn't speak to each other as they headed to their car. They didn't want anyone to overhear them. Waller slammed her car door with disgust. Enclosed in their vehicle, Garcia asked, "So what are your thoughts?"

Waller's mouth curled at the corners. "Carolyn Fazzino really didn't tell her coworkers what was going on at home, that they were separated."

"Maybe she's in denial about him leaving. You know, hoping he'll be right back."

"Four months and still hoping, he'll be right back," she mocked him. "Herman is afraid of us. I mean really scared of us. He wanted to get rid of us. Maybe it's our badges. He sure acts guilty."

Garcia turned the ignition key. "Not just us. He's afraid of his own shadow, like a coward." He backed out of the parking space. "The way Herman is acting, doesn't make any sense. He's not even upset that Carolyn hasn't called in. There must be something else on his mind."

Waller chuckled. "I'm sure his mother loves him; however, I just want to give the fat slob a demerit for something, anything."

Garcia turned the unmarked car onto the four-lane highway. "Take your frustrations out on a candy bar."

"When I gave up smoking, I switched to chocolate, and now you make fun of my chocolate. Once I lured an angry Rottweiler into the back of my patrol car waving a Junior Snickers bar."

Garcia chuckled, but Waller's face was heavy with thought. As she looked through the dusty windshield, she said, "I'm calling in to request a WCPI on this guy. It's necessary to check him out." She meant West Chicago Police Investigation.

Waller put her cell phone on speaker so Garcia could hear too. "Anything on a Hubert Herman?"

Sergeant Dodson looked up the name and told her, "He graduated from Northern Illinois in 2000 with a library degree." After a quick pause, he added, "Oh here's something interesting. He was brought in for suspicion of solicitation of an underage girl two years ago."

Waller answered, "That asinine bugger! I knew there was something. We have to look at him closer."

On the other end of the phone, her sergeant told her, "It says here, charges were dropped."

"He's a dick! No wonder we made him nervous," Garcia said, as he drove west on Roosevelt Road.

"He wanted to get rid of us," agreed Waller.

Garcia stopped their vehicle for a red light and turned to face his partner in the front seat. "Could Carolyn have found out somehow, maybe caught him looking at a porno website?"

Waller speculated, "She might have just walked into his office to tell him she had a dentist appointment when she saw his computer screen."

"He knows it could cost him his job, so one way or another he had to silence her." Garcia shared his theory.

"Would he kill? Or would he just try to can her?" Then on the phone to her supervisor at the station Waller asked, "Should we bring fat boy in for more questioning to put the screws to him, or see what kind of drugs the dentist might have given our missing woman?"

The sergeant answered, "I'll send someone to pick him up. You two keep going. By the time you get back here, we'll have him in interrogation. Go out there and beat the bushes," Dodson said. "We've got to find her."

Waller ended the call with, "Text me the dentist's address. We need to talk with Doctor Carter."

———— ••◉•• ————

Right after Dodson sent the requested address to Waller, his iPhone pinged with a new message: "Could you get us a head of lettuce?" It was a text from his wife. He thought of Diane's skeletally thin frame. She looked like she starved herself, but really, she didn't. Even though she had quit her modeling career after being viciously attacked eight months ago, she still preferred eating fruit, vegetables and salad with no dressing, no desserts, and no cream in her coffee. *If only she could go to the store herself.* Guilt wrenched his heart. *But now that this has happened, I wish the security cameras in that garage would have gotten a picture of her attacker. Or if only we could have taken DNA samples at the scene of the crime, but hundreds of people pass through that parking garage. Then I could put that asshole behind bars, and she could feel safe again.*

"Do we need anything else?" he texted her right back.

———⫸⟪◉⟫⫷———

As Waller and Garcia drove past Seven Gables, both cops glanced over at the restaurant. The parking lot was quiet as they both scanned the area. They assumed the Glen Ellyn cops had picked up the drug dealer Waller had reported earlier. Waller, trying to concentrate on their missing woman case, said, "Let's check with her dentist since her mother and her wacko employer, both said she was getting a crown."

"Great," agreed the younger cop. "Maybe the dentist can tell us if she was sedated on meds." Garcia flicked on their siren and roof lights, so they could run every light to Dr. Carter's office.

As they pulled the unmarked car to the curb by a downtown West Chicago office, they saw cement boxes of inviting blooming pansies on each side of the office door. Waller stepped out of their Ford, and said, "Come on kid."

There she goes again, pointing out that I'm a new detective, thought Garcia.

Soft elevator music played to soothe the patients in the waiting room. Garcia relaxed and tipped his head, nodding to a dark-haired Hispanic woman sitting in the waiting room with a little girl.

"Buenos Dias," he said.

Waller turned to a receptionist who sat inside an arched window and flashed her badge. "We're here to speak with Dr. Carter about a patient."

"I'll see if she can meet with you," the smiling receptionist answered as she rose from her desk chair.

Within minutes, they were asked to come in. They stood waiting in a short hallway until a professional looking woman, wearing a light blue lab coat with short blond hair, came towards them. She grinned with perfect white teeth, like one she would give to patients to calm them. In response, Waller smiled closed-mouthed and said, "I'm Detective Waller and this is my partner, Detective Garcia." Waller reached her hand out to shake.

Dr. Carter politely shook her hand, then Garcia's as the detective extended his arm.

"We're here about one of your patients, Mrs. Carolyn Fazzino. We believe she had an appointment with you four days ago," Garcia explained.

Dr. Carter made a sweeping motion with one of her manicured hands. "Why yes. She had a root canal in preparation for a crown. Is she okay?" Her voice was soft.

Waller took over, smiling she said, "Her mother has reported her missing, so we're looking for her. You might have been one of the last people to see her."

The dentist's fine eyebrows drew together in a thoughtful frown. "She seemed fine when she left here. I numbed her up to do the drilling, but she was coherent. She could drive when she left."

"Tell us about her appointment." Waller had radiated sternness with Carolyn's supervisor, but here she softened. *Was this the same hard-nosed detective who had questioned a man suspected of solicitation earlier? Wow, she could turn on the charm if she wanted to,* thought Garcia.

"Of course, whatever I can do to help. First, I used a jelly substance. Then injected a local anesthetic, that numbed her for the drilling. Everything went fine."

"How was she feeling when she left?" Garcia asked next. He wanted to sound casual, almost chatty.

Dr. Carter gazed at Waller, without really seeing Garcia. Then she came back into focus and smiled. "After that much Novocain, the patient's lips and gums remain numb for a few hours. Later, she might have pain, so I gave her a prescription for Tylenol #3 with codeine, but I don't know if she had it filled. I also gave her a prescription for an antibiotic."

"An antibiotic? Why?" Waller studied the dentist's oval face.

"If a person has an infected tooth, bacteria from the mouth can enter the bloodstream and cause infection."

Waller seemed absorbed in the dentist's details, but Garcia was getting bored when he said, "We're more interested in the missing person than the missing tooth."

Dr. Carter looked wounded as she explained, "I'm trying to *save* her tooth.

"And we're here to save your patient," agreed Waller giving a broad grin. "Could any of that make her confused enough to get lost?"

"Oh dear, no."

"How long was she here?"

"The procedure lasted approximately an hour. She seemed fine; however, she needs to come back in a week to get the permanent crown cemented in place."

Garcia nodded. "Did she say anything about going on a trip?"

"No." The dentist cleared her throat and went on, "I do hope she's ok."

"One last thing, we want a copy of her dental records and x-rays."

Dr. Carter's sweet face became worried. "You think you'll have to identify her body?"

Waller placed her hand on the dentist's shoulder in reassurance. "Right now, we have no idea. We'll just keep them on file, in case." Then the detective looked gently into Dr. Carter's eyes adding, "Thanks for all your help. If anything comes up or you think of anything else, here's my card." She smiled as she said, "Give me a call."

As soon as the pair reached their unmarked car, Waller looked at her chubby fingers and said, "I might change dentists. I wouldn't mind those beautiful hands working inside my mouth."

Inside the Ford, Garcia responded with, "Keep eating all the sugary chocolate and you'll need a dentist."

"*You* should carry Junior Snickers bars for uncooperative dogs and a stash for me," Waller grinned.

Now serious Garcia said, "I don't think the dentist gave her any hallucinating drugs that sent her over the edge. Her mom said she made perfect sense on the phone later that night."

Waller stopped grinning as she said, "The husband could have done something. His girlfriend sure clammed up. That was strange."

"Then there's her alcoholic landlord who gave her drugs for depression or her boss who solicits minors."

"She sure has strange people in her world," Waller agreed. Then her cell phone rang. "Waller," she said into the phone.

"Dodson," was the response on the other end. "Your subpoena for Carolyn Fazzino's cell phone records came through."

"Anything worth looking at?"

"I'll say. She calls a Melissa Tomlin a lot and talks for hours."

Waller sat up straighter. "Then we've got to check her out. It's possible our vic left her car at Diamonds and her girlfriend gave her a ride somewhere."

Their supervisor continued, "Lab tests prove its Carolyn Fazzino's blood you found near her car. We used her toothbrush to get her DNA. Check hospitals. She's hurt."

Chapter 13

CAROLYN'S CAPTIVITY

UNKNOWN LOCATION, EARLY FRIDAY AFTERNOON

Footsteps. Heavy feet are coming closer. Someone is coming to help me. I look up at the circle of sky above, dappled by light. Suddenly there is someone looking down at me. His head looks dark, almost black surrounded by the bright sunshine. Shadows from tree branches hide his face. I try to raise up. I open my mouth, but a squawk comes out. My mouth and throat have gone dry. Finally, a scream wells in my throat. "Help me!" I beg.

"No," a man's voice says. "Shut-up ya fool," he hisses.

"P-please," I plead, terror racing which clouds my mind, my voice raspy with fear.

"You're going to do what I want," he spits.

I coil back. My stomach twists and churns. Panic fills my sub-conscious consuming me. *Don't freak out.* But my next thought is, *why not?*

Hearing his footsteps leave, I look up knowing I am alone. I sit trembling, trying to get my nerves under control, but pure terror takes over. Why is this happening? Oh my God, how can I get out? Panic grips me tighter than ever. Does he want a ransom for me? I don't come from a wealthy family, so *why me?* Will he *kill* me? Tears fill my eyes.

Did that crazy man put me down here? Could he be nearby? If the bastard comes back, can I talk him into helping me? Do I fight the lunatic? Or should I cooperate with him, so he'll help me? What should I do? How do I get out of this? I feel hollow inside as I think about the creep who must have done this. The ground is rough uneven like someone dug this hole out. Him?

A sound, is he coming back? Is it an animal or merely the wind in the trees? Listening for more, I imagine all sorts of wild things with teeth or sharp claws, maybe coyotes. Am I in an animal trap? How dangerous is it here? I must get out. My pulse pounding. Smelling my own fear, the walls seem to close in on me. My panic rises. Anxiety robs the breath from my lungs, forcing me to gasp as the panic attack takes me in its grip. I clutch the bottom hem of my t-shirt tightly in my fist.

I try to get my legs under me. The dirt walls seem to spin in front of my eyes. I drop my head down to my knees waiting for the fog to clear. I feel ringlets of my hair pasted around my face. I'm in a cold sweat of terror. I look at my hands and realize I'm chewing my fingernails, an old childhood habit. I try to get a hold of the dirt sides, but there is nothing to grasp. Frantic fear and hungry grip my insides. Standing on trembling legs, I try to raise up on my toes reaching my arms up over my head. I still can't reach the top. With my right hand shaking, I find a dry wisp of root about shoulder height that immediately disintegrates in my hands. I jump, which makes my right knee hurt like Hell. In pain I try jumping again but put more of my weight on my left leg. This time raising my arms overhead to grab something, anything up there. But there is no way I can reach that high. The sides of the pit are too steep. I scratch at the dirt. I cannot find a handhold, cannot pull myself even a few inches without sliding back down.

Afraid and desperate I try to dig my fingernails into the hard-packed dirt sides of the tomb. Frantically I dig, trying to gouge out tiny bits of dirt. My nails fill with dirt. Then one brakes close to the quick, ripped in the soil. I scream silently as my nail tears under the strain. I use different fingernails because I must get out.

Suddenly I touch something that moves under my fingers. *Ick*! Are there worms or bugs in here with me? This isn't going to work. I need to get a foothold. I need to dig. I look around. No sticks. No stones. Even my car keys could help me dig if I had them. He must have taken everything, even my phone. I can't call anyone. There were some mints in the bottom of my purse, but where is my bag now?

I must get out of here. Then a new thought comes to me. I can use my earrings for a tiny digging tool to chip away at this hard dirt. All I need is a foothold. My hands quickly go to my ears. No earrings. That's right, I always put on my jewelry after my morning shower. I left my apartment before showering. Stupid, stupid: you are so stupid. My nerves strain with agitation.

Then I hold my shaking hands out in front of me. They are trembling uncontrollably. That's when I notice my wedding ring and pinkie rings are still in place. A ring with a large stone could be used to scrape the dirt sides of this tomb, possibly make a foothold. But no, I chose a recessed diamond when Vince and I went looking for an engagement ring. How stupid!

If he wants money, wouldn't he take my jewelry? This isn't a robbery. Then why? Why is he keeping me alive? What does he want? Who is this man? Maybe if I can get on his good side. Maybe bargain with him. I'm scared, although I shouldn't show that to him, if he ever comes back again. What can I offer him to release me? I don't have much in the bank and I've seen his face, he'll kill me. I hate him and what he has done to me.

I need to think logically. I managed to pull myself together after Vince walked out, so I know I can do it again. Think! Why did I need that damn coffee? I didn't even eat breakfast. *Stupid. Stupid. Stupid. I run* my tongue over the tender area in my mouth. The appointment for the crown really threw me off.

I did give Tux some milk before I left for the store. I pulled on jeans and t-shirt. Grabbed my purse and left. I should have stayed home. First stopped at the Kup for coffee. Feeling better, I drove a few blocks to Diamond's Grocery to get grounds for the next day.

In a hurry, I parked near the front door. There was no one around.

Oh, except a man smiling, inviting. He had a nice face, good complexion. What did he say? But, *oh my God,* now I remember, he raised his hand. There was an explosion of pain. That's why my head aches so much. I was *foolish and stupid* to let a stranger come close to me. What did he do to me? What happened? My mind is totally blank. Maybe hours lost. Did he do this? Why? My throat tightens.

Vince please save me, but he doesn't know I'm here. He won't be looking for me, after all we said to each other. Maybe I should have told him the truth before we got married. I'm so sorry for all the yelling. A lump is forming in my throat just thinking about him. He didn't hear my doctor. He didn't feel my pain. He's gone. He isn't looking for me.

I must believe someone is trying to find me. My mother is probably worried since I haven't called in a few days. Melissa will miss me immediately. When Melissa gets worried enough, will she call Vince? Maybe not. She's such a good friend. She was as mad at him as I was when he left. One second can change everything in your whole life, like Vince leaving and now this bastard. Why? One minute and everything changes. I'm never, ever going to be the same again.

The FBI could search for me, like on TV. Please someone look for me. Don't let them forget me. I look upward at the steep dirt sides. I'm so alone in this trap. Fear that no one will come, grips my insides. An icy chill, colder than the air, closes about my shoulders. I wish I had long sleeves. This t-shirt is too thin. I wrap my arms around my body trying to hold any body heat inside and curl into a ball, hugging my knees to my chest.

Stop acting like a frightened little girl. There's too much time to think. I close my eyes. Oh my God!! I'm not religious, but I pray. *I'm lost. Please let me live! I promise to be a better person if you get me out of here.* But no one comes. I've got to do this; I've got to escape this grave *myself.* Suddenly I have a new idea. I pull off my tennis shoe and try to dig with its heel, but the rubber sole merely rubs the hard dirt wall. I try the side of the shoe, but it's too soft. In frustration I use the shoe to madly pound on the dirt walls. I get so mad; I drop the shoe. My fists pummel the dirt blindly until my hands are bruised, my arms too exhausted to move. It's not working. In pain, I collapse. Fingertips bloody and throbbing from fruitless attempts at digging. Arms hang loose and can't move.

I need help. Swearing out loud to the dirt sides I yell, "God damn you!" but my voice is catching. I'm flooded with dread and adrenaline. Suppose that creep never comes back? I clench my fist in rising anger. He might be the only one who knows I'm here. Will I ever see *anyone* again? No one cares enough to look for me. It's up to me. If I'm going to get out, I'll have to do it myself. The woods and loneliness of the pit are caving in on me, overwhelming me. I'm scared. A crazy, frightened laugh that isn't mine at all, comes from me. It sounds like a mad woman until my laughter finally dies.

Chapter 14

BEST FRIENDS FOREVER

Friday 3:45 p.m.

Detective Waller said, "Let's check with her BFF. Both her mother and husband said Carolyn's best friend managed a Victoria's Secret inside Stratford mall."

Detective Garcia drove to Bloomingdale next. As Garcia parked, Waller marked their time of arrival in her iPad for the inevitable report they must turn in later.

While walking through the mall the lead investigator told her partner, "Ms. Tomlin will either know where our gal went, or she'll be so concerned, she'll be a sniveling wreck because her best friend is missing." But as Waller walked into the pink and black decorated store her eyes lit up. She thought, *wish I got this kind of assignment every day.*

Garcia, a single guy, also went into Victoria's Secret with a grin on his face. He too seemed happy to get this assignment.

A clerk was helping a customer with perfume samples to their right. Both shopper and clerk looked up as the detectives stepped inside the store. Even though she was helping someone else, the sales lady quickly asked, "May I help you?"

Lesbian Alicia Waller wanted to shop, but business first. "We're looking for Melissa Tomlin."

Judy, the clerk, simply pointed towards the back of the store. The pair walked straight past the angel wings, lacy garter belts and sexy maid outfits. They saw piles of rainbow satin and pink corsets trimmed with white lace.

An auburn-haired woman stepped out of the back room carrying a few more yoga pants for the store display. She looked up to see the two detectives coming her way. Her long curly waves brushed her shoulders. She gave the young detective a big smile and set her items down on the nearest table.

Garcia took a few steps in her direction, and asked, "Melissa Tomlin?"

Melissa had a soft, happy voice with a trill in it as she asked, "Officers?" She was slender with full tempting lips and a lush body.

Waller saw the way Melissa looked at her partner. Instinctively she knew with a little persuasion this person of interest would open up to him.

Garcia answered, "I'm Detective Garcia." He waved a hand towards his partner. "And this is Detective Waller. We're investigating the disappearance of Carolyn Fazzino."

"Have you found her? I've been so worried," Melissa excitedly asked.

"No, not yet. We're trying to find her."

Sadness showed on her face. "She's my oldest and dearest friend in this whole world, but I haven't heard from her in days."

Garcia's voice sounded hopeful as he said, "We're pursuing a number of leads." However, that could mean they were clueless. "Could we ask you a few questions about her?"

Judy completed the sale with the last customer, and moved towards the rear of the store, her head cocked slightly to eavesdrop.

Nosey, Waller thought, *I've got to keep the prying-ears salesclerk busy so the best friend will talk to Garcia.*

As if on cue Melissa answered, "Sure, but can we find a place to sit down to talk? I've been in these new heels all day."

Carlos Garcia lowered his eyes to her heals, as Melissa went on, "There's a Red Robin in the mall. Things are slow right now." She turned to her employee. "Judy, I'll take my lunch now. I'll leave my phone on. If you get busy, just call."

Judy looked doubtful. Melissa was always dieting, and it was after three o'clock.

Waller wanted to keep the other clerk busy. She glanced down at the nearest feminine merchandise, then raised a lace camisole. Quickly Waller asked the clerk, "Do you have this in a larger size?"

Judy saw a potential sale, so smiled brightly in front of her boss. "Yes, we do." She reached under the display counter to slide a cabinet drawer open, revealing more of the same lingerie.

Waller turned her attention back to her partner asking, "You need me, or do I have time to do a little shopping?"

Detective Garcia, sensing he was being asked to talk with this person alone, answered, "Sure."

Garcia and Melissa Tomlin walked out of the store. Her animal print leather heels clicked through the wide mall. Her green top clung to her seductive curves. They walked to the Red Robin making small talk about the great July weather they were having, but Garcia was thinking, *this good-looking store manager with the great figure is an eleven on the Carlos Garcia scale.*

A loud chatter of mingling voices in the restaurant would have made it hard to talk, so Garcia asked for a booth away from the noise. As they sat, Melissa brushed her hair off her shoulders. Her delicate features and clear green eyes made him think of sex. Melissa ordered a salad and specified a black coffee. Then explained her choice to Garcia by saying, "I spend hours at the gym and never eat carbs."

Even though he had eaten lunch with his partner two hours ago, he wanted to befriend this person who would know a lot about their missing woman, so he ordered a burger and coffee to lengthen his time with her.

As soon as the waitress left them, Garcia rubbed the back of his left little finger along the lower edge of his chin and proceeded to start asking questions. "How long have you known Carolyn?"

Melissa flashed him a genuine smile. "Forever. The Hendricks lived just a block behind us." With her perfectly manicured burgundy fingernails flashing through the air she said, "We grew up together, walked to school together. Carolyn's my best friend. We've never gone this long without talking to each other."

"When did you last speak with her?" But he was thinking, *she is every man's wet dream in one sleek little package.*

"We called each other every night, but Monday morning was the last time I actually spoke with her. She had a dentist appointment, so wasn't going to work. I did text her that night to see how she was." Melissa reached for her phone, scrolled a bit and said, "Here it is. Carolyn wrote back, 'Mouth sore, going to bed, talk tomorrow.' But she never called me, then Mrs. H. called in a panic Wednesday morning looking for her."

"Tell me about her mother."

"Mrs. H. is very protective."

The waitress sat their food in front of them.

Melissa said thanks, then turned her attention back to the detective saying, "In fact, when we were in college, at Northern, her mom used to tell us girls, 'nothing good happens after one a.m.'" She laughed. Melissa kept looking at his face. When their eyes met, the air had the promise of excited thunder.

Act professional, he had to remind himself. "Tell me about Carolyn. What's she like?" He glanced down at his plate and noticed the hamburger came with fries.

"Hmm." Something thoughtful crossed Melissa's face. "She's quieter than me; like she didn't have a date for our junior prom until I told Paul Philips that Carolyn wanted to go out with him, then he asked her."

"Did Carolyn get along with her husband?"

Melissa twirled a small section of her highlighted hair, but the whole time looked at the detective. "Sure, she did. Vince is hot."

"Was he fooling around?"

"Oh no." She picked a raw onion ring out of her salad and crunched half of it and pointed the crescent-moon remainder at Garcia. "He only had eyes for Carolyn."

"But they fought?" He took a bite of his burger.

She speared a piece of lettuce. "Not 'till they were married a few years. Carolyn was really happy at first."

"What did they fight about?" Garcia asked.

Melissa matter of factly said, "Carolyn doesn't want kids."

"What do you mean?" he questioned.

"I mean she doesn't want to go through that whole birth thing." She paused, then shrugged. "I'll tell you what happened. Before Carolyn met Vince, she had an occasional pain in her stomach. At first it wasn't bad enough to stop her from eating, but she would mention it to me when we were together. Then one day, the pain wouldn't stop. She was back from college, living at home then, so her mom called the doctor's office to describe the pain. The receptionist told her to come in."

Garcia watched Melissa intently as she explained, "First thing the doctor asked was if Carolyn could be pregnant." Melissa threw her hand into the air for emphasis. "She didn't have a boyfriend then; no one-night stands. The doctor told her the pain she was describing was similar to contractions. Right then, Carolyn decided she would never have kids. But it turned out to be three large kidney stones. The doctor told her she had twenty-four hours to pass the stones or they would have to operate. She was scared to death." Melissa took a sip of her black coffee. "It took over thirty-six hours before they finally passed, but they really hurt. She swore, she would never go through that kind of pain again."

The waitress came by to ask if everything was okay. "Fine," Garcia answered quickly, for he wanted to keep Melissa talking.

As soon as the waitress stepped away, Melissa continued, "Carolyn met Vince. They dated. Carolyn told me she was in love. I assumed she told him she didn't want kids. They moved in together. A year or so later, Vince proposed."

Garcia nodded to indicate that he understood.

Melissa put the fork near her lips and pulled the piece of lettuce off with her teeth. "Carolyn and I planned the perfect wedding. I threw her a big bridal shower. It was her day to be "queen," have it all about her; the planning, anticipating and count down to the big day. I even helped her write all those tedious thank-you notes to acknowledge the guests after their wedding. Everything was wonderful. They were both so happy in love, then Vince started talking about starting their family. That's when she told him she didn't want to get pregnant. That's when the fighting began. She's my best friend, but she deceived him."

What Vince said, makes sense now. Garcia took a bite of his hamburger even though he wasn't hungry.

"Carolyn told me that's when she explained all the pain she had gone through, but he just didn't get it."

A man walked past their booth holding a toddler's hand. Garcia had an image of Vince as a loving father, then his dreams were crushed. Garcia swallowed then asked, "So they fought?"

Melissa nodded. "Vince didn't want to adopt. He insisted it had to be his. Carolyn told me, 'he wouldn't be the one giving birth.' Vince started yelling that 'having a baby wasn't the same as kidney stones,' but Carolyn was firm. 'No babies.' She'd even told me she wasn't 'a baby lover." Here Melissa made little quote signs with her fingers for emphasis. "Carolyn even asked me, 'How does he know anything about kidney stones or giving birth?'"

Garcia was watching her face, interested in the story.

She continued, "I know my best friend is a princess. Maybe that's why we get along so well. We're both high maintenance." Then to explain, she added, "For example, we both go for manicures every two weeks."

Garcia smiled and reached for a couple of his French fries since they were just sitting there on his plate.

"She's a little bit spoiled, being an only child. I probably noticed it because I come from a family of three kids where my folks can't help me financially. Mrs. H. helped her out after Vince left, only when Carolyn needed just a little more for her rent. A couple times her mother even treated her to a massage or hot rock therapy. Carolyn doesn't have to go looking for a better paying job." She hesitated, then continued, "I don't know why I'm telling you all of this."

Garcia knew the manual said to establish a rapport with the person you are questioning, so they open up. "Yeah, I know what you're saying. I come from a large family. Five of us kids, so I get envious when I see the help my friends get from their folks."

"I'm glad you understand." Desperation sounded in Melissa's voice as she said, "I love her. She's my best friend in the whole world. I can't imagine she would go anywhere without telling me."

He deepened his voice with authority, as he told her, "When people disappear on purpose, they take what they love with them. So, what does she love?"

"This is wrong, all wrong. She wouldn't disappear."

He attempted to avert his eye, an impossible feat because he couldn't take his eyes off her. "Tell me about Vince."

"Vince's temper really upset Carolyn. They fought, first about the baby thing, then about everything. Neither one willing to back down. Then after six years, he moved out."

Garcia was listening to her as if he was looking at the Dalai Lama. *Our missing person lead a fairly quiet life working in a college library; however, she wasn't perfect by any means. She lied to her husband and they fought.* Then he paraphrased the situation, "So Vince was really upset."

"They were both upset, but Vince left her, the louse. Maybe he has her, but it doesn't make any sense." She looked at him and maintained eye contact too long. Then she continued, "I know Vince was mad, but he wouldn't harm her. Would he? Have you talked to him?"

"Yes." It wasn't normal to give information to someone the police were questioning; however, this woman was different. She had really opened up to him about her best friend's personal feelings, so Detective Garcia confided, "We've talked to him. He says he doesn't know what's happened to Carolyn."

Melissa shook her curls side to side. "Maybe I should be looking for her?"

Detective Garcia could sense the honesty in Melissa's responses.

"Leave it to the police. We have a team searching for her. Maybe she needed time away to think."

She looked thoughtful. "Carolyn has always done her thinking with me. We bounce ideas off each other. She's not a strong person." Tapping one finger against her perfect lips she said, "Like, I've tried to talk Carolyn into going to the gym with me. Oh, she came a few times, but she complained her shoes gave her blisters. She's a pampered house cat if you know what I mean."

Garcia carefully asked, "Was she seeing someone new, since Vince left?"

"She talked with a few men, but that was it. They're not legally separated, so she hasn't gone out with anyone new yet. I think she was just trying to get her bearings." Melissa stabbed another piece of lettuce but didn't raise her fork. "I kept telling her to date. I even offered to fill out her profile on Match.com or some other Meet-up website. I told her, 'You have to open yourself up to the world's possibilities, but she kept saying, 'I've forgotten how to do the whole single thing' or other times she said, 'maybe, but it's too soon."

"Could Carolyn have left town to make her husband worried enough that he'd come back to her?"

"Nothing like that. Carolyn's not manipulative or mean. She's really a good person. She would never ever leave town without telling me. I'm worried. This isn't like her." They sat for a minute in silence as Melissa looked at her empty plate. Finally, she said, "I'd like to stay, but I should get back to work."

As they stood to leave, Detective Garcia said, "Thank you. You've been very helpful." Handing her a business card, he added, "Please call, if you think of anything else that could help us locate your friend."

Melissa reached for the card, then he saw her smile. "There's something, maybe I should tell you."

"What?" Garcia found himself thinking, *she's a party girl, perfect from head to toe.* He looked up to see Detective Waller standing by the front door of the restaurant looking across the crowd for them. He knew his private talk with Melissa would end as soon as his partner reached them. Without even thinking he asked, "Could we talk more tonight?"

Her stunning high cheekbones blushed faintly. "I guess, but I don't want to get anyone in trouble. It's just a feeling I have."

"We could meet at the Cadillac Ranch in Bartlett about nine o'clock tonight. You can tell me what's bothering you." Garcia said. *That came out like a date offer. Why would I say that? I know seeing her, when it isn't work-related, could be dangerous. Her best friend is missing. She could be a suspect. I shouldn't go out with a suspect.*

Garcia waved an arm to signal his partner. Melissa turned to see who he had motioned to. They both watched Waller nod her head and unwrap a Kit Kat bar while she started to walk over. Melissa looked back at Garcia, smiled, and said, "Okay."

Garcia brushed crumbs from his mustache saying, "I'll get this." He picked up the bill. "It was a pleasure to meet you."

As Waller reached their table, Garcia saw a Victoria's Secret pink and black striped bag in Waller's hand. Melissa and Garcia gave each other a brief glace, but all Melissa said was, "I've gotta run," and headed back to her store.

As the detectives stepped out of the restaurant, Waller said, "I had a great chance to ask the store clerk some questions about her employer. Seems that Melissa Tomlin came into work just minutes before ten o'clock on Tuesday, just in time to open up. The neighbor, Mrs. Butzen, saw Carolyn at 5:45 that morning." Sarcastically, she added, "That gives dear Melissa time to see her BFF and even do something to her. Did you get anything out of Miss Melissa?"

No one in the wide mall hallway was near enough to hear them. "She called Carolyn a princess, however I don't see a motive. She seems worried about her missing friend. She explained why the Fazzinos were fighting," said Garcia. Then as an after-thought, he asked his partner, "You trust Melissa?"

"Yeah, you don't?" she questioned him back.

"No. I mean, I do." He dropped his voice, "I really do," but he was thinking about those beautiful lips and green eyes.

Inside their Explorer, Garcia glanced over at the senior cop, who was deep in thought. "What is it?"

"I'm thinking about our girl. The husband called her a high maintenance queen..."

Garcia interrupted, "Her best friend called her a princess."

"She sounds like a pampered baby," finished Waller.

Garcia turned the key in the ignition. "There's a lot of levels of strength between a strong tough individual and a weak one."

"Yeah. I'm just trying to get a handle on our missing lady."

Chapter 15

CAROLYN AND THE SERPENT

I have a terrible, splitting headache. I think it's because I'm so thirsty. If only my head would stop pounding. There is the anguish of death which I have no defense for.

Out of the corner of my eye, I see movement on the dirt floor. A small black snake is slithering along the ground! It's inching closer. "No, No. Go away." I scream, hoping it will listen. My adrenalin kicks into high gear as it comes closer. My courage doesn't fail me. Suddenly I raise my right foot and come down hard with my tennis shoe on the middle of the black creature. It whips its head upward twisting under my tennis shoe. I raise my left foot to stomp on the small head again and again while my right foot pins it to the ground. Over and over again I pound my left foot on the snake's head until it looks mutilated, nothing like a snake.

Is it dead? Slowly, I raise my right foot that's trapping the creature. It lay there unmoving. I don't want the creepy thing anywhere near me, but I don't want to touch it. I bend to untie my tennis shoe and pull it off, then scoop the beast into the shoe and toss the snake upward trying to throw it out. But my stupid, half-assed toss only succeeds in raising the small snake a couple feet over my head. The devil thing hits the dirt wall and falls back to the bottom with me. Instinctively I jump back to avoid it hitting me. I stand looking at it across the pit. It can't be alive. I stare at it in disbelief. When it doesn't move, I take a tiny step closer. Again, I scoop the reptile up with the shoe and with a snap of my wrist, fling it as high as I possibly can. The snake sails up, out of my pit. A deep sigh of relief escapes my lips. *When did I get that strong?* My heart leaps with exultation at my victory. Then I involuntarily look around the dirt bottom for more. Where did that snake come from? How did it get in here? Did it fall in? That's when I spot a tiny hole where the dirt wall meets the bottom. Timidly, I move closer to look. Maybe it came in there. I try to scratch some dirt into the hole, but a snake can come through dirt. I pick up my shoe, the only weapon I have, and set it over the hole. Success. No more snakes. I push back my shoulders with determination and think of the song "I Am Woman."

In the wild west, did they ever cook snake meat over a campfire to eat it? Maybe I should have kept that snake. But how can I build a fire? The only things I have are my clothes and tennis shoes. Could I burn them? Then I would be even colder at night. Could I have eaten it raw? Oh, it's too late. It's gone. I couldn't stand it near me. What other creepy-crawlies are in here with me?

As if to answer my thought, a mosquito buzzes around my head, and then the tiny vampire bites my cheek. I pull my hands out of my pockets and swat at it to shoo it away, then I remember that crazy TV show called *Survivor* where those people ate bugs. Can I eat a mosquito? All I do, is worry.

More mosquitoes shriek near my ears. I wish I had bug spray. I swat at the near invisible things to get them off my face and neck. Their bites make my skin itch. Biting flies and mosquitoes are leaving streaks of blood on my arms. They get to eat and feed, but not me. I feel the insects swarming around me, nesting in my hair, crawling up my nose and into my eyes. I pull my stringy dark hair over my face to try to cover it from the hungry mosquitoes. I feel cheated, robbed of my orderly apartment and clean clothes.

Why is this bastard doing this to me? I hate him. I've never loathed anyone in my life, but I *hate* him. He is evil to put me into this dirt tomb. Is he nearby listening to me cry down here? He gives me the creeps. Shivering with rage, I wrap my arms around my body trying to warm myself, but it's useless.

Chapter 16

GOOD OR BAD MEDIA?

Ruth's hands shook. She had been making frantic phone calls for three days to everyone she knew. Someone must have seen her daughter by now. The last person she spoke with, her minister, had promised to pray that Carolyn would come back soon. Ruth, her eyes red and puffy, had just disconnected her cell, when she noticed the red low battery sign. She ran to her bedroom to retrieve the charging cord. She plugged it into the nearest socket and looked at the next name in her contact list, that sweet lady she met in Florida. Her phone suddenly rang. Startled, she stared at the unknown number displayed on the screen. Hoping it was finally her daughter, she quickly answered, "Carolyn, where are you?"

"Ruth Hendricks?"

Hesitantly she answered, "Yes."

"This is Valerie Inglewood, of Channel 7 News. We understand your daughter hasn't been seen since Tuesday. We want to help you find her."

"Yes, but how do you know that?"

"Our police scanner, and we work with local police precincts. I want to report what actually happened. We'd like to interview you for our Breaking News segment."

"Oh, no. I can't do that." *I think the police officer said something about the media. I'm not sure.* "I have to keep looking for her myself." She reached for a tissue to blow her nose. *But I don't know what to do.*

"You should go public, Mrs. Hendricks, so everyone can watch for her. By now, someone, somewhere, has seen your daughter. You want people to look for her, to help the police find her."

I'm so scared something awful has happened to her. "The police haven't even called me back." She sniffled. *I don't know what else to do.* "You're right. I'll do it for Carolyn."

"Can you meet me in front of your daughter's apartment building in an hour?"

———◎———

On Hampton Avenue, Bernice noticed the Channel 7 News van pull up out front of her apartment building. She picked up the nearest cat, a calico. "Look Cally Cat," she said as she held the feline up to the window. "What's going on down there? It's hard to see from here. I should probably check it out. I'll let ya know." She gently placed the cat on the floor and ventured out to the landing to get a better view.

Crews were setting up cameras. Bernice watched all the action. Then she recognized Carolyn's mom emerge from her car. Bernice waddled down the steps as fast as she could to see what all the fuss was about. As she reached the sidewalk, she pushed her sweaty wet hair from her forehead. It was a hot sticky July afternoon in the Chicago suburbs. Soon, someone was patting Ruth's cheeks with foundation make-up and running a comb through her hair.

"Make her look a little paler, but keep those red eyes," a man dressed in all black was shouting.

Forty minutes later, after cameras and lights were in place, a pretty, young newswoman with a head of wavy brown hair and perfect white teeth was speaking to a camera. "This is Valerie Inglewood of Channel 7 Breaking News. Carolyn Fazzino, a 29-year-old woman, was last seen early Tuesday morning in the parking lot behind this building. We have her mother, Ruth Hendricks, with me right now."

The frantic mother's hands hung limp at her sides. She looked from beautiful Valerie Inglewood to the cameraman posed with a huge camera on his shoulder. She really should say something, anything, but she didn't quite know whether her voice would manage it. There was an awful dry taste in her mouth. Her cheeks were burning so much they hurt. She felt like crying. Her baby was gone. Her heart was pounding so hard in her chest that she didn't think she could speak.

Bernice stood in the background staring wide-eyed as the newswoman spoke.

The camera swept to the distraught mother as she let out a sob. Her eyes seemed to be magnetized to the camera in front of her, but she managed to sniffle. "Please come home Carolyn. I love you." Her throat did an involuntary gulp. "If anyone knows anything, please call the police, anything at all. Someone must have seen my daughter by now. Please, please, I beg you, call the police right away if you've seen her. We need your help." Ruth couldn't help herself; she burst into tears.

Ms. Inglewood snapped, "That's a wrap, boys."

The cameraman standing right in front of her brought the heavy camera down off his shoulder.

"Valerie, you-hoo Valerie," Bernice shouted trying to step over some cables on the ground. Then she called out, "I was the one who knew Carolyn Fazzino was missing. I'm the one who went to the police station. I reported it."

Valerie turned to see a heavy-set woman puffing hard as she came to a halt next to the newscaster.

The older woman tried to catch her breath. She smiled broadly and tried to run a hand through her red hair. It seemed to give the thinning hair an even wilder look of chaos. "I can tell the people in TV land al..."

"We're done here. You can talk to my assistant." The reporter abruptly turned on her heels, leaving Bernice with her mouth gaping.

A camera back at the station zoomed in on a large headshot of

Carolyn. The segment showed up on the four o'clock news.

Sergeant Dodson immediately called his detectives working on the case to inform them.

"Shit. I told her not to go to the press. This will bring out every nutcase and goofball claiming to have seen her," said Detective Waller. "We'll be chasing wild goose leads from now on."

⊶⟨⦿⟩⊷

Miles away, a large man was polishing furniture in his country living room. His long sleeves were rolled up, revealing round scars up and down his arms. He turned his shaved bald head to look at his TV screen in disbelief. He spoke to the headshot of a brunet woman on Channel 7 Breaking News. "They're looking for you, Mother, but don't worry, they'll never find you. I have ya in a secret place." He sprayed more lemon polish over the already spotless coffee table, then looked back at the TV. "But why do they call you Carolyn? Stupid, stupid people. They don't get anything right."

Chapter 17

DON'T STARVE CAROLYN

I must have fallen asleep but sleeping fitfully; an image of Vince appears in my dream. We are on a date, walking along the Batavia River Walk. Sun is shining on Vince's black hair as it falls in his chocolate brown eyes. We are laughing and holding hands. Then it fades to one of those Elgin restaurant patios. My hand curled around the stem of a wine glass; birds singing quietly.

Then the birds get louder, somewhere above me. I try to fight waking up from the dream of such happy times. My mind wants to weave innocent images. Their chirping and squawking, mocking my fear and loneliness. Are they laughing at me? They are free while I am trapped. I swallow, dry and sticky. I toss restlessly on the ground. I'm terribly stiff and foggy, almost light-headed and so thirsty.

I look down at my fingers. My nails broken, ragged, bleeding, and sore from trying to dig at the hard dirt sides of this pit. I've been chewing on my dirty fingernails, almost down to nubs. The tips white with a tinge of blue.

My leg muscles cramp from sitting. I stretch my left side first and then my right, pulling each joint, one at a time. Sliding my feet closer, I use the dirt side of the pit to help me get up. My legs try but reject my body for they have lost all feeling. I kick my lower limps to restore blood flow. Then I crawl to the other side of the hole. Finally, I'm able to stand. But when I unlock my knees, my legs wobble, and I almost fall. Am I faint with hunger? I don't know.

I've never been this hungry and I feel quite light-headed. Am I being melodramatic? Vince used to say I was, when I told him I didn't want to give birth to an elephant?

I struggle trying to remember the smell of Vince, the taste of his lips. Our beginning together had been so happy. Where did we go wrong? Was it my fault for not telling him the truth? When he learned I never ever wanted to get pregnant, he became livid. Why didn't I tell him before we got married? Because I loved him so much? Because I didn't want to lose him? I made a mistake when I didn't tell him right up front 'no kids.' When do you tell a guy that news? First date, first month of dating, when you move in together? I deceived Vince. All the fighting and yelling was too much drama. Sometimes I said things I didn't mean. Our feelings got hurt and then everything just spiraled out of control. He abandoned me and then my pride stopped me from calling him.

I moan out loud, rocking my head in my hands. How can I ever fix the mistakes? How could something that felt so wonderful, go so wrong? What can I do so he'll forgive me? Maybe he needed a time-out, or my marriage could be over. So here I am, by myself. Now this, captive in this damn pit. Am I wallowing in self-pity?

My pants feel sticky in various places. I probably smell, no shower in days. I assume I smell like a cooped-up animal in a dirty cage. Another day in this hole, I'm going to lose my mind if I don't starve to death first.

I think of strong pioneer women who moved across the U.S. to go west, how tough they must have been back then. I'm such a pansy now, even childbirth scares me. I've got to be tough like those brave women traveling in covered wagons.

Suddenly, a twig snaps up there someplace. The birds stop their racket as I jerk my head upward. What's moving up there? A bear, cougar, or wolf? Blood pounds in my ears. My gaze drifts along the ledge of soil far above me.

A man's face is there, looking down at me. He shouts, "Give me your hands."

Perhaps I have been rescued. There's a spark of hope. I don't know if I'm going to laugh or cry.

"I have a sandwich for you."

My empty stomach aches. Instinctively, I start to do what the strong voice instructs. I raise one arm up for the sandwich. "Please help me. Please get me out of here. I'm begging you." I plead desperately with him.

His venomous voice full of defiance says, "Raise your hands higher."

That voice, the same voice as the man who wouldn't help me. But his face is in shadows. Is it him?

That's when I notice he's holding something. I see the glint of shining metal in his right hand. I gasp at the sight of a large hunting knife aimed at me. Without thinking I inhale a panicked breath. I know something terrible is about to happen. Fear floods me, sending warning signals to my brain. I jerk my hand back down just in time to see the blade swing. I try to scream, but the noise doesn't come out. Does he want to kill me? A shudder of revulsion moves over me. "NO!" I resist. Anger mixes with my fear. "I won't do what you want! Don't do this." I'm appalled at the tremble in my voice.

He scares me more than I've ever been afraid in my life as he says, "If you don't, my face is the last you'll ever see on this earth."

My pulse races. Sobs catch in my throat as my heart thumps relentlessly. I try to suck air back into my fear-pinched lungs.

He lets me cry for a while, but it must have bored him.

A little loose dirt falls on me, so I try to cover my head with my arms. Then I realize he is throwing small rocks down at me. I tremble from head to toe. I feel warm urine wet my jeans. Then fury takes over like it always did with Vince. "You can't do this to me! I'm not an animal!" I sob. "Fuck you," I yell.

Dirt stops falling around me. I open my eyes. There's a jar near me. He must have thrown it. Spilled peanuts lay around me on the ground. My intestines feel like a tight knot. My stomach does a slow flip-flop as it growls. I wipe my dirty hands off on my jeans, but I can't get them clean, so decide not to use my hands to touch the food. Instead I pick up the jar. There're only a few peanuts left inside, but I shake them into my mouth. It's the only food I've eaten since I've been here. I can't stop eating the tiny morsels of nourishment until my mouth becomes so dry that the peanuts stick to my tongue. I hold them there, savoring the flavor. Before I know, the jar is empty! My hunger returns in full force and there's no way of appeasing it. I look at the nuts in the dirt. I don't care if the peanuts are dirty. I pick one up off the ground and wipe it off on my t-shirt before putting it between my lips. The grit of dirt crunches in my mouth, but I chew anyway.

A wild swirl of black fear and hot frustration pounds in my head. Now that this creep is gone a fresh stab of hopelessness fills my mind. I feel the sickness of despair. I'm totally breaking down. I pick up more nuts, putting them in my mouth. I sit in terror in this pit hour after hour, trying to think of a way to escape, to hope. I don't ever want that bad man back here, but he is the only one I've seen, so maybe he is the only one who knows where I am.

I eat more nuts. I still have hope of getting out, but my hope is turning to despair. I try to think of joys in my life. My job? That's laughable. No, the best time was when I dated Vince, when we moved in together and our wedding. I try to remember happy times like Saturday mornings when Vinny and I could snuggle in bed for an extra hour or two.

I eat another peanut. Oh, my God, food. Who's feeding Tuxedo? Vince? No, he left me and Tux months ago. He wants children. Before we were married, I wasn't honest with him when he brought up kids. But when I told him how I really felt, he became so frustrated with me. And I yelled, 'Why can't it just be you and me, be happy?'

Miserable, I curl into a fetal position on the dirt bottom. At least the pit shields me from the cold wind. Will I die alone? Screaming, "Damn it! No one cares!" I pound the dirt floor with my bunched-up fists and shudder. Survival, I must hang in there. I need to be tough, stronger than these tears.

The physical pain of utter weariness is so great: pain, hunger, thirst, and despair. Yet despite all this, I want to live, not die. To keep up my courage through the weary waiting, I pray, "God, just get me out of this. I'll call Vince. I'll apologize to him when I get out. I'll be a better person." Outlandish promises, but it's the only thing I can think of doing.

I look at the spilled nuts on the ground. Picking up another of the grimy peanuts, again I try to wipe the dirt off on my soiled clothing. Do not look at it. Hungry, I shove it in my mouth. I chew filth but there is a nut prize inside.

Then in frustration, I lay on my back and kick my legs at the dirt sides. Am I trying to crash the dirt down on me? This is so futile. I'm so pathetic. I sense my rising panic and hopelessness.

Chapter 18

HE LOVES ME

Bernice Butzen stood outside watching all the action until Valerie Inglewood and the news van left. She walked over to Ruth, who had just gotten to her car, to tell her how well she had done on TV.

Ruth was so distraught; she couldn't drive home just yet. She could only mumble a weak, "Thank you."

"Now me, I might have smiled a little more right into the camera, like the news lady did." Bernice tried to explain. "Well, next time Dear, you can do that."

Ruth turned towards her. "I don't really care what I look like. They must find my baby. In fact, I can't stay here wasting time. I've got to keep calling people who can help." With that she pulled the driver's door closed.

Bernice slowly climbed the stairs to her apartment. *I was going to invite her up, so we could sit and watch for Carolyn together. Keep each other company.* Once inside, she dropped into her favorite chair. She watched Felix, her orange cat, sunning himself in the living room window, looking around with a sleepy air, expecting caresses, but certainly he wasn't going to trouble himself. Bernice sat in her rocker absentmindedly petting Penelope, a grey and white cat. It was too quiet in the apartment for Bernice. She liked people around her, needed people. She pushed her glasses up to look at her neighbor's front door. No one on the landing. Then Bernice brought out her opera glasses to peer through the curtains because it seemed extremely important. *It's not prying.* Nobody was there. She slid her backless slipper off her left foot to inspect her chubby toes. She felt lonely. Bored, she reached for her phone and pressed speed dial, then zero, three.

After a couple rings, a sweet voice answered, "Hello, Aunt Bernice."

"Oh, I didn't surprise you. These newfangled phones tell you who's calling every time, don't they?"

"You are a wonderful surprise." Diane knew her aunt, her late mother's only sister, could be a little eccentric. "How are you?"

Bernice's voice rose. "Well, we've had some excitement here in our building this week. My neighbor is missing. I had to go to the police station on Wednesday. I didn't see David there. I looked around for him."

"He was working. Maybe he was busy with someone else."

"Must have been, but I got to talk with a Detective Garcia. He was very nice. He and Detective Waller, a woman, came back here. They looked all through my neighbor's apartment. Carolyn hasn't come back yet." Feeling important she added, "They've asked me to help them by keeping an eye on the place and I'm doing just that."

"You're good, Aunt Bernice."

"Yeah. The policemen even gave me their cards. I put them up on the refrigerator with one of my cat magnets."

Diane's voice sounded distant as she said, "I can picture that."

"But dear, I'm calling to check on you. How are ya doing?" Bernice had tried to see her niece in the hospital after she had been attacked and beaten eight months ago. Neither Diane nor Sergeant David Dodson had allowed any visitors into her hospital room. Bernice even tried to visit after she went home, but still Diane insisted she wasn't ready yet.

"I'mmm..." Diane's voice trailed off.

Bernice broke the silence that followed. "Honey, you're an emotional basket case. You've got to pull yourself together. Come over.

Just get in that car of yours and drive across town. I'll make you a nice cup of tea."

"Oh, no." Diane answered too quickly. "I just don't feel well enough."

"You have to get out. Be more like me, talk with people. See folks. You and I, we're extroverts. We like to be around people." She watched her Siamese trot across the room and slink under a small end table.

"I'm not ready, Aunt Bernice." Diane sounded insecure. "I'm too afraid. Maybe next time. I'll see."

Bernice, trying to think of a reason she could see her niece, but also wondering, *how badly were you hurt?* blurted, "You need a friend or a pet you can talk to. I talk to my cats like they're people. I tell them everything. I could loan you Charlie. He's a great listener."

"Thanks, Aunt Bernice. That is such a generous offer for you to give up one of your pets for me, but I can't let you do that. I have David to talk to in the evenings when he's not busy."

Bernice worried, *where was her husband that night? Police Sergeant and all, but he wasn't there with her to protect her.* "Well, ya try to get out of that house. Just step outside." *I get so frustrated with her when she doesn't give real answers.*

"I do, Aunt Bernice. I do go out on the back deck."

"That's great honey, but you need to talk to others, like me. I can even confide in strangers. You can open up, too."

"Thanks, Aunt Bernice. I'm doing weekly phone sessions with a therapist. I'm getting better."

"Okay dear. You know ya can call me anytime, day or night. I'll talk with you."

"I know. I can always count on you."

With that, they said their goodbyes.

As the late afternoon sunshine faded, Bernice glanced once again at her neighbor's front door. Then she stepped around Cally Cat, and into her kitchen to make herself a cup of Earl Grey tea. As she ate a chocolate croissant and sipped her tea, she remembered the day the young couple had moved into the apartment next door.

Bernice had been reading one of her many romance novels when she saw a good-looking man out on the front landing, so she hurried over to the window to watch. The handsome man was unlocking the apartment door right next to hers. Bernice glanced down at the bright yellow house dress she was wearing, told herself it was lovely and yanked open her front door. Hearing a door opening, the young man had turned as Bernice took a step forward on their shared outdoor landing. He smiled. Bernice smiled even broader. "I'm Bernice Butzen," she offered as she moved forward. She barely came up to his shoulder.

He extended his hand to introduce himself. "I'm Vince Fazzino."

She felt a spark as their hands and eyes locked. As she stared at his thick black hair, she said, "This apartment has been empty for several weeks. Are you moving in?"

"My girlfriend and I are." He had glanced past her towards her front door where a tabby was looking out her screen door. "Oh, I see you have a cat."

She noticed his long brown eye lashes hovering over his gorgeous brown eyes. "I have several cats."

"I hope your cats don't bark and disturb the neighbors, do they?" he teased her.

Bernice giggled.

Then he added, "We have a lot in common. My girlfriend has a cat. We're hoping he likes me as much as she does." He chuckled. "Oh, here she comes now."

A brunette in her mid-twenties was coming up the stairs carrying a table lamp. They made quick introductions, then Carolyn said she had to set the heavy lamp down and she carried it inside their new apartment.

Bernice offered to hold their front door open as they moved in, but Vince had set the closer to hold the door instead. Bernice stood at the top of the stairs looking over their furniture as each piece was brought up. Both Vince and Carolyn were polite, saying a few words as they carried box after box up the stairs stepping around their new neighbor. Bernice remembered, the great looking stud stopped intermittently to ask her how long she had lived there and a few other questions. She could have talked with him more. Carolyn seemed more determined than Vince to get their belongings moved into their new apartment, but she was always smiling as she stepped around Bernice.

That night Bernice felt jealous while she heard their bed squeaking and thumping.

———————

Early the next morning, Bernice was out on the back-landing pouring water into a saucer for the stray cats when Vince came out his door. She felt her cheeks burn with embarrassment thinking about the intimate noise she had heard the night before. Vince must have noticed her rosy cheeks and said, "Good morning. My, your makeup is flattering so early in the morning."

Bernice didn't wear makeup to feed the cats. Stunned by his comment, but she quickly recovered. "Good morning to you too, Mr. Fazzino."

"Oh, don't call me that. You can call me Vince. We're going to be good friends."

A couple days later, Vince greeted Bernice with, "Hi Doll-face." He shot her a wink. Bernice knew she had a sweet face and she loved the attention the younger man showed her.

Carolyn became friendlier after they moved in, stopping often to chitchat with her. Bernice wanted to know as much as she could about Vince, so she found ways to ask so it didn't look to obvious. She asked where *they* grew up, but when Carolyn simply said she grew up right here in West Chicago, Bernice had to ask about Vince and how they met.

Over the next few weeks when Vince saw her outside, he would complement her hair or her dress. Sometimes pouring it on pretty thick like, "My, your hair is exceptional today." On another occasion, Vince complimented, "Wow, all the ladies in this building look so young." That left Bernice blushing again. Several times he would say, "You look marvelous today Bernice." What was she to do, except believe him?

Bernice, a woman who didn't hear flattery often, took it seriously. *He really likes me*, she thought.

Once Vince had taken her hand, then gallantly kissing the back in Royal fashion, while saying, "Hello there, beautiful lady." He certainly knew how to charm her.

Bernice didn't wash it for several days, letting her dishes pile up in the kitchen sink.

———◦((◦))◦———

About a month after they moved in Vince brought over half a chocolate cake for Bernice. He said, "Carolyn baked this. We've eaten a few pieces, but now she says this dessert is going right to her thighs. Would you like the rest?"

Bernice had eagerly reached for the plate of homemade cake. "Thank you so much, Vince." With heart palpations she thought, *he brings me gifts.*

That night Bernice wrote in her journal, *he really does love me.*

Often when Carolyn baked desserts, they would share half of it with her.

Bernice could clearly see he had the hots for her with all his gifts. *It's a sign when both of my loves start with the same letter V, first my Victor and now Vince. We're meant to be together.* She had to let him know how she felt about him, so she carefully constructed a message, which took her days to get perfect.

Dearest Vince,
Please come over <u>anytime.</u>
Your lady in 202

She had sprayed it with her, 'Evening in Paris.' While she was sure he and Carolyn would be eating their dinner, so Carolyn wouldn't see her, Bernice quietly tip toed down the back stairs and placed her love note under his windshield wiper.

———◆———

In the middle of the night as Bernice lay in bed smiling, thinking about her true love, the wind picked up. She never knew a gust blew her note away.

The next evening, as Vince returned home from work, Bernice waited on the landing for him. As he got closer to her, he winked saying, "Good evening, my Lady." Bernice tingled with pleasure. Then he opened his apartment door and stepped inside his apartment. She knew he wanted to come over but couldn't get away because of his little girlfriend.

Bernice went out the next day to buy a jazzercise DVD to start exercising. But by the end of the day, she decided Vince liked full-bodied women just like her. *He's never said I should lose weight; in fact, he brings me baked goods. He likes voluptuous women.* Soon the plastic wrap on her new exercise DVD was collecting dust and cat hair.

As Bernice lay in bed at night listening to the young couple next door's squeaking mattress, she wished Vince was making love to her. *He probably really prefers full bodied women over that skinny little thing he's living with. I know he really loves me because of the sexy things he says to me.*

She dreamt of Vince lying beside her. His arms wrapped lovingly around her, but in reality, it was simply a couple of the cats who snuggled with her.

No one in her whole life had ever flattered Bernice like Vince. Not even Victor. He might have a little, at the beginning, but not in fifty years. Now she felt alive with excitement and sexuality. *Victor won't mind; I'm sure he wants me to be happy.*

Over time, Bernice convinced herself Vince loved her the most, but couldn't tell his girlfriend. When Carolyn had seen Bernice outside one day and showed her the new engagement ring, Bernice knew this beady-eyed brunette *must be insisting on marriage.* Bernice tried not to show her disappointment in their upcoming wedding. She laid in bed the entire honeymoon week, absolutely ill. After they returned from Cancun, the tanned Vince continued his praise and flattering remarks, so Bernice knew everything was the same between them. His marriage still bothered her a little, but she put it out of her mind. When she heard them fighting a few months later, she smiled to herself.

One of Bernice's hobbies was to read obituaries. Then go to many of the visitations and funerals at the local Norris Wallen Funeral Home. She loved the variety of free food. She even baked something herself for the occasions. She would make friends by talking with anybody who would listen. Once she told a bereaved widow, "I have a special man who loves me dearly. Oh, he worships the ground I walk on. He just can't leave his wife yet. She yells at him all the time. She's so mean to him."

The widow's smile disappeared. Her eyes opened in astonishment. *"You're* having an affair with a married man?"

Bernice saw the surprised look, so knew she had to explain, "Why yes, and proud of it. I'm a cougar because he's a younger man, kind of high-falutin, but he loves me." *Maybe that came out a little too bragging.* So, Bernice tried to explain, "You might find someone who says great things to you too. It can happen. It happened to me."

The widow squinting an eye in disbelief, then interrupting Bernice, she turned to the next person in line saying, "Why cousin Roger, so good to see you."

The Saturday Vince and Carolyn were screaming at each other, Bernice heard Vince storm out of his apartment. As he slammed the back door, she thought, *this is it. This is what I've been waiting for.* Bernice felt elated when the man she loved, left his wife. She knew he was coming for her. Then when he stomped down the back stairs, she turned to her long-haired cat saying, "Charlie, don't ya worry. Vince is just going that way, so Carolyn won't suspect it's me he's leaving her for."

Hours, then days, went by. Bernice told her Siamese, "Vince doesn't want it to look obvious to his dumb wife that he's in love with me. You just wait Sammy; he'll be back for us."

After weeks of missing him terribly, she told her black cat, Ebony, "*He's looking for a place, the perfect love nest for the two of us and all you darling cats. We'll be so happy together.* After some time, and he still hadn't come to get her, she imagined, *my Love is trying to get a divorce before he whisks me away.*

Bernice had been faithfully watching the neighbor's front door through her lace curtains. She turned off "One Life to Live" and listened to the usual noises of her apartment, the ticking of the living room clock and the hum of the refrigerator. Now she rose from her rocking chair. Her backless fluffy slippers stepped around the coffee table. There were so many Harlequin romance paperbacks piled on top, one could barely see the embroidered doily on the low table. She walked into her bathroom and looked at her image in the mirror. She took off her glasses as she spoke out loud, "I look just like Diane. People can tell we're definitely family. I was that pretty when I was younger. Well, maybe not so tall like her." She smiled adoringly at her reflection. "Let's see what's going on. We'll just take a look for old times' sake, even though no one's home," she said to the nearest tabby, as the whiskered feline meowed in response.

"Shush now Tommy, ya know the rules. No speaking."

She put her glasses back on, reached to the side of her mirror and pulled out the small paper plug that covered a tiny peep hole she had made between their two bathrooms. Bernice had visited the past tenants that lived in the apartment, so she knew the two apartments were identically laid out, but flipped back-to-back with their wall-papered bathrooms, one on each side of this center wall. She moved closer putting her eye to the hole where she could clearly see into the Fazzino's bathroom. She smiled remembering Vince's naked muscular body. *No one there.* Bernice stepped back from her homemade peep hole and remembered the times she had looked in only to be disappointed when it was Carolyn.

Where did Vince go when he moved out? Now Carolyn's missing, too. Maybe if I can find her, then I can get Vince back into my life again. Bernice turned to see Carolyn's cat, Tuxedo, sitting on the small bathroom rug licking his front paw. "Where would your mommy go?" Bernice bent to pet the cat. "Carolyn said 'I've got to run to the store. I'll be right back.' She's never lied to me. If she really went to the store, which one, Tuxedo?"

The cat purred contently.

"You're right, Tux, grocery stores. That's the only thing open at that time of the morning! Of course, I should have thought of that right away. I have to check those out."

She went back to her living room to look back at her lover's front door. No one. She glanced down at the nearest cat, a tabby. "I've got to look for her, but I shouldn't leave. What if one of them comes back? Well, maybe I can, if someone else stands guard for me."

The sky was starting to cloud up. The weatherman had predicted rain, but it wasn't going to stop her from helping her man. Bernice decided to use her cell phone to call another neighbor because her land line cord wouldn't reach to her front door and she couldn't miss a chance to see if Carolyn or Vince came home. As soon as Bernice heard someone pick up at the other end, she yelled, "Yoo-hoo, Teresa, ya busy, dear?"

"Hi Bernice, oh, just trying to decide what to make for dinner tonight," the short dark-haired neighbor answered. "Maybe waffles."

"I have to run out. Can you come right over?" Bernice's voice was rising with excitement.

Teresa, used to her friend's quirky behavior asked, "To stay with your cats?"

"Carolyn Fazzino is missing. I told you, her husband moved out several months ago, so I *need* you to watch to see if either of them comes home while I'm out. The police want me to report if they return." Then to make sure Teresa would agree, she added, "You can make waffles here, at my place."

Reluctantly Teresa gave in. "I could, but Tim is at soccer practice right now. He loves waffles. Can he come, too?"

Bernice thought of Teresa's bean pole teenager who played loud, awful music. He probably ate twenty-four hours a day, but this *was* urgent. "Sure, Tim's welcome, but come right away."

Accepting an invitation to a free dinner, the single mother said, "I'll send Tim a text and be there in a couple minutes."

Bernice quickly applied a thick layer of fire engine red lipstick. Then she pulled out a box of Bisquick and a bottle of maple syrup from her pantry. She was just setting them on the counter as her doorbell rang. Soon Bernice had her 5'4" petite neighbor inside.

Within minutes, Bernice was saying to her, "I appoint you, Teresa Triston, as our official neighborhood watch. You can see Vince and Carolyn's front door from my apartment. If either come back, call me right away on my cell phone. You have my number?"

Teresa nodded in agreement.

Excited, Bernice went on, "And keep my cats company, too. Feel free to talk to them as much as ya want."

As Bernice went down the back stairs to the parking lot behind the building, she had a creepy thought: What if someone was watching her right now? *Could there be "eyes" on our apartment building, just like in the TV crime shows?*

She opened the front door to her car. Her crocheted granny square afghan was carefully laid to hide the worn front edge of the seat. As quickly as she could get her large body situated on her brightly colored handiwork, she started her car. She pulled out of the parking lot to drive across town.

Bernice saw two squad cars when she pulled into the Diamonds parking lot. There was Carolyn's tan car, sandwiched between them. *I must see this.* She pulled into a handicapped spot because it was closer and opened her driver's door. Yellow police tape had been strung up around the car to keep people away. Bernice knew that was for other people. "Did you find her? Did ya find her?" She yelled as she picked up her pace to get closer.

Police investigators were taking samples of brown stuff on the pavement near the Honda. Others were removing the seats. Another was vacuuming the trunk. A uniformed officer stopped Bernice. "Ma'am you'll have to step back to let the officers do their job."

"That's Carolyn's car. I'd know her car anywhere. Did you tell Detective Garcia you found Carolyn's car?" Bernice pushed her body forward, stretching the yellow caution tape.

"He knows ma'am."

"Did you find Carolyn? She's been missing. I'm the one who reported her. I could probably help you if you'd just let me get closer."

"I'm not at liberty to say ma'am. If you need more information, you can call the station." With that comment, she could tell, he was dismissing her. Bernice was not one to be sent away so easily. She was on a mission. She watched as officers went inside the store. She followed. While the police interviewed the manager, Bernice stood nearby to overhear, thinking, *reporters should be here soon. I would love to be in front of the camera.* She fluffed her dyed red hair with her fingers. But no reporter showed up. Bernice thought of calling them herself, but she was too busy following the officers outside as they left the building to even get her phone out of her leopard bag. She stayed in the parking lot, until a tow truck hooked up the vacated car and hauled it away. She wanted to follow, but she was too slow getting back to her car.

Chapter 19

CAMERA FOOTAGE

FRIDAY 5:00 P.M.

Detective Garcia pulled the keys from his pocket and put them into the ignition. As expected, the engine turned over. He piloted the car back to the station, so they could write up their interviews before their shift was over. They had to convert three iPad pages on each person they had interviewed into a single page twenty-four-hour crime report. It was a quick ride to the station. When they got back, they found that Bernice Butzen had phoned. The message from the 9-1-1 operator read, "Neighbor hasn't seen Carolyn. Wants to know what you found out. She's a talker."

"She's a wack-a-doodle," Detective Waller responded.

Chuckling Garcia agreed. "Her apartment is a kitty store on steroids."

Not wanting to face another long drawn out call with the nosy neighbor, the two headed for the breakroom where Garcia poured a cup of what looked like mud from the very bottom of the office coffee pot. Waller wrinkled up her nose at his cup as she helped herself to a 7-Eleven Store chocolate covered doughnut that had been sitting on the counter since early morning. As they stepped out of the breakroom, they saw detectives working the computers in the admin office, pounding out reports of their day's activities.

Two cops discussed a hot car list in slow monotone voices. Someone pulled a sketch of a wanted man off the printer. Another cop asked a middle-aged woman to sign four copies of a list of missing items from her townhouse. Normal confusion.

Waller began filling in the blanks on the first series of lab forms, "bloodstained black top parking lot where we found the missing car." She requested blood and trace evidence analysis and special latent print analysis on the victim's car. She turned towards Garcia to explain, "The FBI has been maintaining fingerprint records since 1921."

Garcia sighed. He already knew that fact, but he listened to her without comment.

Police officers were working on Waller and Garcia's missing woman investigation, punching up criminal records for every name obtained in the preliminary canvass, looking for any known sex offenders, and kidnappers. The staff was trying to eliminate some from the list of suspects. Secretaries were typing reports dictated by officers. Administrative assistants were typing search warrants and dealing with telephone and face-to-face inquiries from reporters. If it was a homicide, Dodson would assign more detectives to the case, request help from the homicide and special tactical section. However so far, it was only a missing person.

One of them, Detective Arnold Turner, who was nearing fifty, turned to see Waller and Garcia as they walked past. "How's the Fazzino case going?"

"Nothing definite yet, just a lot of hunches," answered Waller.

Turner with a strong square face continued, "As we started to tow her car in, that woman who reported her missing, showed up. She was all excited."

Garcia's forehead wrinkled in disbelief. "It's surprising the gossipy neighbor would show up where the vehicle was found." He looked at his partner. "Coincidence?"

"Maybe, but certainly questionable," Waller answered. "Is she hiding something?"

Carolyn's photo had been shown to all workers at Diamonds

who had been on duty the day she went missing. If they were currently off work, Sergeant Dodson made the officer go see them at their home. His orders were, "Don't miss anyone."

Turner's brown hair with grey around the temples and a slight thinning spot on the back of his head, crossed his arms in front of himself and said, "Oh, we finally finished questioning everyone working at Diamonds. No one remembers Mrs. Fazzino coming into the store on Tuesday."

"So, the parking lot is a strange place for her to leave her car," said Waller.

Turner explained, "Well, now Dodson's got some of us running down the telephone tips that followed the TV broadcast."

"Anything?" asked Waller.

"Oh, like, 'I have the killer at my house;' or 'my boyfriend took her." He chuckled. "Hey, we had a ninety-year-old with failing eyesight claimed to have seen the missing woman go into a church."

Waller knew the anonymous calls and false sightings were being checked out, however it was disappointing that none led anywhere.

They stopped by Jake Nelson's IT office. "Anything on Carolyn Fazzino's computer?" asked Waller.

The twenty-five-year-old frowned as he answered, "Occasionally she checked her e-mails and texts. No meet-up dating sites, where she could have met some weirdos. She watched a bunch of National Geographic animal documentaries online." Sarcastically he added, "She's a real thrill seeker. Some games occasionally evenings or weekends. She shopped for some Land's End clothes and Soft Surroundings, but that's about it. I can dig deeper to see what she bought, but really, I'm looking for a needle in a haystack. I checked to see if Carolyn used social network, Facebook, Snapchat, and Twitter. Nothing since she went missing, but plenty from the husband, who has been reaching out to family and friends. He set up a Facebook page asking if anyone has seen Carolyn. Sounds like Mr. Fazzino is worried."

Waller firmly placed her hands on the desk. "So, what is it?" Her voice turned more caustic. "Is the cocky SOB visibly distraught about his missing wife?"

"We broke him when he admitted to having the girlfriend." Garcia reminded her.

"Yeah, low and behold, we find out, he has a new girlfriend." She dug her right hand into her pants pocket and came up with a miniature Reese's cup. "So, what else is he hiding?"

Garcia tossed out an idea, "Maybe the spouse did do something to her. He didn't even want to tell us he has a girlfriend. She's a suspect, too. She didn't even admit to being his girlfriend. They have a weird relationship."

Detective Donald Matters called Waller and Garcia over to his desk. "I've got eyes on the footage from Diamonds Grocery."

The two stood and looked over his shoulder to view the computer screen. As Matters leaned toward his screen a few of his brown strands of hair were falling across his forehead. The time stamped on the bottom right of the screen showed eight forty-nine a.m. They watched as a man dressed in baggy clothes walked around Carolyn's car. "That looks like Phelps," exclaimed Garcia excitedly. The figure was staring into the front seat of the car, then bent down and picked up a baseball size rock near the driver's door. He slowly walked around, stopped at the passenger window, and threw the rock at the glass. They watched as the window shattered. He reached in and pulled out a purse.

"Back it up to when the car got there, sometime earlier Tuesday morning," commanded Waller.

The computer operator backed the footage up. They watched as a tan Honda Civic parked at 6:05. The driver's door opened. A petite brunet wearing jeans and t-shirt got out. She leaned back into the car. They couldn't see what she was doing. Suddenly a figure stepped into the frame.

"Where did he come from?" asked Garcia.

"From the angle of the camera, we can't tell if he walked onto the parking lot or came in a car," answered Matters.

"More importantly, who is he?" was Waller's question.

A hood covered the face, so they couldn't see who he was,

but he looked to be approximately six-foot-tall, maybe more. He swung at her, hitting her solidly. Blood streamed down her face as she staggered backward from the blow. She crumpled to the pavement. Quickly the hooded figure kicked her car door closed and grabbed her feet, moving her a short distance. He dropped one foot to quickly scoop something off the pavement. His hand aimed for a couple seconds towards the car door then went to his pocket. Then he dragged her out of the camera's view.

"She *was* taken!" exclaimed Garcia. "The blood we found next to her car was probably from her head wound." But he lamented, "With that hood, I can't tell if the perp is male or a large female."

Matters staring at the screen said, "Hard to tell for sure, but I don't think he's wearing gloves."

"He didn't touch the car door," said Garcia.

"What did he hit her with?" asked the more experienced Waller. The excitement encouraged her to reach in her pocket digging for another chocolate.

"Whatever he used to hit her, we need to check if he left prints or DNA," answered Matters.

Garcia stroked his mustache. "Pete Phelps used a rock to break the car window. Shit, he could have used the same damn rock as the kidnapper and messed up the prints."

"Did it look like he picked up her keys and actually locked her car?"

"Could have." Then sarcastically Garcia added, "that's thoughtful of him."

Suddenly they all saw Dodson coming their way through the maze of desks. Detective Matters, while on the computer, ran through the camera footage a second time, so their supervisor could review it. Again, they watched a person in a hoodie near the victim as he raised his hand over her head.

Waller ordered, "Stop. Freeze that." They all stared. Then, she asked the operator, "Can you enlarge it?"

Matters zoomed the camera in, but it did not show the image clearer. In fact, it looked a little blurry. Matters explained, "It's the pixels. The larger I make the image, we lose detail."

They all squinted at the monitor screen as Garcia said, "It looked like a rock in his hand."

Waller agreeing with her partner, added, "approximately the size of a baseball." She ripped the wrapper off a peanut butter cup.

The silent film showed that Carolyn appeared to open her mouth to possibly scream, but the blow quickly sent her to her knees.

Dodson told his team, "She was definitely taken. This is officially a kidnapping." Turning to Waller and Garcia he said, "You both work this weekend."

Waller nodding her head in agreement with her boss asked, "Find anything unusual in her car?"

"Fingerprints on the cardboard coffee cup were Carolyn Fazzino's. The attendant at the Kup recognized her photo. Said she came in alone. Was in a hurry but said most of his morning crowd are in a hurry." Dodson turned towards Garcia. "We've got the homeless guy in interrogation room one. He's only admitted to breaking, entering the car and stealing her purse, nothing else. Now that I've seen this, I'll send someone over to go through his junk in the alley to see if he owns a hoodie."

"He might have gotten rid of it," suggested Garcia.

"The drunk's not that bright," Waller told them. "However, maybe someone might have stolen his hoodie if he took it off." Eagerly she popped the entire peanut butter cup into her mouth.

"He wasn't wearing a hoodie when he broke into the Fazzino car," admitted Dodson. "She was taken three days ago. By now everything in that busy parking lot has probably been contaminated from all the traffic through there. We don't even know if the kidnapper touched anything else other then what could be a rock. DNA evidence or fingerprints around there could be anyone's." Dodson glanced towards the interrogation rooms. "Garcia, you take the homeless guy in room one and Waller you question Fazzino's employer, Hubert Herman, in room two. If nothing else, you can give him a really bad day for preferring children."

Waller was still chewing down the chocolate, as she and Garcia reached the monitor outside interrogation room one to see Phelps slumped in the metal chair. His head laying on the dirty sleeve of his jacket. He looked like he was dozing. Behind the closed door, Waller licked at the chocolate on her fingers and explained to Garcia, "This guy is in here at least once a month for burglary. Most of the time, it's pretty hard to prove its him, and he's right back out."

Garcia opened the door. Stepping inside he said, "It's time to wake up Pete. Tell me what you were doing at Diamond's parking lot."

The toothless man raised his head and rubbed at his eyes. "Don't get in a dither. I only took the money. Bad as I hate to do it. I'm hungry. I duz the best I can."

Garcia wrinkled his nose at the smell coming off the vagrant as he sat across the table from him then leaned back in his chair trying to get a little distance from him. "When was the last time you washed your clothes?"

"Washed?"

"That's what I thought." Garcia felt sorry for the vagrant. He set his mouth in what he hoped was a perturbed look as he calmly asked, "Did you see a car there in the parking lot or nearby alley early Tuesday morning?"

"No, I might of been sleeping." Spittle drooled out of his whiskered face.

In dead seriousness, the detective asked, his voice tense, "You wake up in time to see someone walk over to the car?"

"Na, no one around. I told ya. What ya driving at?" The bum said it simply without expression.

The detective continued, "Well, someone took a woman right there in the parking lot. And you're the only one I see here."

"Yo' barking up the wrong tree." Pete coughed. "Booze made me go to pot. Made me lose my job. But I'm not bad."

"The way I see it, you hit her. You dragged her off somewhere. Then came back for her purse."

"Na. Nobody there, just the car."

Suddenly, Garcia banged his fist on the table, startling Phelps, who jumped. Then he composed himself enough to tell the cop, "Don't get bent out a shape. I don't know where she went."

The interviewer changed tactics. "You own a hoodie?"

Pete loudly snorted through his nose. "Huh?"

"A sweatshirt with a hood that goes over your head, keeps you warm." He reached his hands up and motioned over his head like he was playing charades.

"No," he wiped his nose with the back of his dirty frayed sleeve.

Garcia's eyes opened wide as he realized they could get a sample of his DNA off that dirty jacket. "You ever own a hoodie?" the interrogator asked the vagrant.

"That thang over my head? I can't say." Phelps didn't seem to notice the evil eye look the detective was giving him. "Ya got some food? I'm real hungry."

"Not until you tell me what you did with the woman. Fess up."

"Crap, I told ya, there was no woman. But I need a bite to eat, man. Every time they bring me in here, ya give me a good feed."

"I'm going to bring a lot of shit down on you, if you don't tell me what happened." The interrogator hesitated, giving Phelps time to explain himself. But he said nothing. Garcia tried a different question. "How much money did you take out of her purse?"

That made Pete's knees start jiggling under the table. He admitted, "Maybe twenty bucks, but no woman."

The detective stood. "I want the truth, not one of your cockamamie stories."

"I told ya the gospel truth."

Garcia asked, "That so?" without any apparent emotion. "Okay, Pete. You hang tight." He stepped out of the interrogation room, closing the door behind him. He raised his voice to the squad room, "Can a clerk run out and get this scumbag a burger? Maybe he'll open up when he smells meat and some fries."

Dodson was in the hall. He had been watching Garcia as he interviewed the homeless man. "Good tactic. You can bribe him with a nice juicy hamburger sitting just out of his reach to see if he knows anything more, but I doubt it. He's too dumb to kidnap."

"Hmm, it could have been someone else that took her." Garcia pulled on his mustache in frustration.

"Let me know what happens." With that said, Dodson turned towards his office.

Garcia walked down the hall to the monitor outside interrogation room two where the missing woman's boss, Herman, was whining, "I didn't do anything wrong." He leaned back in his chair and folded his arms.

Waller gave him a sneer as she asked, "What happened a couple years ago?"

"My lawyer got me off 'cause they couldn't prove a thing." He was focused on the table. "I didn't do anything this time either." He raised his eyes slightly to see if she was looking at him. "Aw, leave me alone." He grabbed at his chest. "My heart, I can't take this."

Waller showing her teeth in a somewhat mirthless smile, yelled, "You're having a heart attack because I'm asking questions? When we lock you up, you could fall off your bunk in jail and break your perverted neck."

"No, don't do that." Herman whined. He sucked his teeth and stared at his thumbnail.

Waller swept her pen and notebook out of her way, leaned forward across the table into his face, leaving him nowhere else to look. "You knew Mrs. Fazzino was going to be off work. You were one of the last people to see her. You've got a human resources file on her, so you've got her address. You ever go to her home?"

He raised his eyebrows and shrugged.

"You look like a scumbag, fella, so we've done a background check on you. You're a suspect." She waited for a response, but there was none. "You can plead the fifth, however I got to tell you, your silence about your employee's whereabouts, makes you look guilty of something."

Waller watched Herman's sloppy body. Feeling hatred toward the creep, she thought, *he needs to wear a bra under that shirt.* She was in a foul mood. This case was getting worse instead of better. "Did she ever get any visitors at work? Maybe you saw someone pick her up after work. Her husband or a new guy?"

That got the detective a filthy look. "I don't remember 'cause I don't watch."

"Tell me your side of the story."

Herman with his head bowed, stared at the gunmetal gray table as he said, "There's no fucking story. I don't have anything to say to you."

"I'm a cop. I'm nosy. You're not a decent member of society because you like young girls, so now, I'm wondering if you like vulnerable pretty women too."

"I haven't got a clue what happened to her."

Waller stood towering over the suspect at the metal table and screamed, "You are a lying piece of shit! You've got plenty to tell me."

"I, I can't tell you anything 'bout her, because I don't know where she is, but she better come back to do her job." He stuttered as he started chewing on one thumb, maybe a hang nail. He was nervous as Hell.

Probably because he'd had a run-in with the law before, thought Waller. "I want to know where Carolyn Fazzino is, and I want to know now! Do this the easy way, just tell me."

He shook his head slowly. "I don't know."

"So now you've developed amnesia?"

Waller left the interrogation room, closing the door behind her with a loud bang. When she saw her partner in the hall watching the monitor, she said, "This one's filth and the other one is a real goofball."

Waller turned to look at the monitor with Garcia.

Herman was a supervisor at a college, a man in charge, but in here, in the interrogation room was a creep between these four walls. He sat hunched over in the uncomfortable chair staring down at his fists on the table like he was bracing himself for torture. He permeated the air around him with wrongness.

Garcia was watching him so intently; his nose was practically on the monitor screen. Then Garcia backed a little saying, "My personal opinion is, it's not him. He likes them young, not twenty-nine. He's a sick fuck, but I don't like him for this."

Detective Turner walked towards them as they stood watching Herman through the interrogation monitor and asked Waller, "You got some kind of chocolate candy for a teen graffiti artist I got? We've been waiting for his mother to get off work to pick him up. The law says we got to feed him every few hours."

"What?" Waller asked. Her bad mood took a nosedive. "Just because this sad-eyed gang banger delinquent needs a snack every three hours, why do I have to give the brat one of my Ghirardelli, when one of you could pony up for a Snickers from the vending machine?" To prove she wasn't giving up her candy, she turned away from the monitor and walked to her supervisor's office.

Smiling, Turner explained to Garcia, "He's a youth at risk. Her calling him a gang member could stigmatize him for life. Even arrested is too mean a word for our youth today. He was taken into custody."

Garcia had seen Turner with a kid he recognized earlier. Garcia pulled a buck out of his wallet to hand it over. "The last time I took him home, his mother said I could keep him. Where am I going to take him?" Then he followed his partner into their sergeant's office.

Dodson had begun to read through the statements Waller and Garcia had gathered, digesting pieces of the puzzle. He was playing catch up, working to stay on top of a missing person case that was geographically expanding with every hour. The supervisor's hair sprinkled with silver strands, was asking, "Family?"

Waller reported, "Mother, Ruth Hendricks, fifty-five, hair with artificial red highlights. She's addicted to self-tanner and Crest White Strips."

Garcia who sympathies more with people than his partner added, "Her mother is panicking."

Dodson's enormous fingers picked up his iPad as he read a report. "Carolyn's phone shows lots of contacts, however emails and texts to only a few work friends. Many calls from her mother and lots of texts with a Melissa Tomlin."

"That's her best friend," explained Garcia.

Dodson turned to look at him. "No men? Somehow this seems odd since she's been separated from her husband, and he's already dating. She's a beautiful, young woman."

Waller explained, "We haven't been able to turn up any men. But here's something interesting, credit cards were left in her purse. So far, no usage on any of the cards. We've got a mystery."

"What's the husband's story?" asked Dodson. He was still reading the report in front of him. "He's a long-haul driver?"

Garcia quickly added, "No, mostly local stuff."

Waller with an experienced outlook, responded, "Mr. Vince Fazzino was bracing himself for battle when we questioned him. The guilty ones concentrate all their focus tight. I thought, he could be a suspect because he didn't show any emotion like traditional grief."

"Maybe Vince went through the loss of their marriage four months earlier when he left." Garcia disagreed with his partner.

"Any rap sheet or domestic violence reported?" speculated Dodson.

"Just some speeding tickets and a couple of neighbor's calls about arguments coming from their apartment," explained Garcia.

Dodson stood up to flex his muscular shoulders. "Husband report her missing?"

"No. Says he hasn't seen her in four months, not even a phone call." Waller smirked. "Said he wanted to let things cool down between them. Sounds to pat to me."

Garcia presented a theory, "The husband's girlfriend denied being with him the day Fazzino went missing. Maybe she's the jealous type and she did something to her lover's wife, her competition."

"It's possible the husband and his girlfriend were in this together," speculated Waller.

"What about the landlord?" asked Dodson.

Waller replied, "You mean the hot shot guy that sits in the big office with the nice suit and liquor breath? Says he doesn't know anything; however, his office window looks right out into the tenant parking lot. It's possible he could have seen her leave early Tuesday morning. He may have followed her to the grocery store where he knocked her out."

Garcia disagreed, "That sounds kind of crazy." Then, he lowered his voice, "We don't have any proof it was him."

Dodson was trying to keep his cops from one another's throats, so he listened to the banter with the understanding that every comment could have an edge. His dark wiry brows closed together. "Then get me some proof."

After listening to the order their supervisor dished out, Garcia explained to his sergeant, "We've checked local hospitals to see if she's shown up hurt. No one with her description so far."

"How did the interview go with her employer?"

Waller's feet were planted firmly. "Herman practically cowered in the corner when we walked into his office. He said he was getting ready to phone her sometime to check on her. Real caring guy," she added sarcastically.

Dodson explained, "We found out Herman's been living in a trailer park near O'Hare. His most valuable thing is his elaborate computer. He actually portrays himself on-line as handsome and rich."

"Creep," Waller mumbled just loud enough so they both heard her.

Garcia speculated, "Could the homeless guy have hit her one day, then came back latter to take the money?"

"That's totally out of character for Phelps. He's a petty burglar," interjected Dodson. Then his cell rang. He answered in one ring. After saying "okay" into the phone, he turned to the two in his office and explained, "They searched. Phelps doesn't have a hoodie in his pile of junk that's crawling with roaches."

Garcia explained, "We're going to look into the husband's truck route for any place he could have hidden her body. Maybe they had one huge last fight."

Waller nodded agreeing, then said, "I want to look at that film again." With that comment, she walked out of the sergeant's office without being dismissed.

Garcia faced Dodson. "We checked taxi companies but didn't find a cab that picked up a woman matching her description from that parking lot." Garcia looked at his supervisor for more commands.

"Go," was Dodson's quick reply. As Garcia turned to leave, Dodson added, "Keep me in the loop."

Waller and Garcia watched the film over and over. After the fifth viewing, Waller's eyes opened wide. "Look how stooped over Pete Phelps walked around the car. Then, look at the person who hit her earlier. That's a younger, more agile person."

Garcia nodded in agreement. "Herman is much heavier than the guy that hit her."

Exasperated, Waller muttered, "Neither of the jerks we've got in here took her."

"However, the body type on the camera could be the husband, or the psychiatrist," suggested Garcia.

Waller let out a large sigh. "Or it could be someone we haven't even questioned yet, like Fazzino's girlfriend could have hired a hit man."

"You know, Waller, you might be on to something. Look, he used his right hand when he swung the rock at her head," Garcia muttered.

"The majority of people are right-handed," she said sarcastically.

"It could rule out the left-handed ones."

They stared at the footage for a few more seconds. "It doesn't look like she spoke to her assailant. Wouldn't her landlord or doctor say something to her?" Garcia asked.

"Good catch. You're going to be a good cop someday."

They sat at their desks to divide up the hospitals, clinics, and taxi companies they hadn't called yet.

Officer Matters dropped today's local newspaper on Waller's desk, startling everyone. Carolyn's picture appeared with the head-line "Authorities Searching for Woman." Under the photo, the ar-ticle read, "Missing 29-year-old Carolyn Fazzino, was last seen leaving the Kennedy Apartments on July 8."

"Maybe someone saw something," Garcia responded. "Now they'll come forward."

"We'll be inundated with every nut case out there, thinking they saw something." Waller moaned, then she glanced at the large round office clock on the wall. It was after six o'clock. With authority she said, "It's been a long day. We'll have the night team reach out to the rest of the hospitals and taxi companies." She stood. Waller looked over at her partner.

His face seemed to be agreeing and thinking, *I don't want to be here tonight.*

"We've got zip on this case, no leads at all." She munched on handfuls of M&Ms, pacing the small office like a lion trapped. With her mouth full, she declared, "I want to read over my interrogation reports of all these characters. We've still got too many suspects right now." She threw another handful of candy into her mouth. "How about we go home and mull it all over? We'll come back with a better idea in the morning."

Garcia nodded his head in agreement. He knew they would be working this kidnapping even on the weekend, until they found their missing person. Then suddenly he pictured Al as the 'all-knowing Buddha' and smiled to himself. He was well aware she was trying to teach him so he wouldn't screw up. It was aggravating and reassuring all at the same time. "Sounds good to me. We all need a little time off to come back with new possibilities."

Chapter 20

CAROLYN CAN'T STAND

UNKNOWN LOCATION, FRIDAY NIGHT

Strength is draining from my legs like water from a bathtub. I lower my knees. My stomach growls a low rumbling sound. It could be dehydration. Feeling the grit in my mouth from the dirty peanuts, I will my stomach to settle. I lick my dry lips, try to swallow, but there isn't enough moisture in my mouth. My eyes look upward as my hope is fading. There are no stars tonight.

Exhausted, my eyes squeeze shut against anguish so deep it seems to reach inside and grasp my heart. Wrapping my arms around my abdomen, hugging myself, I worry. I hurt so much that I just want to sleep until I don't hurt anymore. But when I'm on the verge of sleep, I jerk suddenly to a dull wakefulness of fear. Groaning, my hands wave into the air to ward off invisible dangers. Tiredness burrows into my bones.

The pit fills with the deep moan of the wind through the trees above. The night is alive with the mating calls of countless insects. Crickets shriek with rhythmic, piercing monotony. The night is not quiet. The occasional dismal cry of an owl fills me with unspeakable horror. Coyotes howl off in the distance. I think of ravenous beasts like hungry wolves who stalk their prey and destroy them mercilessly for the satisfaction of their own appetite. Please keep the animals far away. I duck down, as small as I can get. I could die in this *God forsaken hole.* My palms are sweaty. My insides start to gag. Every little sound makes me jump. My terror escalates. The sounds up above live and breathe all night long. I wish I could think, but only fear comes.

A far-off rumble. Noise of muffled thunder is coming from above. The tree branches rustle from a breeze as I look up at the small opening to the sky. The sky is an angry purple black. The wind is becoming boisterous, rattling, then howling. It shakes the trees. Branches above me sway about as if they are performing some sort of ghostly dance. I blink furiously and open my eyes hoping to see the glare of a flashlight, someone coming but it's flashes of lightning showing the wind bending tree branches at an awkward angle, and then toss them back. Branches look like giant monsters waving their arms. I hear the creak and groan of trees. I can smell the impending rain in the air. When the first raindrop hits, it is big, fat, cold, spattering on my forearm. Nature herself is playing a horrible, cruel trick. I have no umbrella. No coat. No way to cover up.

Rain drops plop onto my face as I open my mouth to the sky, trying to capture every drop. At first it hurts to swallow, but the water soon feels good as it goes down. I feel no wind down here underground, just the cold rain as it pelts down. Rainwater collects in small beads and runs down my arms. Wet and cold, I worry. Could I catch a cold, or possibly die of pneumonia? No, I'll starve first. What if lightning strikes? Could it reach me down here? I need to save some of this rainwater, but how? Then, cupping my hands together, I try to catch some.

Suddenly there's another bright flash of lightning. I see the empty peanut jar still sitting on the now wet ground. My blue jeans are soaked but I put my legs close together for strength. Holding the jar as high as possible I try to catch the rain drops, but I shiver in my wet clothes. Then I notice my shoes. Drink out of my dirty sneakers? Yes, if I must. Catching as much water as possible is the only thing on my mind now. I need to do whatever it takes to survive.

I set the jar on the muddy ground. Reluctantly, I use the shoe covering the snake hole. I untie my laces and slip off the other shoe. Lining up the shoes and jar in the middle of the pit where they can catch the most rain, I edge to one dirt side trying to stay out of the dredge of rain, but it's impossible to stay dry. I wipe my eyes trying to focus in the downpour but still drink in the nourishment. It's wet everywhere in this hole. Relentless rain is turning the enclosure to mud. Wet clothes cling to my body. My hair falls in dripping ringlets around my face. The ends of my fingers wrinkle, but my head still throbs. My thoughts are bleak during these long, weary hours while the incessant storm rages. No one can imagine such loneliness. I'm scared to death and so cold my teeth are chattering.

Finally, it changes to a slow drizzle. I'm soaked through, freezing cold. Hugging myself to stop the shaking, then I lean against the dirt side. With no will to fight, I am convinced I will not survive.

Chapter 21

VINCE

Jerry Ridder had texted Vince, 'Meet at Tap tonight?'

Vince sent a 'thumbs up' emoji.

An hour later Jerry, wearing his old high school letter jacket, stepped inside their favorite watering hole out of the rain to find Vince already there at the end of the bar. The mug in front of Vince, half full.

"Hey, good Buddy. How's it going?" asked Jerry as he ran his hand through his wet hair.

Vince turned to see his best friend's big smile. "Like shit this week." He didn't mention that he was on his third beer already. "The cops think I know where Carolyn is."

"What?" Jerry responded, then raised his voice to the bartender. "I'll take a Miller Light." He sat on the stool next to Vince. "I didn't even know she took off 'til the cops told me this morning, but I told 'em, you were out with me Tuesday night."

"Yeah at Stone Eagle."

"What's going on with her?"

"I really don't know. God, Jerry, I was pissed when I walked out of the apartment back in March. God, even her damn cat hated me."

165

"It can't be that bad."

"Oh, that cat had nothing to do with it. It was the same old argument between us. I wanted kids. She didn't." Vince turned and looked directly at Jerry. "Son of a bitch. She lied to me. She didn't want babies. 'Messy brats,' she called them. *I thought* she loved me, so I was sure I could change her mind." Vince lifted his mug. "We were fighting so much I finally left."

"I get it."

"I thought she would call, beg me to return, give in, and agree to have a baby. But that never happened." Vince gulped at his beer. "She didn't call me back! Who does she think she is? And now the police are involved. Fuck!"

"She was lucky to have you, buddy. Gosh you used to tell me how the high school coaches begged you to try out for sports." Jerry reached for the dish of nuts and put it between them on the bar.

"I was the quarterback, for God's sake. Popular, especially with the girls." Vince looked down at the nuts. "I was a real heartthrob. That isn't bragging. Girls *called me* for dates. Remember that Molly I was dating during college?"

"The girl that got pregnant?"

"Yeah, that's the one. We only went out a few times, but then she called, to tell me she was pregnant with my baby. She was going to get an abortion. She wanted to know how I was going to support them if she kept it." He drank from his glass again. "I didn't have a job."

"I remember you looked into sales, 'cause you could always talk anyone into buying anything."

"Yeah, but I decided to take a sure thing like truck driving to support a family."

"I hated it when you dropped out of school. I got that nerd roommate after you left."

"Thanks man, but it was too late. Molly had already gotten the abortion." Vince pounded his fist on the top of the bar. "I was so pissed that I couldn't even see her anymore. I couldn't even look at her."

"Women!" Jerry took a sip of his beer. "And you've kept yourself in good shape."

Vince straightened up in the bar stool. Puffing his chest out. "I try. I take pains to keep this." He patted his flat stomach. "I never drink regular beer."

"Well damn, the regular stuff causes beer bellies," Jerry agreed with him.

"But I like an occasional lite beer." Vince finished his drink and signaled to the bartender for another. Only the bartender knew it was his fourth. "I exercise, even lift weights. I play tennis in the summer and racquetball inside when the weather's bad."

"Shit, no one would think you're in your mid-thirties."

"On my last birthday, Carolyn even said she didn't believe it. She said I was bluffing, that I'm really twenty-five." Vince chuckled. "In a few years, I'll be an old man, so I need kids now."

The bartender set another lite in front of Vince.

Jerry assured his friend, "Vince, you'll still be attracting women when you're ninety."

"Hmm." Vince gave a half smile. "I wanted children with Carolyn." Then, exasperated, he asked, "Why isn't life going the way I want?"

"Don't know why you want to get yourself tied down with kids like that." The bachelor punched his friend's arm. "Life gets in the way, good buddy."

"Why did she fight me on the kids? Hell, I had to leave the *prima donna*. I'm still driving every day with no one to talk to. I was lonely. Then there was this cute red-head at one of my stops. Union rules forbid us from unloading our own trucks, so I stand around waiting. I don't want to be in the way on the dock. This one morning, at Plastic Equipment, it looked a lot like rain, I went in the lobby and saw this cute red-head on the phone. She wore this fuzzy purple sweater with a V neckline, lot of cleavage." Vince took a handful of peanuts from the bowl on the bar.

Jerry nodded. "So, you started talking to her. I get it."

"A few days later, we went out for lunch. Maybe it wasn't right."

Vince dropped the handful of nuts into his month.

"Carolyn practically forced you out."

"Yeah, man, so it's not my fault. I could sit and look into Jenny's doe eyes forever. She talked a lot about her niece and nephew, so I could tell she loves kids." Vince took a swallow of beer. "You should see the way she runs her tongue over those puffy lips of hers. After that I timed my visits to that company just before noon to have lunch with the sex pot. The next week I took her to Pattie's Pastries. We got an outdoor table."

Vince drank some more of his beer. "Listen to this. I leaned over to kiss her just as my cell rang." Vince chuckled, remembering. "Turned out to be the dock supervisor, letting me know my truck was loaded. He wanted me back there right away. They had another truck waiting to get into the dock. Jenny thought it was funny. Guess it was. She's beautiful when she laughs. I couldn't help leaning over to kiss her again. She didn't hesitate. My heart did a kind of flip."

"Maybe it was the greasy food." Jerry sounded a little suspicious as he arched an eyebrow.

"Yeah, that's it 'greasy food,' but she didn't slap me or pull away, so I asked her out for a drink after work."

Jerry gave him a head nod as he toyed with his mug.

"A few nights later I took her to a little place in Elgin. I wanted to get to know her better. After the first round, I reached up to touch her face, just a feather light stroke with my fingers. Women love that sort of thing."

Jerry got a big proud grin on his face. "You're smooth."

"She kissed me." Vince rolled his eyes for emphasis and smiled. "So, I asked if she wanted to get a room."

"She was going to be easy." Jerry nodded his confidence in his friend.

"But I wanted her to be comfortable, so I told her to stick with me. I even told her she had a knockout body under those clothes."

"What happened after you got to the hotel?" Jerry sounded eager like he wanted juicy details.

"Well, I pulled the drapes closed, but I could still make her out. I joined her on the bed to kiss her. I had to unbutton the front of her dress. When my eyes got used to the dark, I could see she was smiling. Then she asked if I was thinking of my wife."

Jerry's face looked startled. "What? She asked a question like that when ya wanted to bonk her?"

"Cause I told her the truth earlier, that I was separated from Carolyn, but right then I told her I was only thinking of her. She bought that answer."

"We all want to be loved." Jerry reached for more nuts.

"Carolyn and I are still legally married."

But his bachelor friend sounded optimistic as he said, "Go for it. You've been so miserable with all the fighting between you two. She could have called you, but she didn't."

"You're right. You only live once, good buddy. I could be in love with Jenny. I'd like to live with her. But now, where the Hell has Carolyn gone?"

"Who knows?"

"I couldn't even sleep Tuesday night after the police told me she was gone. They treated me like *I* had done something."

"You?" Jerry was shocked. "You're a great guy."

"I wouldn't hurt her. The truth is I haven't seen or heard from her."

Jerry was full of confidence as he said, "I believe ya, man."

Vince said, "I'm worried about Carolyn, but Hell, where is the drama queen? It was always all about her. Now what's she doing to mess me up? I'm fucking separated, not dead."

Jerry sounded optimistic as he said, "Well, the police are looking for her." With the shrug of his shoulder he added, "so do what you want."

Vince downed the rest of his beer. "Yeah, so I should move on with my life. I want kids. Jenny could be the perfect mother."

Chapter 22

IS THIS A DATE?

Melissa left work early Friday to go to a tanning salon because she reasoned, *Carlos is probably used to dating Mexican girls. He has such brown skin and those long, thick eyelashes; I don't want to look too pale next to him. Latin men are sexy.*

As soon as she reached home, she picked up the remote, pressed power and switched the channel to seven. The news would be on soon. After texting Carolyn for the umpteenth time, she started to look through her mail, a few advertisements and of course, one bill. Then she heard the newscaster, Valerie Inglewood say, "Breaking News. Missing woman Carolyn Fazzino walked out of 202 Hampton Avenue three days ago and disappeared. No one has seen her since Tuesday, July 12th, at approximately six o'clock a.m. Neither her phone, nor her credit or bank cards have been used since Tuesday." The news team managed to find a photo of Carolyn in her bikini and there she was across the screen. The announcer was saying, "Born Carolyn Hendricks in Geneva, IL in 1984."

What happened to you?

The reporter smiled into the camera as she said, "A 2002 graduate from the College of DuPage. The police say they have spoken to a witness. They are pursuing several lines of inquiry. Fazzino is described as a white female, five feet, three inches tall, weighing one hundred twenty pounds, brown hair, and brown eyes. She was wearing blue jeans, a white t-shirt, and gym shoes. Missing Persons

Bureau found her Honda Civic at the Diamonds Grocery parking lot."
The TV scene changed to show a shot of Carolyn's car with police
personnel searching the vehicle. "A grocery clerk believes she saw
a man near the Civic parked right in front of the store, then looked
down to scan the next person's groceries. She was quoted as saying,
"Later, I thought it was odd when the car was still parked out there.
The police have asked me to call them if I see the man around here
again. Friends reported they can't reach her by texting."

They could be talking about me.

"Family and friends are asking if anyone has seen this young
woman. She's been gone more than seventy-two hours. Police are
watching for a ransom note. A Missing Alert is in effect. Anyone
with information regarding Fazzino's whereabouts is asked to contact the West Chicago Police Department's Investigations Section."

Where are you?

The story was getting plenty of national news coverage. This
was her friend. Melissa shivered with worry even though it was
a warm July evening. She tried to pull herself together. *I need to
find out what the police know. I'll ask Carlos tonight. I like a man
in a suit. I dated a Navy man one summer, but this man, Detective
Carlos Garcia, is so much better looking.*

She put on a pale wisp lace thong, underwear for women who
don't need support and her killer tight fitting first-date outfit with
the plunging neckline. She buttoned and unbuttoned the front, un-
decided on how many to leave open. Then checked her pedicure.
If her toes were going to be poking out of the sheets tonight, she
wanted them to look good. She strapped on her knock-off Jimmy
Choo heels because it was the best pair of shoes she owned. She
looked into her bathroom mirror, checking her perfect arched eyebrows. She started to wrap her thick, highlighted hair into a French
braid, but decided it was too formal and took it down. After ap-
plying fresh lipstick, she said to the reflection, "Eat your heart out
Detective Garcia." *Please find Carolyn safe.* Hopeful, she grabbed
her umbrella and went out to her little Eclipse.

Chapter 23

THIS ISN'T A DATE

Detective Garcia thought of stopping at his mama's house for a nice home-cooked Mexican dinner, however this hot tamale could be so much better. Melissa could be a suspect for she was the last person Carolyn spoke with on her cell phone. The police force forbids dating someone who might be a suspect. Could the missing woman have gone to see her so-called best friend the morning she disappeared? *No way has Melissa done anything wrong,* Garcia reasoned.

Was his judgment clouded by that body and bubbly personality? *How inappropriate is meeting her tonight? Am I crossing a big unethical line?* As a police official, he knew he should keep his distance from her until the case was settled. *But that doesn't prevent me from having thoughts about her. I'm a risk taker.* Garcia had his pilot's license. He could even land at the DuPage Airport. He enjoyed sky diving lessons and rock climbing on vacations. *So here I am, getting ready for a date with one hot Chiquita. Should we make it look like we accidently met up tonight?*

He glanced out his apartment window at the rain pouring down. As he was getting ready to meet with a possible suspect, was evidence being washed away? Were vital clues like smears of blood, footprints, possible DNA-loaded cigarette butts disappearing forever? A dead end. He sighed. As he drove to the Cadillac Ranch, he thought about the various people he and Waller had interviewed that day. *Were any of them lying to us?* He could feel the electricity igniting in this case.

Carlos Garcia was there early because he wanted to see her again. Country music played from a jukebox. He ordered while he waited for her.

Melissa arrived fashionably late on purpose to make a grand entrance. She walked in with three buttons undone on her red skin-tight bandage dress that might have been painted on her knock-out body. *Okay, she's hot.* He would have appreciated it more if she had popped the fourth button, but the fact that it came to her mid-thighs was fantastic. He glanced at her beautiful long legs, slim ankles, and four-inch open toe heels, then professionally moved his focus to her face. Her glittery eye shadow and fluttery lashes lit up the room as she entered smiling. She sparkled as she walked towards him. She looked like a dangerous thirty, the unmistakable look of a woman who could be fast and loose. Her eyes seemed happy to see him. As she sat at his table, she asked, "What are you drinking?"

"Tequila."

"Okay, I'll try it." She leaned forward. The earring that showed was a spur studded with red and coral stones and dangling jiggle bobs.

After the pleasantries, he ordered her drink. He exhaled heavily, a breath he hadn't realized he was holding and opened with, "So you grew up near Carolyn. Where at?"

Melissa had grown up in West Chicago like Carlos, but he hung with the Mexican kids. She laughed as she talked about being popular in high school. She said, "Because Carolyn is an only child, she and I become inseparable. I'm the only girl in a family of two older brothers, so Mrs. H. would laugh that I'm more comfortable around boys then her own daughter."

She pulled her cell phone out of her purse, pressed a few buttons, and turned the screen towards Carlos, showing a picture of two happy little girls grinning for the camera. "That's us. I'm so worried about her. She never goes this long without calling or texting me." Melissa gave a broken sob that forced her to wipe her nose and run the side of her thumb past the corner of her eye in an attempt to keep her mascara from running.

He handed her his napkin and smiled at the photo. "Cute." He could see why Carolyn, as a young girl, would respect her friend's strong independent spirit.

The waitress delivered Melissa's drink. She sipped. "It's okay." She smiled. "Carolyn and I did everything together, even attending school basketball and football games together. Did you play any high school sports?"

Melissa was a wonderful listener, turning the conversation back to Carlos, her eyes always on his face. When she spoke, she would ask him a follow-up question, showing how closely she was paying attention or was she changing the subject? He thought, *there could be a lot to her; too bad this is work.*

"Yeah, I was in high school football." *This isn't about me; I have to keep asking questions about the case.* "Was Carolyn depressed when Vince left?"

"She was visibly upset." Melissa's expression was serious. Her gaze lingered on Carlos, as she continued, "Carolyn cried, and I cried with her. She got a prescription because she was having trouble sleeping. She told me, it made her super foggy, and she had to drive all the way to Lombard for work every morning, so she stopped taking it."

"Do you know who gave her the prescription?"

The soft green in her eyes looked inviting. "I don't remember his name, but she called him the 'old codger' who was right in her building."

That's the guy, he thought.

"Carolyn didn't take the pills long. She couldn't function when taking them and had to be sharp at work." Melissa gave him a half smile. "She tried the gym with me. Sometimes we went out bar hopping, you know, looking for guys."

He shifted in his seat. "Yesterday, you implied that something bothered you."

"Well," Melissa hesitated. "You need the absolute truth, so, I never told anyone about this, but once I saw bruises on her arm, up here." She pointed to her upper arm. "Like fingerprints. Like he dug his nails into her. We were trying on clothes at Carson's the day I saw the marks, so I asked her what happened. She wasn't going to tell me, but finally she said, Vince got excited, a little demanding and grabbed her. She said it was nothing." Melissa seemed relieved to tell the detective. Then her eyes were pleading with him. "But that doesn't mean he did anything to her. It doesn't mean that at all."

Vince didn't tell us about hurting her when we questioned him.

"I don't want to get him in trouble. I just think you should know." Melissa let out a sigh as she smiled.

"You're absolutely right in telling me about him." *Maybe he does have a mean streak.* "Could he have abused her? Maybe she left to hide."

Melissa licked her lips and emphatically said, "Oh, no." Then she leaned forward into his personal space. "I was hoping they ran off together. You know, a romantic weekend to reconnect. They're both good people."

"Do you know if she's had any contact with him after he moved out?"

"I'm sure she would have told me if she had."

Grateful, he said, "Thank you for telling me. You really are a true friend. We'll look closer at Vince." *Actually, we haven't stopped looking at him.* He thought of reaching across the table to touch her hand. Instead Carlos asked, "Was Carolyn seeing anyone after Vince moved out?"

Melissa shook her head. "Carolyn was actually a little embarrassed that her husband left her. I don't think she even told the people she worked with. She didn't say anything about her separation on Facebook. She just didn't know how to tell people that her marriage was failing. So maybe she was a little depressed." Melissa sipped her drink again. "Carolyn didn't even give back the rings when he walked out. Doesn't the woman get to rip the wedding and engagement rings right off her finger and throw them at the guy's face in a fit of rage like in the movies?"

Carlos gave a slight chuckle at her humor. "Do you think she has mood swings? Any irrational behavior?"

She looked startled. "No, that's not Carolyn."

"Tell me more about your friend," he said without tying her down with questions.

Melissa sighed. "Carolyn just kept asking me 'how could he do this to me? How could he leave me?' Then she would cry. Once I took a couple bottles of wine over to her place. We tried to get drunk together. A couple weeks later, I suggested we go out to a bar, maybe meet someone, but she wasn't interested." Melissa scrunched up her face. "When she didn't really want to date, I thought she needed closure, so I asked her once if she was thinking about getting a divorce. She burst into tears and said she couldn't think, something about it being her fault. I never mentioned divorce again."

"Can you describe her personality?"

Melissa took another sip of her tequila. "She likes to be pampered. She's my best friend, so I can say she's kind of a princess. Oh, maybe we're both high maintenance. Ya know what I mean?"

"No, not really."

"We go to the best salon in Oak Brook, but we're worth it. Maybe that's why we get along so well. We both enjoy massages and leisurely bubble baths. We get our nails done and a pedicure every two weeks. Most of the time we went together. It's more fun with a friend." Melissa smiled at him. "I love her. She's the best, but it was always about her. Like when her dad died, the first thing out of her mouth was 'What am *I* going to do?' Not, oh poor Dad or thoughts about her Mom. It was about her." Melissa's hand brushed her auburn hair back off her face. "I've called everyone we've ever hung out with, to see if they've heard from her this week. Nothing."

She leaned forward, and Carlos could see more cleavage, but he managed to ask, "Does she like her job?"

"Hmm." She put a fingernail to her lips as she thought about his question. "Well, she likes the ladies she works with. Maybe one of her coworkers in the library might realize that she's not there by noon. She told me one, I think her name is, Mary Ann, called their boss Mr. Mashed Potatoes behind his back, because he has a soft, pudgy body, and enormous belly with flabby white arms. They all love Mary Ann's humor, but their boss is a spineless mush mouth." Melissa's smile changed to a very worried look. "Her coworkers might've thought she got fed up and quit when she didn't show up for work. But I just know, she would have told me if she quit her job."

Detective Garcia had to ask, "Did Carolyn ever say she thought someone was watching her, like a stalker?"

Her beautiful hair swished across her shoulders as she shook her head. "No, she never said anything like that. She would have told me."

For the next forty-five minutes Melissa talked easily about her best friend and all the things they did together. But she seemed to be getting more anxious about her friend as she talked and kept fiddling with her necklace.

Carlos reached for her hand that rested near her glass. When she said, "I'm really worried about her," he placed his hand over hers to comfort her.

He wanted to calm her, so said, "We're close to finding the truth." However as soon as he said it, he realized his mistake.

"Really?" she quickly asked, with a hopeful look across her face.

All he could do was nod his head. Wanting to change the subject, he moved closer to her. He felt her foot brush his pant leg. He kept inching closer and closer, not wanting her to stop. *She smelled so good.* He leaned forward, sharp as a terrier. Melissa took his hand in both of hers and turned it over, examining the creases. He felt an electric charge racing up his forearm as she traced the line on his palm with the tip of her fingernail.

"Your love line," she said tenderly.

His heart seemed to skip a beat as he shifted in his seat. He could feel her breath on the palm of his hand. "I thought it was called a lifeline."

She looked up into his eyes. *Her eyes were green like new summer grass and so easy to get lost in.* "It's your love line, and it's very strong." She tilted her head to one side. Holding his hand, she said, "Okay, Handsome." The look in her eyes said sex.

He should have said something about her involvement with his case, but it didn't come out of his mouth. Instead he thought, *take a chance, do something. She's so damn tempting.* They were so close their lips were practically touching.

Before he could say anything, Melissa reached out a finger, ran it along his mustache slowly, softly and said, "I've never kissed a mustache before. I just want to break the rules to see you."

She's thinking the same thing I'm thinking, so he asked for the check. They hurried out to his car in expectant silence. It had stopped raining, but the blacktop was wet. In the dimly lit parking lot, he took her hand and folded it into his, saying, "You are so beautiful."

At the passenger side of the car, he put his arm around her waist, pulling her into a hug. Then he leaned into her, her hands soft on his chest. From the parking lot lights, he noticed her eyelids flicked rapidly. He kissed her quickly, then a long passionate kiss.

She pulled away slightly to whisper, "Want to see my apartment?"

In answer, he opened the car door for her to get in. It didn't take long to reach her apartment in the town of Stream Leaves. They started kissing in the elevator. The air between them sparked with electricity. Then they raced down the hall, hand in hand. She unlocked her front door and stepped inside.

Once inside her apartment, he pushed her back against the wall and kissed her. He was grateful for a sliver of light from a streetlamp coming through a nearby window. *Oh God, she's unbelievable, like something out of a magazine.* Soon they were in her bedroom.

His heartbeat against hers, keeping time. They hugged like magnets. She made him feel like the most important person in the world. He couldn't stop looking at her as he cradled her head in his hands.

Chapter 24

WET CAROLYN

I wake stiff, cold, sore, wet, and hungry, but at least the rain has stopped. The air is humid. I lick rain drops off my bare arms. My fingers are so cold. My wet clothing stiff from sweat and ground-in dirt. I can feel the bottom of the pit is mud. I'm so hungry. Are there any more spilled nuts? I crawl on my knees and bleeding fingers, feeling, searching through the muck. Finally, I think I find one of the dirty peanuts. It's swollen in the wetness. I try to wipe the mud off on my dirty wet t-shirt. So hungry, I put it in my mouth. I reach for rainwater in the peanut jar. Eagerly I swallow some water to wash the dirt down. Then cough in disgust.

I have a new idea because the rain has softened the dirt. Maybe I can use the jar to dig footholds into the dirt sides of this tomb. Should I dump the rainwater to use the jar as a tool for the possibility of getting out? Get out of here now! I pick up the plastic jar with slippery mud-covered hands to gulp the last swallows of water. With the jar empty, I start digging at the wet mud wall at a spot about two feet off the bottom. If I can just dig a foot hole into this dirt, then I can get one foot up closer towards the top, then maybe make another spot up higher for another foot. I must try.

Finally, I manage a small indentation in the dirt. I raise my foot up to it, digging my toes into the tiny crevasse. Balancing on my left foot, I make my right toes reach higher up and begin a new spot with the plastic jar. It takes forever, but finally there is another tiny foothold. Balancing on my right toes, I try to draw my left leg up to the next crevasse, but suddenly my toes slip, and I'm plunging downward, hitting my left foot hard on the slippery bottom surface. My ankle bends under my weight. Instinctively I cry out in pain. I sit defeated rubbing it. Lifting my face toward the opening, I suck in deep breaths. Freedom is out of my reach. Now my ankle hurts. Fearing the sprained ankle will swell, I scoop cool mud from the floor and pack it around the sore ankle. "No, No. Let me out of here," I wail.

Too weak to stand, too weak to sit, so with frailty I lay down in the tomb. I feel the cold dampness of the dirt floor. I curl up on my side on the muddy cold ground and draw my knees up to my chest in a fetal position.

My mind going around in circles. I'm not safe here, so how do I get out? If I get out of here, I've got to change my life. My mind is confused. Be quiet. Quickly I put my hand over my mouth. I don't want that bastard to know how scared I am. I don't know how close he is. Will he come back? What if he doesn't? The silence is deep, as deep as the grave. I'm numb with despair. The cold ground leaches human warmth. My head pounds with fear of no way to escape.

I wish I was back home in our apartment with Vince, back the way it used to be, a long time ago, surrounded by his love. In my memory, his lips are slightly parted. I can even recall the arc of his mouth in the moment before he would smile. Is he thinking of me? Could this be God's punishment for driving my husband away? I might not ever see him again.

I remember an article I read at work in the medical library where a human being can only live approximately three days without fluids. A few sips of water would make the person stay alive longer, but the rainwater I collected in my shoes leaked out already. With mild dehydration, the person would experience a lack of saliva. My mouth is sticky and dry. There would be a decreased output of urine. I peed a couple times that first day or two, not yesterday or today. There would be deep color and a strong odor in the urine. I can smell the puddle. I think the article said one could live without food for three weeks. I've eaten nuts, dirty nuts, but I've had something. Before death, muscle would break down and be used for nutrition including the heart. My muscles hurt. Are they degenerating to mush? Kidneys would quit functioning without fluids. The body would be unable to eliminate toxins. The person would be unresponsive close to the end. No tears. I think I cried yesterday or was that the day before? How long have I been down here? Oh my God, I'm losing my mind. Is my body shutting down? What if I don't get out of here? With a shaky finger, I try to write in the mud, "V I love you."

Against my will, I can feel my eyes closing, trying to shut out this place. I just need a little sleep. I'll try to figure things out later after I rest.

There have been deaths in our family, Daddy, Uncle Jerry, Grandma. I've never thought of my own death before. TV treats death as a drama to revel in. But dying is no drama. A slow darkness is creeping through my body. My death is cold, hard, painful, and dull. It's going on too long. I'm exhausted and growing bored with it. Now I have too much time to think about whether I'm going to die. Everybody dies. Who decides when we die? I should think of God instead; and how He would help me through this. God, if you get me out of here, I'll donate to the poor. I'll do anything, just help me. Thinking of Him doesn't make me less scared. I feel sleepy. My breath and the beating of my heart is slowing. Is this the final moments of my life? My last conscious thoughts are of Vince.

Chapter 25

BREAKFAST

Saturday morning

Early the next morning, the sound of running water woke Carlos Garcia. Neither he nor Melissa had bothered to close the blinds. Predawn light teased at the bedroom window, casting a soft glow over the bed. He rolled onto his side in the rumpled sheets. He looked at the room that he hadn't seen in the dark last night. An odd shaped perfume bottle on the dresser caught his eye. *I probably have eight to ten different kinds of cologne at home, mostly Christmas gifts from family who don't know what to get me. Melissa has one signature scent.*

The water turned off. The bathroom door opened, sending a puff of steam and the smell of soap into the bedroom. Melissa wrapped in a bath towel that stopped high on her thighs, leaving a long expanse of nicely toned legs, walked toward him. In the dim light, he could see a tattoo on her thigh of a champagne glass, complete with tiny bubbles. He hadn't noticed it last night.

Smiling she sat next to him on the bed.

Tracing his fingertip over her tattoo, he said, "Champagne is classy." He breathed the clean smell of her in deeply. *"Maravilloso."*

She asked, "What does that mean?"

"You are wonderful."

She smiled again and gave him a little kiss. "I'm so hungry. You want something to eat? I could make us a salad."

"I need more than a salad." He folded her in his arms.

"I eat lots of salads. I'm sure I have the fixings for two more." Her voice sounded like a satisfied purr.

He wanted to devour her, but instead he said, "I'm hungrier than a salad. How about if I make us some enchiladas?"

"You cook?" She looked a little startled, but there was a smile too.

"Sure do. If I hadn't gone into law enforcement, I might have started a restaurant with my mother's recipes, however there were several Mexican restaurants in town already."

"Hmm, sounds good right now, but I don't have the makings for anything like that."

"I do at my place. If we hurry, I can make us chicken and corn enchiladas before I have to go into work," he suggested as he started to raise up off the bed.

She kissed him for a few minutes, then she pulled away just enough to ask, "Where do you live?"

"An apartment in West Chicago."

She laced her fingers through his.

I don't want to let go of her, he thought, however he said, "Do you want to see it?"

"Yes," she breathed.

As he put on his clothes, he said, "Bring your salad makings. That will go great with what I've got."

She put on a low-cut top and skinny jeans that hugged her figure. He liked the way she wore her clothes. Standing barefoot in her bedroom she looked into his eyes. He saw her glance at a pair of flats on the floor near the dresser, but instead she picked up the high heels, and put them on. When she stood, they were almost the same height.

They drove as the sun was just starting to come up, the streets wet after last night's rain. He drove her to get her car first and then she followed him. It didn't take long to reach his apartment. He held her hand as they climbed the stairs to his second-floor apartment. Early morning light was peeking inside his kitchen.

They had fun cooking together. He shredded the cooked chicken on a cutting board. When Melissa wanted to help, he explained how to lay the tortillas in a baking pan. He also asked her to mix the chicken, corn, and cheeses together in a small bowl. He filled and folded each tortilla over like his Mama always made them.

Together they sprinkled more cheese over the top. It didn't take long, and their food was hot out of the oven. Soon they were sitting at the kitchen table, eating hungrily. She took a swallow from her coffee and gave him a warm glance over the rim of the cup. "That was delicious, but I'll need to work out for a couple extra hours so that cheese doesn't go to my hips."

"I'm really glad you liked it," he said as he stood. "Let me check out those hips to see where that cheese went." He took her hands in his and gently pulled her up out of her chair.

She smiled and stood. He wrapped his arms around her waist and gently kissed her. He needed to get dressed for work but reached for her hand and gently guided her to his bedroom. "Your ass is a visual deterrent for getting ready for work," he whispered into her ear.

The first time had been a marathon session. It was more relaxed and wonderful the second time. Afterwards, they lay in each other's arms. *I'm so comfortable with her, but it's wrong to be with someone involved with the case I'm on.*

"That was good," Melissa whispered.

He smiled. "Unbelievably great."

Melissa sat up with her back against the headboard. She rearranged herself until they were side by side. There was a silence. Then finally she took a deep breath, her voice dropped, "I don't want to scare you."

My God, she didn't use any protection. He turned to look at her.

"My brother is getting married and..."

He let out his breath.

"I really don't want to go without a date. Would you?" her voice trailed off.

"Anything," he quickly answered. "I could go with you."

"Really? You don't mind? They might think we're a couple; you know how parents can jump to conclusions."

Seriously, he said, "I can act like a couple, if that's what you need."

"You'll be perfect." Her face looked relieved.

She's fantastic. Then out loud he said, "You don't have a date?"

She laughed, "Well, no one I want to take home to my parents." Then quickly added, "You do own a good suit, don't you?"

"Yes. You didn't ask me just because I own a suit, did you?"

She reached for his hand, grasped his fingers, and laced them through her own. "I asked you before I knew you had a suit. There's something about you that feels right."

Chapter 26

JENNY MAXWELL

I couldn't sleep. My husband's even breathing meant he was already asleep. I pulled the covers over my head to drown out his breathing. But it was my inner turmoil that kept me awake.

Yesterday had been a horrible day. First thing at work the police walked in the door. They actually came to see *me* about Vince. The police said his wife was missing. Vince told me he and his wife were separated. There's something weird going on with him. I don't want to get involved with anything crazy. Did those detectives know I lied? They looked at me like I was a slut. My coworkers wanted to know why the police talked to me. I saw their glances when I got back to my desk. I told Ray it was nothing. But I could tell by his look, he didn't believe me.

Promptly at five o'clock, I ran out of the office to get home. I was outside watering flowers before starting dinner when my neighbor, Anna walked over. Being a friend, I asked, "What's up Anna?"

With her arms crossed, she said, "I guess you haven't heard; Tom and I are getting a divorce."

"What?" I hadn't had much time for any of my neighbors, with full time work, three kids, driving them to their activities, and then seeing Vince whenever possible.

Anna wrinkled her nose in disgust as she said, "He was having an affair."

A sinking feeling came over me as I managed to ask, "But you and the girls?"

"Oh, they hate him." Anna's shoulders slumped. "He moved in with some young hussy. The girls hate what he's done to our family."

My stomach fell. I simply stood there, too stunned to speak at first. Then I awkwardly hugged my friend. Finally finding my voice, I offered to help any way I could.

When Sam got home, I told him right away about Anna and Tom. He shrugged it off. Maybe he was worried about problems at work that were more important than what he perceived as neighborhood gossip. But I couldn't forget.

Now, laying here in the dark, I can't imagine what Anna must be going through. I'm just as bad as Tom. I never considered my own family. What if Sam found out about me and wanted a divorce? Oh my God, I don't know what I'd do. Or where I would go. To Vince? Vince is sex. I've made a spectacularly selfish mistake. My guilt kept me awake for hours as my double-chinned neck ached in this position, so I rolled over, then opened my eyes to see Sam's outline.

━━━━━(◆)━━━━━

It all began that first day when this good-looking truck driver strolled into the front office of Plastic Equipment Inc. where I've been the office manager for over three years. A driver with about three pounds of gold around his neck. The muscles of his thighs bulged right through those tight jeans. We spoke briefly. Then he showed up a week later with another shipment, his broad shoulders filling out a blue polo shirt. That time we exchanged names. The third time was about noon. I was just getting ready to leave for lunch when Vince walked in grumbling, "This is a large shipment. It's going to take a while. Is there someplace to get a bite to eat around here?"

"I was just going out myself, over to Red Rooster."

"Mind if I come along?" God, he was sexy with his dark hair falling seductively across his forehead.

"I was going to walk the two blocks," I told him.

"Walking would be great. I sit too much on my job," the hunka-lunka answered.

I realized my heart was racing as we walked along the sidewalk together. That first lunch I found him charming as we talked about traveling.

Vince's, Matthew McConaughey's whispery voice and sexy, smoldering movie star eyes glanced down at my hands. "I see you're not married."

Oh my gosh, I'd forgotten to put on my wedding ring that morning. For some stupid reason, I was tongue-tied and wobble-kneed. I agreed with him, "Right." If I had told him I was married, he would've lost interest. The way he looked at me, I saw exactly what was on his mind. So of course, I couldn't talk about my family. When Vince said he was separated from his wife, that was my chance to come clean, but no, I didn't say a thing about being married. I told him funny little stories about my three kids, but I told him they were my nieces and nephew.

He kissed me at our second lunch. I was startled, he was so fast, but he smelled good. I didn't recognize the cologne. But mixed with his manly scent, he was intoxicating. About a block from my office he said, "Maybe we could go out for a drink some evening after work."

"Oh, I don't know," was my reply, but I was thinking, this great looking guy is interested in ME. I've still got all this baby fat from having the kids. This stranger looked interested in me. Well, he's no stranger now.

My husband never asks, how I am. It's always, "How are the kids? How's Ben's cold? After all these years, I know my husband's not a talker, but I often wonder 'does he think of me at all.' I wanted to feel valued and cherished even though I've put on weight.

Vince and I went out for that first drink. That's when I started wondering, what would he be like in bed? I imagined his hands on my hips. I agonized over this new sexual man, knowing I felt a strong animal attraction to him. I had hesitated some time before that final step, because of my upbringing. But finally, my decision was made. I even lied to my husband saying I had to work late.

That fateful morning, I put on a pair of pink thong panties I remembered were in the back of my dresser drawer. I'm a little heavier now, but I liked the hip hugging silk. I wanted to feel sexy for this new man. I spent extra time on my hair and makeup. I ran out at noon to buy a cute polka dot bra.

I was amazed after that first time in the hotel with Vince to discover that I felt no different afterwards from what I had before. I had expected I would feel something. When I looked in my mirror that night, I was bewildered to see the same woman staring back at me.

Every time I saw him, I felt drawn to him, so it just happened. And then it happened again. We made love like teenagers. I felt breathless with our passion. My heart skipped a couple beats every time. I felt like a sexy lady around him.

Pushing my red hair back off my face, he once said, "I want more time with you."

I think we both wanted it to last, but no, we were always in a hurry. Meeting as often as we could at cheap motels, our affair had been animal-like sex, hot excitement. I never meant it to go anywhere. I just enjoyed feeling wanted. It was as simple and stupid as that. Maybe I should have come clean, told him I was married, but I was so afraid if he knew the truth, he would stop seeing me.

Sam's a good husband. He had been the kid in high school who thought up marching band configurations. Now he's an electrical engineer. He's good at providing for me and the kids. Our friends think we're the perfect couple, so how did I let this happened?

My husband has been so concerned with his career and I've felt neglected, but instead I should be proud of Sam. I've got to focus on him. We've got three wonderful kids. What have I been doing to my family? I risked my marriage because I've been selfish. I have become a cheater. I'm not a good person. I must stop this before anyone finds out. I've been so stupid. I was naive to think there would be no consequences. I can't hurt Sam like Anna was hurt.

Finally, my decision was made. I will stop seeing Vince. I will be a good wife, a better mother. I promise to remain faithful to you Sam from this day forward. I'll work harder. I'll make Sam his favorite dinner tonight, beef stroganoff. I need to show more interest in him and in his job. We can invite his colleagues, even his boss and his wife over for dinner. Socializing could help his career. I'll ask him if he would like to entertain a little. Maybe we should do a religious retreat or weekend vacation just the two of us, away from the kids. I could pry him away and ask my mother to watch the kids. I'll get more involved with my kids. We must be a family again.

I tossed and turned all night. Close to morning, I slept fitfully in a nightmare haze. With a start I woke. Bright, early morning light streamed through the blinds and fell into neat white rows across the bed as the alarm sounded. I opened my eyes, looked around the twilight room. That was a long night from Hell, but my decision was made. I must stop seeing Vince; he was forbidden love. I don't want to hurt my family. I swallowed and squared my shoulders. From the bathroom mirror my face looked deathly pale. I threw on a robe and hurried to the kitchen.

Sam was just finishing a bowl of cheerios. He turned toward me as I walked in and said, "I've got a meeting and I didn't want to wake you."

I looked at him. "But it's Saturday."

"The boss man wants us in there."

"Okay." I glanced around at the countertops covered with Susie's crayon drawings, papers, bills and scattered mail, the disorganized signs of a busy family.

Sam gulped his coffee and stood. Walking towards me he said, "Have a good day." Then gave me a peck for a kiss.

I've got to improve things between us. It didn't feel natural, but I forced myself to place my hands on each side of his face to kiss his lips. *I want a second chance to make things right within my marriage.*

"Whoa, what's with you this morning? Bed bugs get you during the night?" He chuckled at his own humor.

I can't ever let him know what I've done. "I love you."

"Me too, but I've got to go." And he was out the back door. I watched him through the kitchen window as he walked to the garage. The air looked clean after last night's rain. I felt a sudden cold chill pass through my body and shivered. My head ached from lack of sleep or worried how I would do what I had to do. It was dreadful that I couldn't control my trembling lips.

Benjamin walked into the kitchen. Susie, our five-year-old was right behind him. She smiled sleepily up at me. "I want ice pops for breakfast," whined Susie. Soon they were talking in high-pitched voices over the top of one another.

I sat down at the kitchen table while two of the kids fought over the yellow cereal bowl. It was strangely unnatural. I got the impression the children were speaking from a long way off.

I had to break up with Vince the sooner the better. The thought of his arms around me made my heartbeat faster so I can't see him, can't do it in person. He was so irresistible. Don't ever see him again. Just call him, I thought as I reached for my cell. I owed him an explanation, but what could I say? I've changed my mind. I don't want to be this cheating, lying, sneaking mother. No, don't say any of that. I can't tell him; I don't care for him. That would be too cruel. My throat seemed to contract. I can't speak the words. A phone call was not going to work. My pain was so strong, I screamed at the kids, "Stop fighting and eat your breakfast, now."

Suddenly Susie, holding a large box of corn pops was yelling, "Mommy, Mommy is there a prize in here?"

Since no one answered her, she started shoving her whole arm down inside the cereal box. Then pulled out a handful and tried throwing them into her raised opened mouth, missing every single one. The food scattered on the floor.

Angela walked into the kitchen dressed in a mini skirt over black leggings. Black tulling that looked like she hacked with a razor was wrapped around the mini skirt. Sugar pops crunched under her shoes. She picked up Benji's toast right off his plate and took a bite.

My jaw clenched as if this breakfast was a horrible medical procedure to endure. "Just give me a minute and then I'll be all ears," I told them while deep in thought. Vince was an adventure in my dull life.

Benji whined, "Mom, Angela is walking on tippy toes."

"You tattle tale. For your information, I'm practicing wearing high heels. Mom, make him take off his football helmet."

"For your information, I'm practicing being a famous football guy."

"Which famous guy?" his big sister wanted to know.

"Oh, I don't know."

"Ya don't even know anybody famous," she sneered at him.

He thought a minute. "Cutler, I know Cutler, kind of."

Suddenly the smell of something burning brought me back to reality. One of the kids had spread peanut butter on his bread, then put it in the toaster. The smell of burnt breakfast was curled through the air. I grabbed the toaster cord and yanked it from the wall. "What do you think you're doing?"

"I want peanut butter," whined Benji.

"BENJAMIN MAXWELL Stop it," I yelled into the chaos. Are my children demented? No. They're just walking a very fine line between adorable and obnoxious.

My head ached from lack of sleep. "Because I say so," was my automatic response.

Benji started kicking the table leg rhythmically as he ate.

I'm just not wonder woman. I needed to get my problem solved and focus on them. They were whinny and melodramatic. One called the other an idiot. Angela wearing a chunky plastic wristwatch, her backpack slung over her shoulders said to her little sister, "You're so freaky."

I threw my arms in the air more to get their attention than anything else. "Would you three just be quiet for once in your lives?" I snapped.

The eleven-year-old glared at her younger brother. "You were adopted, Freak. I'll help ya pack a suitcase to run away." She huffed and stomped out of the room to the retreat of her bedroom.

Once she was out of sight, Benjamin sarcastically said, "Oh, pardon me for breathing."

I was still deep in thought. If I see Vince to tell him in person, if he touches me like he always does, I won't be strong enough to break up. He's so sexy. I took a bite of dry toast and washed it down with orange juice. I can't ever see him again. I don't trust myself to see him. My only choice was to tell him by phone. We'll never see each other again. We'll go back to our lives. We will move on. I'll be stronger with a text message. Suddenly without doing any rational thinking, with tears dripping down my face, I typed, "Must stop seeing U. It's over!"

I pressed send and sighed in relief. Then turned towards my children. "What's going on?" That's when I saw Benjamin's GI Joe glued to the kitchen table.

Chapter 27

DISTRACTED VINCE

Saturday, 7:30 a.m.

I was pissed that my boss told me I had to work this morning to make up the time I lost at the police station Wednesday afternoon. That wasn't my fault. It was the cops. No maybe it was really Carolyn's fault for taking off and not telling anyone what she was doing. But I didn't want to lose the money.

I loaded the semi in St. Charles first thing Saturday morning. From North Avenue I turned onto 390, heading into Chicago. I'll admit it, I was thinking about Carolyn. How dare she refuse to give me a child. She lied to me. Led me to believe we would have kids someday. It was a total lie. I gave her the best years of my life. As soon as she gets back from wherever she went, I'll explain to her that our marriage was a mistake. The only sensible thing is to acknowledge it. I'll plan exactly what I'll say to her. I'll be kind, smiling, but firm. I'll tell her the years we've spent together are priceless memories for both of us. She might be upset. It's a damned humiliating position for anyone to find your spouse wants to marry another woman. Will she feel like a fool? Carolyn's sensitive. But with all the fighting we did before I left, I know she isn't in love anymore. In fact, she hasn't even tried to reach me, not one phone call or text, nothing in months. It's going to be a horrible confrontation. Even as

I thought of Carolyn, I could feel the palms of my hands starting to sweat on the steering wheel. I swiped my hands on my jeans. I'm so fed up with the arguing and the fear of never having a child to live for. "Fed up," I repeated out loud in my truck to no one but myself.

Where the Hell is Carolyn now? Did she go off to think about our failed marriage? Maybe I'll never hear from her again. She'll move on with her life, so I should too. There might never be closure, no resolution if she doesn't come back. I'm worried about her. This is agony. Nothing is more painful than not knowing what happened to her. Or is she doing this to me on purpose, the drama queen?

I'm sorry about how this has turned out. I don't want to cause her pain, but I need children. For God's sake, I'm in my mid thirty's. I want kids when I'm young enough to play with them. I need heirs, like a king on his thrown. I don't have much now, just a truck driver, but who knows. Maybe someday I'll own the trucking company. It could happen.

It's best to tell Carolyn the truth. She'll be unhappy at first, but then she too can move on. She might do the right thing and give me a divorce. She's got her mother and Melissa to be there for her. It would all be so simple. Everything could be managed. Trembling with anger, I'll marry someone who makes me happy. It would be worth going through the bother of divorce to achieve happiness.

I'm not satisfied with seeing Jenny only occasionally. She's so cute with her pretty red hair. She says she's busy. But I want her more. I could be in love with her. All I think about is how much I look forward to seeing her. I've told her about my separation, so Jenny knows my relationship with Carolyn.

I'll tell Jenny, "Every thought I have is about you. I want you so much more than an hour or two every now and then. I want to marry you. We are two human beings who love each other."

Is that too mushy? That's not the way I talk, but woman like that mushy stuff, especially when you're proposing to them and asking them to have your babies. I can't wait any longer to start having children. Jenny's thirty-six. That's a perfect age to be a mother. It's funny that I'm thinking about our biological clocks, but I can't help it. A man's DNA becomes more important as we get older; or maybe it's some kind of testosterone wallop, but time is running out to make the family I need. I know she wants children by the way she talks about her nephew and nieces so much. We'll have a wonderful life together. We'll have fun with our children.

As I sped along the highway, I was trying to decide how to bring up the marriage idea. Should I invite her to my tiny apartment for a private dinner? Would my shabby Blossom Hotel apartment turn her off? Maybe a fancy restaurant would be better. My nerves tingled with excitement as I planned the proposal at the best restaurant for this exciting grand finale question. I've got this all planned out. I will ask Jenny as soon as possible. We'll be so happy.

Suddenly my cell phone that was lying on the passenger's seat next to me, buzzed. I looked at the screen, a message from Jenny, but this early? That's odd. With my right hand I unlocked my cell, and then pressed the text app. Her message read, "Must stop seeing U. It's over!"

What? My full attention is on the screen. My thoughts are coming fast and furious. What does this mean?

Chapter 28

DREAM DESTROYED

Another driver in a small Silverado pickup truck drove past the rural school campus and read 'Homecoming tickets on sale now' on the Central High School marque sign. He couldn't help thinking about the stories his parents had told him of how they met. How seventeen-year-old Marilyn had her life all planned. Right after high school graduation, she intended to go to Hollywood where directors and producers would beg her to star in their movies. She would become a box office hit overnight like Jessica Lang. She imagined adoring fans surrounding her, begging for her autograph. During study hall she practiced signing her name quickly, so she could accommodate every request. All she wanted was everything.

Marilyn made herself popular with the high school crowd as she attended events and joined clubs. She experimented with makeup, feathering her chestnut brown hair like Farrah Fawcett and shopping for the latest trends. She always got the leading roles in the theater group. Everyone said she was good. Marilyn and her popular friends would lounge against their lockers acting like fashion police, passing judgment on the quiet girl's faded high-top sneakers or their thrift-store sweaters. Maybe she did have a mean streak, but her friends followed her lead, with their own teasing taunts.

At the end of Homecoming week, she was voted Queen by her senior classmates. It took her an hour that evening, staring into her closet of skirts and stonewash jeans, before she decided to wear a bright, neon skirt with a jean jacket. Looking at herself in her bedroom mirror she decided to add a few neon bracelets to each of her arms and oversized hoop earrings.

Later at the football game she had her circle of friends around her. The boys were wearing stonewashed or ripped faded denim blues with long sleeved velour shirts. As the game ended, Gary said, "Hey, there's a party over at Ralph's house. Let's go hang out over there."

The popular crowd always went to parties, so she and her girlfriends couldn't pass this up. The kids at the party were guzzling beer and dancing to tape cassettes like Olivia Newton-John's "Physical" and "Eye of the Tiger" by Survivor. A few were passing pills. Marilyn and her friends were clustered like grapes. As the pills came around, she popped one into her mouth to show off. There had been many simple drinks: Dewar's on the rocks, Jack and Coke, but one of the guys had a paperback, "Bartenders Guide to Drinks" and he tried to make some Tequila Sunrises, and Slow Gin Fizzes. He wasn't very good at making them because if he didn't have the right ingredients, he simply added any alcohol on hand. After trying sips of several of her friend's cocktails, Marilyn chose a Pink Lady, because she was going to be a famous lady someday. As she stepped back from the bar with her drink, she noticed a quiet boy standing off in the corner of the room all by himself just watching the other kids. He looked nice in his corduroy pants which were in style in her People magazines, but she didn't recognize him. She stared briefly at the nice-looking dark-haired boy. He shyly started to smile. But Marilyn turned to smile at those around her instead.

On her next trip to the tabletop bar she told the kid who was playing bartender, "The Pink Lady was yummy."

"Ya want another like that or want to try something different?" he asked as he handed her the paperback guide.

She looked through and selected the next drink in the alphabetic listing, which was a Pink Squirrel. As the evening moved along, Marilyn lost count of her drinks. She was having fun flirting with the boys. Local girls flicked their hair, sat on one another's laps, shrieked, and joked. They talked about how to get beautiful skin, what your face really says about you, and their plans for Christmas break. Someone said they weren't going home until they were thirty. Everything was hysterically funny.

During a lull between records Beverly said, "Girls, get out your lipstick."

"Why?" Marilyn asked.

"I read in *Glamour*, if ya keep your lipstick pointed, it means you're sexy. But if you use the tube flat, then you're not sexy."

Marilyn couldn't even remember what hers looked like. She reached for her purse, pulled out her fuchsia lipstick.

Beverly reached over and quickly pulled off the top. There in front of everyone Beverly screamed, "Oh no, yours is straight across. You're not sexy, Marilyn."

"I am too," Marilyn protested. "Well, look at you, a pink lipstick with a purple dress." She pointed a finger at Beverly.

A good friend of Marilyn's stuck up for her and said, "It's just a dumb article. It doesn't mean anything."

Marilyn needed to change the subject. The next cassette started playing Joan Jett's "I Love Rock 'N Roll." Standing up, she laughed saying, "Let's dance."

Again, she noticed the same nice-looking shy guy watching her. As her friends talked, she gave him a fast wink. Soon she was dancing with a couple girlfriends while holding her Singapore Sling. Suddenly someone tripped, bumping into her. She spilled some of her drink on the young man who had stepped out of the corner. "I'm sorry," she apologized, then gave him her biggest smile, adding, "It's all over you, I'll get a napkin."

Feeling awful about the mishap, Marilyn rushed off to look for something to wipe him off. He followed her to the kitchen. Once there, they found paper towels. She ripped a handful from the roll and dabbed at his shirt to clean him. The music was so loud even in the kitchen; it was hard to hear each other. She smiled and shouted, "I don't think I know you."

He had to yell to be heard also. "I'm, I'm here with my cousin.

He invited me." He gave her a big smile back.

"You a senior, like me?"

"No." He hesitated, but still yelled, "a junior. I don't know anybody else here, except Don."

Marilyn understood if she went back into the family room, she would just end up drinking more with her friends. Knowing she was already tipsy, she decided to stay in the kitchen away from the drinking crowd. She shouted, "What's your name?"

"Harland. Yours?" he answered as loud as he could.

"Marilyn."

"Did ya spill your drink on me on propose to get to meet me?"

She couldn't hear him over the loud music. The alcohol was hiding any inhibitions she had. She wanted to keep talking with him, so she shouted, "You want to go outside where it's quieter?"

He leaned towards her ear yelling, "Sure. I can show you my cousin's new Chrysler."

They ducked out the back door off the kitchen. He walked her about a half block down the street. There the car shone in the streetlight. She hadn't brought her jacket out with her and was getting cold. Harland invited her to sit in the car. "I wish I could start it to turn on the heat for you, but Don's got the key. We're just lucky he left it unlocked."

Once out of the breeze, and inside she snuggled into his shoulder to warm up. "I'm so cold. Put your arm around me." Her common sense was clouded in her inebriated state.

He hesitated, but then did as she instructed him. He took a deep breath and said, "You, you looked so fantastic in there dancing."

"Why didn't you dance?"

"Oh, I don't know any of you."

Then she thought of the others inside, how they made fun of her for not being sexy. She turned to look him in the face asking, "Do I look sexy?"

Huskily he whispered, "What? Why you're the sexiest girl ever."

"I thought so." She kissed him on the lips in one fast move.

He kissed her back, but much longer.

Yes, I am, thought Marilyn. Marilyn's girlfriends often talked about sex. One good friend had told her how wonderful it was to be with her boyfriend. Marilyn was curious. She put her hands on his shirt and started to undo a button. *I'll prove I'm sexy.* He didn't stop her, so she kept undoing buttons. Then she touched his warm chest, noticing just a few hairs.

They kissed more. He touched her arms.

She felt like she ruled the world. Lustfully she pushed Harland's hand down to her thigh.

With obedience he stroked her legs.

It electrified her. She pulled her panties to one side.

He felt her with hesitating fingers.

I can be super sexy, if I want to be, she thought.

"Should I take my shoes off?" he whispered.

"I don't know."

He reclined the seat and got on top of her. Soon he was asking, "Am I hurting you?"

She didn't answer him as the car seat gently swayed and lurched.

Sometime later when they were done, she was silent, shivering, and feeling awkward. The pain she felt forced her to realize this was a mistake. She wanted to go back inside with her friends as soon as possible. She straightened her short skirt and asked, "Will ya take me back to the party before my friends miss me?"

She never noticed how he slowed to kiss her again in the darkness. Instead she walked straight ahead determined to forget this incident and return to the party.

Harland was smiling as they walked back inside the house.

Once back in the kitchen, he ripped off another paper towel and wrote his phone number on it. Handing it to her he asked, "Marilyn, what's your number?"

She was too embarrassed over what had just happened out in the car. She glanced around, finding no trash can in this strange kitchen, she shoved his number into her pocket and quickly made up a phone number for him.

He wrote it down. Carefully he folded the paper towel, placing it in his back pocket. Only the next day, when he tried to call her, he found it was a business number.

But her dreams collapsed in the backseat of that car when she missed her next period. Then her breasts were sore. In fear and desperation, a tearful Marilyn called Harland, "I... I think I might be pregnant."

There was silence. He couldn't believe the prettiest girl at that party was calling him back, even if she had waited over two months. Hesitantly he asked, "What are ya going to do?"

"I, I don't want this. I can't have this."

"We could get married. It's going to be okay," he tried to soothe her.

"This is a mistake, ya fool. How can we do that?"

"I help my dad on the family farm now and eventually I'll take it over. We'll manage."

Abruptly she hung up on him. When Marilyn found out he wanted to be a wheat farmer just like his father, she saw Harland as a man with no ambition.

A girlfriend told Marilyn about a cousin of hers who said abortion clinics were dirty. Where many girls got sick even dying from infections and horrible complications.

She also heard a rumor at school that pickle juice, cinnamon, cod liver oil, and large amounts of vitamin C could terminate a pregnancy, so she stopped at the local grocery store and bought six jars of pickles, the largest bottle of cod liver oil, three containers of cinnamon, six bottles of vitamin C and a bag of navel oranges. The checkout clerk looked at her strangely but said nothing. As soon as she got home, she opened the first jar of vitamins. She started swallowing them down with the cod liver oil, but promptly gagged on the horrible oil. Thinking, if the pickle juice could do what she wanted, then the entire pickle would be better yet. Taking a fork in her hand, she proceeded to shovel the sliced pickles into her mouth and chewed as fast as she could. The saltiness was horrible, but it HAD to be done. Then she peeled oranges one after another, dumping mounds of cinnamon on each section and ate them as quickly as she could. By the time her mother got home from work, Marilyn was in the bathroom vomiting everything up.

Her mother heard the retching and flung open the bathroom door. "What's going..." then she saw Marilyn on her hands and knees before the toilet. "What's wrong? Are you sick?" Then noticing the strange collection of groceries on the bathroom floor, she started yelling, "What's all this mess? Are you drunk, young lady? At, at this hour of the afternoon?"

Crying Marilyn had managed a second time to say, "I think I might be pregnant."

Her mother screamed at the top of her lungs, "How can you do this to me?"

—◦《◉》◦—

Later that month Marilyn found herself before a justice of the peace with their parents as witnesses. Sure, Harland had saved her from the disgrace of being a pregnant teenager by marrying her quickly; but moving her to his parents' farm, what she called 'this God forsaken hole' had been hellish torture for her. The pregnancy had been awful as she got fat and lost her cute figure. She yelled at Harland, "I hate these ugly stretch marks all over my stomach. My breasts hurt. My body is ruined forever, thanks to this baby." She would slap her protruding stomach for emphasis.

"You'll change your mind after the baby comes," he assured her, but that didn't happen.

When the screaming baby arrived, she took all her frustrations out on the infant. She left him crying in his basket as she put her hands over her ears to try to block him out of existence. She yelled at the helpless little creature, "You've ruined my life." She felt trapped under mounds of dirty diapers with a colicky baby. It was his entire fault she had dropped out of school. Now she would never ever get into acting school. Her dreams of Hollywood were long gone.

Marilyn was a sad woman who could drink all by herself while Harland, who didn't want to watch, would stay outside as much as possible plowing and planting the fields.

She wore nothing that could be construed as suggestive. Her clothes looked like dull shapeless bags as she became unhappy with her life. She didn't bother with makeup because she felt, who cared out in the country? Who would see her? She didn't stay in touch with her school girlfriends after she moved out of town. They went off to college leaving her behind on an isolated farm. *Jail would be better than this Hellhole I'm in.* She felt her life was a failure.

She didn't make friends with the other farmers' wives because she didn't want to understand their lives. A neighbor woman called her when the baby was just an infant, asking if Marilyn wanted to visit their quilting group on Tuesday mornings. With the baby screaming in the background, Marilyn had yelled, "I don't sew," and hung up on the cordial offer. A member of the local women's club had phoned her once letting her know of an up-coming bake sale, when Marilyn snapped, "Don't you know that sweets are junk food?" Marilyn disliked and resented everyone.

Every day for the rest of her life Marilyn thought of leaving her pathetic husband, her troublesome child, and that lonely country life she hated, but she didn't have the energy to leave.

———————⟫⟨◉⟩⟪———————

Mom you should have left, thought the pickup driver.

Marilyn would scream at the top of her lungs at the three-year-old to go to bed. Harland saw how this affected their son, so he tried to intervene by taking the little boys' hand, walking him to his room, helping him get ready for bed and reading bedtime stories to him. His father would make him sandwiches with peanut butter then sprinkle extra salted peanuts into the gooey peanut butter telling the child, these were his special sandwiches, just for him. It was Harland who taught him to brush his teeth. Harland's only recourse was to stay to help his only son, who he loved dearly.

The little boy's first memory of his mother burning him was at lunch time when he was five. *Why? I was reaching for my milk. I'm sorry I spilt your drink.* His mother flew into a rage screaming at him. "Stop making work for me! You're such a slob! Ya disgust me!" with her deep two-pack a day voice. She gave him a stern disappointed look and yelled, "You are sloppy. I have to clean up after you. Don't make me hurt you!"

She grabbed her cigarette out of the ash tray, waved it in front of him, took a long drag on it, glared at him and then grabbed one of his little hands. She always dressed him in long sleeves, so yanked one sleeve up and purposefully held the burning end of the cigarette to his bare skinny arm.

In pain, he screamed out.

"Clean this up!" She laughed at him.

He grabbed the dish towel off the counter trying, but he smeared her gin and tonic even further on the table. Then she burned him again. "If ya tell your father," she hesitated, "or anybody, I'll hurt you even more than this."

He knew his mother hated him.

The pickup driver was aimlessly driving with the early morning traffic, turning occasionally at an intersection, whenever a whim struck him and thinking of his childhood.

By the time he was nine he could anticipate when she would get mad. Her brown eyes would squint at him. Her mouth would tighten into creases. He watched her hands for he knew what those hands would do. With one hand she took her burning cigarette from her mouth. Her other hand moved towards him. He knew what was coming, so he would try to pull away. But she was too fast and grabbed his arms to burn him.

As the youngster got older, he realized her abuse was only

inflicted when his father left the house. He wanted to be outside with his father. He begged his father to take him out. When he was ten, Harland taught him to feed the chickens. As he got older his father taught him to pick up eggs carefully putting them in the egg basket, to drive a tractor, to farm and to hunt in the woods. The child heard his mom and dad's big arguments about his up-bringing in the evenings. He sensed that it was his fault his parents fought all the time, but his father was fighting to protect his son.

Dad taught him to shoot squirrels and rabbits and how to skin the carcasses for their supper. His dad encouraged him with praise and positive feedback, "Good shot, my boy."

The memories of his dad, he liked: repairing fences, feeding the squealing pigs, hunting in the woods, and gathering eggs in the hen house. A bond developed between father and son. He loved his father, but never his mother. She hurt him over and over.

The little boy quickly learned the best way to get along in life was to keep a low profile. On the farm, he had no close neighbor children to play with. He would entertain himself, pulling a wing or two off a helpless fly. At school he watched the other children from the edges of their games. He wanted pals to play with. There was one little boy, George, that talked to him at recess during third grade. The other kids called George, "the Germ." So, what if he smelled a little. They would sit together at the back of the school playground, watching bugs. The two boys pulled off a leg or wing and watched as the insects tried to deal without the naturally es-sential. But in the middle of that summer, George the Germ and his parents moved away.

He wanted the kids to like him, to praise him, so he took one of his toy army men and crammed it headfirst down the throat of an eight-inch rubber alligator. He used some of the old red barn paint to splash around the miniature body. After gluing it in place, he presented it to his favorite teacher, Mrs. Anderson. She looked horrified. Recovering, she managed, "This is very unusual. Thanks."

He expected her to display it proudly on the top of her desk, but she hid it in her top drawer. At lunchtime, Mrs. Anderson phoned his mother asking her to stop by after school that day. His teacher wanted to ask the boy's mother if he was having any problems at home. But Marilyn never bothered. She didn't care how he did in school. After that incident, he avoided attention to the point where he appeared stupid.

⸻ ◆ ⸻

Now, driving aimlessly he thought of 1996, when a stray, dirty dog had wondered into their barn. His father had warned him wild dogs could have rabies. The thirteen-year-old knew the mangy thing was bad. In his childlike imagination, he told the dog, "I'm Zorro." He swung the pitchfork fast. He watched red blood ooze out of its head. Then he grabbed a rusty hatchet and swung fifteen times. He didn't mean to cut off the dog's leg, but the dog snapped at him. He found himself madly chopping and slicing the dog. Its ribs cracked. He was filled with rage. It was "good" to get rid of the irritating, troublesome pest. He buried it behind the tool shed where no one would find it.

Now he stared at his scarred forearms. He recalled a gym class when kids asked about the strange marks on his arms. The child with scars calmly explained, "I had smallpox when I was a kid."

They didn't know anybody who had smallpox, so they believed him. He couldn't tell anyone about the cigarette burns, so he wore long sleeves, even in summer. One of the reasons he left high school was because he didn't have the social glue to keep him there. He would rather stay away from people, stay home, but not in a house with an abusive, evil mother.

Chapter 29

ACCIDENT

The pickup driver was snacking on dry roasted peanuts and day-dreaming of his past. Suddenly the jar slipped from his grip and spilled across the pickup's empty passenger seat. Nuts all over. *Mother will get mad at the mess.* His truck swerved as he reached for the jar. Tires screeched as the drivers tried to control their vehicles. A witness watched in horror as a head-on crash became inevitable. Then there was a horrendous screaming squeal of tires, and a bang, a sound that seemed to echo forever. The crash, so loud, it was terrifying. A witness, eyes wide with horror, stared toward the sound of the collision. Soon there was quiet except for the hiss of a radiator venting into the air.

The collision sent the black Silverado 4x4 pickup flipping through the air, rolling sideways into the deep ditch, onto its top, then rolled again settling on its wheels. Metal crumpled like tissue. The steering wheel smashed into the driver's body, pinning him into the seat, causing internal injuries. The driver's left shoulder crushed. The accident banged his kneecaps hard on the dash. He sagged in his seat, spittle flecked at his mouth and he gagged. He was white as a sheet, scared, pawing at the steering wheel. Then he tried to reach the lever to move the seat back, to release its tight grip on his body. He pushed with all his might at the crushing steering wheel to help him breathe. He gasped and wheezed while struggling for air. Fragile nerve endings ruptured. Oxygen-starved cells burst blood vessels. His eyes were vacant, then his eyes changed to a greenish pallor. Purple burses formed on his chest as the blood pooled under his skin. Convulsive spasms caused his fists to clench. All his bone, muscle, and fluid screamed in silent flurry. He felt all the muscles of his body contract violently, caught in a spasm of reflex action. At the same time, he felt his groin fill with warm liquid. It was his urine. He could not control the muscles of his body. He often felt outside of this world and now it was true. His body twitched spastically and did not surrender willingly.

The witness stopped and dialed 9-1-1. Then he got out of his car to run towards the damaged trucks. The distinct smell of blood in the stale air caught the witness's nostrils. He was the first person on the gruesome scene. He threw up.

Chapter 30

THE HUNT

The 4 x 4 pickup driver stopped making an effort to release the steering wheel. His eyes came to rest on the steering wheel as the dash pushed in on him. He thought of another torture where people had crowded around him close, bumping and shoving him in its grip at a bus depot a couple months ago.

The station was stuffy and busy with people of all sizes, shapes and ages, a few hooded gang members trying to look tough, tattooed losers, and slow-moving suitcase seniors, but the tired women with dead eyes intrigued him the most. No one spoke to him. He remembered feeling the sweat under his arms as he tried to get past the mass of people and make his way to a vacant bench. The frame squeaked under his muscled weight. He noticed the cameras in the bus depot watching everything. Some days he bought a *Daily Herald* newspaper to look busy. On that particular day he pretended to read the *Chicago Sun Times* on his iPhone, but really, he was watching those people like a piranha on an attack mission. He spent time sizing up the women who reminded him of his mother.

Not to draw suspicion to himself, he moved to the coffee shop for an hour or so. After another train pulled into the station he paid for his coffee and mingled with its passengers. Then he spotted the timid looking woman as she got off the Metro bus. Wearing skinny jeans, sweatshirt and a backpack slung over her shoulders, that made her appear like she was trying to look younger than she was.

Seeing her doe-like eyes darting around the Chicago station, he reasoned, *she's not familiar with this place. She's never been here before.* Her chestnut brown hair reminded him of his mother's. *I must stop her from hurting me.* Because of course, he had to do something.

He watched her go to the vending machines and drop in a few coins. She grabbed a Coke and drank with gusto. *Mother is thirsty.* He reasoned; *she could hurt me.* The decision, she's the one, was handed down to him by some logic, not his own, which he had no control over, but he had to obey. It was so easy. He simply walked up to her asking, "Hey, didn't we go to school together?"

Startled she turned to him. "College?"

The clean-shaven guy was actually a high school dropout, but he wanted to keep her talking. "Yeah. I'm sure we took a class together."

"Maybe." She chuckled. "Northern's a big campus."

"Sure was. So glad I'm out of there now."

She smiled. "I'm really not out yet, decided to transfer East for my masters."

"Wow, I'm impressed."

They talked small talk for a while, even exchanging names. He gave a fake name. He smiled broadly as his muscles bulged under his shirt. "Tammy, can I buy you a drink? They got a place just around the corner."

She eyed him cautiously then gave in. "Oh, why not?"

"Let me help ya with that bag." He pointed at her backpack.

After two drinks she got brave enough to ask why he had no eyebrows. "A buddy dared me to shave them." He smiled. "There was alcohol involved. What can I say?" They both munched on handfuls of the bar peanuts and exchanged cell numbers.

"Can I just tell you; I can see pain in your eyes. You're sad. Something wrong?" he asked.

Her eyes blinked downward. "No, I couldn't possibly bother you with my problems."

He tried to show his most sympathetic expression. "You look

troubled. You're cute, so I want to help. Do you want to talk about it?"

She smiled at the compliment. "Oh, I'm afraid I have bad news for my dad."

"I'm a great listener." Concern sounded in his voice.

Slowly she lifted her chin to look at him and gave a slight sigh. "I have to tell him I failed a class. I came to tell him in person."

He sensed he was gaining her trust by the way she had confided in him. He reached for her hand. "It's going to be okay. I'm glad you're here and we met. I'd like to go out with you sometime."

"Oh, I'm just passing through, not staying."

"Well, how about now? How 'bout we get something to eat, to call it our first date?" He motioned to the waitress for the check.

Tammy stared at his shoe-black eyes. "Oh no."

He heard her stomach growl. He smiled for he knew she was hungry and probably scared.

She put her hand across her stomach and laughingly said, "Stop that."

"What else ya doing? You got time to eat. You're hungry. I've been watching you eat peanuts." He nodded towards the almost empty dish on the bar between them. "You need something better. I know a place just about a mile from here. Come on," he urged.

That's all it took. Suspicion fought with hunger. Hunger won. She got into his Silverado pickup.

As she buckled the passenger seat belt, he switched on the radio to a soft music station. She leaned back in the seat as he maneuvered his truck through the streets of Chicago.

"I've changed my mind about the restaurant in town. I want to take *you* to a special place."

"No, you don't have to do that." But she smiled.

"You deserve the best." Once he got onto I-90, he sped up.

She watched out the side window as houses got farther apart.

They made casual small talk during the drive out to the country. But confused he thought, *why was mother at a bus depot? Was she trying to get away?*

After he went through the town of Evergreen and was out in the country, Tammy finally spoke up asking, "Just how far is this restaurant?"

He didn't answer, but instead calmly turned down a side road lined with trees, driving for another couple of miles.

"Is it down here?"

His chiseled features turned more severe, as he turned onto a gravel road and stopped his vehicle; he quickly reached his right arm under his seat and grabbed his knife. Before she could even react, he touched the knife's safety lock which immediately flicked open the blade to its full seven and three-quarters inches. His impulse was to strike.

Tammy's eyes shot open, becoming saucers of fear as he swung the blade into her soft stomach. He saw horror in the tense lines of her face. *Mother is mad at me. She's going to hurt me.* Blood oozed through her sweatshirt. She looked down at herself, dazed, like she couldn't believe what was happening.

His face emotionless, but his eyes flashed fire as he calmly yanked the knife out.

Blood spilled out faster, the stain widening. Her arms shot up in protection, her right hand flew to the glass window, fingers spread, then banging for help on the glass. She pressed the seatbelt button and it released as he plunged the knife again. Frantic, she brought her hand to the door handle. She pulled, opening the passenger door, and jumped off the seat. As her feet hit the ground, she clutched at her painful middle.

Mother is trying to get away. He opened the driver's door and bounded around the front of the truck.

Tammy tried to run along the side of the road. The gravel was loose and slippery. She moved to the short weeds along the roadside. "Help me, help me!" She screamed, but there was no one coming, no cars.

He quickly caught up to her and brought his knife down hard into her back.

She stumbled.

He grabbed her right arm. His fingers dug into her arm. Yanking, he swung her around.

There was no way for her to escape his tight hold.

The victim brought her right foot upward and kicked at his legs. Her tennis shoes did little to stop him. She fought, kicking, and scratching his face. Tammy opened her mouth to scream more, but the shock of what was happening didn't even seem to be registering with her brain.

He lunged the knife at her again.

Her sweatshirt fabric was turning red and wet, beginning to darken and glisten.

The attacker cut her arms as he swung madly with the weapon. "You could hurt me," he yelled at her over and over again. His voice loud as his vision dimmed with rage. He could feel his knife hitting the bones in her arms. Her actions of fighting back threw him into a mad furious rage. Red splatters were flinging through the air.

She screamed, begging to be let go, but the blood still flowed. He was vicious as he silenced her. Then she had that look, like a deer in the headlights, as she realized, he would kill her. Hyperventilating and shaking uncontrollably, her voice filled with sadness, she said, "No." Then she put her energy into the scream, "No! Not yet!"

Somehow it was magic the way the blood and soul oozed out. Her sweatshirt transformed from grey into a glistening rusty red hue.

Finally, he watched her unmoving body slump in the ditch. The air was filled with the scent of human tissue and blood like a butcher shop. He looked up and down the disserted country road. No one. But someone could come by later and find her. He must hide her. He looked around. The nearest farmhouse was at least a hundred yards set back from the road. Nice long driveway. If he picked her up, he would get more blood on his clothing. He grabbed her ankles. Dragging her bloody body to the nearest culvert. Then he noticed her hands. The hands that hurt him when he was a child. He had to stop those fingers from ever hurting him again. Slashing wildly, he cut off the fingers. He pushed her inside the eighteen-inch culvert, using his foot to push her deep inside the galvanized metal. He went back to his pickup truck, where he spotted her backpack on the floor of the front seat. He calmly carried her belongings to the culvert. Using her backpack, he pushed her further into the dark tunnel leaving her canvas bag with her. He calmly looked down at his clothes at a streak of red spatters across his chest. He had another shirt in his truck. It took him a minute to remove his stained shirt and stuff it into the culvert. He rearranged stems of tall weeds over the galvanized opening in the ditch.

"You've just had the shittiest day," he laughed as he wiped the dripping blade through the grassy weeds. He felt an arrogant pleasure in getting rid of mother so easily.

Once again, he walked back to his truck. After the killing, he felt relief. Calmly he returned the knife under his seat. He finished her off, but too quickly. He wanted those exciting moments to last longer. If only he could have saved her somewhere, kept the excitement going longer, maybe a cage or hole in the ground. But his laughter ended abruptly as his attention came back to the present. He heard his mother's words, "You're such a slob. Clean this up." That was months ago.

Now he looked down at the steering wheel pushed into his body and the blood on the seat next to him. He had to go home immediately to get peroxide and ammonia. This was like Mother's blood that day on his truck seat. The blood was on him. He felt waves of nausea as he watched it, but he could not look away.

Chapter 31

NICE BOY

He didn't make it home right away when Mother's red blood got on him a few months ago. There was a big interruption to his plans. He was on his way home to get cleaned up, actually only a couple miles from home when he saw Dale Lathom parked on the side of the country road.

His neighbor stood beside his beginning-to-rust Impala, the wind blowing his dry white hair. The trunk was open, but the old man was looking at the front tire.

He wanted to ignore him, just get home, but what if the geezer recognized him whizzing right past? Would that look weird? "Shit," he said out loud to no one. He slowed his pickup truck and pulled onto the shoulder of the blacktop just in front of the Impala. He backed up a little, then stopped his vehicle, and turned off the ignition. Reluctantly he opened his pickup door to step out with a big fake grin on his face. "Everything okay, Mr. Lathom?" he called out.

The seventy-nine-year-old farmer with the weather-beaten nose turned his tanned face. "Oh, my boy. It's great to see you."

The younger man, his head perfectly shaved and his face smooth, reached out his hand in a friendly gesture.

Mr. Lathom reached his gnarled fingers forward as the men shook. The man with frayed bottoms to his coveralls asked, "What happened to your face?" Lathom was pointing an arthritic finger at him.

"Oh that." The younger man quickly raised a hand to his face, *Mother hurt me.* "Oh, I caught a coon in one of my traps. Darn thing was still alive."

"You got to be careful. They can have rabies, ya know," said Lathom with the white cotton socks and dark scuffed work shoes, one of which was slit.

Could be a bunion. "You're right. I'll be more careful next time." He brushed at his cheek. *Got to change the subject.* "Why did ya stop here?"

"I've got a flat tire. Seems I've misplaced the handle to my jack, but I've got the jack." They both looked at the distressed flattened front tire. "I'm thinking of just driving it home on the flat, just go really slow."

"You can't drive on that. You could damage the rim. Ya really need to take the flat into town to get it fixed."

"Oh, I don't know if the garage is open."

The ancient guy doesn't even know what day it is. "It's Tuesday afternoon, sure they'll be open. I could call them to get ya right in." The good Samaritan started to reach for his back pocket to get his phone out.

"I suppose I should get it fixed. You're right. I'll call them. I got me one of those small phones in the glove compartment. It's for emergencies. Guess this is time to get it out to use it." He chuckled.

"If ya haven't used it much, it probably needs charging." In a flat tone he said, "I'll make the call for you."

"Okay," he relented.

His helpful neighbor made the call to Goodyear where they said to bring the tire right in.

"Thanks a lot for getting me in so fast. Hey, I haven't seen much of your folks lately," he said with his chipped tooth smile.

As casually as he could, the young man answered, "Didn't ya hear? They finally retired and moved to Florida. They got a little place down there away from our bad winters," he easily lied.

The elderly man's thin white eyebrows pulled together as he said, "Your dad always did like fishing, but I didn't know the snow bothered them."

"Yeah. They're happy down there." He glanced at his watch. *When is this guy going to stop with the third degree?*

"Good for them, but that leaves you running the farm all by yourself." His stooped shoulders sagged a little more.

"I don't mind."

"Maybe you should hire Grant Magden's son. He's looking for a job."

He didn't want anyone poking around his place. "I'll see." A pause. "Do ya have a spare?" he asked, quickly changing the subject.

"Yeah. It's still in the trunk."

They both moved around to the back of the car where the younger one reached in to pull out the spare. He bounced it a little on the side of the road. "It seems to be in pretty good shape. It should get you into town. Let me get my jack to help you." With the shoulders of a blacksmith, he knew he would be doing the work for his neighbor anyway.

"Oh, that's wonderful. I heard ya were gone for a while serving our country. You've always done the right thing, my boy. Did I ever tell you about Korea?"

The killer rolled his eyes as he turned his head away. *Oh boy, here he goes with his war stories.* "I've heard about it." Then he added, "I'll get my jack." He opened the pickup truck's passenger side door to reach behind the seat. That's when he noticed Lathom's eyes go wide. He followed the staring eyes to see what he was looking at. There was blood splattered on the seat. The killer immediately knew he had slipped up. Fear surged into his stomach. He glanced towards Lathom who was staring at the red splatter. The thirty-one-year old's throat tightened. His fists balled in nervous anticipation.

"What happened here?" Dale Lathom said in a fearful tone as he pointed a finger towards the truck seat.

Will he figure out it's Mother's blood like Father did? "That coon," he explained as calmly as he could, but he was breathing fast and hard. His knuckles holding the door turned white.

"Ya didn't throw it in the back of the pickup?"

Trying to think fast, he answered, "Had seed in there, so I tossed the raccoon inside. Guess that wasn't the best idea. Pretty messy." *Hope he won't notice that it's fresh blood.*

"You got to get that cleaned up before it draws flies."

"Yeah, uh flies."

Out of the blue, Lathom asked, "How long your folks been gone?"

The younger man's whole body stiffened. *Why is he still asking about them?* He began to reach for the knife he kept under the seat, but slowly he answered, "They moved out, just before the snow came last winter." *This is my fault; I didn't clean the mess up.*

There was a long pause in their conversation as Dale seemed to think about his answer.

This was a clusterfuck of major proportions. If he had to stab him here, anybody coming down the road would see it. His eyes narrowed dangerously. The liar watched the man's head of white hair. Then he saw the senior smile. He relaxed as he dropped his knife, pulling his arm back and swung the door closed as quickly as he could, thinking, *that was close.*

While his helper jacked up the car, Mr. Lathom broke the quiet asking, "You miss the army life? Your buddies? I got to hand it to you, ya sure did your duty to fight and protect our country. Did ya hear that Ben Flatter's kid got shot up bad? He lost a leg."

"Yes sir, I heard that."

"He's in some rehab place now. Ben says he's getting one of them new artificial legs."

The young man glanced down at his own legs as he removed the tight lug nuts, saying, "That's rough."

Lathom made small talk as his quiet helper managed to pull the flat tire off. The spare was smaller, but it would get Dale to the garage about six miles away. It took a while, but he got the spare on.

"Thanks a lot for doing this for me." Lathom patted his savior's back warmly. "Don't know what I would have done if you hadn't stopped to help me. You've served our whole country. Now you've helped me." Dale thanked him and smiled wearily, like he had done all the hard work himself. "I owe ya a beer for helping me. You come over sometime to collect. We'll chat some more."

Not if I can help it, he thought, but politely mumbled, "Sure thing. We'll do that some time."

They said their goodbyes as the younger man walked back to his truck chuckling to himself; *he believed every one of my lies.*

He opened his door and slid in, looking at the blood-spattered passenger door. He heard his mother say, "You are a slob." *I know better. I'll go straight home to clean this up.*

He turned on the ignition and edged onto the highway. His fear mounting as he thought, *Mother is mad about the dirt.* Within a couple minutes, he turned into his own driveway. He parked the vehicle. Then went inside to get ammonia and rags. As he stepped into his childhood house, now his own home, he saw the image of his mother standing in the kitchen with her hands on her hips.

In a childish voice, he begged, "Please don't hurt me. I'll clean it up."

She gave him a stern disappointed look because he forgot to clean the truck. He heard her deep tone. "Stop making work for me! You're such a slob! You disgust me!"

While she yelled, he slowly walked into her bedroom. He was afraid, but he knew what he must do. He opened her dresser drawer and took out a pack of cigarettes. Removing one, he put it to his mouth. With a Bic lighter, he lit the end.

He tried to turn her screaming out of his mind. "You are sloppy, and I have to clean up after you. Don't make me hurt you!"

Blind impulses welled up in his body. He watched her fingers take the cigarette from his lips, moving it closer to him. He stared at those hateful hands as she held the weapon of torture to the flesh of his arm between some old healed cigarette burns. Screaming out in pain, he watched her image fade.

Chapter 32

GIVE ME YOUR HANDS

Saturday 8:00 A.M.

His truck leaned dangerously to the side. There's been an accident. There was blood everywhere in the trailer cab. He looked at the blood on his clothing, where the steering wheel pushed into his ribs. He heard his mother say, "You're such a slob. Look at the mess you've made."

He looked out the truck window at a group of trees on the side of the road. They reminded him of the woods where his dad took him hunting when he was a boy. That woods was his haven, land left untouched by human intrusion. He loved the thick woods of his childhood summers with their tall trees and thorny wild raspberry bushes because no one went out there. Those trees had been there for hundreds of years. He remembered digging a hole in the woods surrounded by those trees.

For weeks he had been digging a deep pit, swinging the shovel into the hard earth repeatedly as he thought of bringing it down on her head. The dark shadows, thick bushes and weeds didn't hamper his morbid thoughts. He shoveled perhaps a foot into the earth. He rolled his long sleeves up, something he never did in public, because his arms displayed the old round-holed burn marks. Under his shirt he hid his military abs, perfect defined muscles, but pale white skin never exposed to sunlight. Out there, deep in those dismal woods, no one would see his ugly scars. As he looked at his old wounds he yelled, "I hate you. I tried to please you."

He remembered expanding the hole steadily like the ripples flowing out from a pebble that broke the surface of a still pond, then he widened the dirt oval. Once he was about two feet down, the ground grew moist and dark as he started hitting rocks and tree roots. He dug out the small rocks. Pounding with his shovel, he broke through roots. Good thing he brought the twelve-foot ladder and bucket out to the woods, so he could carry all the dirt out of his profound pit.

He even took a file out there so he could sharpen the shovel blade. He used the file to smooth out tiny nicks from hitting rocks. After he honed the edge to razor sharpness, he stepped back into the hole and continued. For days he dug as mounds of earth formed around his hole.

He remembered taking a deep breath, then stood looking down at his work, six feet long and about three feet deep. *Not big enough. Mother could get out, must be deeper, wider, must keep going.* It was a lot of work with little breeze through the trees, so his sweat-soaked camouflage clothes clung to his muscled body. Sweat dripped off his forehead. His pulse pounded in his temple. A flash of blood surged through his arms and shoulders.

The broad-shouldered man worked hard, digging the monstrous trench. His hands blistered inside the gloves. His shoulders ached. The hole got deeper as the piles of dirt surrounding the hole grew higher. Clammy sweat poured down his back. His adrenaline and aggression kept him digging, shovelful after shovelful for his man-made grave, piling the loose soil and rocks around the top.

Afterward he looked around at his handiwork and felt confident it was deep enough no one could escape. *I'll keep you here Mother, so ya can't hurt me.* His self-made mission completed a pit about ten-feet-deep and seven-feet-wide. After he climbed out, he pulled the ladder up, tossing it to the side of a huge pile of dirt. To him this represented a great symbol of his strength.

I'll make you suffer, he thought as he looked at the loose piles of dirt circling the pit. This hole was hidden in the thick woods, deep enough that Mother can't get out. His trap was complete. Taking his pressed white handkerchief out of his back pocket, he wiped the sweat off his forehead, then he carefully wiped dirt off his hands.

Trees cast jagged shadows across the surrounding piles of loose dirt. The undergrowth was inked with shade as he trudged through the trampled weeds to his truck. The dense woods looked dreary as the sun started to set. The green undergrowth was murky with decomposing leaves. Tree branches looked grotesque as the shadows steadily deepened with gloom. The air turned cooler as the sun went down. The sky darkened into smudged charcoal. Now he was prepared. He must find mother before she hurt anyone else.

It didn't take him long to reach the two-story, red brick house set back from the country road. He wasn't even aware of the lightening bugs darting across the lawn. Instead of seeing joy in the country, he aggressively scraped the dirt-caked sides of his work boots through the crabgrass lawn trying to get as much dirt off as possible and muttered to himself, *"You're dirty. Get cleaned up, you slob."*

He remembered walking through the back porch. Just as he unlocked the kitchen door, he heard a scratching noise. Glancing to his right, he saw a small rodent struggling in a mouse trap, its front paw caught. He felt power surge through him. *He was in control of this despicable dirt, vermin,* he thought as he brought his boot down hard. Bones crunched; blood spattered. He felt powerful. He was in control of something, even if he couldn't control his mother.

He imagined Dad patting his arm saying, "You are a really good boy."

Mud and mouse blood were on his work boots. Before going to bed that night, he took a brush to them, getting them back to the high gloss spit-shine quality he always kept his shoes. He also changed clothes and laundered them before bed, so no one would think him dirty and hurt him. After scrubbing the floor with bleach to clean up the blood, the thirty-one-year-old showered and scrubbed until his skin turned red. Once clean, he made something for his dinner. His favorite treat was a peanut butter sandwich with extra peanuts sprinkled in the butter, then cut off the crusts like a little boy would prefer.

He ate his simple meal alone. As he finished his supper, he wiped his mouth with the back of his hand and felt the stubble. He hated the itch from new growth. He liked his face clean shaven. He liked everything free from dirt like Mother insisted.

As he stood in the bathroom shaving, he looked into the mirror. He inherited his mother's chestnut brown hair, which he shaved off to feel clean. *Mother taught me to be immaculate.*

Every night he walked into his living room and dropped to the carpeted floor, where he did his regimented one hundred pushups. Afterwards he sat in his dad's old recliner worn around the edges, but clean, in fact, very clean.

Right after the ten o'clock evening news he went into another of his daily rituals as he stepped into his third shower of the day. He scrubbed his nails with a stiff brush to rid himself of dirt until his cuticles bled. Then he stretched his raw fingers before the steamy mirror whispering, "I'm clean now, see Mommy."

But, where are you? He had to find his mother before she hurt anyone else.

No, that's not right. I did find you. He stared down at his right hand, as if he could see the rock that had been there just a couple days ago. He thought of last Tuesday when he stopped at Diamonds grocery store on Route 38 to buy a jar of dry roasted nuts to munch on later. He often took the Elgin O'Hare Expressway but sometimes he drove the back roads into Chicago to the bus depot. He remembered parking his pickup in the alley. As he walked towards the front of the store, he saw the woman with chestnut brown hair in the parking lot.

She was getting out of her car. The cool morning breeze blew her shoulder-length hair. It looked unkempt, like Mother's. She looked up at him, her face plain. Mother was annoyed. She was angry with him, like always. He saw her hands, the hands that used to hurt him over and over. Was she reaching for cigarettes?

She's going to hurt me. He had to stop her before she hurt any-one. He must have picked up a large rock, for it was in his hand. He walked straight for her. Then raised his arm up and swung.

Once he knocked her out, she laid unmoving. He kicked the driver's door closed with his boot. He quickly bent down, grabbed her by the ankles, yanking her backwards. Her head scraped against the pavement as he dragged her by her feet to his truck. He placed Mother on the passenger's seat. This very seat right next to him here inside his truck. Here where his chest hurt, and he was having trouble breathing.

Then yesterday she was on a TV news report. 'Missing,' they said. He had to check on Mother, make sure she was still in the woods, in his domain, where she wouldn't hurt him. He automati-cally grabbed a jar of roasted nuts out of the kitchen cupboard. He munched on them during his walk out to the woods.

It didn't take him long to reach his hole. And there she was. His blood pulsed as he watched Mother down in the pit. He was at the top, ground level looking down at her. Dirt and blood smeared her face. Her face was muddy where her tears had mixed with the dirt. *She's mad again. She hates me.* She was biting her lip. Her eyes looked wild and chestnut brown hair disheveled. He could feel his heart pumping wildly. She looked mad, her eyes puffy, and her lips dry and parched. They were the hands that kept hurting him and hurting him. He hated those hands. They're mean. He had to stop those hands. "Give me your hands." He yelled.

That's when she looked up at him.

He could feel the blood pulsing in his neck and sweat at the base of his spine as she looked at him. He knew he must destroy those hands to save himself. He had to cut mother's hands before they burned him. Adrenaline and anticipation fired his blood as he lied, "I have a sandwich for you."

She started to raise her arm, but suddenly she pulled her arms down to her sides, out of his reach.

He swung but missed.

She wouldn't reach up to him.

His rage overtook him as he yelled, "You're such a slob." He spat, "You're sloppy. You're filth." Words he had heard over and over from her. He was coiled like a spring, nervous energy radiating. "Ya have to do what I say."

He heard a desperate edge to her voice, a horrible noise when she screamed for help.

But he told her, "You can yell all ya want out here. No one will hear."

A tornado of red anger sprang up in his chest. He spit at her, then kicked some loose dirt down the hole. He was mad. Rage came, like a wave of heat throughout his body. He wanted to throw something, but not the knife. She couldn't have his knife. He worked himself up into a frenzy he couldn't control. He picked up a few rocks, hurdled them down at her, then flung the only other thing he had, his opened jar of dry roasted peanuts down at her into the dirt hole. They spilled in the dirt. The words he heard his whole childhood come out of his mouth, "Look at ya! Go on look. You're dirty and disgusting. You're sloppy. Ya disgust me. Don't make me hurt you!"

He backed away from the hole thinking, *she's not cooperating. Why doesn't she listen to me? She talked back.* Mad, he turned storming off. Several feet from the dirt piles he yelled back, "You're not supposed to say 'No!' You should do what I say."

He stomped down the trail upset, muttering, "Crap. Damn it, Mother. You must do what I say. I always did what you told me."

He quickly hiked back to the farmhouse. *That's a good place for Mother.* He laughed at her. *She can't hurt me now.*

He went back to his clean house. Eager to clean himself of the dirt out there in the woods. He immediately went to the bathroom, looked around to ensure everything was in place then picked up his razor. He shaved his face clean of all whiskers. He had a system, his way to shave the top of his head. He looked into the mirror, his cranium bald and gleaming. He quickly undressed and stepped into the steaming shower, where the hot water streamed down his body as he stooped to carefully shave his legs of hair, smooth like a little boy. *I must stay clean, so Mother won't get mad.*

———«(●)»———

But now I've made a mess in the truck. Blood everywhere and I can't get out. Mother is in the woods all alone. She can't get out. No one on the highway had even an inkling of the terrible struggle which raged within his tortured soul. Beyond conscious thought, his frenzied instinct to survive fought its doomed battle.

Chapter 33

SOLITUDE

Sergeant David Dodson realized he had a high heel fetish by the time he was twenty. At thirty-five, David had alimony and child support to pay his ex-wife and a ten-year-old son. Because of the cop's salary, he needed to moon light. His fellow cops called it "easy money to babysit those cheesecakes," when he got the job working security at runway jobs in Oak Brook. The police detective loved watching the models' calves in their high heels. That's where he met Diane.

As a teen, Diane thought her hair too straight and had wished for curls. At least she had wanted some curves on her body. She'd been gawky, flat-chested, and towered, six inches above the tallest boys. Kids used to make fun of her thinness, calling her skinny, and bean-pole, like there was something she could do about it. But not anymore, for Skinny grew up to be a high fashion model. When the talent scout had spotted the seventeen-year-old at the Woodfield mall's food court, she assumed the guy was playing a trick on her until he handed her his business card.

Within a couple months, Vogue booked her for their fall on-line catalog and for the Dutch magazine, Rika. Diane posed for Raf Simons spring Christian Dior collection just a couple weeks later.

She soon became one of the most sought after faces in the business, working at the high-end fashion house of Mary-Kate and Asley Olsen. In New York she modeled for Alexander Wang. She had gigs around the world. The five-foot, eleven-inch top fashion model worked Paris Fashion week wearing Dries Van Noten, the Belgian designer's fashions. She had multi-million-dollar contracts, endorsements, and campaigns. She worked for the French fashion house of Balenciaga at the Paris Observatory, where she wore hand-braided miniskirts and buttery leather dresses.

Five years ago, as David and Diane simply rounded a backstage corner too fast, he ran into her. He felt like an idiot. She had just come off the catwalk and stumbled on the Sophia Webster sandals with the pop pineapple print four-inch heels. He grabbed her to keep her up. The high heels drew him in. Little did the detective know she was wearing Hedi Slimane and the coveted Saint Laurent designs that day. He, with his muscular barrel-like six foot, three inch body was in awe of her slim one hundred sixteen-pound model figure, long legs, flawless skin, cute little nose, and shiny stick-straight blond mane. He couldn't believe his ears when this stunning woman had actually agreed to go out for coffee with him. They had such a good time talking about their different lifestyles, but soon they found they had so much in common. They both loved classical music, both vegetarians and loved long hard workouts at the gym, for both had to stay in good physical condition for their jobs. They started working out together.

Diane was turned on by his boyish grin that brought out the laugh lines at the corners of his brown eyes. His laughter was deep, rich, infectious, his nose stolen from a Greek statue. He always asked her to wear heels on dates when they weren't running through the park together. Diane loved to be the center of his attention. Soon both fell in love. She enjoyed sex with David. He showed her how to love her tall lean body. Diane wanted to share her exciting fashion life and world travels with him, so they honeymooned in Paris. They bought a home in West Chicago near David's work. She continued to work and travel until the attack.

Now the police sergeant held their back door for his wife and her miniature schnauzer, Trixie, as they stepped out on their deck to share their first cup of coffee in the early morning refreshing air. The July day was going to be a hot one, but now this early morning was cool, quiet and pleasant. David already dressed for work in a starched white shirt, blue striped tie and his badge that read 'Sergeant Dodson.' Diane wearing black pajamas with a pink sash and high-heeled slippers for David still liked his wife wearing stilettos around the house. They enjoyed their half hour of peace out on their secluded deck. The day was warming up beautifully. Each sat on a deck chair.

David looked over at his wife's slim hips and honey-gold eyes. Her lips, pink as cotton candy and just as sweet. She was pale and beautiful even without makeup, her face flawless from every angle. Birds were happily singing in the leafed-out tree branches that engulfed their deck.

That was as far as Diane would go in their back yard, feeling safe the neighbors couldn't see her through the thick green leaves. Diane's blond hair gathered in a neat ponytail, which emphasized the ex-model's jutting cheekbones. "You didn't sleep well, something on your mind?"

He was holding the morning newspaper in one hand, but ignoring it, he answered, "Yes, we're looking for a missing woman who was last seen Tuesday morning."

With the cup handle held tightly between her thumb and index finger of her right hand, she carefully sipped the hot liquid. "It upset you?"

"This just doesn't feel right," he hesitated. "She's only twenty-nine."

"Oh, no," she shivered remembering how fast beauty can disappear.

Birds chattered in the nearby trees. David glanced at his watch.

"Oh man, it's late. I've got to get going." *Should I tell her the kidnapped woman lives in her aunt's building? I don't have time now. I'll tell her tonight.* He pushed himself heavily to his feet. He stood, threw what remained of his cold coffee into the grass and hitched up his pants. He bent to kiss his wife's lips as she placed her left hand on his meaty right cheek and kissed him goodbye.

"The sooner we solve this one, the sooner I get some sleep, so I've got to run. You have a great day."

David headed for the garage to get his car thinking; *I should have been there the night she was attacked.* Most nights he had driven her home after work, but that night he stayed home to watch the World Series.

Diane's therapist had tried to explain to him, that victims like Diane, can be overwhelmed. They could have an intense fear of the crises ever happening again. He called it post-traumatic stress syndrome, prolonged shock and emotional numbness with the victim experiencing nightmares, trembling, helplessness, and fatigue. They must find new ways to deal with this dangerous stress. But how long will it take Diane to learn new problem-solving techniques and face the crisis head-on? And if she can't, the doctor also told David, "If the victim won't let go of their grief, their pain could bury them, drowning in their suffering."

Diane sat there with her fingers, at least the ones she had left, wrapped around the cup of coffee. She looked at their schnauzer curled at her feet instead of her deformed hand.

Chapter 34

BREAK OUT, GET OUT

Saturday 8:05 a.m.

"Have a great day," Diane thought of David's words, as she sipped the final wash of coffee carefully holding her mug with her right thumb and index finger, the only digits left on that hand. After the caffeine, she knew it was useless to go back to bed to hide. She knew her work-obsessed husband would be working late as usual, but what did she have to do all day?

She looked at what remained of her right hand, remembering the excitement, spotlights of the photograph sessions and cat walks of her past, all abruptly ended for the model eight months ago, after the attack. The life she had known, was over, ended in THE attack in an Oakbrook parking garage. Her poised self-confidence had been shattered that night as she walked with long strides towards her car. She just wanted to get home.

Suddenly, someone had come up behind her. There was pain in her left shoulder that dropped her to her knees. He had stabbed her shoulder. She turned holding up her hands to fight off the blade. He pushed her down on the cement floor, straddling her body. With his heavy weight, he used his knees to press down on her stomach. The hard hand over her mouth prevented her from screaming. It was so large; it was over her nose too, preventing her from breathing. She kicked and tried to scream. He shoved her scarf into her mouth. She gagged. He pulled her hands up to his face. In the dark shadows, she couldn't see his face well, but it was emotionless, no expression, as though he were in a trance. It was too dark, to even see the color of his eyes. She thought he was going to bite her hands, but he tied them together. He was saying something, but she couldn't remember what. His monotone voice had absolutely no expression. She saw a long blade held to her throat. Then the excruciating unbearable pain in her right hand. It felt like a thousand knives of agony tearing into her flesh. She lost consciousness.

The injury exposed bones in her fingers, but there wasn't enough tissue around the wounds to stitch them closed. A surgeon operated to shorten the bones, so her wounds could be stitched closed. They also stitched her shoulder wound.

When she woke in the hospital, David was sitting by her side. He looked wrinkled and tired, like he had been there for days, with his head bowed and shoulders slouched. They were told, her three fingers were not found at the scene. If they had been, emergency medical protocol was to put them in a plastic bag, put them on ice, and transport them with the patient to the emergency room in case they could be reattached. But all three were missing.

Rape crisis unit on the police department and Victim's Services came to speak with the model. She pulled her heavily bandaged hand under the covers and screamed, "I wasn't raped. I'm disfigured, just leave me alone!"

David wanted to take care of her wellbeing. He felt guilty for leaving her alone, not driving her that horrible night. Many friends tried to visit her in the hospital. But she couldn't stand for them to see the horrible huge bandages, or her beaten face. Soon David had asked the hospital staff to put her in isolation with a sign on the door reading "No visitors." Especially reporters were not allowed in. David was her teddy bear protector and savior. Coworkers sent flowers instead. She laid in her hospital room with the shades drawn, her hand felt on fire, the pain so bad. She still remembered the first time the doctor removed the bulky bandage; her horror at the stump of a hand. After that she felt ruined, destroyed, horribly violated. She wasn't whole anymore.

An occupational therapist came into her hospital room to perform active range of motion exercises to the uninvolved joints, her thumb and pointer finger, but Diane wouldn't show him her hand, keeping it firmly under the covers. David had asked him for a list of exercises she could do on her own. The therapist provided pages of strengthening exercises, crucial to restore hand function for the patient to perform tasks for daily living as quickly as possible. Then he said, "You're so lucky, you didn't lose the thumb for grasping items."

"You idiot! I can't model like this." She had screamed at him as she threw the printed pages at him. He ran from her hospital room.

David did everything in his power to catch whoever did this to his beloved. The police said the attacker was possibly after her rings. She was wearing a ring with three small diamonds on one finger and her late mother's opal ring on her middle finger. Perhaps he cut her fingers to steal the rings. The police watched pawn shops for her jewelry. But the thief didn't take her more valuable engagement and wedding rings on her left hand. He had taken a couple smaller rings on her right hand. It just didn't make any sense, but she felt robbed of her career, her life. The rings were never found.

David wanted to console Diane's anguish her first night home from the hospital. Sergeant Dodson felt defeated since he hadn't been able to find the criminal who attacked and deformed his very own beautiful wife. Then silently, he lay down beside her on their bed and wrapped himself around her. For the first time since seeing her hand, her heart and mind calmed. Just for one blessed moment, they found a place that held love, not loss. Lying all night, holding Diane, he'd dared to hope the worst was over.

In the morning as David stood at the side of their bed looking down at her, he said, "I want everything to go back to the way it was, just like that." He snapped his large fingers.

She stared at his hand in mid-air and said, "I can't even do that tiny gestor, like snap my fingers anymore." She pulled the blanket over her head as the tears came again.

The psychiatrist on the force told David, "The victim could feel the sudden death of her fingers when there was no way to say good-bye, but if Diane perceives the trauma realistically, has adequate support resources from you, her husband, from her friends, peers, community, and she develops adequate coping mechanisms, then the odds will be in her favor to cope with the crisis and adapt to the changes in her life."

David tried patiently to explain to her, "He didn't take your purse or cell phone, so he doesn't know where you live." That made her feel safer at home. Diane remembered begging David to cancel their cleaning woman, pleading that now she wasn't traveling, she would take care of their home. No one was coming in. Diane needed to mend. Maximum medical improvement is sixty to ninety days to heal her hand. The mental healing was so much slower. She still had night terrors, but at least she didn't need David with her twenty-four/seven like she did right after the attack.

Her fellow models had been close pals. Now she blogged, twittered, Facebooked with lots of Cyber friends, but she didn't see anyone. Her long ago friends called it an unfortunate accident. *It wasn't an accident! It was an attack!* The ex-model had typed on her Facebook page, "Let the younger girls take over." Implying it was her age, when in reality, she was at the height of her career. Her life was shattered.

Now she looked at the empty coffee cup and rose from her deck chair. Trixie stood with her. She reached her long elegant left hand out to open the back door. As they both stepped inside, sunshine fell across the hard wood floor. She laid her right hand on the stainless-steel kitchen sink. There it was, only the thumb and index finger left on the damaged hand. She was only ninety-seven percent of a woman. For a right-handed person, she was unable to give a typical handshake to every individual she would ever meet.

Though she had called a therapist immediately after leaving the hospital, it didn't work very well because it was so overwhelming. She remembered the therapist's phone conversations. She would never go to his office. He kept repeating, "Lives change in an instant."

"Without three fingers, my life is utterly ruined," she wailed.

"You were not in control of those events." His voice always soothing.

Tears of shame rolled down her face as she said, "I was mutilated."

"You did not cause him to attack you."

"I was getting paid a lot to look perfect. Well, I'm not perfect anymore. I'm a monster!"

"There was nothing you could have done to prevent this tragedy. Learn to breathe deeply and slowly to give yourself confidence. You can do things in spite of feeling scared."

Was he even listening to me? "Agents are going to see me as flawed, as handicapped." Diane also told her therapist, "I was the kid in high school who made curfew. I followed the rules, but still this happened to me."

"When fear disrupts your ability to go to work and to engage in activities you love, you have a phobia. Acceptance and commitment therapy involve opening yourself to uncomfortable situations."

Memories of that night entered her mind. Sadness at losing her career turned to outbursts and depression, even thoughts of suicide. But David was always there. She couldn't do that to David. *I've got dark shadows but stop looking at the shadows. I'm trying to look at the bigger picture, the beauty. It should fit together.* She Googled articles that said nighttime would be especially difficult. The authors wrote that it was essential to experience a rebirth to fully heal. What she took from the experts was everyone heals in their own way and at their own pace.

At first, she was paralyzed with anxiety and fear. Privately, she was mortified that a task like being seen by people, so effortless for others, roused such anxiety in her.

Peapod delivered groceries to the front porch and collected the check taped to their front door or David picked up a few things. It wasn't perfect, but with Amazon.com, AmazonFresh and David stopping at a drug store occasionally, they were managing. Her world was her home. She felt destroyed, loathing herself, insecure, and withdrawn. *I was a madwoman, weeping all the time. I felt scared.* She tried to heal by watching a YouTube instructional video done by a meditation teacher that said, "Victims should be overjoyed that you lived. Promise yourself to make the most of this second chance by living life to the fullest. Fear is destructive. Yes, it happened. Now it's time to move on."

Diane's friends called saying things like, "I'm sorry this happened to you." And "You're such a strong person. You'll get through this."

David told Diane she could be a strong hedge tree with deep unfathomable roots. *Why can't I be half as strong as he is? I know this is not the end of the world. I want to be a survivor.*

The dining room blinds were tipped to show tiny slates of light. Diane could feel the warmth of the sunshine streaming through the window. A housefly buzzed desperately in the window overlooking the street. *It must have come in when we opened the deck door.* The fly kept buzzing and bumping into the glass. *Even the fly wants out. I should want out of here as much as it does.* Diane slowly walked closer to the window watching the sun slide towards her slippers. She looked longingly out the window to see happy little sparrows splashing in a brown puddle in the parkway. *Even they're happy.* A few puffy clouds drifting in the bright blue sky, a beautiful summer day. A woman walked by with a small dog prancing beside her. *They're both smiling. Even the dog is happy to be outside. I'm a recluse in my own home.* She started pacing up and down the room. Trixie following, then Diane stopped to drum the fingers of her left hand on the table.

Her large wet eyes, looked out the window again, seeing manicured lawns. She was torn by the most terrible conflicted heart a woman can ever know, to get out or to hide forever. She wanted outside in the fresh air so badly, but she was heavy with fear. She climbed the stairs to their bedrooms. Frustrated, she started opening doors. Fashion magazines were staked in the guest room closet.

I could clean that out. Oh, it's too nice a day to be stuck inside. She slammed the door closed. *What am I going to do?*

She took a nice long bubble bath since there was no need to rush through a quick shower. She had plenty of time to get ready for her day. As she leaned back in the tub of hot water, she thought about her therapist's words over the phone the day before, "You're stuck in a closet."

At the time, she had argued with him. "No, I'm not. My home is nice. It's not a closet."

He had simply told her to think about it. Now she started thinking, *maybe he meant a closet in my mind. He could be right. I've built my own personal closet.* Diane had lived in a world of fashion for so long, her closet filled with metallic clothing, but she couldn't wear them anymore. Now she wanted to be invisible. David gave her the comfort and sympathy she so needed, but he's at work and I'm lonely. She dressed in white designer jeans, put on an intricate white-on-white embroidered top with long sleeves, long enough to just about cover her right hand. She had ordered several of these designer shirts online because of their extra-long sleeves.

She stepped in front of the mirror, took small scissors, and carefully trimmed her bangs with her left hand, something she's been doing for the past eight months. There was no way she was going to her salon with gabby beauticians anymore. She missed mall shopping, beauty salons, even grocery stores, and family gatherings. She looked at her white-blond hair and pale eyelashes.

She was still diligent with sunscreen, an old habit. First, she hydrated her skin, so the makeup would glide on. She applied her professional makeup expertly over her pale face, first her Marc Jacobs Marvelous Mousse primer foundation. She liked Flower Glisten in pearl shimmer for her fair skin. A flesh colored liner on the inner rim of her eyes made the eyes look larger, wider awake and the whole face fresher. Her eyelashes were wispy and pale without mascara. She applied nude smoky eye mascara for daytime. She layered shades of beige and brown shadows to build intensity. Lip liner applied correctly made lips seem fuller, even younger. Her new

Almost Pink gloss flattered all skin tones. She did this makeup routine every morning, even though she hadn't gone out of her house for the past eight months. Her honey colored eyes were thoughtful. She glanced at her right hand. If only a little makeup could conceal THAT deformity. She took an inappropriate amount of time with her hair, brushing it out and letting it fall to her shoulders, straight as a pin.

Fifty minutes putting on makeup, her own stalling tactic and she knew it. But she also was trying to feel good about herself. She needed to improve her self-image. She'd been damaged. She knew all the tricks to prevent the inevitable. Her stomach cramped with anxiety. *But this perfect makeup job isn't to be left inside this house. It would feel heavenly to get out of here, after David tossed and turned all night. It's true I don't have a great deal to do any morning after getting my makeup on. Go, go out* she tried to convince herself. *Even Aunt Bernice has told me to get in the car and drive. Take Trixie. Don't disappoint the poor dog. I've retreated inside myself much too long, but how do I get out? I feel broken inside and out.*

It was a beautiful day, but she pulled on a cream-colored glove over her thumb and index finger of her right hand. The other three fingers of the cotton glove flopped emptily. She remembered David's words as he pleaded, "Take a chance Diane. You were the center of attention. How can you shut yourself up and throw away the key to your life? Get out of your own jail. Face that door. It's not locked. Go through the door."

I've been such a burden to David. He's so stressed at work that he's not sleeping well, and he's got me to worry about. But how can I help him? I should make his life easier for him. If I could go out more than just our secluded deck, maybe get in the car, go somewhere. She put on sunglasses and straw hat to protect her face from wrinkles.

She remembered her therapist saying, "Face your fears."

She turned her stunning face towards the small animal curled on the bathroom rug. "Trixie, do you want to go out?"

The miniature dog quickly rose to her feet and scampered down the stairs. In the beginning when she tried to leave the comforts of her own home, Diane would throw up, running back to the kitchen sink. Good thing there was the garbage disposal. *Get a grip on this.* Deeply and achingly she was sorry for herself. Never had she felt so pitiably lonely.

My therapist said, "Take a deep breath. Count to five. Bring out your courage. You had courage to step on that runway stage. You worked at it. You did it before. You can do it again."

I was a model, but who am I now? She willed her feet to move, then Diane followed the schnauzer down the stairs and to the garage door. *I'm not staying in this house one more day. I need to quit focusing on what I lost and concentrate on what I have left. I've tried to be invisible long enough.* She opened the kitchen door to the garage. "Trixie, do you want to come?"

She and the little dog walked to her car. She opened the door. Trixie hopped up onto the seat. Diane got in. She'd probably sat in her car at least once a week for the past three months. Slowly, she reached her good hand up to the automatic garage door opener. She'd done this step before, but only a couple times. She hesitated with panic but pushed the button. The large overhead door rose. Holding the key between her thumb and finger, she started the Escalade. David used her car occasionally and had the gas tank filled. *Thank God for David. I couldn't possibly go to a gas station.* Diane breathed deeply, regularly, from her solar plexus. It worked. Slowly the terror ebbed. Taking hold of the steering wheel in a death grip with her thumb and finger, she said to Trixie, "We're in this together. Wish us luck."

She placed her left hand on the steering wheel naturally. She put the car into reverse, took a deep breath as if she were about to plunge into deep water, and backed out slowly. "Let's try a ride again." She spoke softly to Trixie as the dog stood on the seat beside her.

It was a perfect day, sunny, warming up. Ever so slowly, she edged the car down the seventy-foot black top driveway, looking right, left, and the opposite side of their quiet tree-lined street.

Then four doors to the south, someone stepped out her front door. Diane hit the break and ducked her head. She watched the woman put a letter in her mailbox, then turn and go back inside like it was no big deal.

My therapist said, "Push yourself. You can do this." *I need to take my life back.*

With her heart racing and sweat forming across her upper lip, she pressed the garage door button and watched the big overhead door slowly lower. She wanted to run back under, back inside to safety, back into David's arms. *He's not home. You can do this.* As the garage door closed, Diane scanned the street and homes again. No one. She let out the breath she'd been holding. Then looked at their perfect lawn and privet hedge, with bark mulched flower beds where roses obediently bloomed thanks to their landscaper. She eased out of their driveway. Steering with her good hand and lowering the damaged one, she slowly backed into the street. *They can't see my hand down here on my lap. I'm well groomed, neatly dressed, and my mind is as organized as my garden.* The narrow street was sunny and quiet. The maple trees whispered.

Glancing in the rearview mirror, she put the car into drive and edged forward. Her whole frame shook with anxiety at the very thought that someone might see her. She turned her slender neck side to side to watch for people. It was quiet, no one walking, a car drove carefully down the center of the road between a couple parked vehicles. The driver too busy to look at her. She inched forward into a sleepy, tidy, and affluent neighborhood with lots of young families. Her gaze was steady, her left hand firmly on the wheel and her right firmly on her lap.

A bend in the quiet tree-shaded street soon hid her two-story home. She headed south to sneak out of her subdivision. Soon she turned off her street. She avoided the small shops and cafés of the downtown area, making the car go past houses with the same cookie-cutter design. *I'm afraid to keep driving, but now more afraid to turn around.* The body of the car surrounding her, protecting her from people looking, seeing her flaws. Somehow, she made it out of town. The houses got farther apart. Then there were fields between the homes. Driving forward, she drifted over the long white concrete ribbon. The freeway shrank down to a country road. She kept driving further into the deep green of the countryside. The ride through the sunny farmland was peaceful with a few wildflowers on both sides of the country road.

Diane felt exhilarated, giddy freedom in the car. With sweat beading across her forehead, she glanced at the car's temperature gage, seventy-four degrees outside. She pressed buttons to lower the windows slightly, enjoying the warm summer breeze. She took off her straw hat, freeing her blond mane to feel the wind through her hair.

She kept her remaining two gloved fingers curled inside her long sleeve, and watched the traffic, what there was of it that far out of town. It was a quiet road with only an occasional car passing by. The country terrain was green grass sloped ditches with green corn or soybean fields and occasionally a pasture. A herd of cows didn't even look up as she drove past.

Diane realized she and David had driven this country road when they went out to Northern University to see Annie. Diane and Annie, David's niece, were close, so when Annie went off to DeKalb to college, her aunt and uncle had driven out to see her once a month to take her out for a meal at a nice restaurant. Diane's mind drifted to the long-ago fun times riding through farm country on their way to visit his niece.

There wasn't anything prettier than farm fields in July. *Don't stop. You can do this.* Trixie watched out the side window entranced by the motion of the car. Here in the country, the fields were comforting with patches of woods or a farm placed here and there. Suddenly a speed sign for twenty-five miles per hour warned her, she was nearing a town. Someone was mowing their lawn. *I can't stop.* It was such a small town. She made it right through, then the peace of the country again. She sighed with relief.

Only a mile or two past the tiny town, the small dog whined.

Diane's eyes panicked. "You have to go <u>now</u>? Oh no Trixie, we can't get out here." *But it's too far to make her wait until we get home.*

Diane slowed down at a large metal white mailbox. Hand painted in black was the name 'Eisenberg.' No vehicles of any kind in the wide gravel driveway. Drawn by something beyond her control, she flipped on the right turn signal and turned into the driveway. The first few feet were black top, but it changed into a gravel driveway. The tires scratched over loose stones.

In the car, the dog whined again. She switched off the ignition and looked around carefully. No one, so she timidly opened her driver's door. Trixie hopped across her lap. The small dog squatted as soon as she leapt from the car.

Diane looked around everywhere to make sure there was no one present. Slowly she emerged from the car. She pulled on her white sun hat to protect her face from the Illinois sun. Then together they stepped across the gravel drive that led up to a house. Diane's shoes crunched across the gravel as the tiny dog noiselessly trotted by her side. Huge oaks and maples surrounded the farmhouse. The home had an old lived-in look. The front seemed to be in constant shade with nondescript windows. The house was set back with a commanding view of its surroundings, outbuildings of sheds, red barn clad in weather-beaten shingles and two silos were circling the driveway. A red two-car garage was located about twenty feet from the two-story brick house. No sidewalks. Some wild geraniums grew beside the garage. A gentle breeze brushed her long blond hair across the right side of her face. The sky was an intense blue. The air was warm and clear. The country greenery was beautiful. There were so many shades of green. Some were almost a deep velvet, others so light, they verged on yellow. She had been cooped up inside her house way too long. She took pleasure in the distance she had covered. She had left the rush of modern life behind and entered an untouched world. The feeling of freedom was so exhilarating, she had to smile.

Diane stood for a few moments staring at the house. It wasn't the thick lush manicured lawns of the city. Instead it was thin weeds and crabgrass. It looked green from a distance, but up close the uneven lawn was pitted. The overgrown lawn gradually turning into a hayfield. She waded through the ankle-high grass.

Tall bushes shrouded a shadowy sagging front porch. The old red brick of the walls looked eminently picturesque. It looked poetic and peaceful in the sunlight. She breathed in the scent of dirt, grass, and sun. Yes, the smell of sun where she was soothed. She felt the sweet-smelling summer air scented with freshness that only the country could give.

A small porch led to the front door. She didn't even try the weather-worn door, because she really didn't want to see anyone or go inside. The only sound was some birds in the clumps of oaks and maples. For a long time, she stood there, content to take in the scene, but gradually the spirited birds beckoned her towards the trees. As she drew near, crows scattered from the trees with a clatter of wings. *Such freedom*, she thought. The open land thrilled her. Trixie trotted beside her. The moment they rounded the corner of the house, the yard opened up before Diane's eyes.

Chapter 35

COUNTRY ROAD

Murphy Hartman had been farming his whole life. He took over his dad's two-hundred-acre farm. He'd seen some strange things happen in his fields, flooded areas where the crops died out or higher ground where the sun had baked his crops, but never had the end of his driveway flooded like this. Sometimes the ditch by the road would fill with water, but this spring was the highest he'd ever seen the water get. And the really strange thing about it was how the water only filled up on the one side of his driveway. He gave the water several weeks' time to seep away like it always had in the past, but really it just seemed to be getting worse. He got onto his lawn tractor and drove down to the road. After parking at the end of his double-wide gravel-driveway, he got a clear view of the high water over the west end of the culvert. He walked to the other side of his driveway. Nothing but a trickle of mud and water. With his t-shirt straining against the spare tire around his waist, he bent down to look. Whiff, what a stench. No way could he reach the middle to pull out whatever had crawled in there to die.

He called the highway department. They sent out someone to look at the problem. Once they discovered the body, they turned the scene over to the county police.

Late Saturday morning Sergeant Dodson called Detective Waller and Garcia's vehicle. "They've got a Jane Doe at the county morgue that could be your vic. Description might fit your missing woman.

Get over there pronto."

Garcia placed his third cup of coffee, after his night out with Melissa, into the cup holder of their car because he didn't want it spilling on him as they quickly drove over to the morgue.

Dr. Somerfield with white streaks growing in his hair, was waving his arm in the air as he talked. "This was a female, twenty-five to thirty years of age, approximately five three to five four in height. I examined the victim's clothing prior to removing it from the body. None of her clothing was tailor made. In other words, all of it was junk. You could purchase it anywhere, Walmart maybe."

Garcia put a hand over his eyes, pressed his finger to one temple and his thumb to the other and sighed. "Same age as Mrs. Fazzino."

Detective Waller grimaced as she stared at the body. "This looks like it's been dead quite a while."

Somerfield nodded as he said, "You're right. I estimate one to three months."

An audible sigh escaped from Garcia as relief flooded his face. "Been dead too long to be our gal."

Sarcastically Waller said, "If it had been her, it would have been case closed, however we've still got work to do."

"Could you identify this one?" asked Garcia.

"Water causes wrinkling on the skin. Relatives will not be able to identify her because the skin was altered so much. However, we got lucky because there was a backpack with the girl's body with an ID. We even found fingerprints inside the flap on the backpack."

Somerfield looked down at his iPad notes. "They match a missing twenty-five-year-old girl, Tammy Burton from Iowa. Her parents thought she was still at college in New York, so they didn't report her missing for a couple weeks. The detectives on the case were blaming her abusive boyfriend for her disappearance, however her roommate said she was going home to Iowa."

"The State Police lab is sure it's this missing girl?" Garcia scratched at his mustache.

"Identification of the remains was positively established through DNA-PRINT which was a paternity-type testing of her hair and bone which established she is related to the Iowa parents." He showed them the screen of lab results. "Tammy's boyfriend recognized a picture of the necklace she was wearing around her neck because he gave it to her last Christmas. Their report shows they questioned the boyfriend till they were all blue in the face. What they didn't understand was why the roommate would stick up for the boyfriend."

Waller speculated, "Maybe the roommate really believed she went home."

"Now they believe her friends since she showed up in Illinois." Somerfield said.

"When was the last time she was seen alive?" Waller sounded skeptical as she stepped around the table.

Somerfield looked back at the body as he said, "The roommate told us she saw her six weeks ago. The boyfriend said, she failed a class and was going home to tell her parents in person that she wanted to drop out of school."

Waller sucked a deep breath of air in, then asked, "Was she sexually violated?"

Somerfield grunted. "No semen, however, it's possible animals and insects got to it." They heard the doctor's voice rising as he added, "The crime was done too long ago to be sure."

"Finally, there's closure for her family," Garcia said sincerely.

"Both shoes were found in the culvert, but apparently one shoe had come off her foot somehow. The sock was starting to decompose," the coroner said with dismay. "Tammy's blood pooled in her lower extremities, her legs, so in my estimation, she was standing or sitting when she died. She was found lying inside a culvert, so she didn't die in there."

"What could have happened?" Garcia wanted to know.

Somerfield said, "Her cell phone was still in the back pocket of her jeans, so it doesn't appear to be a robbery."

"How was she killed?" asked Waller.

"Tammy Burton's autopsy showed her windpipe had been severed. The blood loss would have been enough with that kind of injury to cause death. There was very little blood in the culvert, so she was killed somewhere else. Cause of death was stabbing wounds from a large, possibly a hunting knife. In Ms. Burton's stabbing there were multiple wounds to the stomach and arms."

"Well, you can also see the personality of the offender at crime scenes," stated Waller. "For example, when you see a facial assault on a victim, most of the time, it's personal. The murderer is somebody who knows the victim and is mad as Hell at them."

"By hiding this body in a culvert, and the missing fingers, they indicate murder by stabbing," said Somerfield.

Waller gulped air. "Missing fingers?"

Waller and Garcia exchanged a confused look.

"After examining the bones of the hands, we could tell, the female fingers were not gnawed off by animals. They were all straight cuts. The bones were sliced off smooth. Possibly sword, machete, ax, strong hunting knife or a cleaver was used to cut the women's fingers off."

"That's really strange," said Garcia.

"However, there was a bloody shirt in the culvert with her. The blood matches the victim, but it's a man's shirt. It's possible she owned a man's shirt, so we tested the DNA on the inside of the shirt to see if anyone else wore it."

"Could be the boyfriend and then we bring him in for questioning," Waller said.

"It didn't match her boyfriend," Dr. Somerfield said. "But we got lucky. We got a DNA match from an Army data base on the shirt that was found with her body. The shirt was worn by a Thad Eisenberg, age thirty-one."

"It's a strange, interesting case but this obviously isn't our missing woman. I'll call it into Dodson." Waller phoned their supervisor and filled him in on Somerfield's findings about Tammy Burton, the woman's body found in the culvert and explained she had been dead too long to be Carolyn Fazzino.

Only to be told, "We're shorthanded. There's been an accident with injuries out on 390, so I want you two to bring the Eisenberg man in for questioning."

Soon Garcia and Waller were driving their police cruiser west on Route 38, siren yelping and emergency lights flashing. Garcia kept one eye on the road and one eye on the computer screen between them on the dash. The radar equipment was showing the way out to the Eisenberg home. Waller sitting in the passenger seat ripped open a KitKat bar as she pressed the button to close her window trying to close out some of the siren noise. Loudly she asked her partner, "Is there something between you and that suspect, Tomlin, I should know about?"

Garcia tried to look shocked, but he nervously fingered his mustache instead and said nothing.

Waller continued. "You're going out with her, you fool. She could be messed up in this disappearance."

"She didn't do it." He kept his eyes on the road as they sped ahead.

Waller's tone was sarcastic, as she said, "Oh, now you know who did it."

"No, but she didn't."

"It's none of my business who you see until she's part of this case." She momentarily hesitated. "Well, I won't say anything, if you won't talk about me and the dentist."

"Doctor Carter? I didn't see that coming."

"Yeah, the eye-candy with the long elegant fingers. However just to let you know, she called me, and it wasn't about this case." She tore a little more of the wrapper, exposing more of the chocolate candy. "You know that I like professional women, don't you?" She took a bite of the candy bar in her hand.

Garcia shot her a glance as Waller smiled.

Chapter 36

EISENBERG HOME

SATURDAY MORNING

Detective Garcia slowed their vehicle and pulled onto the farm driveway. They parked next to a white Cadillac Escalade. The 1920's brick house was heavily shaded with trees. Four wooden steps led up to a small screened in porch. No doorbell, so Waller knocked. When there was no answer, she banged on the door louder.

With a puzzled look on his face, Garcia said, "If that's his car, he ought to be home."

"Let's run the plates to make sure." Waller quickly returned to their car with Garcia following close behind.

After a quick call into the precinct, they learned the white Escalade belonged to a Diane Dodson.

Waller's next call was to their Sargent. "We're here at the Eisenberg farm. No answer at the door, however there's a Cadillac Escalade here registered to your wife."

"That's impossible. Diane won't leave the house." David tried his wife's cell phone. It went to voice mail. Then he dialed their home number. It also went to their answering machine. He was back on the phone with Waller. "Find her," he yelled. Then in a rush he shouted, "Diane's car is at the home of a possible killer. Since we've got his clothing and DNA found with a dead woman, I'll get you a search warrant for that house."

"Waller quickly added, "There's a barn and garage too."

"I'll request a subpoena for the whole damn farm." Dodson called a judge himself and texted the search warrant to his detectives. Unable to sit in his office, he left the precinct house. With the siren blaring, he urgently sped home hoping to find his wife and thinking, *Diane is so fragile.*

⸺⸺●((●))●⸺⸺

Garcia discovered the detached two-car garage was unlocked out there in the country. He raised the door. No vehicles, spotless, no leaves in the corners like his garage at home. The workbench on the right side was completely cleared. Tools, rakes, and shovels all hung carefully on the back wall. There he found a house key hanging on a nail. Waller was circling the house when Garcia yelled to his partner, "Think I've got our key."

Wearing rubber gloves, he opened a screen door. They both stepped into a small porch with its collection of coats on pegs over a long wooden bench and boots lined up perfectly. Waller's eyes scanned newspapers neatly stacked with their edges lined up. Inside were old rooms with yellowed flooring and tired appliances, but spotlessly clean, too clean for such a tired looking house. A polished Formica table sat in the middle of the kitchen but no dirty dishes in the sink. Not even a glass or cup. Dishes were stacked neatly in the cupboards. Rooster salt and pepper shakers sat on another shelf. The white and chrome gas stove gleamed. A couple jars of dried peanuts lined up like solders on one Formica countertop.

Built-in bookcases separated the dining room and living room. No books, but small figurines were evenly spaced on the shelves. Old-fashioned lamps, their shades aged a golden yellow and an outdated 1970s davenport and small end tables filled the living room. The only frills were the many framed photos setting on the end tables of a young man in his Army uniform, his face serious.

"These crocheted doilies on the arms of the chairs look like my grandparents' home," commented Waller.

A white tiled bathroom was scrubbed perfectly clean, like a hospital room, no dirt, too neat, too orderly. The scent of soap hung in the air. Detective Garcia said, "this place smells of window cleaner and bleach."

Waller had the feeling the person who lived here was addicted to neatness. "This house is obsessively clean!"

They climbed stairs to the second floor. One bedroom had an old flowered bedspread and matching curtains over the two windows, nothing out of place. They also looked in closets for Diane Dodson. Another bedroom had a cowboy printed blanket over a perfectly made bed. As Garcia looked at the tucked in sheets as tightly as a soldier's bunk, he commented, "He was in the military."

A clock radio with flip numbers sat on a polished bureau which showed its dark grained wood. Neat stacks of books and sharpened pencils were on the desk. His shoes were spotless in his closet, all facing forward, lined up perfectly right shoe next to its left shoe partner. Perhaps it was his army background, but this guy was obsessively compulsive. The room felt cold. Actually, the whole house had a cold sterile feel.

Even the basement had no clutter. One room of the basement had been painted gray, but the other cement walls were original cement gray. They found at least twenty bottles of peroxide, ammonia, and bleach lined up on the shelves.

"Strange. What's he running, a hospital?" asked Garcia. "This place is spotless."

"The trouble is, I don't have anything else to go on, just a bad feeling in my subconscious," commented Waller. "I can't ignore a bad feeling."

Chapter 37

SILVERADO TRUCK DRIVER

Route 53 and 390

The first sixty minutes after an injury are called the "golden hour" because more than seventy percent of all deaths occur within that time.

Soon there was the wail of sirens, the dizzying smell of spilled gasoline, with the thrum of traffic in the west bound lane. Black and whites surrounded the collision. A cop's stomach lurched, but he kept his breakfast in place as he looked into the 4x4 pickup. He quickly said into his cell phone, "Send an ambulance and cutting equipment."

The driver's door of the pickup truck was punched in twenty-nine inches in on the victim who was slouched over the console, a broken and pulpy mess. His body contorted into something less than human. Blood started to flow out his mouth and nose as he heard his mother's words, "You disgust me. Don't make me hurt you."

His head hung to the side as he thought, *Mother, you can't hurt me. Ya can't get out of the woods.*

An emergency medical technician tried the passenger door of the Silverado cab, but it was jammed. They call it the hot zone. It was decided to cut through the metal to take off the roof of the truck's cab to extricate the victim. The jaws of life arrived on the scene by a fire rescue truck. Firefighters stabilized the small truck by putting wooden blocks under the tires.

A fireman climbed into the back of the pickup. He wanted to calm and reassure his patient before the jarring noise of the hydraulic cutting tool started. The only way to get to the victim was through a small window behind the diver's head. A cut was made through the glass. The window was pried out the opening. The firefighter laid the glass in the bed of the truck and calmly said, "We're here with you." He reached his hands inside to feel the man's neck. "There is a pulse," he yelled to the other emergency personal. But he could see the victim's chest was in a vise-like grip between the seat and steering wheel.

The patient's breathing, shallow; his wheezing was loud from a fragment of rib bone which created a huge gash into his lung. He was fighting for air. Blood was filling his chest cavity. The firefighter said, "Stay with me."

They wanted to protect the purple, swollen face from any broken glass or metal pieces that could fly towards the victim during evacuation. From ground level a heavy-duty blanket was handed up to the Medic in the back of the pickup. It was difficult to get it through the small window opening. He asked the injured man to help pull it inside if he was able. But the victim's long fingers only made flickering movements.

The firefighter struggled, but finally got the entire blanket inside the cab. With only his arms reaching through the small window, he carefully shook it out enough to cover the injured bald head. The fireman firmly put his hands to the side of the victim's neck, so the patient didn't move in case there was a neck or spine injury. Other firemen hooked the jaws of life, spreaders to a portable generator. The grinding metal on metal drowned out the EMT's calming words as he said, "Easy, easy. We're going to get you out."

Finally, saws broke through the roof. Then they started on the steering wheel. Extraction seemed to take forever before the victim was pried out of his truck. The medical professional couldn't tell the victim's age. He checked vitals that were barely there as he said, "We're here with you."

One pupil was abnormally dilated. His chest sagged inward against his lungs.

The EMT started an IV and pumped him with seizure-stopping benzodiazepines. A tube was inserted into his trachea and air was forced into his lungs with a mechanical ventilator. The same voice full of authority said, "At least two or three ribs are broken. He can't breathe. Could be a punctured lung that's leaking air."

Quickly they had him on a stretcher and into the ambulance. An EMT worked on him as a cardiac arrest, all the way to Northwest Community Hospital. At the emergency entrance the victim's eyelids flicked slowly. Then the eyes had the stale look of death. An ER doctor grabbed electric defibrillator paddles and pressed them against the victim's chest. "Clear."

A quick jolt made the prone body jerk involuntarily. Something about his face changed, as if a curtain had been drawn across it. His mouth opened. The tracing on the monitor was still flat. "Again!"

His life did not pass easily from his body. But the results were the same. He was gone. Death was demeaning. His face in death had a loose amiable expression, in spite of the blood oozing out of his mouth.

One began to go through his pockets looking for an ID. Then a hand explored the dead man's wallet. They contacted the Cook County morgue and transported the body there.

Chapter 38

VINCE'S SEMI-TRUCK

Vince's semi ECHO truck topped a hill at a high rate of speed and began to swerve as he tried to comprehend the text message on his screen. The world exploded in sound; the side window shattered before him. He placed his hands on the dashboard to brace himself as the window came hurdling into the truck cab. He gave an involuntary yelp of fear. Splintered glass flew everywhere cutting Vince's cheeks like razor blades.

The semi spun wildly into a field as debris littered the road. Soon his eighteen-wheeler, with the hood bashed in, was parked three hundred yards off the road.

Vince felt as if it was raining inside the truck cab. Blood oozed from various places on his face, crawled down the corner of his mouth and glistened on his chin. He licked at something warm and sticky on his face. It tasted like iron and salt. *Blood*, he thought. He was aware of the pain in his head. He understood instinctively that the left side of his head was awash in shards of glass. For a moment, he tried to catch his breath. He tried to move his arms to reach for his face. Then his body felt strangely sluggish. The world seemed to grow almost pleasantly hushed.

A paramedic opened the driver's door and Vince sagged to his left. The medic caught him, then took his pulse. "Can you hear me?" shouted the paramedic, flashing a light in each eye. "Can you hear me?"

No response. The trauma to Vince's head was severe with jagged glass in his eyes and face. The EMT did not remove any glass for fear of causing further injury. Instead he carefully put an air mask over the bloody face and quickly slipped a breathing tube down the trachea of the injured patient. Then he placed his hand on Vince's arm in a reassuring jester. They used roller gauze to wrap around Vince's head gently covering both eyes with the sterile dressing. They looked for additional external bleeding, then for spinal injury. An IV was started. Soon someone was carefully lifting him gently. He knew he was being carried on a stretcher. The pilot with excitement in his voice asked if he had ever flown in a helicopter before, but Vince couldn't respond. Soon he could hear the whap-whap-whap of the helicopter rotors as they became magnified like the clapping of giant hands.

While flying they drew blood from Vince's right arm. Paramedics were concerned that his airway was open. The medical helicopter became blood, glass, cut-off clothes, and a ventilation bag. The suction tube was full of blood.

It seemed like minutes later paramedics were landing at Central DuPage Hospital. Vince was breathing in big gulps as they lifted him out of the helicopter. New hands, many new hands were on him. The hospital was all activity. He wanted it quiet. He wanted to sleep. He passed out again.

The doctor listened to the medic's report as he checked the patient's abdomen for internal bleeding. The EMT told the doctor about the two trucks, what kind they were, how they looked, that the other driver was entrapped and didn't make it. At the hospital Vince's paramedics disappeared.

A doctor was shining a tiny pencil-thin light, but Vince's one eye saw a torch. *What's happening?* A doctor asked him to follow his fingers back and forth. The doctors asked questions he couldn't answer and told him things he wouldn't remember. "What did you have for breakfast this morning? Do you know the day of the week? Do you know the date?" A nurse with a laptop was asking about health insurance, allergies and next of kin. He was rolled off the backboard.

Blinding lights, nurses, doctors, x-ray techs, surgeons, and cops trailed in asking questions. Clear bags with cord drawstrings were filled with his clothes, wallet, watch, rings, phone, belt, gold neck chain, and shoes. Forgetting that his wife was missing, he gasped, "Tell Carolyn, I, love her," as they wheeled him very fast.

"You can tell her that yourself," assured the nurse.

Vince was wheeled through a door off to surgery. Lights overhead seemed too bright. Fingers were pulling at his eyelids and a blindingly bright light appeared. He heard the hum of equipment. The pain in his head dulled and became distant with the morphine drip.

They cleared his throat of glass and elevated his jaw because there was a problem breathing. He missed the x-ray machines and of course the operating room as they tried to save his eyes. Because of the large amount of bleeding, Vince was given two units of O negative blood and plasma products through an IV, then they cross matched four more. Shock made his skin look pale, bluish, and clammy.

⸺⸻«◊»⸻⸺

Melissa turned her iPhone on at work in the Stradford mall. The news media announced, "Semi-trailer crashes on Elgin-O'Hare at approximately eight forty this morning. The Addison Police department and Addison Fire Protection District responded to the ramp off 390 and 53 (Rohlwing Road) to investigate a motor vehicle crash involving a semi-truck and a Silverado pickup truck. An ECHO Global Logistics truck was traveling east on the Elgin/O'Hare when it struck a vehicle traveling north on Rohlwing Road. The driver of the pick-up truck was pronounced dead on arrival at Northwest Community Hospital in Schaumburg. The ECHO driver was transported to Central DuPage Hospital where he is in critical condition. We cannot disclose the victim's names at this time. The Addison Police Department continues to investigate the cause of the motor vehicle crash, but a spokesman from the department said, "Clues indicate it was caused by a driver texting."

Melissa thought *Carolyn's husband, Vince works for ECHO Logistics. But they have many drivers. I hope it's not him. I'll call Carlos as soon as I get home to see if he knows anything about this accident.*

————————⊲⟨◉⟩⊳————————

What neither victim saw was all the uniformed personnel, the Crime-Scene Division that went to their accident. Because there was a death, there was an investigative team. One of the cops shook a can of spray paint in his hand. He drew white paint lines around everything in the highway, a man's shoe, tires, and debris. They closed off the road to study the paint lines to re-create the scene.

Departmental photographers mulled around the wrecks, taking pictures from every angle. Some photos were taken at ground level. A drone was used to take aerial shots to show location of the vehicles. Several overlapping photographs were made. Totally accurate photography and measurements were critical. These professionals would determine fault.

Before entering either vehicle, vacuum sweepings were taken to minimize the likelihood of contaminating the vehicle with foreign mater, possibly brought in by the investigator. Then the vehicles were searched.

A small quantity of dried blood was found between the passenger's seat cushion and the seat back of the pickup truck. The investigator submitted the seat and back cushion with the driver's blood samples. The results indicated the blood could not have come from the driver and it wasn't animal. Then whose blood? They started checking nation-wide data bases.

Investigators found a knife on the floor of the pick-up truck. A cop wearing latex gloves, used only his fingertips to pick up the knife, holding it by the edges of the knife high up near the handle because that area is too small to hold prints. It was a steel Banshee knife, weighing 3.97 ounces. The blade was three and a half inches long. The closed handle measured four and five-eighths inches. Overall length was seven and three quarters inches, with "Guidesman" written on the blade. The knife had a safety lock with a spring speed opening. During impact it slid forward, out from under the truck seat. As the investigator put it in a plastic bag, he asked, "What's he doing with a knife like this?"

The older policeman with graying hair at his temples suggested, "Well, he was dressed like a farmer. Maybe farmers use knives for something, like cutting rope."

"He's a farmer, not a cowboy. But would he need such a large knife?" was the response as they listed all items on their reports.

A hydraulic lift was used to examine the undercarriage of both trucks. Weeds were found on the underside of his pickup truck. A forensic examination revealed small plant material like seeds, leaves, pigweed pollen and ragweed pollen. But nothing out of the ordinary; it was his farm vehicle.

Chapter 39

FREAKY FARM

Diane found a wild over-grown rose and herb garden behind the house. A rutted farm lane crept through a few straggling bushes. She felt carefree, like a kid. She loved the solitude, tranquil, blue sky, and isolated feeling. Tiny green apples the size of mothballs filled the apple trees. She walked through the orchard, just following the quiet country lane to wherever it took her. Her footsteps were quieted by the softness of the grass and weeds. Wild green swaying grass and white wildflowers grew in knots along the lane. It was silly, she knew it, but she felt freedom, so started swinging her hips as she took a path which was nothing but dry, trampled earth, cut by two sets of tire tracks.

The lane was hugged closely on both sides by shrubs and trees which Trixie sniffed. Keeping close to the low line of shrubs, she felt safe from the view of passing cars. A red winged black bird sang happily in a nearby tree. Sun filtered through a canopy of trees. Streams of light and shadows dappled and danced across the woodland floor on both sides of the lane. A few green leaves ruffled a little. Spots of gold shimmered through and waved. Shadows fell across the grassy ground. She enjoyed the sweet scent of this summer day as a few crickets chirped. This far from the house, there wasn't a sign of humans anywhere. She walked noiselessly along as the vegetation thickened on both sides of the trail. Trees on each side gave Diane the feeling she was walking through a tunnel in the

woods. The brush seemed to be an impenetrable tangle of bram-
bles. There was the far off sound of wind in the treetops. Heavy vegetation of vines, small saplings and low tree branches covered the
woods floor. It was thick underbrush, with some trampled weeds.
The quiet stillness enticed her to take a few steps off the path and
into the woods.

It's as if one entered the dark forest of a fairytale. There she saw
a bush of beautiful red raspberries and realized she'd only had coffee so far today. *It must be past lunch time. I'm hungry. They should
be washed, but out here in the wild, no one sprays chemicals.* She
removed her sunglasses inside the thick trees to better see the berries. She stepped further into the woods to pick one and popped
it into her mouth. Exquisite. Then she picked one more and held
out her left hand with a berry for Trixie. The dog's soft little doggy
goatee brushed Diane's palm, tickled her hand as Trixie smelled the
berry, but the dog refused.

"Fruit is not your thing. You don't know what you're missing."
Diane picked and ate more. The bush was loaded with berries.
For some reason, the berries on the other side of the bush looked
plumper, so she lifted one knee high over the weeds. *Why did I wear
white jeans?* She maneuvered through the bushes and took hold of
each berry with fingertips so gentle, not a single one was bruised.
That's when she saw the bent-over grassy weeds. *Someone has
been here,* she thought with a start. *Probably picking berries before
us.* She picked a few more of the juicy morsels. *Could I take a few
home for David, but what do I put them in? The juicy berries would
stain my pockets or straw hat if I used that to collect the berries.*

She moved from bush to bush picking and eating more berries. The trees grew denser. Trixie followed her as she stepped over
a low pile of decaying logs. Though it was midday, the sun shone
bright and the air was a summery seventy-six degrees out on the
lane, here in the forest the day had darkened to a twilight gloom.
Trees suddenly so dense, it seemed dusk had instantly fallen. Tree
branches above gave off gloomy shadows. The air was close and
windless. The silence hung among the trees like a dark cloud. She

felt as if these trees had trapped years of dankness where any-thing could be incubating, waiting. With her adrenaline spiking, she stared into the gloom of the thick vegetation.

By now insects had caught her scent and were swarming, greedy for blood. Diane was grateful she'd chosen to wear long pants and a long-sleeved top that morning. Her unprotected face was turning into a blackfly feeding station. Birds stopped singing. The quietness engulfed her. Her body stiffened. She wanted out. Even though the berries tasted wonderful and she was hungry, she turned to leave, to retrace her steps back to the lane.

Suddenly the little dog was barking insistently. Diane immedi-ately thought of wild animals. "Trixie come here. Come on baby. Don't you start tangling with anything out here." *I should get her back to the car.* Obediently the dog stopped in her tracks. Her bark-ing changed to a low growl.

Strange, she thought. *This gives me the creeps.* She shuddered, one of those shivers that come over you when you're not even cold, but you can't stop yourself. Could something be hiding in the thickets? Her palms were sweating. She quickly wiped her hands on her pants. It was so overgrown with natural camouflage. Anything could blend in perfectly against a background of dry grass and dead leaves on the wooded ground. Then the small dog was sniffing at a dead snake covered in flies. Diane became suspicious of things around her. Diane's eyes searched the ground for more snakes lurk-ing, waiting to slither out. Not finding any, she stepped forward to pick up her small dog. She sensed a breath on the back of her neck. Were there invisible footsteps sneaking up behind her? Quickly she turned to look. She saw the flicker of leaves that could be the wind or someone. *Are demons lurking nearby?* Diane felt a strange lurch of doom, every instinct said, 'get out.' *Could this place be haunted?* Her legs were shaking, and her heart beating so hard she felt it inside her throat. She couldn't give in. *No, face your fears,* she told herself.

She peered into the gloom staring at the shadows so long her vision blurred. She blinked her eyes to clear them. Then she saw a narrow cutting in the thicket, no more than a thinning, really. Diane looked in the direction Trixie faced growling and saw something dark through the underbrush, low like piles of dirt. *But what would be digging out here?* She could smell the earth in the air. She looked around with a great deal of curiosity and some horror at the gloom and despair of the place.

Diane had to make herself move. She carefully stepped through knee high weeds around bushes, then quietly climbed over a small pile of packed dirt. A deep hole was revealed on the other side of the dirt mound. She saw that piles of excavated earth ringed the perimeter of a trench, extending over seven feet across. The sides seemed to plunge downward. Her mind was racing, *why would anyone dig way out here? Maybe there are wild animals? Would bears dig like this?*

She thought she could smell urine. A sense of dread and bile rushed up her throat. *I don't want to look.* But something was drawing her forward. Diane with her eyes wide in horror looked deeper into the pit.

A figure was lying weak on the dirt floor in that airless thickness, trapped. It was filthy with mud-covered jeans and t-shirt. Diane could smell the fear, the scent of an animal awaiting slaughter and other bodily functions coming from the dirt hole. The figure's brown hair was a dirty tangled mass. The body's profile was hollow, shadows hung beneath her eyes, dark as bruises. A film of sweat and dirt covered every inch of her skin. *Is she dead?*

"Are you ok?" Nothing, so Diane yelled louder, "Hey, wake up." With urgency she reached her good hand into her bag for her smart phone. She dialed 9-1-1.

Dispatch received the initial telephoned complaint. "Sycamore emergency police."

Diane screamed at the top of her lungs, "Help, Help me!" She heard her shrieks but didn't recognize her own voice.

"Where are you?" asked a calm voice from the phone.

"Help. I'm in the woods. There's someone here," she screamed. The dirty body moved slightly. Misquotes were epoxied by sweat to her bare skin which left welts on her arms, neck, and face.

"Are you ok?" Diane yelled down. It was a dumb question; of course, she wasn't alright. "Who are you?"

A dirty arm moved slightly. The body slowly turned its head to look upward. Her eyes too filled with fear and dehydration, to cry. Insects swirled and buzzed her face. She gave a painful gasp of relief. She opened her cracked and sore lips to talk, but nothing came out. Then tried to get up, but she looked weaker than a baby bird.

Diane knelt on the ground and extended her good hand to the girl. She *keeps staring at me, but does she see me?*

On the other end of the phone, the emergency operator heard a female voice asking, 'are you, all right?' But she couldn't hear the answer. She was trained to respond calmly in emergency situations, so she held on. Not hearing anything more, she asked, "Who is this? Do you need an ambulance?"

Diane couldn't reach the person, so quickly laid her lean almost six-foot body across the ground to get lower and extended her hand again. Then, Diane remembered her phone, she dropped in the dirt. She quickly reached for it. Her voice sounded urgent, "There's someone here in the woods in a hole. I can't get her out. Send someone, yes an ambulance."

"Is anyone injured?"

"I can't tell but send paramedics."

"What is your address?"

"I don't know where I am." Diane was panicking.

"We can track your phone. Leave it on," instructed the emergency personnel.

The figure below ground only got out a choked whisper that didn't sound like words at all. "A, Angel."

Diane heard the sound and turned back to the girl below ground. "I've called for help. The police are on their way."

The figure incessantly licked her lips like they were cotton, then her shallow voice emerged asking, "Am, I, in Heaven?" Her body had turned to a piece of brick that was cold, heavy, wet, and aching. "Please help me before he comes back." She tried to raise herself up on her elbows, which acted like spaghetti arms.

Diane stood to look around for a branch or stick that could help, hoping a ladder would magically arrive.

Slowly the young woman in the pit asked, "Ar, Are you an angel?"

Diane realized; the dirty figure was looking at her as the sun shone off her long straight blond hair. Whoever this was, thought she was an angel in white, beautiful, standing there looking down at her.

"Oh Heavens no. You must be delirious. I'm not perfect."

The victim's throat sounded like a dry pipe. "Take me to heaven, away from this nightmare, this Hellhole." The hollowed eyed victim was trying to get to her knees.

"Can you jump to reach my hand?"

But the victim had no energy.

Diane needed her husband, Sergeant Dodson. She had to tell him everything, so she shouted into her phone. "I'm putting you on hold. I have to make another call." She dialed David's number.

Sergeant David Dodson was standing in his own empty garage, barely able to comprehend that his wife's car wasn't parked there. He answered his cell phone on the first ring. Seeing her name pop up on his screen, he shouted, "Where are you?"

Rapidly she fired, "I'm at a farm."

He was still shouting, "Are you alright?"

"Yes. Yes, I'm fine, but there's a woman in the woods."

"What? What farm?" he shouted. "Are you sure you're alright?"

Excitedly she tried to explain, then David said he would be there. The minute she pressed the disconnect button, she knew people were coming. They would see her hand, her mutilated fingers. She began to pant. She fought back the panic even as her brain was yelling at her to hide because people were coming. Things were lighter and darker, back and forth. Her heart was racing. *I must run. I must hide.* Then there were some minutes she didn't remember well because the weeds and trees were tipping and spinning out of control. Diane wobbled and reached for a pile of dirt that was coming up close to her. But when she moved it was only to put her left hand out to steady herself against the loose dirt. She held on, trying to catch her breath. She strained to hear something other than the blood rushing through her ears.

Her ears attuned to the slightest sound, heard the distant wail of a siren. *They're coming. They'll see me.* With her heart pounding, she plunged the deformed hand into her jeans pocket. *Be logical.* For just a second, she closed her eyes. She concentrated on controlling the air going in and out of her lungs. Diane stumbled forward, back through the trampled weeds to the woods edge. The sunlight was so bright. She had to cover her face for a moment just to get her bearings, just as the ambulance turned onto the lane. She waved her left arm and phone frantically over her head to direct the police. Diane could feel the perspiration on her forehead. *Please David be the first one here. Help me.*

But it wasn't her husband. Dispatch had put out an all alert bulletin explaining a woman had called in an emergency, saying she had someone who needed an ambulance immediately. A tracking device gave the location of a Thad Eisenberg's home.

Detective Waller and Garcia were just exiting the old farmhouse. They were walking across the driveway to look through the barn next when they heard the radio dispatch report crackling out police calls.

Dispatch asked if they were near anyone within listening range.

"We're clear," Waller said into the mike.

Dispatch said, "We've had a request for an ambulance for a female victim." She gave the country location.

"We're at the address. Where's the emergency?" Waller yelled into the radio mike. Then she looked at her partner, and slowly said into the mike, "Is it a DOA?"

"Unknown at this time," was the fearful answer. "Is there a woods nearby?" the dispatch woman asked.

Both detectives were turning their heads, then Waller pointed across a field. "There."

Garcia added, "I saw a lane off the road that heads back in that direction."

"We'll take the car down there," Waller demanded as she got into the front seat.

Garcia pulled his driver's door closed and started the engine. They backed out onto the country road and turned down the farm lane. Approximately a quarter mile down the lane they could see a thin blond woman frantically waving her arm. Even though Garcia had never met her, he knew this was an ex-model and he recognized her as the beautiful woman in the photo on their sergeant's desk.

"That's Mrs. Dodson."

Right behind them came an ambulance team with their tubes, monitors and bottles of IV fluid.

Diane turned her back on them to return to the person in the hole. More police cars were arriving.

Garcia parked and quickly he and Waller walked into the woods to follow Diane who was frantically pointing. Then they saw the woman at the bottom of the hole. Waller yelled to a paramedic to hurry. Once the EMT looked down into the hole, he quickly asked for a confined space rescue technician. Static crackled from a paramedic's walkie-talkie. Cable was released from the back of the fire truck. Another fireman dropped the other end of the strong rope over the side of the pit. A specially trained firefighter scaled down into the deep ditch in seconds. The technician in the pit examined the victim. Then yelled up to his coworkers, "She's alive."

Everyone was moving so fast, so efficiently. A nylon sling harness was put around the body. Then he attached himself to the patient. An auger lifted them both up.

Garcia standing at the top of the pit, couldn't contain his excitement. "Oh my God, that's our missing woman! She's been found alive. I've completed my first kidnapping case." He could hear his voice climb an octave with emotion as he took a step back to allow the paramedics to haul her up.

Detective Waller looked upward and in a proud tone said, "Thank you, Jesus. I haven't lost. We can become heroes of the week solving this case already."

Under his breath, Garcia mumbled to his partner, "We didn't find her. Our sergeants' wife found her."

The victim was put on a stretcher, then lifted into the back of the EMT truck. A paramedic stuck her arm with a syringe and attached an IV to give her nourishment.

Someone yelled, "You really want to step on it."

Ambulance doors slammed. A five by ten rolling memorial to the abruptly and tragically injured pierced the air with a long loud burst of siren. Lights flashed as it sped over the dirt terrain, then turned left at the blacktop road towards the nearest hospital.

It seemed to Diane they were off at a speed close to a hundred miles an hour. Diane stood in the weeds, straining to follow their progress down the road first with her eyes and then with her ears as the ambulance disappeared out of sight. Within minutes quiet reclaimed the peaceful farm. And Diane was aware of her heart rapidly beating.

David Dodson saw his wife's car in the driveway. The farmhouse looked to be approximately a quarter mile away from the woods. Several police cars were parked askew a hundred yards from the house. He saw light bars strobing in the sunshine from two police cruisers bookending a farm lane, an ambulance and a windowless truck with big blue letters ILLINOIS POLICE MOBILE UNIT printed on the side and a county sheriff vehicle parked on the farm road. He drove down the lane quickly, dust billowing behind his tires. David found his wife standing still, in a shaft of golden light. He pulled his vehicle to a stop between two police cars. As he got out of his car, he surveyed the many official looking uniforms.

A state trooper greeted him and said, "A woman, Diane Dodson, out for a walk in the woods, stumbled across a large tomb. They hauled out that missing Fazzino woman, breathing, but dehydrated. They're taking her to Central DuPage Hospital."

David was pie-eyed as he stared at his wife at the edge of the woods. He kept looking at her. He couldn't believe she had left the house! And driven an hour out of town. She had done it, but how? He kept staring at her as if trying to see what she was really thinking. Trixie barked, ran in circles and wagged her tail as David Dodson approached his wife. He unconsciously glanced at his wife's right hand, seeing a cotton glove, he smiled at her. When he got close enough, his mouth moved, however nothing came out of it at first, then finally he asked, "What were you doing out here, picking daisies?"

Diane managed a faint, "Picking berries." Softly she added, "I needed to do something." Strength ebbed from her. Her knees wobbled, giving way.

David moved to Diane's side. He gripped her shoulders tightly taking her in his big strong arms. Not speaking, he let his body absorb the tension and fear she was feeling.

The sturdiness of his shoulder comforted her. She felt herself relax and flow into his solacing strength.

Detective Waller stepped up to her supervisor to explain, "The victim matches the description of the missing woman, but so far she's not talking."

David's hand gently stroked the side of his wife's face, tracing a line with his thumb from her forehead to her lips. "You found her. You saved her," he said. "Oh darling, you are so brave. It's my fault, I wasn't with you the night you were hurt."

Diane looked up into his eyes. "You can't protect me from everything."

Dodson smiled at his wife, then got serious as he turned to his detectives. "While I was rushing out here, the hospital and the morgue called. They identified the victims in today's accident on 390. A Vincent Fazzino is going to need a lot of plastic surgery. But they don't know if a plastic surgeon is going to get him back to normal."

Waller was the first to react. "Vince Fazzino, the missing woman's husband?"

"The very one," was Dodson's answer. He looked at his two detectives as he said, "But the other guy was Thad Eisenberg. He didn't make it."

"The man we came to pick up for questioning?" asked Garcia.

"The possible murder suspect?" Waller asked.

"That's the one. The identification of the body was based on his driver's license and owner registration of his vehicle. We can't release his name until notification is made by his next of kin. We're trying to locate his parents." Sergeant Dodson went on, "He was an only child. Informing them that they've lost their son will be tough."

"Really hard," Diane sympathized.

"We'd like one of them to identify the body, but if we can't find them, then we'll ask a friend."

Garcia turned his head towards his partner and asked, "What are the odds of Mr. Fazzino killing a murderer in a vehicle accident?"

Waller sucked air in through her teeth as she said, "One in a million. And then his wife is being held captive on the guy's farm?"

"Maybe one in a gazillion, however that could make him a hero," answered Garcia.

Waller's voice rose, "Eisenberg's accidental death saved the state from prosecuting him, the trial, the lawyers' appeals and finally years later, his execution. In Illinois, he would have gotten a lethal injection if he had lived."

"Put like that, it's kind of cynical." Garcia took a long sigh. "But I wish we could have questioned him, to get his motives."

Chapter 40

SINISTER WOODS

Detective Waller asked Diane to come to the station to make a written statement. She pushed her right hand deeper into her pocket and turned to David. "I can't go in there."

Sergeant Dodson suggested they question her right here while everything was fresh in her mind.

Garcia started, "I'm sorry about these questions, but you are an important witness." He bent to scratch the ears of the miniature schnauzer by Diane's side.

Diane tried to explain, her voice soft and insecure, "I know I was trespassing, but it was so peaceful and quiet here."

"Did you kneel down on the ground?" Waller was watching Diane carefully.

Diane cast her eyes downward, then hesitantly said, "I suppose, I could have. I don't remember."

Garcia's calm voice said, "That's quite understandable. It must have been quite a shock."

Diane sucked in her breath. "Yea. Will she be okay?"

No one could answer her.

A ladder and shovel were found approximately ten feet from the hole. A detective from the Crime-Scene Division said, "The rain we had Friday night might have washed away any fingerprints and DNA there might have been on the items."

But they would search the tools anyway. This physical evidence was not wrapped in paper, cloth, or plastic because that could destroy fingerprints. Instead, Garcia wedged the shovel firmly in a strong box, so the surface wasn't touched by the packing. Nails were used to fix the objects in the boxes. He placed the ladder in the trunk using a strong box to hold it secure so both pieces of equipment would go back to headquarters to be tested.

Waller asked Diane, "Did you touch the shovel or ladder or anything else?"

"I didn't even see them." Diane said. Then excitedly she added, "Actually, there was a narrow path, like grass matted down between the lane and the hole in the ground. I thought maybe animals or maybe someone else had been here picking berries."

The path was soon marked with stakes. They literally walked Diane through her version of the events. She ended up telling her story three or four times.

As soon as Detective Waller and Garcia left Dodson and his wife standing in the lane, Diane turned toward her husband and whispered, "No one asked about my hand. Didn't anyone care?"

In response he said, "You're a hero. You found the missing victim."

"But there are too many people. I need to get out of here."

He put his arm around her shoulders. "I'll drive you home."

"No David. You should stay. Besides, I've got my car."

"Then I'll get a patrolman to drive you to your car, if you're sure you're strong enough to drive."

She smiled at him. "Yes. I'll see you at home later."

He watched her and Trixie get into a patrol car that drove her down the lane toward the farmhouse where her car was parked.

Next Waller and Garcia were standing at the edge of the deep man-made pit. With Waller's eyes wide open she said, "It takes a while to wrap your head around a scene like this."

Then they heard Dodson's voice barking, "Mark this clearing

into grids, so we know the exact location where evidence is found. Don't forget to look up in the tree branches. Then divide this entire woods into grids to search for evidence, or footprints. Are there any signs of a struggle? Like the ground trampled?"

Search teams began walking the grid Dodson mapped out in a clearing. A sketch artist took measurements, made initial crime-scene sketches at the location, and later would make detailed crime-scene drawings at headquarters. Paths taken by subjects and vehicles would be demonstrated on the drawings with colored pencils on graph paper.

Lab techs were taking photographs of the bottom and dirt walls. Policemen looked at the pit as if it were some abstract work of art; stared at it from every conceivable point of view in search of deeper meanings and textures. Dodson said, "Take aerial shots showing the location by panning the area and zooming in on the hole and location where the shovel was found."

Because of the smell of urine in the hole, the police were taking regular intervals for a cigarette to cover the stench. Garcia, a non-smoker, wanted a breath of summer air. The small pit took nearly two hours to cover.

Dodson demanded, "We've got to find out who did this. See if there are any loose hairs on these dirt piles or in the weeds. There's an off chance the lab might be able to identify some trace evidence."

Garcia gave their sergeant hopefully some good news. "Tiny dark threads were found on some berry bush thorns. They've been photographed, identified with location, bagged and removed from the scene."

Waller said, "I noticed Diane was wearing white jeans."

"It's possible these dark blue threads are from whoever trapped Carolyn here or the victim's jeans. Let's hope the lab can find out whose clothing they're from," Garcia said.

Someone asked about any tire tracks in the lane. "Good question but," and Waller made a heavy sigh, "tire and footprints near the hole were destroyed in last night's rain, which is a real shame."

Garcia added, "The fresh footprints around the hole are only Diane Dodson's and the emergency crew that rescued Carolyn Fazzino."

The local sheriff showed up with members of the press. Waller leaned over to Garcia and said, "I wonder if it's an election year for him."

Dodson also noticed the news truck pulling onto the lane. "I don't want a lot of foot traffic through here to mess up any print evidence. Secure the perimeter of this entire scene with tape. Put a few patrol officers around the boundary. Refuse entry unless their presence is absolutely necessary." He assigned a uniformed officer to maintain a crime scene logbook to record the names, dates and times of people entering and leaving the sealed area.

Garcia dropped his police bag with 'scene of the crime' tape and paraphernalia on the ground. Soon yellow plastic tape was strung up around the path Diane had taken and around the entire pit just like the police would have strung if it had been a grave, but it was a crime scene. It could have been a murder.

Waller calmly leaned over to her partner and said, "The media will be all over this like flies on shit."

Waller started a spiral search pattern beginning at the side of the pit and walked away approximately three feet. She started circling the deep dug up area. Then she raised her voice, "How big is this fucking woods?"

A local cop a few feet away answered, "Probably five or six acers."

Chapter 41

SKELETONS

Detective Waller looked up. Standing still, she allowed her eyes to examine the entire area around the hole and path leading to it. She was carefully looking around at bushes for anything out of place. Detective Garcia stepped through the knee-high grass-like weeds still damp from the rain the night before. Both detectives poked through weed clumps looking for signs of disturbance, like a discarded beer can. They walked about four feet apart. Weeds pulled at their pants as they stepped around green growth coming through the rotting leaves. The woods had an unwholesome smell mingled with damp, dirt, and decay. Approximately fifty feet away from the pit, Waller complained, "I'm sweating so much out here, I'm probably leaving salt stains on my shirt collar."

Garcia glanced towards his partner. "That's too much information." He stepped forward without looking down and suddenly tripped as he stepped into a small hole. His knee buckled. He looked down to see what he had tripped on. It looked like more loose dirt, possibly an animal digging, then he saw what looked like little dirty bones poking through the dirt and dried leaves. "HEY, OVER HERE." He looked closer, saw dirty nails attached and realized they could be human bones. Garcia grimaced and licked his lips, like an animal that's tasted something putrid. He rubbed his hands down the front of his jacket, unconsciously, like he was trying to wipe away the feel.

Several officers complied and got through the undergrowth as fast as they could. As they looked at what could be bones, talking among detectives was reduced to whispering. They could hear their own hearts beating. The silence was so strange. To break the tension, Waller whispered to her partner, "Did you know that in the 1500s, grave robbing was common among medical students, so they could dissect human bodies?"

"Really?"

"It was a learning experience for those people," Waller explained. "Good thing we have a chief medical examiner who does autopsies now."

Police oversee all crime scenes; however, the medical examiner was in charge of the body. It couldn't be moved without the ME's permission. They called him.

Dr. Somerfield responded within the hour to the country woods. This was serious. He wanted to see where the bones were found. The position of the body could determine if the victim was killed there or somewhere else and moved after death.

Another technician took photographs as dead leaves were brushed away to reveal what looked like dirty toe bones sticking out through torn soiled fabric. With his gloved hands, Somerfield pulled away soft soil until he found a foot. He brushed more leaves and dirt aside. A leg, then a body was found! Even through his rubber gloves, the black puffy skin of the arms felt ice-cold. A sickly stale raw meat smell filled the air.

Waller whispered, "This could be a homicide now, instead of only a kidnapping."

Garcia was taking notes of how the victim was laying, the position of hands, arms and legs, even the condition of the soiled clothing.

Somerfield slowly uncovered a gaping mouth.

The open eyes seemed to look through Garcia. It felt like the gaze paused briefly at the core of his soul. It was trying to see his inner-most thoughts, as if asking for his help before moving on to infinity. Garcia horrified wanted to look away. However, after finding a body, his anxiety heightened because he didn't know what to expect next.

While the ME covered the hands, or rather the palms of the victim with clean paper bags and fastened them with tape, he explained, "We don't use plastic bags for biological evidence, like blood, because the bag could accelerate the deterioration."

Garcia remembered the training manual saying that rigor mortis started at the face. A homicide detective was narrating and videotaping by panning the entire area, then focusing and zooming in on the central scene.

Waller turned from the image and spotted an area with new growth, just to the left of this body. Weeds were only an inch or two high, much lower than the surrounding undergrowth which was knee-high. "Let's dig down here." She pointed to the area. Waller found a second buried body.

Into his phone Dodson said, "We need the K-9 unit out here now. Especially the cadaver dogs."

Waller under her breath, said to her partner, "Why the hurry? They're dead."

The sergeant continued, "Also bring out thermal infrared photography equipment to detect the heat of any decomposing bodies. I want photos of this entire area, the woods and path from here to the house. Look for any possible entrance or escape routes of the perpetrator to and from this crime scene."

He waved an arm towards the nearest farmhouse located a quarter mile away. Soon a police helicopter was flying overhead taking aerial photographs to relate the scene to the surroundings like nearby farm buildings and neighboring houses. The whir and flash of cameras was amplified.

More yellow crime tape was strung between trees around these bodies. The investigators worked within the circle, bowing down like some pagan ritual.

Probing was done with a steel rod five feet long with a tee-handle at one end and a sharp point at the other. If the ground was soft, the rod was left in place to be inspected more.

What an investigator thought was a leg covered by blue jeans was actually blackened, decaying human bone and rotting flesh. A foul smell filled the air as they uncovered the bodies.

Waller told Garcia, "The dead smell gets into your hair and into your sinuses. Wash your hair before you go home tonight. You don't want to sit down to dinner smelling like that? Lemon or citrus-scented shampoo helps. Eating horseradish or strong peppermint can help, too."

Garcia turned his head away instinctively, then decided that action wasn't very macho, he joked to his comrades, "It's three months until Halloween."

"This isn't a Halloween prank," Waller said dryly. The woods turned sinister after bodies were found. "A killing field," she exclaimed. "And, it just got a Helluva lot worse."

Garcia responded with, "This is certainly going to ruin my sleep tonight."

Waller trying to explain the detective's psychological buffer between life and death said, "Don't let yourself think of it as human beings; it's evidence." She sighed, "But this is a colossal clusterfuck. I want to click my heels together three times to make this woods and my headache go away."

Skeletons were photographed with a thirty-five-millimeter camera and placed in heavy body bags, with the clothing that was found on the bodies. Death is heavy. It smothered the living with unanswered questions. All bones were carefully collected and packaged in new paper bags for DNA samples. All tools and instruments had to be sterile to prevent cross-contamination. The coroner's investigators placed each victim into a separate body bag. Then transported them to the morgue.

Detective Waller and Garcia walked the lane so they could look closer at the vegetation. They found oil and gasoline traces on the weeds. They clipped the vegetation and put it in evidence bags. When a truck was driven through the tall grass and weeds, there might have been a transfer of oil or gasoline from the underside of the truck to the vegetation. A lab test could determine if this oil matched the kind Eisenberg used in his truck.

Garcia turned and faced Waller. "Forensic botany could help us identify plants found under his truck that could match the plants in this lane."

With an empty tone to her voice, Waller said, "It's a farm truck. He probably used it all over his blasted farm. He probably walked the whole thing too. That doesn't prove anything."

"Not definitely that it was him, however if the oil belonged to another truck it could point to another kidnaper."

"Right," she agreed with him.

"Go back a decade in the old homicide files looking for any unsolved murders or disappearances involving young women when you get back to the station." Dodson instructed them. They would contact National Crime Information Center (NCIC) and the FBI database regarding wanted persons, missing persons, and criminal histories.

Garcia turned to his partner. "I'll check Thad Eisenberg's Facebook and Instagram accounts. He may not be a pillar of integrity."

A portable generator was brought to the woods to supply high-intensity lighting after the sun went down. Television cameramen, one from each of the three networks, were hovering along the main road, not allowed to park in the driveway or drive on the lawn. Around midnight as personnel were leaving, Dodson ordered, "Post a guard. I don't want any nosy neighbors or lookie-loos checking out what's going on here."

Dodson had his tech department go through Thad's cell phone, only to have the officer report, "There's no address for his parents. No calls from Florida, actually very few contacts. This guy is a real loner. Perhaps he used his landline." However, phone records from his landline number showed no Florida calls. The only calls were incoming sales calls. *The parents didn't try to contact their only son. Maybe they had a falling-out.*

Chapter 42

SCARS

SUNDAY MORNING

Suddenly Detective Waller's cell rang, waking her. She fumbled for her phone laying on the bedside table and mumbled, "Shit. You know what time it is?"

"After seven," the male voice said.

"Well, I didn't get to bed until five o'clock, so this better be great news." She pulled herself to her elbows.

"This is Doctor Somerfield, from the DuPage County Morgue. I'm calling about a thirty-one-year-old male accident victim that was brought in Saturday morning."

Waller raised her voice, "Why call me in the middle of the night?" Because to her this felt like night. But at the same time, she was using her hand to shade her eyes from the sun streaming in the bedroom window.

"Because, you've got to see this."

"He was D.O.A. wasn't he? He's not going anywhere." Reluctantly she was lowering her feet to the floor.

Forty minutes later Detectives Waller and Garcia stepped inside the County Building. The hall ended with two doors. One had INQUEST ROOM in block letters. The other opened into a small office where florescent fixtures filled the room with cold light.

Waller reached in her back pocket and pulled out a hair band. With both hands, she bunched her hair into her left fist. With her right, she wrapped the band around her straight dark hair.

Gene, the lab assistant gave them each a cup of coffee.

Somerfield, the heavy-set coroner wearing paper booties on his feet while safety goggles hung over his white lab coat, was eating a jelly donut. "He's in the cold room."

Waller with Garcia holding a clipboard were led across the tiled walled autopsy lab, through another door to a large refrigeration unit. It looked like a walk-in meat locker with temperature dials and a massive stainless-steel door. Air conditioning churned from the ceiling. Hanging on the wall beside the big door was a clipboard with its log of deliveries. This was a roster no one wanted to be on. The pathologist opened the door as wisps of condensation drifted out. They stepped inside to see a row of gurneys. Only four had body bags, their contents covered in white plastic. In front of them were spotless white tiles with a gleaming stainless-steel tray of scalpels and other instruments. The smell of antiseptic and cleanliness gave way to the smell of death and the damaged.

Somerfield washed his hands at the side sink, then he walked up the row of stainless-steel gurneys scanning the various tags. He stopped at the third body covered with plastic higher at the head and sloped down to the feet. "Here's our guy, delivered at eleven a.m. Saturday," he said as he unzipped the bag low enough to reveal the white bald head, and the upper half of the torso.

Reluctantly the pair of detectives stepped up to the table. The body had been undressed and washed. The waxy pale body lay naked. As the plastic parted, they stared down at the cold albino-white corpse showing the damage of the accident, an unsightly mass of burses. The Y-incision on his chest was stitched together with mortician's rough sutures. They knew body parts had been removed, examined, and put back.

Matter-of-factly, the coroner's voice continued, "Death was internal loss of blood, shock and a ruptured spleen, secondary to traumatic hemorrhage of the lung." Doctor Somerfield glanced at the detectives and explained, "He suffered three broken ribs on his left side. All were broken inward. A splinter of rib punctured his left lung. He bleed to death but had a lot of trouble breathing at the end. His death was not peaceful, not instantaneous. It was lingering and painful."

"He was trapped in his pickup," Garcia explained to the doctor.

As the coroner looked up at the detectives, dark circles looked more pronounced under his eyes. "We think of our hearts as protected inside a sturdy cage of ribs, however all it takes is the squeeze of the steering wheel to do this. We're made of such fragile material."

Waller turned to the coroner. "ID on him said he was Thad Eisenberg, age thirty-one."

Somerfield said, "We found a fingerprint match on the government military file."

Garcia simply nodded his head. He knew all military services store a small amount of genetic material of each recruit so there would never again be an unknown soldier.

The doctor licked some sugar off his lips and then went on, "His body is totally devoid of body hair."

"What?" came out of Waller's mouth. She took a small step closer to the table to see.

"All hair on his body was shaved off, so we could not clip a sample from his head, chest or groin. I've noted scars and other identifying marks and that's what I want you to see." He pulled the plastic down farther at the sides to reveal the dead victim's arms.

As the detectives took in the damaged torso, they saw the round scars up and down the arms.

Waller picked up a nearby microscope to look closer at them. "Are they burns?"

"Old burns, done with cigarettes. Most are completely healed, so it was probably done when he was a boy," the pathologist explained. The doctor switched on a hand-held black light and pointed towards the wounds. "However here on the inside of his left arm are some new ones that aren't healed." He turned the arm over revealing the burnt flesh. "I'd say, he was tortured by someone in the past couple of weeks."

"What a horrible secret." Garcia responded, "I wonder what his childhood was like. But who was still doing that to him?"

Waller didn't feel any sympathy towards the dead man. She was there for the investigation and asked, "Anything of interest in his stomach?"

"The contents were all peanuts, the dry roasted kind to be specific, however nothing that would impair his driving. Toxicology of both drivers demonstrated nothing out of the ordinary. The manner of death was accidental." He looked up at the detectives to continue. "I've also been looking at Thad Eisenberg's hands. I was hoping to match dirt from the woods or DNA from one of his victims, but the bad news is, they were scrubbed clean, especially under the fingernails, just calluses which could be from farming or from digging."

"That proves nothing." Garcia shrugged.

"His home was exceptionally clean when we went through it. I started wondering if he had some kind of compulsive disorder to keep it that clean," Waller told them.

Garcia was troubled. "It's just a car accident, but how did he get those scars and dead bodies burried on his farm?"

"Speaking of dead bodies." Waller paused to look closer at Somerfield. "The whole woods has been searched and most of it dug up. What could you learn from those skeletons?"

"My autopsy technicians have been investigating the remains." The coroner knew the police and the media wanted detailed reports. "They're in the next laboratory."

All three stepped into the adjoining room. Mingled sick odors could be tasted when inhaled in this area. Dr. Somerfield announced, "We've been working round the clock to identify the human remains and get you some answers."

Waller set her jaw. "Looked like two bodies out there."

"Right, one shallow grave, with two bodies." Somerfield rubbed his hands together, grinning. "Let's get started."

Garcia whispered just loud enough for his partner to hear, "I am alive." He gave a little head nod to the first sheet covering the remains. "You are not."

They stepped closer to a lab table covered with dark plastic sheets. The two higher bulges under the plastic were obviously two rounded heads laid side by side.

"When a body is buried in a shallow grave with loose earth, worms attack it almost immediately. Twenty-four hours after the bodies were dumped in the woods, animals attacked the nose, ears, stomach, and belly areas. Within three days of death, the entire body would show signs of decay. Warmer temperatures increase decomposition. Colder temps slow it down." The doctor pulled back each sheet.

"In other words, bodies hold together better through the winter then in summer?" verified Waller.

"Right. I've seen bodies skeletonize in as little as two weeks during the muggy heat of summer," the coroner assured them.

Garcia was staring at the doctor as though he could see bugs, then he took one look at his coffee and sat the three-quarter filled cardboard cup on the nearest counter.

Somerfield didn't seem to notice the detective's loss of appetite. Instead he took a big swallow of his own caffeine and continued, "Remember they were found in July in Illinois. Soft-tissue damage made it impossible to recognize the two skeletons." Somerfield pointed towards the bones.

Detective Waller asked, "They look badly decomposed, but can you identify them?"

Somerfield had his reading glasses on the end of his nose. His voice slow and heavy, "We got lucky with bone fragments that eventually added up to two skeletons."

The harsh lighting brought out the deep creases around Somerfield's eyes and mouth. "We had excellent support from the state crime lab in Chicago. Their forensic pathologist could deduce an amazing amount of information from the skeletons long after an autopsy was impossible." The doctor shook his head. "Let me tell you what we've been able to make out."

Waller looked pale, but said, "That's why we're here, doc."

They all looked down at the table.

The doctor shifted his feet. "We relied on the pelvis bones to confirm sex. Pelvis size and form are different for men and woman. We found a male and a female skeleton."

"Could you tell what race they were?" asked Garcia. He wanted to look away from the badly decomposed bodies.

"Race was easy to peg. On the ground beside the skull we found the hair mat where it had sloughed off. She had straight brunet hair. Plus, the shape of her mouth with teeth that were quite vertical. No forward protruding. Clearly, she was Caucasian. Using the Trotter-Gleser formula for white females," Dr. Somerfield looked back down at his iPad. "I estimated the combined lengths of the femur and tibia to be sixty-three to sixty-four inches long." The coroner waved his hand over the first gurney. "This skeleton is a white female who was between forty-five to fifty-five years of age at the time of death. The male skeleton was around the same age at the time of his death."

A tiny hiss of breath escaped from Garcia. "Can you tell, who they were?" He looked up. His face was pulled into a grimace.

Somerfield leaned closer. "The good news is it takes approximately ten years to destroy DNA from bones. DNA showed these are family members of Thad Eisenberg."

Waller snapped her fingers. "The deceased victim in yesterday's accident? The guy you've got in the next room?"

"Right. We swabbed the inside of Thad's cheek, to verify the skeletons found on the farm are related to him." Somerfield rubbed his eyes with his thumb and index finger.

Garcia told them, "A wedding ring was found on the hand of one of the victims with the initials H. E. on the inside."

Detective Waller pinched the bridge of her nose between her fingers, squeezing her eyes shut with a grimace. She muttered, "That could be Harland Eisenberg."

"I should have more lab results within twenty-four hours." Somerfield smiled. "But, step over here, I've got one more thing to show you now." They walked to a nearby counter where an old shovel laid across the white surface.

"Is that the one that was found in the woods?" asked Garcia.

"That's it. Since it rained the night before the shovel was found, it was wet, and no clear prints were found. However visible cracks showed in the wood." Then Somerfield turned a strong light on over the handle. They could see smudges. "Grease and perspiration in the cracks, match Thad Eisenberg's DNA."

Garcia snapped his fingers. "We've got him."

Waller's cell rang. She read the screen, "Illinois State forensics lab."

A police official told her, "One of the photos taken inside the Silverado truck shows blood on the passenger seat."

"So?"

"The blood is between the seat cushion and the back of the seat and it's not fresh blood."

Sarcastically she said, "Maybe it dried faster than the rest."

"Between the cushions? With less air getting to it. It should have dried slower."

She turned to her partner and said, "Let's go look at that pickup truck that was in the accident yesterday."

Chapter 43

SILVERADO PICKUP TRUCK

As Detective Garcia and Waller reached the West Chicago municipal garage a team of experts had just completed analyzing everything in the dead man's truck. Detective Turner approached them as they walked in.

Garcia stopped in his tracks. "What's up?"

Turner stood in front of them. "The Silverado truck belonging to Thad Eisenberg was interesting. Peanuts were found scattered on the floor of the pickup."

"Probably spilled during his accident." Waller was sounding exasperated. "We just left the morgue on that case."

"I used a vacuum cleaner over the front seat and floor to collect microscopic evidence." Turner explained to both detectives. "DNA evidence proves Carolyn was in the Eisenberg pickup truck. I found a couple of her hairs and trace fiber evidence."

Waller told them, "We need to talk with her to see if she remembers being in there."

"Dirt from the floorboard of the suspect's vehicle was a match to oily dirt that could be found at bus depots. It could have been deposited there from shoes worn by Eisenberg or Ms. Burton. So, we looked at the Burton woman's tennis shoes that were buried with her. We found motor oil on the bottoms, the kind you can find in bus stations."

"We start looking at the bus stations around here first. Then expand our search outward." Waller was already pulling up a list of bus stations on her laptop. "We'll call every one of these if we have to."

Bus station personal completely cooperated with the detectives, sending them their surveillance videos. They got lucky. Camera footage of the metro station showed Thad hunched over on a bench two days before Tammy's New York ticket had her changing buses in Chicago.

"Thad Eisenberg was hanging out at the bus station." Garcia's voice rose a little with excitement.

"A woman from Iowa, found dead in Bleakville. You're telling me, she met up with Thad Eisenberg in Chicago?" Waller's voice was doubtful.

They kept watching the footage. Minutes later she exclaimed, "She sure did. We've got proof. Bus depot camera footage showed Eisenberg speaking to Ms. Burton."

"There were no decent prints on the cloth seats of his pickup." Turner's voice got excited. "But the lab said there was an unusual smudge on the inside passenger window that wasn't affected by Friday's rain."

"Probably one of the firefighters resting his hand on the glass when they were trying to get the driver out," suggested Garcia.

Turner shook his head. "Not any of the rescue team. Fingerprints are Tammy Burton's. There was a fingerprint card on file when she and her friends were arrested for underage drinking at a teen street dance even though her fingers were missing, we can prove she was definitely in his truck before his accident. And it gets better, the blood found between the seat cushions is Tammy Burton's blood," Turner added.

"She was there." Waller smiled broadly. "We've got him even though hydrogen peroxide and bleach were used to clean the inside of his truck. He didn't clean between the cushions well enough."

"He did a lot, however fingerprints and blood testing exposed him. You brought justice to Tammy Burton's family," announced Turner.

"Both women were in the Eisenberg truck. These two cases are related." Garcia was excitedly pulling on his mustache. "Burton was hurt in his truck. Then he got blood on his shirt."

Waller finished his statement, "And that bloody shirt was hidden with her body in a culvert."

"If it was an accident, he didn't have to hide her and the shirt." Garcia's eyes were wide with excitement.

"That makes Thad Eisenberg look really guilty." Waller smiled and snapped her fingers.

"And we've gone over the Fazzino car." Turner was smiling now. "Good thing we got it towed into our garage before it rained Friday night. The partial boot print we found on the car door, matches the boot tracks on the shoes Thad Eisenberg was wearing when he died."

"That's right." Garcia pointed his index finger towards his partner. "In the grocery store security footage, he kicked her car door closed."

"The size of the figure in the grocery store camera footage matches the shape of Eisenberg's body." Waller told him, "He kidnapped Carolyn Fazzino."

Chapter 44

POSITIVE IDENTIFICATION

Detectives Garcia and Waller had an architectural drawing of the farm and woods taped to the police station wall which graphically showed the crime scene. Aerial photographs illustrated the outdoor scene. Death photos and autopsy reports were scattered over their desks.

First thing Monday morning, Waller and Garcia were phoning dentists in nearby towns. The eighth phone call struck pay dirt. Dr. Jackson confirmed that Mr. and Mrs. Eisenberg and their son, Thad, had been patients of his. He agreed to give them dental charts and four bite-wing X-rays of their teeth.

Within the hour everything had been electronically received on their police computers. "The teeth and fillings matched dental records of x-rays by the Eisenberg family dentist. They were indeed the Eisenbergs," said Sergeant Dodson.

Waller tapped her pen off her teeth. "The dentist said the male was fifty-one the last time he saw him and the female fifty-two. They are Harland and Marilyn Eisenberg."

"Wow," was the first thing out of Garcia's mouth. "He buried his parents on their own farm. Did he lose his marbles?" He nervously fingered his mustache. "So, no priest or minister said anything, like a funeral service for them. Was he a sicko?" He asked no one in particular.

Looking at the photos of the teeth, Waller said, "By the way, the woman's teeth show, she was a smoker."

Chapter 45

CAUSE OF DEATH

Detective Waller pulled out her cell and dialed the morgue.

As soon as Somerfield answered, she put him on speaker and barked at him, "You got any more on those skeletons found in the woods? Like how long have they been out there?"

"Both have been dead for proximately the same length of time. We used insect evidence and vegetation like weeds growing through their garments to determine how long the bodies had been in the Eisenberg woods. We linked the decomposition stages and insect development to compute time since death. We can tell, the two bodies were out there from eight to twelve months."

For a moment Garcia thought his bowl of cereal he had for breakfast was going to come up. He didn't want to embarrass himself in front of his veteran partner who also looked a little peakid. Garcia swallowed back a sour taste of milk and Cheerios and questioned towards the phone, "You can't tell us any closer than months when they died?"

Somerfield sounded weary, "Wish I could, however time of death calculations are tough outside. Warm days in June and July, but cooler evenings, so the body temperature changes." He sighed, then continued, "Now their clothing was in a better state of preservation than the bodies because cotton fabric can last four to five years. The male was wearing a wool shirt, which could indicate it was cold when he died, maybe during the colder months. By the way, his leather shoes could last out there for twenty years. However, the victim's upper clothes, from the waist-up were full of slashes and blood probably drew the wild animals and insects to the bodies."

For the moment, Garcia thought he saw a great insect thrumming against his desk ready to attack. A revolted look crossed his face as he said, "It was the toes that I saw first."

"When you tripped," added Waller sarcastically as her mouth formed a slight smile. "Good police work, Detective."

Ignoring his partner's kidding Garcia asked, "Have any idea how either of the vics died?"

"They were found out in a woods. Possibly a hunting accident, but both of them?" was Waller's question. "And no murder weapon was found in the woods."

"Not a gun. I searched the clothing for evidence of gunshot residue. None and no bullets found." Somerfield assured them.

Garcia leaned his elbows on his desk and explained, "We found out from the family doctor that Thad's parents had no prior history of medical problems."

"The skulls were intact," said Somerfield. "No evidence of fractures at the cervical canal. This rules out death by blunt trauma to the head. No fractures along the spine or injury to the backs. I'm sending my files over to you right now."

Waller started to open a drawer for a candy bar but changed her mind about eating.

Garcia leaned in and pulled Mr. and Mrs. Eisenberg's files up on his computer screen and read, "Death was due to multiple sharp objects. There were a lot of breaches in the clothing of the victims that could have been made by cutting implements such as knives, scissors, hatchets, or other edged weapons."

"Yes," agreed the coroner. "All tears were photographed, measured, and marked as evidence in my report."

Waller pulled up a report on the Burton victim and said, "This compares to the same way the body found in the culvert was attacked, where Thad Eisenberg's shirt was found with the victim."

Garcia continued reading off his computer screen, "The male was stabbed four centimeters left of the sternum into his heart. A few wounds could be from sharp animal teeth; however, many were too sharp and neat to have been made by animals." He glanced at his partner then went back to reading the lab report on his screen. "A sharp object nicked the arm bones and the ribs of his parents, actually groups of wounds. This says the killer's crimes were committed in a frenzy."

Waller reading the Burton report said, "Same with this vic." Her eyebrows rose.

"We x-rayed the skeletons and found a tip of a broken knife point in Marilyn Eisenberg's third rib. The killer was stabbing her so hard; it broke," Somerfield explained.

"My educated guess." Waller sat up straight, finally turning and looking Garcia in the eye. "Is a sword or knife was used."

"All three victims were bludgeoned to death?" Garcia sounded angry.

"Yes," answered Somerfield on the phone.

"Your report said, there were tears, rips or cuts into Burton's clothing." She clicked on a screen showing two side-by-side generic body profiles, one of the front and one of the back of the body. The marks were the wounds numbered from one through fifty-three. "It looks like a connect-the-dots puzzle," responded Waller.

"Oh brother." Garcia placed his elbows on the desk and rested his chin on his combined fists. "My conclusion is that he hated her with a vengeance."

Waller still staring at the screen commented, "Wow, that's overkill. You have to really hate someone to stab them that many times."

"This report on the couple says the knife blade was approximately four inches long. The slash and stab marks appeared random and were different lengths and depth," he said.

"The killer was up close to each victim." She sat more hunched over her computer screen.

Garcia continued reading the report of the parents. "Look at the scattering of red marks on the outline's arms. These are defense wounds to the bones in their arms and the palms of their hands, particularly between the wrist and little finger. All three were trying to defend themselves."

Waller crossed her arms. "The chipped bones on the skeletons could be from knife wounds." Then she speculated, "The defense injuries on the male victim demonstrates there was evidence of a struggle."

Garcia clicked through a couple more screens and stopped. "Both females are missing all their fingers."

I wanted to look for broken fingernails that might have been damaged if they put up a fight, however they're gone," said the coroner.

"Maybe they're actually defense injuries caused when the victims instinctively raised their hands for self-protection." Waller raised her hands in front of her face to show her partner what she had in mind.

"All ten? I doubt that." Garcia shot her theory down.

"Animals?" Waller speculated out loud. "We thought if wild animals dug up the grave and bit them off, possibly carried them away, so they used ground penetrating radar to see if we could find all of the person's body parts."

"We even sifted through the earth out there looking for the smallest bone fragments." Garcia looked away from his screen for a minute.

Somerfield told them, "A couple of the female's toes were intact, but several of the other toes were scattered in the area."

Waller pointed to the computer screen on her desk showing an aerial view of the woods. "These red and orange survey flags mark the location of every bone we found."

The detectives studied the diagram.

Garcia leaned back in his desk chair. "We located all of the male's digits but couldn't locate any of the female's fingers."

Waller looked at her own hands. "Strange. Fingers missing on only female victims. Could missing fingers indicate some kind of satanic murder?"

Garcia's thick eyebrows drew together as his forehead wrinkled. "Did he cut off the fingers, so we wouldn't be able to identify his victims? You know, to remove their fingerprints. Ever read *Gorky Park* or see the movie?"

"Years ago, I saw the movie," Waller answered. "Isn't that where the killer even shot the vics in their mouths, so the Russian police had trouble identifying their teeth?"

"Right. But to hide the identity of these people," Garcia pointed at his computer. "Our killer could have just cut off the end of the digits, instead he or they, if it's more than one killer, cut the entire fingers off." He held his own left hand in the air and with his right, made a quick slicing motion across his left knuckles. "Those fingers were amputated, cut off with a sharp instrument."

"I've got more, my friend. Do you remember the knife found in Eisenberg's truck?" asked Waller. "Was that knife sharp enough to cut off the bones of the fingers?"

"Extraordinarily sharp," was the answer Garcia was waiting to give.

An a-ha moment crossed Waller's face. "A knife never runs out of ammunition. Attackers can strike again and again repeatedly."

Garcia was quick to add, "However a five-inch blade isn't unique. One could purchase that kind of folding knife in any hardware store around here and when it broke, he could easily buy another."

"No blood found on his knife, totally cleaned off. Only Thad's fingerprints were found on the weapon. No one else's."

"No weapon sharp enough to make the wounds, was ever found in the woods," added Garcia. "So, the knife that was found in his truck was probably the weapon he used. And he carried it with him in his truck when he was driving."

Waller questioned, "Mm-hum, if he wanted to stop us from identifying the bodies, then why put the Burton girl's backpack with her ID near her body?"

"Possibly, he didn't look in the backpack." Detective Garcia mused.

Waller gave her partner an evil snake-eye look as she answered, "Then he's really stupid."

"Maybe he removed the fingers from the females because they scratched him, and he didn't want his DNA under their fingernails," speculated Garcia.

"Then we're dealing with a smart killer." Waller was sarcastic this time.

"It doesn't make any sense that he would cut off female fingers to hide their identity, however not the one with something so obvious as a wedding ring with initials." Garcia was thinking out loud.

Waller speculated, "Either he didn't know about the initials, or he never meant to hide identity of anyone."

Nervously Garcia pulled at his mustache. "You think the mutilations were souvenirs he collected?"

"It's possible, maybe the fingers were trophies. The male victim had his fingers. There was some of the son's DNA under fingernails on his right hand. So then why didn't he take off the man's fingers, when we know he fought his attacker?" asked Waller.

Garcia's eyes widened. "The son's DNA was found under his father's nails? Really? Could the son have killed his own parents?"

"The same son that was killed in a highway accident this weekend?" Waller clenched her teeth tightly together then said, "We can nail the bastard with the microscopic particles of the suspect found under the fingernails of the male skeleton."

"Dark fibers were found on the raspberry bushes in the woods and we matched them to one of his shirts hanging in his closet, but it had been laundered. He not only drove down the lane, he walked in the woods, too." Garcia stated.

Waller unwrapped a candy bar and explained, "The lab tried to compare dirt near the pit with the bottoms of the work boots Thad Eisenberg was wearing when killed on I-390 or even spare boots found in his home, but all of them had been scrubbed clean of dirt and mud."

"No proof with the shoes," Garcia mumbled defeated.

"After examining all these wounds," Waller said. She covered her mouth with her left hand deep in thought. "I'm convinced the burial site in the woods is not where the couple was murdered. These wounds were severe. There should have been a lot of blood."

"After this many months would blood still be present?" Garcia asked.

"No," was Somerfield's answer.

Waller shifted her weight. "I want to know where they were murdered."

Chapter 46

FARMHOUSE

Detective Waller raised herself out of her office chair as she said, "We start with the nearest building, which is the Eisenberg home."

The first thing they spotted as they stepped into the back porch, was a dark hoodie sweatshirt hanging on a coat hook. It looked like the one worn by Carolyn Fazzino's kidnapper in the Diamond's security footage.

The house, yard, and entire farm were searched again, but differently. They wanted to know if it was the scene of a crime. They looked through the entire house for fingerprints. Dodson wanted to know if anyone other than the dead owner had been in the house. Maybe he had an accomplice.

Waller and Garcia took a vacuum to the entire three-bedroom house from basement to attic, in closets, inside the refrigerator and freezer, even vacuuming for hair or dust on curtains throughout the house looking for evidence of other people. As they did each room Garcia put the dust particles into separate evidence bags and marked which room it was from. When they were done, they turned the vacuum bag's contents of loose fibers and other trace evidence over to the white coats for sifting in their fourth-floor labs. Nothing of Tammy Burton or Carolyn Fazzino was found. The only fingerprints found in the farmhouse were Thad's, but many surfaces had been wiped clean with no prints at all. With a little exasperation in

Garcia's voice, he exclaimed, "We assume he never took Tammy Burton or Carolyn Fazzino inside his home."

There were no loose papers, no telephone messages or notes, nothing scrawled on pieces of newspapers anywhere in the home. No computers or laptops. However, they did find a set of keys that did not belong to the home or the damaged Silverado truck. After a call back to the station house, they determined the keys belonged to a Honda Civic, Carolyn Fazzino's car keys found in Thad Eisenberg's drawer!

They also spent hours searching for another possible murder weapon in the toilet tank, freezer, refrigerator, oven, under rugs, high shelves in the bedroom closets, between and inside mattresses, drawers, taped to the bottom of drawers, inside sugar and flour canisters, and inside an ornamental clock on the dining room wall. They looked for secret walls and floor panels and searched the barn and garage. The only knife found had been the one in his truck. It could have inflicted the wounds that killed Tammy Burton and the Eisenberg couple.

They found a lot of cleaning supplies. The odor smelled like bleach and ammonia throughout the home. Waller commented, "Bleach will destroy DNA."

"His home carpet looked clean enough you could eat off it." Garcia stated.

However, when they took up the bedroom carpet, they found blood on the subflooring. They discovered the killer tried to remove blood spatters with bleach in a bedroom on the first floor. The female clothing found in the closet of this bedroom, identified it as having been a woman's room. Two bedroom closets upstairs held male clothing. The walls and floors of the lower bedroom appeared to be immaculate to the naked eye, but the detectives sprayed the area with luminal which reacted with the iron in hemoglobin causing blood spatters to shine fluorescent with a bright blue/green glow that could be seen in a dark room. Luminol will react with the iron for approximately ninety seconds, so they photographed the glowing bloodstains quickly. There was so much blood that two bodies could have been killed right there.

"The medical examiner said the bodies were found wrapped in cotton fabric and the downstairs bedroom had new sheets." Waller speculated, "He could have wrapped them in their own bed sheets, then dragged or carried them to the back door." A thick swipe of blood on the kitchen floor and down the back steps showed up with Luminal which proved her right.

"Thad Eisenberg did everything he could to cover up his murders." Garcia said, "Maybe he moved them after dark so no one driving by saw him carrying bodies out the door."

Waller stopped to unwrap a small chocolate bar as she said, "Reliving a murder through the eyes of the killer is disturbing, but it's the only way to see exactly how the murders were committed. This guy was able to organize things in his environment."

"I wish we could have talked with him to see what went on in his head. Was he organized there too? Too bad we couldn't have interrogated him." Garcia used his left hand to scratch at his mustache.

Waller turned her head towards her partner. "Him dying saves the lawyers and jurors a court hearing and saves us taxpayers lots of dough prosecuting his ass and then feeding him for the rest of his life. He saved us a lot of trouble. But if you want to know what made him tick, we can talk to a police profiler.

Chapter 47

PROFILE

Detective Garcia hardly thought about his drive to the station Wednesday morning. He was so preoccupied with this case. As soon as he saw his partner he said, "We've got Eisenberg, however I'm going to call the local police department anyway."

"Good idea," Waller assured him. "Sometimes they know more then what shows up on the computer reports."

"This is a village that most people simply drive right through on their way to someplace else. Isn't even on any tourist map. The thing is, this is a safe place," the Bleakville cop said into his phone as he leaned back in his office chair. "This is such a sleepy little town that we all come out in droves for each other's garage sales." He chuckled at his own joke. "We get our Saturday night drunks that end in overnight jail time till they sleep it off. Teens doing pranks or stupid stuff, but kids will be kids. We get some speeders, maybe a burglary, or some family squabble, but that's our police blotter. We're a small community. My God, we still have a volunteer fire department and it works for us." Then he added, "Some of the folks out here, don't even lock their doors."

"What can you tell me about the Eisenbergs?"

"For a while Harland Eisenberg was on the volunteer fire department. Mr. and Mrs. Eisenberg and their son were quiet farmers. They grew corn, soybeans and raised some chickens. Marilyn Eisenberg never got involved with the local ladies bake sales or rummage sales, but that stuffs not for everyone."

After several more phone calls, Detective Garcia learned that gas station and grocery store clerks saw the family around town, but to everyone else, the Eisenbergs were pretty much invisible.

"Thad's schoolteachers said he was average in class. He was quiet one minute, then lashed out with little to no guilt, mean and self-centered, with no close friends either. He dropped out of school to enlist. Teachers always hoped he would get his GED. Army buddies said he could be charming one minute, then snap and become vicious the next," Garcia told his partner as he used his left hand to smooth his mustache.

Detectives interviewed surrounding farm owners to see if there were any witnesses, like a neighbor who saw lights out in the woods after dark. The closest neighbor, an elderly man, Dale Lathom admitted he often fell asleep while watching TV at night. When they asked him specifically about Thad Eisenberg, Mr. Lathom told them, "Thad's friendly, respectable, nice guy, and quiet. He even changed a tire for me, very helpful. Thad's the all-American boy and he has a girlfriend."

Detective Waller perked up, "How do you know he had a girlfriend?"

"I saw some long brown hair in his truck."

Other neighbors agreed with Latham. They liked Thad, said he was a great guy, and real quiet.

Waller snorted, "He could certainly fool some people."

Garcia and Waller provided raw data from the pickup truck, woods and autopsy to federal agents trained in psychological profiling at the National Center for Analysis of Violent Crimes. A profile of the killer was prepared by the FBI's behavioral analysis unit. Soon Randy Wright, an agent from Quantico, Virginia who specialized in psychological profiling techniques, was seated at a table in the small conference room with Detectives Waller and Garcia inside the West Chicago police headquarters. Spread out on the table in front of them were reports and photographs of this case.

After the introductions, Randy jumped right in. "This guy wasn't in the VI-CAP list, the violent criminal apprehension program system used to identify serial murderers and the type of individuals who would commit a certain crime." He paused for effect, then went on, "This offender probably was unmarried. He would have been a master at a false front, presenting a reasonable even placid exterior. He didn't look like a killer. He looked like a normal guy. He wasn't considered odd, different or dangerous by his peers. Many serial killers are able to remain undetected for long periods of time." Agent Wright ran his right hand through his unruly sandy colored hair and told them, "Serial killers have been described as intelligent, charismatic, street wise, charming, and generally good looking."

"However, most people have secrets," Detective Waller answered.

Wright agreeing said, "Serial killers feel no guilt. None at all. They rationalize. They blame others. These killers are mobile individuals capable of traveling miles in search of the "right" victim. Serial killers love to drive always looking for a specific type to kill."

Both detectives watched the profiler as he went on. "Possibly the victim may have initially felt safe or comfortable with the offender and gone willingly with him. He usually demands a submissive victim, but he masks a horror underneath."

Wright smirked as he said, "Killers regard themselves as all-powerful and all-knowledgeable. He may have experienced hallucinations. He could project his fantasy onto other women when he killed. Serial murderers are childlike, changing quickly, acting like stars. They feel they were born to do anything they want. The victim in this instance may not have responded to the offender as he thought she would initially have acted. His difficulty in controlling her may have led to the victim's death. It is possible the offender killed the victim within a short period of time of meeting her."

"In Mrs. Fazzino's case, she didn't even speak to him. He just came up to her and knocked her out," said Garcia. "We saw that when he grabbed her on the security footage."

"Cops have briefly spoken with Carolyn Fazzino and she says, she didn't know Eisenberg," explained Waller. "But we want to question her further."

"So, it was a crime of opportunity." Agent Wright brushed at his shoulder to dislodge a couple light colored hairs that had fallen on his navy jacket but kept talking. "In the mind of the serial killer, he experiences great pleasure in exerting power and control over his victim, including the power of death. He is excited by the cruelty of the act and will engage in physical and psychological torture of the victim. His pleasure is derived by watching the victim writhe in pain as she is humiliated and tortured. The serial killer operates in an emotionally detached manner." Wright picked up one of the manila folders off the table. While waving it in the air, he said, "Many of these killers maintain respectable life-styles."

"His home was spotless. He cleaned with ammonia and bleach maybe to get rid of the blood." Waller told the FBI man.

Wright said, "That could be his desire to control everything around him, to control his world and the people in it. His obsessive neatness is just one part of that desire for control." Wright reached for a photograph of the hole in the woods. "You can tell he spent a significant amount of time digging this pit. That's telling you, he was comfortable there. It was his comfort zone. However, the killer really doesn't have any type of satisfactory relationships with anyone. He felt unloved by one or both parents. I suspect Thad Eisenberg had a mother fixation if it was his mother who burned him. He felt things were bad in his life because of women. Serial murderers are frequently found to have unusual or unnatural relationships with their mothers."

"Then what about the man buried out there?" asked Garcia. "DNA proved it was his father."

"Perhaps his dad walked in when he was killing the mother," speculated Waller. "Maybe caught him in the act and he had to silence his own father. He was a serial killer that we didn't even know we were looking for."

Wright told them, "Childhood abuse may not be the sole excuse for serial killers, but it is an undeniable factor in many of their backgrounds."

"You think something like he had to be perfect or he got beaten by an unfit or alcoholic mother?" Garcia asked.

Waller nodded in agreement. "It's possible, he slashed at his own mother with a knife until she was dead. He used such force and determination that Tammy Burton's liver was cut in two."

The profiler said, "Many serial killers are experimenting with their victims. This killer had a chilling disregard for people. His mind was clearly contaminated."

Garcia turned towards the profiler and suggested, "His heart was made of stone."

"What heart?" was Waller's response. "He was a terrible fucked up mess."

Wright ignored the banter between the partners and went on, "Serial killers are extremely manipulative. They are quickly able to gain the victim's confidence with their verbal skills. If the victim is female, she may resemble other female victims in some aspect, body size, hair length and color. In his head, he thought there was a connection to these women."

"You said victims could resemble each other? That's interesting because Burton, the single female victim, had approximately the same color brunet hair as his mother." Garcia held up samples of the hair he had brought into the meeting. Visually the detectives could not distinguish between the two samples of dull medium brown hair color.

Waller released a low whistle, then exclaimed, "Carolyn Fazzino also has the same color hair. We should look at unsolved stabbings to brunet women. Go back five, maybe ten years. Check the whole country. It's possible he's been doing this for a while."

"Most of the serial killers interviewed by the FBI's Behavioral Science Unit reported the killers had been victims of child abuse at the hands of a female parent. These women are similar in size and all the women victims had brunet hair the same color as his mother." Wright taped his pen on the corner of the conference table a few times.

Garcia said, "Our coroner said the killer committed his crime in a frenzy."

"The many stabbings even after death, demonstrates he felt great rage at his victims. He could have been in denial that his mother was dead."

Waller interrupted, "Okay, your point is well taken. Water over the dam, or under the bridge, or whatever the Hell that saying is. We got him. Dead, and he's off the streets."

"Was there a hollowness to his character?" Garcia still wanted to know more about what made the killer tick.

"Oh yes, he regarded humans as worthless annoyances to be dealt with and then forgotten. This guy killed someone he knew. Maybe he hated his mother's hands. Maybe he was trying to cut them off," said the profiler.

"That's sick-o," muttered Waller, her face showed disgust.

Garcia's fists clenched as he asked, "But what *makes* them do this?"

"Profilers or doctors believe a primary key to understanding serial murderers could be in their hypothalamus and in the limbic system because they regulate emotions and moods. A serial killer has no social or psychological attachment. Someday DNA may be able to predict a serial killer."

"You mean like it's something in the genes?" speculated Garcia.

"In the future, what if they test all fetuses to find out what could eventually go haywire in their brains, so they add some kind of tiny device in the baby's brain to prevent mental retardation, periodontal disease, Alzheimer's or killer?"

"Wow, are our brains prewired at birth? Are the serial murderer's decisions predetermined?" Garcia's eyes opened wide trying to understand that concept.

Randy Wright could tell them, "Brian circuits begin developing before birth. However, a male doesn't reach maturity until the middle of his late teens. Maybe a certain chromosome arrangement could become violent for criminal behavior or maybe they lack a chromosome."

"He wasn't even on our radar," Waller said calmly.

"So many times, a serial killer becomes tomorrow's media celebrity," stated Wright.

Garcia turned to his partner and asked, "His type of crime was slashing, cutting and mutilation. What if he wasn't working alone?"

"Then there's another sick fuck out there someplace," was Waller's answer as she looked at Garcia.

Wright told them, "Many a murderer commits his own murder, which makes it the last significant thing he'll do in his life."

"Do you actually think he created that accident to take his own life?" questioned Garcia.

"The serial killer tends to increase his killings to maintain an equilibrium. The fantasy and psychic high they get increases to more bold and frequent attacks. This type of killer never stops killing. They keep on going until they are arrested, or they die. In my opinion," the profiler hesitated for drama. "There is no cure for the sadistic psychopath except life in prison or death."

They thanked Randy Wright for coming in to speak with them. It had been an interesting training session they might use in future cases.

As they walked back to their desks, Garcia asked Waller, "Wouldn't it be great if serial killers could be trained to benefit society? Maybe qualified psychiatrists could work with killers to have them join the armed services. Maybe there's a place for them."

"Are you fucking nuts?" Waller's face registered horror, then she turned towards her desk. Her face turned into a huge grin. Heaped on her desk was a large pile of miniature Milky Ways, small boxes of Milk Duds, Hersey bars and Snickers. She got a clownish grin on her face and cried, "Gold." As she scooped up the fabulous candies of Miniature Musketeers, Twix and Snickers candy bars she said, "Mine, all mine." She looked like she could fall face first into the pile of candy. Instead, she ripped open the cellophane around a Ghirardelli dark chocolate and gobbled it down. "Haven't had one of these in a couple days." She laughed out loud. "Did you do this?"

Garcia smiled, "They're a thank you for not telling anyone I'm seeing Melissa Tomlin."

Waller lowered her voice, "You tight with her?"

"It's good." He gave a slight nod of his head.

"You were paired with me to get some seasoning." She chuckled. "When you came up, I thought you were gonna be bad at this. You know, no good at all, but I was wrong. You got what it takes. You've done a helluva job. You're going to be a good detective. You read people. You're okay. I don't admit that often." Waller kidded her partner, "However, I'm going to keep on your case to make you better."

"I'm grateful to have had a hand in finding a serial killer posthumously to get those three some modest measure of justice."

Waller agreed, "It's not a happy ending for the Eisenberg family but it's satisfying." She reached for a second candy. "It wasn't easy for me coming up through the ranks of an all-boys network like I did."

"You're a good teacher." Garcia smiled. "I've learned a new lesson everyday working with you, Alicia."

She lightly punched him on his upper arm. "Go ahead and call me Al. I know everyone around here does behind my back."

Detective Waller picked up her cell and quickly dialed Sergeant Dodson's office. "We've been going over a lot of surveillance tapes from bus stations and parking garages including the Oak Brook garage where your wife was attacked eight months ago. We see Thad Eisenberg at the garage two days before Diane was attacked."

"What's he doing?" Dodson practically shouted.

"Walking through at nine twenty a.m., then at eleven thirty-seven a.m., and again at two forty-eight p.m."

"Let me see that." Dodson was out of his office and running down the hall towards Waller and Garcia's desks before he even disconnected the call.

After viewing the footage, the sergeant said, "Looks like he's just out for a stroll with nowhere special to go."

That evening as David Dodson stepped into his own home, he thought, *she's too fragile. What once were long elegant hands, perfect for piano lessons, are gone, but I've got to tell her what we suspect.* David had to confront her. He put his beefy hands on each side of her face and looked deep into her eyes.

"What is it David? What's wrong?"

"Diane, the woman you found, lived in your aunt's apartment."

Fear gripped her. "Is Aunt Bernice okay?"

"Fine, however the man who kidnapped Carolyn Fazzino was a serial killer. We uncovered two bodies out there in that woods and another one just a few miles away that we can prove he killed."

Diane's face contorted, "A killer?"

"Every one of his female victims were missing their fingers." He reached for her mutilated right hand. Holding her palm softly in his own hands, he continued, "We have proof he was in the same garage two days before you were attacked."

Horror crossed Diane's face. She couldn't speak.

David continued, "The only thing that doesn't work for this theory is the profiler said he was picking women that resembled his mother. All were brunets except you. He seemed to attack women with brown hair like his mother, but you're blond."

Diane's eyes went wide. "Oh my God, I, I was wearing a brown knit cap. My hair was up that night, David. I pulled the hat down over my ears because it was so cold in January."

The room started spinning. Diane's left hand reached tighter for David for stability, for comfort, as he said, "Thad Eisenberg might have been interrupted before he took all your fingers, or maybe your hat came off during the struggle and you didn't look like a brunet to him anymore."

"Oh my God," she gasped. The floor was spinning out of control. She clung to her husband for balance.

David wrapped his arms around her slim body to steady her and said, "I want to rip that bastard limb from limb, but he's already dead. Monsters don't play by the rules."

"The young woman in the woods." Diane gulped. "She could have been his next victim."

"Yes, and he could have killed you. I'm sure he thought he was getting away with it, with all the killings." David kissed her cheek. "I sit in my office all day on my fanny, but <u>you</u> found her."

Chapter 48

AFTER SURGERY

Vince dreamt of blood. He woke feeling drugged and alone. He felt surgical tape over his eyes, face, and most of his head. In the darkness, his senses gradually returned, but his focus remained on his head and aching body. He dozed on and off. He winced as he tried to feel his face through the bandages. His head pounded in pain. It felt large and hot. The stitches in his face pulled. His lower back cramped from inactivity. He turned painfully onto his side. That is when he realized there were wires connected to him. One wire was attached to one finger of his left hand. His hands and arms felt deeply bruised; his arms slashed with cuts. Vince didn't know how many days or nights he had laid in complete blackness with bandages over both eyes. The only sound was the faint hum of a monitor somewhere behind him.

The hospital came alive with more sounds during the days. The nurses and doctors came and went sometimes tapping softly at the door as they pushed it open and other times suddenly at his bedside without making a sound to warn him. Some didn't want to wake him if he was sleeping. When awake, he could feel movement in the room: orderlies, housekeepers, doctors, lots of nurses. He occasionally heard them speak in low, grave voices. He'd been told he wouldn't die, but after days of virtually no food but plenty of meds and IV bags of something and too many doctors and nurses, he wouldn't have minded a prolonged blackout. At times he wanted to rip off the tubes and wires, just bolt from the room. But he couldn't see. He was helpless and depressed.

What if he could never see again? Vince had lost one eye. A plastic surgeon would be called in to try to reconstruct his face. He had asked several of the friendlier nurses if he would be scarred, but all responses had been vague. Many things were vague. Vince had decided he was dying no matter what they told him. He wanted to die.

The concussion caused constant ringing in his ears that made him mumble. The doctors denied this. The nurses just gave him another pill. They changed his meds frequently to see how he would react. Try this one for pain. This is an antibiotic. Then the pain pills were making him constipated, so this new pill to poop. *Just let me die.* Dozens and dozens of pills. Then he was aware the doctors were giving him less morphine. He wanted to sleep until the pain was gone or until everything would go back to when he and Carolyn first met and dated. But when he woke, it was still pitch-black. Vince overheard police talking about a death. He worried it was Carolyn.

Chapter 49

HOSPITAL

When Carolyn Fazzino reached the ER, the ceiling lights flickered past her as the gurney rolled down the hall. A nurse had glanced down with concern on her face. The wheels squeaked. The nurse panted a little as she pushed the gurney through the double doors. Different lights glared overhead, harsher, blinding. Carolyn closed her eyes. She was in and out of consciousness.

The shock-trauma unit moved into position and whisked her into trauma room one. Six people swarmed over her, a dozen hands working in unison to stabilize her. They were wearing gloves. They took her clothes off; a gown was draped over her body. As the ER personnel undressed Carolyn, they put each item, each shoe, each sock in a separate bag and labeled each bag immediately. Since her clothing was dirty and slightly damp, it had to be packaged in paper, so the moisture would continue to evaporate, otherwise the items could rot. Clothing with blood on it, like her torn jeans, was a special problem. It would be spread out in a police interrogation room and allowed to dry. It would not be folded. They did a head-to-toe examination to look for injuries, bandaged her head wound, cleaned her scraped knee, listened to her breathing sounds, listened to her slow heart rate and blood pressure, even palpated her abdomen. A nurse with a soothing voice asked if she had been raped.

"What?" Then hesitantly Carolyn responded, "No, No, I don't think so." She started to raise up.

The person put one hand to her forehead, as if she was dizzy, then she laid back down. "We can bring in a rape kit to see."

Electrical wires attached to circular patches were taped to her chest and upper arms. A blood-pressure cuff was wrapped around her left arm and inflated. The senior ER resident quickly placed his stethoscope on Carolyn's chest asking, "What's her blood pressure?"

"Seventy-five over thirty, pulse fifty-five," one of the nurses answered.

Her blood pressure was low, so they raised her feet slightly above her chest. Doctors checked her breathing and checked her core temp. She was covered with a warm blanket to prevent loss of body heat. "Bring the portable machine over here, get a head and chest x-ray now."

Carolyn was dehydrated. Tests revealed that her potassium was low from eating next to nothing for six days, so the emergency doctor had her admitted. Blood and fluids were forced in rapidly through large 18-gauge base needles. One hand hooked to an IV drip pushed meds and nutrients into her veins. They were concerned about environmental exposure. X-rays of her swollen ankle showed it was sprained. She was diagnosed with hypothermia and malnutrition, but she was one lucky lady to be a live witness. Her body relaxing because she was safe inside, in a bed. Her fingers raking the blankets to make sure they were there.

Then Detectives Waller and Garcia were around her asking her name, asking who had taken her. The detectives videotaped Carolyn's story. She lifted her head from the pillow. She couldn't answer many of their questions, like, "How did you get to those woods?"

With her voice swathed in wool, she managed, "I, I don't know how I got to that hole, but I saw a man in the parking lot, and I saw him in the woods." She couldn't give height because she was in a deep hole when she saw him. She thought he was huge. "Large body type, strong, white male, twenties or thirties, bald, good looking," is how she described him. "I'll recognize him. I'll pick the bastard out of a lineup, just give me a chance."

Garcia used a military photo found in the Eisenberg's home and a set of six photos of similar looking men. She didn't know who took her from the parking lot, but she recognized the man she saw in the woods. She identified Thad's picture as the man who looked down the hole at her, swung a metal object at her, and threw nuts, the only food she had eaten. He was the only person she saw while she was trapped in the underground hole, but he wouldn't do anything to help her get out.

"Did he ever talk to you?" asked Waller.

"Not a lot. He told me he had food, a sandwich for me, but then I saw a blade. It wasn't food. He tried to stab me with a knife, maybe a large kitchen knife." She did an involuntary shudder. "He called me, 'Mother.' He had this kind of unbelievable sneer that seemed to twist his face."

Once the detectives were in the hospital hall and out of Carolyn's earshot, Waller said, "No rape, no sex. He stabs his victims with a knife again and again. It's a case of overkill if there ever was one. He was working out something in his sick fucking mind while he was doing it."

"And he called Mrs. Fazzino, mother," added Garcia as he played with his mustache. "What type of personality would have done that?"

"Sick," Waller answered her partner. "Really sick."

Inside the hospital room, Carolyn hugged herself, shivering. A nurse put out a soothing hand, patted her leg through the blanket. Carolyn asked for coffee. Reluctantly the nurse handed Carolyn a Styrofoam cup. It was hot and strong. Carolyn felt it running down her throat, into every vein of her body waking her up. That is what she wanted days ago. It seemed like a hundred years ago. She had been so scared for so long. It was impossible for her to believe she was alive. She gulped at the coffee not caring if it scalded her as she swallowed.

"I'll see if you can have some soft foods," the nurse cooed. With that she stepped out of the room.

Carolyn didn't know how many minutes passed before her mother hurried into her room and to her bedside wrapping her arms around her daughter.

Ruth had lost weight and sleep in the last six days. Her cheekbones poked out sharply through skin that had faded to papery grey. "Are you okay? Oh my God! You had me so worried." Ruth swiped a hand across her eyes, leaving a streak of warm tears on her cheeks. "I don't know what I'd do if I ever lost you."

"I'm fine," Carolyn mumbled. She breathed in deeply. "I'm going to be fine." Every minute she tipped more coffee down her throat.

"Thank God!" Ruth left out a sigh that could probably be heard down the hall. "The strange thing is that Vince is in this same hospital."

Suddenly hearing Vince's name, cleared some of the fog out of her clouded mind. "What? Why is he here?"

"He's been in an accident. Bad accident. At first, they didn't think he'd make it, but he's come through surgery."

Carolyn was so confused she didn't even know who was talking. "An accident," she repeated. She felt like someone took away her heart. "Where is he?" she asked.

Instead, Ruth explained, "The police said he went through the windshield." What Ruth wasn't telling her daughter, was that the impact came at a point less than two inches from the driver's steel side support post. If Vince had struck that, he would have been killed or left permanently comatose, a vegetable with arms and legs.

"What?" Carolyn was not understanding.

"The doctor said there's a long gash in his scalp and face, but mostly there was so much glass in his eyes."

Please, Carolyn thought. *Please pull yourself together, you stupid bitch. It's not always about you. Get up. Find out what happened to Vinny.* Shakely, she asked again, "W-where is he?"

"Sixth floor," her mother answered. "But things don't look good for saving his eyes."

Slowly Carolyn raised herself up into a sitting position on the hospital bed. The sides of her bed were up, and she was hooked to an IV. "Get this off me." She managed to say.

Ruth glanced at the IV bag. "The nurse said it's Dilaudid. I think that's important and they said your electrolytes in your blood are out of range or something like that. You *need* those vitamins."

"Get it off." Carolyn struggled to sit up. "You're sounding too much like a mother. *Now* let me go see him." Slowly she slid her legs up under her body. Every movement hurt, but she had to see him. On her knees she could reach the IV bag.

As she started to reach for it, Ruth could see the pain and determination in her daughter's face, so she reached up and gently unhooked it for her.

"Thanks, now get me out of this bed."

But Ruth couldn't figure out how to lower the side of the bed. Determined Carolyn crawled down to the end and slowly lowered her feet to the floor. As she tried to stand, she felt every muscle in her body seize up, every nerve ending protested. She groaned but staggered to her feet, unsteady as a newborn calf. That's when she became aware of the hospital gown, she was wearing that was open at the back. *I've lost my dignity along with everything else, even my husband.*

At that ill moment, a doctor came through the door. Quickly he moved to get his patient back into bed. He took ahold of Carolyn's arms.

"Do not fucking touch me, you patronizing asshole." The stress made Carolyn's voice rise half an octave.

The doctor jumped back startled. "Look, it's not unusual..."

But Carolyn was addiment, "I want to see my husband." Her voice caught, but she went on, "I want to go home. That's what I wanted when I was in that God forsaken hole and that's what I want now!" She felt her anger rising. "This hospital is a fishbowl world compared to where I've been for days in the ground."

"I understand you're upset, and the police want to talk to you some more, however I'd like to examine you to make sure you're up to speaking to them. I can only do that if you're calm. Do you understand Carolyn?"

She nodded her head mutely.

The doctor checked her pulse and blood pressure against the readings on the machine. He passed a small pen light across her eyes, then asked, "How do you feel?"

Calmer, she answered, "I have a little nausea. But I want to see Vince."

"What day is it?"

Not knowing how long she had been in the woods or how long the examination or police had questioned her, she spat, "I don't care. I've got to see my husband."

"Well, you seem to be doing remarkably well. We'll put something in the IV to settle your stomach. I'll also send in some warm broth." He hung his stethoscope around his neck and put his little pen light in his front pocket."

"I must see Vince."

"Hmm." He looked at a computer screen on the counter. He was stalling, trying to decide. "I'm not convinced you're up to it Carolyn." At last he let out a long breath, a frustrated sigh and swiped his badge across the screen to sign off. "Very well. Only half an hour. I'll get an aide with a wheelchair. You're not strong enough to walk and you should keep your sprained ankle elevated." The doctor patted her shoulder.

She looked at the sensory probes attached to her chest and an IV in her left arm. "Can I get a shower?"

"Of course, I'll get someone to help you." With that he was out of the room.

Soon a nurse held her hand as she stepped unsteadily into the stream of water. Carolyn hung onto the grab rails. The nurse left the door ajar just a crack. The warm water and soap were Heaven to her. After Carolyn turned the water off, she stepped out. She grimaced as she stepped on the sore ankle. The nurse helped towel her off and secured a black boot to stabilize her ankle.

Carolyn glanced at the steam covered mirror. The nurse saw the look, so used a small towel to wipe at the condensation on the glass. Carolyn slowly took a couple steps towards the mirror to look at her reflection. A face she didn't recognize stared back at her. She'd always been kind of plain, not like Vince who could turn heads. Besides a face filled with swollen mosquito bites, some she had scratched, now her pale cheeks were sunken, with dark circles under her eyes. The hallowed-out eyes were the worst, but she was out of that horrid hole. *I'm alive,* she thought. *Vince is hurt. He's here.* The sterile bathroom walls were crushing in. If she didn't move, she felt she would explode. It was that thought that made her pull on two hospital gowns, one with the opening in the back and another with the opening in front, like a robe.

An aide brought a wheelchair.

Even though her entire body ached, she insisted, "I can walk."

"No, you're too weak. Also, you need to keep that ankle up."

It didn't take long for the aide to get Carolyn into the wheel-chair. Now her only aim was to see her husband once again. Her mind was fuzzy, but Vince was hurt. He could have died. "Take me to him," her voice sounded hoarse as she spoke to the aide. She turned towards her mother saying, "I need to do this by myself."

Ruth nodded, "I'll wait here for you."

The aide hooked the IV bag on the back of the wheelchair and raised the footrest to lift Carolyn's booted foot. She pushed Carolyn out into the hall to face the world, up the elevator to the sixth floor and into Vince's room.

The room was quite dark, the curtains drawn. He laid there in the white hospital bed. Carolyn motioned for the aide to leave her. Using her hands, she inched the wheelchair closer inside his dark room. Machines hummed and whirled all around him. Vince's breathing, ragged and shallow.

With her heart throbbing she inched closer to his bed.

His head was covered in white bandages especially the left side of his face and chin. Cotton stuck out around the white gauze tinged with red blood seepage covering his eyes. Both eyes covered by protective cups. What wasn't covered in white bandages was skin a strange waxen color with many small cuts and scratches. It was as if the tape bandages were holding everything in place. His face, what she could see of it, was puffy and bruised with an antiseptic smell about his head. A five o'clock shadow showed around the bandages on his chin.

Someone had tried to get the blood out of his dark hair, but there were matted clumps. His hair sticking out in weird peaks, was more messed up then she had ever seen before. His lips were a bloodless pale with small scratches on the top lip. But he was still Vince. She knew the ridge of his nose, the hollow beneath his bottom lip where sweat beaded on summer nights.

As she arrived at the side of his bed, she was sure her pounding heart would wake him. He lay, not moving, only a few feet from her touch. She wondered if he was sleeping or maybe drugged. It was intensely private, the way he did not move or notice her arrival. His breathing was short.

Carolyn so nervous, she was about to throw up. Her heart was literally rattling her rib cage, it was beating so hard. Softly Carolyn whispered, "Vinny? Is it you?" Carolyn closed her eyes and imagined all the ways she wanted to touch him, how she wanted him to touch her, but she didn't want to hurt him. Instead, she reached her hand out to his arm and ever so lightly touched him.

He groaned, then stirred. "Carolyn?" the weak figure answered in his confused restless sleep. "Are you really here?" Vince's voice was weak, but so familiar.

She took a deep, shaky breath and leaned forward to hear Vince through the bandages. Her heart swelled in her chest, overflowing with love, relief, and fear. "Vinny," the name was out of her before she was aware of making it.

"Am I dreaming?" he whispered.

Carolyn shook her head, then realized Vince couldn't see through all the bandages and cotton over his eyes, she spoke up, "No. It's me." Her voice was gentle but insistent. Her eyes filled with tears.

He whispered. It came out thick through the damage and the bandages. "Something happened." He was fighting to raise up, but the drugs and his weakened condition didn't allow much.

"Hush, you need rest." Tears were running down her cheeks.

"Don't cry," he said softly. "You're real. You're really here." He hesitated. "I, I didn't know you were missing," Quietly, weakly he went on, "not until the police told me." He caught his breath. "Then I heard the alert on the news, so I knew it was real. I should have been there." He gulped a few times. "A nurse said they found you." He paused to catch his breath. "None of this would have happened if I had been there."

"Vince don't die." It was all she could say.

His arm raised up like he wanted to touch her to make sure he wasn't dreaming. She reached for his hand. The hand she knew so well without even looking at it, as tears streamed down her face. She kept holding him as they wept. She grew calmer, a quiet flow of tears. Finally, her breathing eased. "How do you feel?" Her throat croaky, but she didn't care about her.

"The police told me; you were held by a serial killer. I could have lost you forever." The silence between them swelled filling the room. "I, I was in an accident. The cops told me the other man died. I wish I had too."

She let out a gasp and grabbed a tighter hold of his hand. "Don't say that. Don't you ever say that Vince. We both lived. We both lived for a reason. I feel very alive."

"But why live, blind?" The pain lacing through his words. "I want to die, but first, I can tell you that, I love you."

"I know you've got a sore head and all, so take your time. Think really hard about this. Apologies aren't easy, but our differences," she trailed off. "I didn't even go after you when you walked out that day."

"I'm so sorry." With a weak voice, he managed, "I wasted so much of our marriage arguing with you."

She listened to his breath, as he drew in and out of his nose covered with bandages.

With tears in his voice, he softly said, "I was so unkind to you. I was a fool, a complete bastard."

Carolyn couldn't find words, so gently lifted his hand to her cheek. She bent toward him to kiss the bandages. He smelled of disinfectant, rubbery goo bandages and vaguely of Vince. She remembered his smell during their first kiss after the movie, Erin Brockovich. Vince had kissed her. He tasted of buttered popcorn and a hint of chocolate. She had saved that kiss and his manly scent as a memory. It came back to her now. That kiss was a lifetime ago when two kids believed in a happy ending. And she gave him a tender kiss on his injured lips. She wanted to cradle his face close to her but was so afraid of hurting him.

Under his bandages Vince only saw black, but he reached his bruised sore arms up towards her. He felt her, circled his arms around her waist and pulled her to him, then rested his palms on her back, not letting go. His voice calm, "I want retribution. I want to get the guy that took you, harmed you. Have him arrested, beat him up. Ya know an eye for an eye."

"In a way, you've already done that. Now I'm going to take care of you." She gripped his hands tighter. "I lived four months without you. No more."

"Caroline, I love you. Just love me half as much as I love you."

"With all my heart."

"You'll be with me? Even though…" his voice trailed off. He gulped and finally said, "I can't bear the thought that I might never see your face again."

"I don't look very good right now, but I'm stronger than I thought. Strong enough to endure starvation and strong enough to have a baby."

"What?"

"I killed a snake in that hole. I am strong Vince. If I can survive killing a snake, I can survive having a baby. Piece of cake." She snapped her fingers to prove it to him. "I found strength; I never knew I had." She arched her back, so she was closer to his body. Her arms went around him.

Timidly he asked, "Really?"

"Well, if the doctor gives me something for the pain."

They both chuckled.

And she said, "Like the song, I Am Woman."

"Hear me Roar," he added.

"One day at a time," she murmured.

"With my eyesight gone, they won't let me drive the trucks anymore. That's all I've ever done. How can I work and take care of you?"

"It doesn't make any difference. You will find something else. Maybe you will be a stay-at-home dad, while I work."

"Maybe I'll get some worker's comp from the trucking company."

"I've achieved nothing in my life except loving you. You are the best thing. I've had plenty of time in that Hell hole to ask myself, how I could let you go. I'm so thrilled to be back with you. I want a baby with you. Do you want me back?"

"Oh yes."

She squeezed him tighter. She knew reality was waiting somewhere out there, outside this hospital. In a remote corner of her mind she knew they had been too distant, that had to change. There was nothing they could do about the past except learn from their mistakes. Her head was resting against his shoulder. His grip grew tighter and he pulled her in to him. He reached for her hand in an absentminded gesture. Knowing that he couldn't see her, she put her hand in his, then he raised it up to his lips which gently brushed the back of her hand.

A light knocking on the door caused them both to stir. Detective Waller stepped into the hospital room, followed by Detective Garcia.

Waller spoke first, "We wanted to see how you were both doing."

Carolyn sitting in the wheelchair right next to Vince's bed, straightened up.

Garcia said, "We stopped by your room. Your mother said you were with Vince. I'm glad you're here together."

"Who is it?" Vince asked since he couldn't see through the thick bandages.

"It's the detectives that were working on your wife's case, Mr.

Fazzino." Garcia stepped up to Vince's hospital bed. He reached taking Vince's hand and they gently shook.

"Waller and Garcia," Vince responded. "You thought I took her."

"We had to rule out all possibilities," Waller explained to him. "How are you both?"

Carolyn and Vince never let go of each other. Carolyn looked up, giving the detective a weak smile. "We're going to be okay."

"That's great to hear." Garcia absentmindedly fingered the left side of his mustache. "We wanted to check on you both before we officially close your case."

Weakly Vince managed to ask, "How, how did you know my wife was missing in the first place?"

"Oh, it was a neighbor, Mrs. Butzen, who filed the missing person report on her," Garcia answered.

"Oh my God," exclaimed Carolyn. "Bernice? I'll never, ever call her a Smelly Old Cat Lady again. How can I ever thank her enough?"

"Get her another cat," Vince suggested.

The detectives didn't stay long, but Carolyn stayed at her husband's bedside. When a nurse brought in a dinner tray for him, she also called the kitchen to get Carolyn's tray delivered to Vince's room, too. They were both allowed soft foods. He was so weak, Carolyn spoon fed him between bites of her own food.

After two bites, Vince asked, "What is this pureed stuff?"

"The absolute best pudding and mashed potatoes I've ever had."

"If you say so."

Chapter 50

MY HEART IS BACK

The day Carolyn was released from the hospital, her mother drove her home. Carolyn had to shoo her mother out of her apartment saying, "I just need a good night's sleep in my own bed. In the morning, I'll go back to the hospital to be with Vince."

After Ruth reluctantly left, Carolyn found herself hobbling on her booted sore ankle from room to room of their tiny apartment just looking at everything, the walls, the furniture, every item. In the kitchen, she paused, to open the coffeemaker. The paper filter was already there, like she left it so long ago, a whole week, but it felt longer. She drummed her fingers on the top of the coffee machine. She still didn't have any coffee. This time she went next door to ask Mrs. Butzen for coffee and to retrieve her cat, Tuxedo.

As Bernice answered her front door, she said, "Oh, bless my soul, come in Carolyn. Come in." Bernice's shapeless flowered house dress hung to her ankles barely touching her green clogs.

Carolyn stepped inside her neighbor's apartment saying, "I can't thank you enough, Mrs. Butzen, for going to the police."

A calico cat was entwined around Bernice's legs. "Oh, Darlin' I just knew something was off when ya didn't come home." Bernice patted her arm. "I keep an eye on my neighbors." She led the way into her flower-carpeted living room. It was cluttered with furniture, stacks of romance novels, lemon drops on her coffee table and cats, but it felt like a sanctuary. Sammy, the Siamese was patrolling the sofa.

"It was nothing and kind of fun to talk to those nice police officers. Sit down, sit down. Just move those books over. I'll make ya some hot tea and you can tell me everything." She scooped a limp cat off the sofa.

Carolyn sat on the warm spot the cat had unwillingly left.

Coffee was what Carolyn really wanted, but Bernice was so sweet, Carolyn couldn't say 'no' to the offer of tea.

Bernice rattled around in her tiny kitchen for about five minutes, yelling back to her guest, "I'm so glad you're okay. You had me absolutely worried about you, Dear."

"I'm going to be fine." Carolyn called back to Bernice in the next room.

Tuxedo, who heard his owner's voice, came running into the room. He took one look at her and hopped up on the couch next to Carolyn. As the cat sniffed her, Carolyn softly said, "Hello there, Tux. Did you miss me? I sure missed you."

With that comment, the black and white cat curled himself onto Carolyn's lap like old times.

Bernice came back with two cups on a tray. She looked around the room, then sat the tray on top of a stack of books on her coffee table. Gazing at Carolyn, she said, "Don't you two look cozy together? Guess that's what Tux needed, your lap. He just paced around here, like he couldn't get comfortable. Even though every inch of this place has cat hair; it should have made him feel at home."

Soon Carolyn was sipping the sweet hot liquid.

Bernice sat in her nearby chair. She leaned her soft body forward asking, "Did he?" Her voice faltered, "Did he hurt you?" Bernice folded her hands as if to say, I'm hungry for every juicy detail.

"Yah," Carolyn's voice was angry.

Bernice's eyes shot open. "Did he rape you, Dear, or touch you? You can tell me everything." There was a hopeful sound to her voice.

"No, not like that." Carolyn wanted to calm her. Out of the corner of her eye she watched Charlie on the back of the sofa. His tail switching like a charmed snake.

Bernice gulped. "Did he violate you?"

Carolyn was trying to sound tough, but her words came out frightened, cracking on every word. "I'll never be the same, Mrs. Butzen. The guy that took me was a criminal, a killer."

Bernice reached forward and patted Carolyn's arm. "Oh, you poor little thing."

Carolyn looked into Bernice's round face and admitted, "I felt powerless. It was pure terror."

The elderly woman sat her cup down pulling Carolyn into her arms. "You're going to be okay now. Come Hell or high water, I'm here for you and Vince."

"Thank you so much." Carolyn hugged her back as Penelope slinked across the room.

Bernice said, "It still gives me goose pimples that I was the last one to see you before you got taken. Well, when Vince gets home, I can help him out while you're at work. I've always been a little sweet on him." She took another sip of tea and tried to stop herself from sighing.

"You are the absolute best neighbor and friend ever." Carolyn did an involuntary shudder. "We still don't know if the doctors have saved Vinny's eyes or not."

⸻ ◆ ⸻

Across town, Sergeant Dodson's workday over, he leaned back in his home recliner. He was thinking about turning on the Bears game when Diane turned on the run-way music and stepped out of the downstairs powder room wearing nothing, but a large feathery boa wrapped around her slender body and her highest heels.

"Ta-da," she seductively said over the music. Diane jutting her right hip and shoulder forward in an exaggerated model's runway walk, the strut that has ruled catwalks around the globe.

David startled, sat in his leather chair, and watched Diane as she strutted the thick cream carpet of their family room.

The pink boa draped over her shoulders, circled her thin right arm with the end tucked carefully between her thumb and only finger, concealed the missing fingers of her right hand. She was all soft lines and smooth skin.

He met the gaze of her warm honey-gold eyes. He never tired of watching the sheer length of those legs.

She strutted to the music, hips exaggerated, walking straight towards her husband. Diane was beautiful. Her moves were as graceful as he remembered her on stage.

"I can still wear my wedding ring," she said as she waved her left hand through the air. "Just call me lefty." When she reached him, she leaned forward to give him a movie love-scene kiss. She told him, "Everyone has a part of their body they don't like. They each have something they would like to change. Everyone thought I was perfect. Then after," she hesitated. "After what happened, I found me imperfect. Now I'm just as human as everyone is."

His arms instinctively tightened around her hips tugging her closer. His fingers brushed across her bare thighs. He leaned forward and gently pulled her down into the chair with him. He continued kissing down her body.

She gripped his bulging biceps.

This increased his desire higher.

Together they unbuttoned his shirt and dropped it to the floor.

⸺⸺ ((◊)) ⸺⸺

The next morning after Sergeant Dodson left for the station, Diane showered. She dressed in a chambray Gap camisole, a flowered pencil skirt and Napa leather sandals. She was just stepping out of their bedroom when the doorbell rang. Diane stopped in her tracks, startled. Her first thought was, *No one should see me.* Then slowly she took a few steps forward. Soon her flip flops flapping noisily, she hurried to the window beside the front door to peek through the side window. Looking out, she saw a woman she didn't know, then just maybe it might be.... surprisingly, it's that woman from the woods. Diane quickly unlocked and threw open the door keeping her right hand behind the door.

"I'm Carolyn, Carolyn Fazzino. I wanted to thank you. Thank you for my life. I think he would have killed me."

"Come inside, please."

Carolyn stepped into the house. "Just when I gave up all hope of ever getting out of there alive, you saved me."

They stood in the entryway facing each other as Diane said, "When I saw the way you were laying in that ditch, I didn't think you were alive. But then you moved. You seemed so weak when they got you out, I didn't know if you would make it to the hospital."

One tear slipped down Carolyn's cheek. "I thought you were an angel saving me. Later I had to ask the police who you were."

Diane shook her head no. "Angels are perfect. I'm no angel."

Recognizing the fact that she would probably be dead right now if Diane hadn't found her, Carolyn said, "You saved me." Carolyn bit down hard on her lip, but the tears came anyway, silently spilling down her cheeks.

Instinctively Diane reached out wrapping her thin arms around Carolyn. Then she realized she was comforting someone who was more tormented than herself. Diane gulped. Her flow of tears started. What had happened was inconceivable. Their world had turned violent, harming good people.

"To me, you are a hero," Carolyn said as she pulled Diane tighter into her arms. They held on together. Carolyn pressed her face against Diane's shoulder, as though trying to burrow her way into some safe place where no one could find her.

They stood like that holding each other a long time, until Diane said, "Come into the kitchen. I've got tissues in there."

They moved into the next room where Diane got tissues for them both. After they blew their noses, they sat at the kitchen table facing each other. Diane asked, "How are you really feeling?"

Still sniffling, Carolyn managed, "I don't think I will ever like moss or worms or dirt ever again."

Diane smiled at Carolyn's attempt to make a joke. Then seriously she said, "I was so worried about you, Carolyn that I actually forgot about my hand for a time."

"Your hand?"

Hesitantly, Diane held out her deformed hand.

Carolyn let out a small involuntary gasp, but then quickly said, "Face your fears."

Diane told her, "We are both lucky ladies to get a second chance. We're different people now. We're stronger. Neither of us has to be afraid."

"We've developed new strength to deal with new things in our future."

"Touché." They both smiled.

Carolyn swiped her hand at a stray tear. "This was an opportunity for me to take a closer look at my marriage. Vince and I are back together. My heart is back. He needs me. We treat each other with kindness and comfort."

"How is he after the accident?"

"The doctor said he could lose his eyesight."

Diane gasped, then said, "Face your fears."

"We really don't know about his eyes, but I will be there for him. I'm strong now. I've changed. We're hopeful he can eventually get a cornea transplant. The doctor also told me that Thad Eisenberg signed a form when he was in the army to be an organ donor. That killer's eyes will go to someone at the top of the list and Vince will move up. We're hopeful."

"I hope so too." Diane said, "Vince will have you, so take care of yourself; you hear."

Carolyn added, "I'm going to watch my surroundings very closely. That was stupid to park so near the alley."

"It's not your fault," Diane told her. "No one is ever safe from a serial killer because his violent determination isn't human."

Carolyn smiled. "I guess."

Diane had a sudden new thought. "Do you sew? I'm thinking of buying a sewing machine."

"I took sewing in high school." Carolyn told her.

Diane explained, "I have trouble finding really long-sleeved styles. I want my blouses to come down over my right hand. I've been watching You Tube videos on sewing. I think, I should be able to follow a pattern. I could kind of roll or fold up the left sleeve a little. Would that look crazy?"

Carolyn told her new friend, "Not at all. You could even buy larger sized tops for their longer sleeves. I can show you how to take in the sides to fit your slim body."

"You would do that for me?" Diane asked.

"Anything." Carolyn was smiling.

"Will long sleeves ever be popular in the summer?"

"Whatever makes you comfortable. That should be in style now."

REFERENCES:

Dr. Bill Bass and Jon Jefferson. Death's Acre. 2003

Rod Englert. Blood Secrets: Chronicles of a Crime Scene Reconstructionist. 2010

Steven Egger. The Killers Among Us. 2001

Barry Fisher. Techniques of Crime Scene Investigation. 2012

Connie Fletcher. What Cops Know. 1990

Vernon J. Geberth. Practical Homicide Investigation. 1983

Vernon J. Geberth. Practical Homicide Investigation. 1990.

Kevin Hazzard. A Thousand Naked Strangers. 2016.

Lee Lofland. Police Procedure & Investigation: a guide for writers. 2007

Sean Mactire. Malicious Intent: a writer's guide to how murderers, robbers, rapists and other criminals think. 1995

Helen Morrison, M.D. My Life Among the Serial Killers: Inside the Minds of the World's Most Notorious Murderers. 2004

Adam Plantinga. 400 Things Cops Know. 2014

David Simon. Homicide: A Year on the Killing Streets. 2006

Keith D. Wilson. Cause of Death: a writer's guide to death, murder & forensic medicine. 1992

Anne Wingate, PhD. Scene of the Crime: a writer's guide to crime-scene investigations. 1992

AUTHORS NOTES AND ACKNOWLEDGEMENTS:

I want to express my infinite love to my children: Deborah Wells Lee and Richard Ronald Wells for turning out so well. Every day I'm proud to be your mother. My precious grandchildren: Kyle Richard Wells and Andrea Faye Wells are the bright lights of my life. You are dreams come true and my reason for being. Thank you to my husband, Ron for letting me pretend to write and suggesting I let others read my dribble. Thanks for allowing me to attend all those writers' groups when you so often wanted to do other things with me. I love you.

My love of books started when I had a chance to pick my own reading material during my summer teenage years. My reading continued while working for Pat Ulery at the Warrenville Public Library. Thank you, Pat, for being such a dear friend who made me laugh through the writing process. Pat believes in me and that is appreciated more than you know.

A thousand thanks to Mark Petrovich, retired Hoffman Estates policeman, for the many crime books you loaned me. They were invaluable. Also, for happily fielding my endless, naïve questions as I badgered you with official protocol questions regarding our police force. You always took the time to help me.

I want to thank Sergeant Kyle Rybaski of the Bartlett Police Department for all the Citizens Police Academy training and for answering all my writers' questions. The training was invaluable.

Thanks for the ride-along with Officer Max Puente. I was so excited; I couldn't stop talking.

Thank you to James Povolo, retired Chicago policeman for answering my many questions about our police activities. Thank you to Beth Orchard for the crime books you loaned me. They were a fantastic source of information and I also want to thank Detective Tom Alagna of the Bartlett Police Department for explaining how a real missing person case would be handled.

Thank you, Christi Konieczny, retired Lower Merion, Pennsylvania detective for sharing some fascinating true stories. They are better than fiction.

Thank you Eve Lomoro for telling me I can write and encouraging me to join her writers' group. That was the beginning. Thank you, Jeanmarie Dwyer-Wrigley, who offered take-no-crap advice showing me how scared a victim would really feel. The Schaumburg Scribes read hundreds of drafts of this book over eight years. They are probably glad I have moved on to book two.

Thank you to my many friends in the Bartlett Creative Writers, Bloomingdale Writers, DuPage Writers, Hanover Township's Life Stories, the lively No Ordinary Women Writers, Poplar Creek Writers, and Write Time Writers in the writing community who read chunks of the many versions of this book to offer advice and critiques. Thanks for reading the beginning pages and wanting to read more. A fiction writer never hears more encouraging words than those. I'd like to thank all my writers' groups who taught me point of view and organization. Their encouragement and advise on how to adjust my story enhanced its clarity.

For technical help, I owe a great debt to John Paul Clayton, EMT-P who helped with all your medical knowledge and who faithfully answered all my questions. Thank you to my good friends: Kelly Lovewell, Jean McNelly, Wendy Molof, and Kathi Stelmach, for their medical advice. Many thanks to my editor, Stephi Cham, for your vital feedback on this book. You are brilliant and made my story so much better. I am very glad to have you as my net. I will call you much sooner with my next manuscript. Thank you to my smart, eagle-eyed readers John Maes, Ilene Goldman and Alice Refvik. Susan Chisum's love, confidence and continual support have made writing this possible. My characters benefited from Deborah Wells Lee's lists of formal versus informal writing.

Thank you to my nephew, Scott Brittan for your service in Bosnia and Afghanistan to protect us all and for your military lingo. Thank you to my niece, Sara Norris FBI DEA (Drug Enforcement Administration) Senior Forensic Chemist, Clandestine Laboratory Coordinator and Field Training Officer for all your forensic details.

Thanks to Clint Kramer for the needed trucker advice. Dear friends, Kathy and Tim Sleep who hosted my very first crime/mystery reading, I thank you for the fun.

Thanks to the late Marilyn Donovan who encouraged me to keep writing just a week before her death and thank God I listened to her. I owe the genesis of this story to Adeline Dobbins posthumously for her great off-beat ideas and a big twist to this story even before it was completed in my mind. She gave me a wonderful solution.

I borrowed the names Catherine Wells and Irene Pelletier in the hopes my favorite people live forever on these printed pages.

I love you all.

I hope my details are plausible. But in reality, I know of no buried bodies in any hidden woods in, near or around the Chicago suburbs. Bleakville is of course, fictional, so don't try to find those dreaded woods.

CPSIA information can be obtained
at www.ICGtesting.com
Printed in the USA
LVHW021137031120
670573LV00001B/66